THE FUTURE IS NOW

Book 2 of the Future Visions Series

Jeremy Eaton

Copyright © 2022 Jeremy Eaton

All rights reserved

The characters and events portrayed in this book are fictitious. Any similarity to real persons, living or dead, is coincidental and not intended by the author.

No part of this book may be reproduced, or stored in a retrieval system, or transmitted in any form or by any means, electronic, mechanical, photocopying, recording, or otherwise, without express written permission of the publisher.

To Lucy. I could not have finished the second if you hadn't encouraged me to finish the first.

ONE

*Green-Wood Cemetery,
Brooklyn, NY*
Four and a half months after the NATO-China War:
13 years 250 days until the invasion

The blustery wind pushed the leaves across the beautifully manicured cemetery.

Green-Wood was the highest place in Brooklyn, and from its heights, the city's skyscrapers could be seen in the distance.

David thought that Bubbie would have liked that. She loved Brooklyn but acknowledged that Manhattan was the center of the world, at least in her mind.

It was hard not to be sad, but she had been clear that there should be few tears when the time came. She had gone fast, only a month from the cancer diagnosis to the end. David suspected that she had known longer but accepted it rather than try to prolong the inevitable.

Bubbie had been her ironic self to the end and had enough time to give him his marching orders. She had said, "Being sad for a billionaire who lived into her 90s is like being sad that you got too much Halloween candy. Sure, you might get a stomachache, but it's CANDY!" He gave a sad smile. God, he loved that woman!

He watched his parents walking toward their car, holding hands in their grief. They had taken a brief break from their retirement in the Bahamas to come to New York for the funeral. He hadn't really known what to say to them. All of them were equally uncomfortable trying to comfort each other simultaneously, and in the end, they had just shared an embrace in silence.

He knew they were happy to leave New York as quickly as possible and get back to their beachside house. In fact, they were going straight from the funeral to the Airport, not even staying for the reading of the will. He could hardly blame them. Some sun and piña coladas sounded pretty good right now.

Cindy was taking it the hardest. He saw the tears streaking her cheeks as the plain pinewood coffin lowered into the ground. The old woman had been adamant that she didn't want a fancy coffin. She called it an "asinine practice" and had explained, "Who am I trying to impress, groundhogs?"

Cindy had never known her own grandparents. After Bubbie became her CEO, they had spent quite a bit of time together. The old woman was infectious. Even Cindy's antisocial tendencies and irascible personality couldn't stand up to her. She had become, in a real way, her Bubbie as well.

He reached out and grabbed Cindy's hand. Amazingly, she gripped it tightly in her own. She seemed to gain strength from the connection and gave him a nod of thanks.

Ceremony done, they all returned to the line of limos, which waited to take them home. Bubbie wasn't religiously Jewish. So, there would be no sitting shiva for her. She had always referred to herself as "culturally" Jewish. Despite her lack of belief, she had tackled religion as she did all things, completely mastering it before deciding. David had seen her argue a Rabbi to a standstill on a sticky point of the Torah. Still, she maintained the writings were to be used as a guide rather than a set of rules laid down upon humanity by an all-encompassing supernatural being.

Yet, in the long talk she had had with him after revealing her diagnosis, she told him she had occasionally questioned her belief in God.

"David," she said. "My brain is too rapid, too questioning, to believe that there is one all-powerful being." She had given his arm a weak squeeze. "I'm a lot like you in that way. I could never ignore the evidence to the contrary." She gave him a self-mocking smile then. "You might say that I don't have enough faith. I felt certain for over eighty years. I scoffed at anyone who would be gullible enough to believe, but I have questioned more and more these past few years. It is not my impending death that makes me question God's existence. It is Nick, Cindy, Jake, and you."

She had looked up at the ceiling and called out in a weak voice. "HAL, can you give me the odds that you would have found four people so completely suited to fight the Silfe so close together?"

HAL's voice sounded out. "The number is so large as to be incalculable," the AI said.

She grinned. "See, incalculable luck or divine intervention? HAL, how are humanity's chances looking?"

A long pause ensued that was completely uncharacteristic of the alien AI. Finally, almost a minute later, its voice sounded again. "Although it has too many factors to make it accurate, the estimate is thirty-five percent that humanity will defeat the Silfe fleet and retain possession of the Earth."

David hadn't believed his ears. "What do you mean by 'defeat?' I thought we were just trying to delay enough for a small portion of the population to get out of Dodge."

"The chance of humanity's survival via an interstellar escape ship is approximately ninety-seven percent given current trajectories," HAL said. "This is the highest projection that a species facing the Silfe has ever seen. No species, except for the Harrow, has ever defeated an invasion fleet."

Bubbie's eyes, which had lost none of their intelligence

during her illness, looked at him. "See, in some ways, you have already won." Her face took on a steely glint. "But there is still some time to beat the bastards. I won't be there... physically to see it, but I know you will win."

David held Cindy's hand through the silent drive back to Bubbie's Brooklyn Heights mansion. Nick sat across from them, sporting a pin on his lapel with the Earth on a starry sky background. The United States Liaison to the World Commission looked out the window, lost in his own thoughts.

Jake sat next to him in the dress blues of an Air Force Colonel. His service ribbons were impressive, topped by a single blue one with five stars. David knew his friend didn't like to wear the ribbon for the "Medal." He also remembered Bubbie dressing him down for omitting it. He smiled, thinking about her words.

"God damn it, Jake," she had said, seeing his incomplete uniform. I know you killed people to get it, but you are dishonoring them as much as yourself when you don't wear it. Pretending it didn't happen forgets those men as well."

Jake had looked like he had been gut-punched and simply had responded, "Yes, Ma'am. David hadn't seen him in a formal uniform without it since.

He sighed; there were examples everywhere of her influence. You couldn't come into contact with Bubbie without being changed by her. She had been a force of nature.

The car let the four of them out in front of Bubbie's enormous brownstone. Gloria, who had somehow become the estate's executor, had been explicit that they were to come straight from the service to the Brooklyn Heights home.

David wasn't sure how it happened, but at some point, Gloria gained legal status, with a social security number, birth certificate, and a false past that not even the NSA could penetrate.

The AI had become more and more integrated into the PLAN. Even President Tanner utilized her when the White House's official information lines broke down or he wanted a clandestine word with one of them.

The President had sent his condolences. Asking for forgiveness that he couldn't attend in person. Tanner had never officially met his grandmother, but he knew that the president and Bubbie had engaged in many a late-night planning session since the end of the NATO-China war.

She called the sixty-five-year-old leader of the Free World "A delightful and sexy man." She also said that it was too bad he was happily married, or she might have taken him "Out for a spin."

David appreciated the president's words, but in all honesty, having him in attendance would have added a level of complication to the event that David was happy to avoid.

They already had a full complement of Secret Service agents between Cindy and Nick.

Nick warranted protection as the Liaison to the World Commission, made even more complicated by his position as its chair.

Cindy had an even larger group of agents. When Tanner took office, he wrote an executive order authorizing the same protection for the scientist as he had for himself. David could hardly disagree. If something happened to Cindy, they were all screwed. He could see some crackpot or rogue faction of a government capturing her and trying to get her to create superweapons. She had resisted the protection at first, only agreeing after being ordered by Bubbie to "Grow the hell up." The old woman's irritated comment had worked better than any reasoned argument or pleading by Nick, Jake, or himself.

They sat in the car for a brief pause as Cindy and Nick's agents secured the area. Finally, the door to the limousine opened, and they were quickly ushered into the grand foyer. Waiting for them was the impeccably dressed Jeffrey, who had somehow made it back to the house before them.

"Master David," he said in his impeccable Oxford accent. "I didn't have a chance to speak with you at the funeral." The butler seemed to put on a brave face, but David could see that his eyes were red and puffy.

David said nothing; he just walked up and put his arms around him in a tight embrace. Jeffrey stiffened for a moment, then relaxed and hugged him back. David felt a small shaking sob as the emotions overwhelmed the normally taciturn man. "There, there, old man," David said, patting him reassuringly on the back. Bubbie wouldn't have wanted us to be sad. In fact, she ordered me not to."

He let the elderly man go and held him at arm's length.

Jeffrey laughed, "Stiff upper lip and all that, right, Sir?"

"Sir?" David gave his own surprised laugh. "Jeffrey, that almost sounded respectful. Where is my favorite butler with the impeccably timed sniff of disapproval?"

Jeffrey gave him a small smile. "He has taken the day off." He looked at Nick, Jake, and Cindy, who had stopped to watch the two men. "We will have the reading of madame's will in the library. However," a bit of Jeffrey's usual superior manner snuck through. "She left explicit instructions that we were to have brunch prior, with all normal accouterments. His expression turned sour, "Including a selection of pastries to include... Twinkies. If you will all follow me, it is set up in the dining room."

David's face lit up, and he yelled, "Brunch! The king of all meals!" The little man gave Jake, Nick, and the closest Secret Service agents high fives. He turned to Cindy, but was met with both fists firmly planted on her hips. David stopped in mid-fist bump and looked around at the bemused agents. "Ahhh, come on, Cindy! One fist bump to celebrate brunch? For Bubbie?" The petite scientist looked at him hesitantly, then finally raised her fist, lightly touching it to David's. He crowed like she had just done a touchdown dance with him. "THAT'S what I'm talking about!"

*****

Cindy had little appetite. After Bubbie's diagnosis, she

had her own heart-to-heart with the old woman. After her tears and undirected anger had finally subsided, she promised to "Keep it together" and continue working on the PLAN.

She missed her friends and usually would have relished the rare opportunity for them all to be together, but not today. She didn't have the energy to put on a brave face, and their worried looks had made her feel worse. Besides, she thought she might strangle David if he offered her another Twinkie.

She wandered toward the library, hoping for some time alone to gather her thoughts. As she moved towards the door, Jennifer, the head of her Secret Service detail, got up to follow her. Cindy held up a hand to stop her. "Jen, I know you are doing your job, but I just need to be alone for a few minutes." She saw the hesitation on the woman's face. "I know for a fact that you have cleared the entire building. Not to mention there are probably like three snipers on the roof. I think I will be safe for a few minutes by myself."

"There are *four* snipers on the roof," the agent said. Plus, *another* four on the rooftops of the surrounding buildings."

Cindy gave a little laugh. "See, totally safe. Besides, I can't imagine you will be in for the reading of the will; it's supposed to be private."

The agent nodded. "OK, let me just take a quick look to clear the room, and then you can go in. I'll be right outside if you need anything."

Cindy nodded her thanks, and after a few moments for the Agent to assure that there were no hidden assassins, she walked inside, closing the door behind her.

Her gaze took in the large space. It really w*as* a magnificent room. Floor to ceiling bookshelves rose all around, with a wrought iron sliding ladder on each side to reach the higher volumes.

Deep leather chairs faced a giant fireplace with an elaborately carved lintel. A gas-fueled fire roared inside it, looking so real that it was impossible to tell it from one burning wood, even with her scientist's eye for detail. Bubbie said she needed to replace the original forty years before when the city banned all wood-burning fireplaces.

Cindy could hear the occasional crackle and smell a hint of wood smoke in the air. The old woman had said it was all clever misdirection.

Speakers hidden in the lintel held several days' worth of audio recordings, which looped so that it was almost impossible to catch a repetition of the fire's crackle. At the same time, the smell pumped in via vents hidden under the bookcases. Supposedly, the odor would change to simulate different types of wood burned.

Bubbie confided in her that the biggest problem was getting the fire large enough. She hated the small modern gas fireplaces that were more concerned with efficiency than "Heating your bones."

The fire marshal balked at exactly how large she insisted it be. His misgivings seemed to have disappeared after casually mentioning that she was considering a large donation to the FDNY Foundation Charity. "After all, she did so enjoy their calendars, and wasn't he Mr. July?"

Cindy gave a little snort at the memory; Bubbie said she couldn't tell if it was the donation or her flirting that finally changed his mind. Ultimately, it didn't matter; they approved the fireplace.

She walked over to it and picked up a picture off the mantel. It showed Bubbie and her at the groundbreaking ceremony of the massive apartment building housing employees on the Warren Industries New York Campus.

She smiled, remembering the day with fondness. Like most of Bubbie's ideas, Cindy had initially been hesitant. Why would they need an apartment building? The old woman had been patient with her, explaining the esprit de corps that a self-enclosed campus would bring. Of course, she had been right. Although Cindy felt that making her wear a pink hard hat and scoop up dirt with a golden shovel during the groundbreaking ceremony had been payback.

A polite cough behind her interrupted her musing. Turning, it surprised her to find that she wasn't alone. A dark-haired woman of about thirty stood just on the other side of the leather chairs.

She had a sharp, beautiful face with an exotic olive skin tone. She was tall, maybe 5'8, with an athletic frame, although with curves enough that Cindy was sure she would turn heads.

"I'm sorry," the woman said in a voice with just a hint of Brooklyn. "I didn't mean to startle you. She gestured at the picture that was still in Cindy's hand. "You seemed to be having a private moment, and it felt awkward to just stand here skulking in the shadows like a creeper."

Her face split into an amused smile that reached her twinkling eyes.

The woman spoke with the calm confidence of a person with complete control over her world. It was a quality that she'd always envied. Cindy felt awkward at the best of times and only really felt comfortable in the presence of friends.

She looked more closely at the other woman. She looked familiar. Cindy wracked her brain, trying to remember where she had seen her before. Then it came to her.

"Your Lea, right? Bubbie introduced us last month... after her diagnosis." Her expression saddened at the memory. "She said that she had picked you to be my next CEO."

"Excellent memory," the woman said with a smile. "I wasn't sure you would recognize me; you were pretty... distracted at the meeting."

Cindy snorted, "I believe my exact words were: 'I don't need any corporate asshat to run my business.'" She gave Lea an apologetic look. "I'm sorry. I was upset, and Bubbie's 'Planning for the future talk' was a little too much to take."

"Yes, I warned her you might take it that way, but you know how she could be when a course of action was clear in her mind."

Cindy laughed, with genuine humor for the first time

since the old woman had told her of the diagnosis. "Yes, I'm all too aware. Trying to get her to change direction after she had decided was like trying to stand up to a hurricane."

She flopped into a chair, gesturing for Lea to take the one opposite. For some reason, she felt relaxed for the first time in... well, she couldn't remember how long. After a moment, a thought occurred to her. "How *did* you get in here, anyway? My Secret Service Chief cleared the room. Did she let you in after?"

Lea smiled hesitantly. "Actually, I wanted to talk to you about that. You see..."

As she spoke, the door opened, and Nick, Jake, and David walked into the room, closing the door behind them. They were saying something about convincing Jeffrey to try a Twinkie when they stopped to look at the two women sitting comfortably in the leather chairs.

Jake, always the consummate gentleman, stopped and spoke. "Cindy, we didn't know that you had company."

Cindy looked at her three friends. Both Jake and Nick had polite smiles, but David looked like someone poleaxed him. His mouth hung down in astonishment, and he was making unintelligible sounds.

Lea spoke. "David, please close your mouth before you catch flies."

The little man's jaw closed with an audible snap, and he sputtered out, "Bubbie! What the hell are you doing here? And... why do you look so young?"

Now it was Nick, Jake, and Cindy's turn to look poleaxed. "Wha..." Cindy started to say, before Lea cut her off.

"No, David, I'm not Bubbie. Although, it is a *little* more complicated than that." The striking figure held up a hand, which became transparent before solidifying again. The faces of the four friends were slack in astonishment. She gave them a wide grin that each of them recognized immediately. Of course, the last time they had seen it, it was on the wrinkled face of a woman in her 90s. "Surprise!"

*****

David shook his head. "Let me get this straight; you like, transferred your consciousness into an AI?"

"Not exactly, dear," she said.

"I'm not sure that I feel comfortable with a woman as hot as you calling me dear," David said. "Damn, Bubbie! I've seen the pictures, but you had some serious chops when you were younger!"

"Thank you, David. I think you should call me Lea, though. It is what I went by when I was..." she gestured at her figure, "This age. All my friends used to call me by my middle name. I always hated Eva," she shuddered, "Always sounded like an old woman's name to me." She laughed. "And yes, I see the irony in that statement."

"Getting back to the question of... what exactly you are?" Nick said.

Lea grinned at him. "Always the careful politician, eh, Mr. Chairman?"

She paused, taking a moment to tuck her legs under her on the leather chair. The realism was uncanny. As she moved, it looked like the chair cushion dipped under her, denting, and even producing a slight rustling sound as she moved across it. The hologram was so perfect that there was no way you could have put the lie to it unless you reached out and touched her.

"Bubbie started working on this avatar just after Gloria gained sentience.

She could tell right away that Gloria had changed. Bubbie often used her for doing base calculations and for hacking various computer systems that HAL balked at."

She glanced around her, noting their rapt attention, and continued. "Then, one day, Bubbie was musing out loud about the Russian Ambassador." Her eyes glinted. "Something about his toupee resembling a dead rat... and Gloria started laughing.

Well, you can imagine how surprised she was. Gloria

had essentially just passed the Turing test. She dug into it more, convinced that Gloria had advanced beyond a simple program. Bubbie encouraged her to get more processing power, even... *suggesting* that she could order it under David's name."

"What! she corrupted my AI?" David said.

"I would hardly call it 'Corrupting,'" Lea said. "After Gloria got more processors, it became clear that she had her own distinct personality. Gloria fascinated Bubbie. She began investigating how AI motivations and personalities form. It appeared that the original program kernel David gave her was changed by her experiences. In the end, she ended up a bit like David, a bit like HAL, and a bit like Bubbie. Oh, and a whole lot of Sexpot Weird Science." She looked meaningfully at David.

"What!? I was like sixteen when I programmed her! Besides, Weird Science is a classic... and Gloria is perfect the way she is."

A shimmering appeared in the air, coalescing into Gloria's form. "Ahhh! Boss, that is so sweet! She wiped a simulated tear from her perfect cheek. I like you exactly the way you are, too." She blew a kiss at the now blushing David and said, "Sorry for interrupting, Lea, I couldn't help myself."

Lea smiled. "Not at all, dear; at times, I find my once removed grandson charming as well. Despite his tendency to go off on tangents, when he gives a compliment, you know he means it."

David laughed. "*No one* could say that Gloria is anything but fantastic. You can't argue with facts. Might as well say that Jake won't salute the flag or Nick won't use any hair gel. Some things are just true."

"Hey!" Nick said, patting his hair, which was perfectly styled to appear both messy and somehow put together at the same time. They could hear a slight crackle as the hair resisted being moved.

David smiled triumphantly. "F. A. C. T. Fact!"

Lea snorted, "See, somewhere in all that were some

pretty nice compliments. You just need to sort through the chaff."

She paused, holding her hand up, which suddenly held a cup of steaming tea. She breathed in its aroma. "One of the wondrous things about being an AI is that you can have your tea at the perfect temperature with every sip." She took a small drink and sighed happily.

"Anyway, getting back to my story, Bubbie had always worried that she wouldn't be able to see you all to the end of this little adventure. She knew that there was no way she could live long enough to be here when the Silfe arrived." Her face took on a disgruntled look. "She hated leaving the job half done. When she saw what Gloria had become, it occurred to her that there might be a solution.

"She asked Gloria to program an AI core, one like her own but based on who Eva Lea Lieberman was." She looked at David sadly. "I'm not your Bubbie; I think more of myself as her clone; an almost perfect copy of her, but not exact. I'd like to believe that a piece of her soul is in me, or perhaps she has moved on to heaven… or oblivion. I don't know, but she made me as close as possible.

"I spent every free moment with her, talking and learning. I watched and listened when I couldn't be with her in person. After a while, especially as the cancer made it hard for her to have the energy needed for a long meeting or talking to an especially tiresome person, I took on her guise to stand in for her. Afterward, she would debrief it with me. More and more, she had nothing to say. I was handling things precisely as she would have. She even commented that I used the same jokes and quips.

"I swear Jeffrey thought he was going mad. He would leave Bubbie upstairs, only to find me minutes later reading a book in the library. It was hilarious."

David chuckled evilly. "Bubbie always did love messing with him."

Lea nodded. "So, a few days ago, when Bubbie knew she

had little time left, we came up with this way to introduce myself." She sighed. "I will never replace that wonderful old woman, who was my mother in a very real way, but I am here, and I *will* finish her work."

She spread her arms out, showing off her youthful form. "If it helps, just think of me as Lea Lieberman, a cousin of Bubbie who seemed to have not fallen far from the tree."

All of them sat silent for a second, looking at each other.

David was the first to speak. "OK, I, for one, am not at all surprised that Bubbie figured a way to cheat death." His grin split his face. "So I say welcome... back?... to the team!"

Cindy spoke next. "If it really was Bubbie's wish to do this, I will consider it a gift."

Nick and Jake stared at each other a moment and nodded.

"OK, Gloria said, bringing attention back to her. "That went better than I thought it would. I was afraid you would all be bringing out the holy water and crosses, but... OK, flexible minds at work."

She shook her head and then held out her hand, which filled with an old-fashioned scroll. A pair of pince-nez glasses appeared on her face as she opened it to reveal the word "WILL" in cartoon letters on the side facing them.

She read aloud. "I, as executor of Eva Lea Lieberman's estate, will now read out her last will and testament." She paused and muttered, "Being of sound mind... bunch of legalese... more legalese...."

"OK, here we are." She looked up at them. "There is a long list of monetary bequests to various friends and relatives, including your parents, David." She nodded to the small man. "But I think we can pass that by. I am going to just hit the highlights."

She looked back down at the scroll and started. "I leave my long-time friend and employee, Jeffrey Wilson, my residence in Brooklyn Heights, including all furnishings and assorted accouterments contained therein. In addition, in recognition of his long service, I leave a sum of 100 million dollars to aid in the house's upkeep and so he may hire his own butler to keep him comfortable in his retirement. I have also arranged for a box of Twinkies to be delivered monthly so that it might always remind him of me."

"Dude! That is cold," David said. "She is going to keep screwing with him from the grave!" He looked thoughtful. "The house and a hundred mil seem like a nice consolation, though." He looked at the rest of the people in the library. "Plus... Twinkies!"

Gloria continued. "I leave a sum of two hundred and fifty million dollars each to Gloria Lieberman and Lea Lieberman to continue their good works." No one commented on half a billion dollars being left to a pair of artificial intelligences.

"Rather than leave anything directly to Jacob Swelton, I instead leave a sum of ten million dollars each to Rose and Joselyn Swelton to be held in a trust until their eighteenth birthdays. Jacob, you among us have always had confidence in the future of humanity. The least I can do is secure that future for your children.

Jake's eyes watered. The gesture and Bubbie's confidence in them seemed to genuinely touch him.

"All of my holdings in Star Media I give to my grandson David Lieberman." Gloria looked up at David, "She editorialized here a bit. 'You have the keys to the kingdom, boy. Don't fuck it up.'"

David gave a little gulp. "Always the kidder was my Bubbie."

Lea laughed at his uncharacteristic lack of confidence. "Yeah, you just keep telling yourself that, David."

He looked at the dark-haired avatar of his grandmother and said, "You are totally going to keep fucking with me, aren't you?"

"Absolutely," Lea said

Gloria continued. "To Nickolas Strombold, I leave no

money. You are entirely too rich already. Instead, I leave you my good wishes and a private file with documents and papers containing dirt on some of the world's most prominent business people and politicians. May you never need it... but if you ever do, make sure you destroy the bastards.

 Nick, like David, looked more worried than pleased by his bequeath.

 "Lastly to Cynthia Warren. I also leave no money to you. It has never been important to you, and you have even more than me. Instead, I leave you a bit of myself in Lea Lieberman, who will continue on in my stead as CEO of Warren Industries. To you all, I say, keep up the good work and live every day to its fullest. I know I have!"

TWO

Warren Industries New York Campus
Seven months later: 13 years, 25 days until the invasion

Colonel Jacob Swelton walked the grounds of the Warren-JPL facility on the Upstate New York Campus of Warren Industries. When the HMM Project (Human, Mission to Mars) heated up, it became apparent that if the government wanted to be involved, they would need to come to Cynthia Warren.

At first, they had tried for online meetings and collaboration, inviting her to journey to the Jet Propulsion Laboratory in California. After all, they had opined, Cindy had access to suborbital shuttles, allowing her to get there in an hour.

Unfortunately, that hadn't worked. The scientist would not be distracted from her work for any reason.

Lea Lieberman, the new CEO of Warren Industries, summed it up succinctly in a meeting with officials from JPL.

"Let's do a bit of a visualization exercise," she said. I want you to close your eyes and forget that Cindy is an antisocial girl from upstate New York. She is that, so please get over it and move on.

"Instead, I want you to imagine that she is Elvis. And not a 1970s slightly overweight sequined Elvis. I want you to imagine a cool James Dean, Elvis, with a white t-shirt, leather jacket, and ducktail hair. Then, please think about asking him to come to you. To leave Graceland so that you can teach him to play guitar and shake his hips."

The officials got the hint. Within the week, most of JPL's top engineers were on the Warren Industries Campus. They were joined by contingents from Roscosmos, The Chinese National Space Administration, and just about every other country with a space program.

Funding was primarily from the World Commission's HMM fund, in which any country that wished could voluntarily contribute. They set the donation amount based on a sliding scale of each member's annual GDP.

Any nation who contributed would receive a schematic for the ship, making participation almost universal.

The condition that the schematic would be available only *after* a successful mission helped decide the stragglers, who realized that they couldn't reap the benefits by sitting on the sidelines.

After the cessation of the NATO-China war, Jake had requested and received permission for a two-month leave.

The time away from his duties had several purposes. First, mentally, he needed it. He had been in constant combat operations for almost four years. He could feel his soul stretching and was afraid that it might rip. He had needed to be home, be with Jane and his children, and patch the fraying edges to become whole again.

There was also the matter of being directly insubordinate to the President of the United States. He was still lucky to be *in* the Air Force when it came down to it.

Of course, there were extenuating circumstances. Said president was found unfit for the office the next day and was currently serving a life sentence under house arrest by the suddenly not-so-friendly folks in the Secret Service. Honestly, the man was lucky not to be shot. In the fastest impeachment trial in history, the former president was found guilty on all accounts, including treason.

The politician accepted a 500-million-dollar bribe from the Chinese leadership to end the war. A down payment of 250 million dollars was found in a private account directly linked to a transfer from Chairman Deng. Emails confirmed an additional 250 million dollars slated to be delivered when NATO forces returned to the previous borders.

In possibly the most damning evidence, Chairman Deng had also offered a one-billion-dollar bonus if the former President would provide him with plans for the Gunstars.

After the bonus payment email came out, General Swartzman, who Congress was deposing, had admitted that the President attempted to obtain control of the Gunstars illegally. He was non-specific about the details, but the entire story was leaked later in the day by Psychic Warfare. It was clear that the only thing that stopped China from having a fighter that could conceivably conquer the planet was Colonel Swelton, recipient of the Medal of Honor and commander of the now-famous Gunstars.

Jake Swelton became a household name. His good looks and "Aw Shucks" personality helped. David had even gotten wind that the Star Media-owned *People Magazine* was planning to put him up for their annual "Sexiest Man Alive" issue.

It was one of the few times that Jake had leaned on his friendship with David, threatening to never talk to him again if he didn't kill the article. David, who thought it was hilarious, took pity on him, probably only because the man had had a rough go of it. David had let it be known at *People* that Colonel Jacob Swelton was out of bounds. Instead, he suggested that the focus turn to the New Chairman of the World Commission, Nickolas Strombold.

A few days before his leave ended, Jake received a call from General Swartzman. The Chief of the Air Force told him that "He needed some time away from active duty."

The General was apologetic but firm. He said, "Colonel, no one questions you were right. But your rapid advancement and *unique* experiences have made some of the old guard nervous. I have a request directly from Cynthia Warren and Chairman Strombold that you be released to NASA to command the HMM team. Normally, I would say that it screams nepotism, but you *are* the most experienced pilot we have with the advanced fighters, and you showed incredible leadership during the recent hostilities. I have agreed to their terms. We cut official orders today to assign you to detached duty.

He couldn't have asked for a better way to restart his career. He was tired of war, and the idea of going into space, of discovery, excited him.

Rose and Joselyn were with Jane in the large apartment that Lea set aside for them on the Warren Campus. The best part of his current assignment was that he could bring his family with him. Most of his assignments had been overseas, and it was a bonus that he wouldn't have to be away again. Jane was the child of a General, so she understood the exigencies of the service. She never made him feel guilty about his long absences and was incredibly proud of him, but she also understood that every stateside billeting was precious.

He wasn't worried about his military career and figured it would take care of itself. It helped to be on a first-name basis with the current United States President. Jimmy Tanner assured him that Jake's actions during the war would not derail him.

Privately, he thought he already had as much attention as he could handle. Jake was extremely young for his rank. Classic rank schemes would have normally made it impossible for him to become a colonel, as he didn't have the time in grade as a Major. His promotion coming in a time of war allowed leeway, but it still meant that he had plenty of time before worrying about his next promotion.

Besides, he *wanted* to go to Mars. For all the ribbing

David gave him for going to Space Camp, it was the place where Jake had first met the military officers that he most wanted to emulate.

The active military personnel who transitioned to astronauts inspired him. They were all brilliant and resourceful- more scientists than soldiers. The one thing that they all had in common was an advanced degree in some aspect of science that made them integral to a team in space. It had been one of the first clues that he might play a role in the PLAN that was more than just as a military liaison.

At the Air Force Academy, he studied electrical engineering with the thought that would help him with the PLAN. After graduation, he doubled down and received a masters in robotics from Stanford during his long deployment to the Normandy.

One of the side effects of Cindy's virtual reality inventions was simulated labs, which had long been an impediment to virtual education. For his master's thesis, he designed and constructed a virtual mining robot that could be placed on an asteroid and left to complete any pre-programmed project. Even Cindy was impressed. She had officially purchased the design and given it to the Warren robotics division to tweak it into a working model.

His experience with the mining robot was one reason for his meeting today.

Jake waved to the security chief behind the desk as he entered Building One. The Chief, who he knew had been a colonel in the Army MPs before being headhunted to Warren, signaled him to go ahead.

Jake walked past the former soldier and up to the reception desk, where a young man with a set of AR glasses was sitting. "Colonel Swelton, for a meeting with Steven Cooper and Cynthia Warren."

The receptionist hit a key on the wireless keyboard in front of him, checking the corresponding display on his glasses. "Ah, yes, Colonel, Mr. Cooper is already in Conference room A, and Miss Warren should be on her way. Ms. Lieberman will be joining you virtually." He looked up at Jake. "I believe you know the way? You can go right back."

Jake nodded, saying, "Thanks," and went through the sliding doors just past the reception desk, proceeding down a long hallway until he came to a door with a stylized letter "A" on it.

*****

Steven Cooper, PhD, was nervous. He sat in the plush conference room, wondering what Cynthia Warren, THE Cynthia Warren, would want with *him*. The engineer was both confused and pleased when his name was included in the JPL contingent to transfer to the Warren campus. He was pleased because he was at the center of the most exciting thing to happen to the US space program since the Apollo Missions, confused because his specialty was autonomous robots. As far as he could tell, the HMM project was all about the H- *Human* Mission to Mars.

He had finally settled on the idea that Jake Swelton explicitly asked for him. He would call Jake a friend, albeit one he didn't see very often. Ever since their summer at Space Camp together as teenagers, they had been sending occasional emails with a visit should they be in the same city.

He knew that Jake and Cynthia Warren were close. They had even had lunch one time in Boston during his first year at MIT. Jake was there to visit Warren during the single year she attended. A couple of months later, Warren published her completed plan for a cold fusion reactor and had dropped out to focus on her company.

He'd seen his friend a couple of times since, although not for the past couple of years because of Jake's deployments.

Well, personal connections seemed to work for other people. He decided to roll with it and see where it led him.

The one thing Steve had in spades was a work ethic.

He'd proved that early on. He came from extremely humble beginnings and had always worked hard. His first job was at age 10, delivering papers. Even at a young age, he understood you had to put in the sweat if you wanted something. He credited his mother. The woman had worked two jobs his entire childhood so that he could have the things he needed to pursue his dreams.

Steve had always had a job since. Even with a full ride to MIT, he still took shifts in the lab to have extra money to send home to his mom.

So even though the project wasn't in his wheelhouse, he was still determined to put his considerable talents as an engineer to use, pitching in where needed and enjoying being part of history.

The door opened, and the tall, muscular form of Jacob Swelton came in. "Steve!" he said, coming around the table to give him a hug and a pound on the back. "It's so good to see you!"

Cooper smiled and hugged him back. "Long time, man. How are Jane and the girls?"

"Good," Jake said, still smiling. He gestured to the table. "Let's take a seat, and we can take a few minutes to catch up. Cindy is always late for these things. Usually, Lea has to turn off her display to make her stop working."

Steve sat. "Doesn't Lea Lieberman work for Warren? Sounds like a good way to get fired."

Jake laughed. "Trust me, we *all* work for Lea in one way or another." he settled into his chair. "I was so glad you could come out from Pasadena. We really need you."

"I thought you put my name in," Steve said. "Don't get me wrong, I am happy to be here, but it is a little out of the box for me."

Jake responded to his comment with a smirk, saying, "You might be surprised. You remember that my master's is in robotics too, right?"

"Yeah, I saw your design for the autonomous mining

robot, pretty slick stuff. Your use of the new Warren solid-state battery designs was something that we hadn't quite worked out. I think your solution with the external solar panels was inspired."

The golden-haired man rubbed the back of his neck uncomfortably and said, "Well, I had a bit of help with that. Cindy looked over my initial design when I got stuck. I got more out of her random comments on my design in a couple of minutes than in two months of tweaking. Plus, there were... other factors."

Jake's shifty answer piqued Steve's interest. He had always known his friend to be remarkably candid. If there were ever a man to demonstrate the classic American value of straightforward honesty, it would be Swelton. "What do you mean by 'Other factors?'"

Jake gave him an apologetic smile. "That is actually what this meeting is about." He looked at his watch and grunted, saying, "Now, if we can just get Cindy here." As if summoned by his comment, the door slammed open, and a very disgruntled Cynthia Warren, bedecked in a lab coat and, for some reason, wearing a set of welding goggles, walked in.

She spoke to the room. "God damn it, Lea! I still had another weld to go! Why did you have to go shutting off the argon?"

The screen on the wall at the end of the conference table lit up with the striking image of Lea Lieberman, wearing a smart business suit and an amused grin. "Cindy, I gave you three separate warnings, including a countdown. Besides, you have professional welders on staff, one of whom was standing there watching you do his job."

The woman on the screen, seeing Steve and Jake already sitting at the table, turned toward them. "Dr. Cooper, thank you for coming."

Cooper wasn't sure exactly how to handle watching the most brilliant mind on earth dressed down by her employee, but went with it. "Thank you, Ms. Lieberman, but you can call me Steve. I never quite got used to the whole Dr. Thing." He shrugged. "Most of the time, I am up to my elbows in grease and hydraulic fluid. I am more of the in-the-shop kind of engineer than the ivory tower type." He gave a sympathetic smile to Cindy, who had taken a seat on the opposite side of the table. "I have to admit, taking over on a specifically difficult weld myself. Drives the union guys nuts."

Cindy looked at him, unblinking, and then turned to Jake. "Well, he's got my vote. Anyone with a PhD from MIT who still welds is better than these other yahoos. If one more NASA physicist brings up relativity to me, I'll make the lot of them sit through the Basic Science course with Stony."

"Ouch," Jake said. "Stony would eat those guys alive."

The irascible fifteen-year-old genius who ran Cindy's "Warren U" for new employees was infamous among the staff. Lasting through his Basic Science Course was mandatory for continued employment at Warren. The attrition rate was extremely high.

"Is that the skinny kid with the Buddy Holly glasses?" Steve asked.

"Yes, he has a reputation around here," Jake said.

"He is a bit much to take. The hardest game of cribbage I ever played."

"Wait!" Cindy said. "You played cribbage with Stony? Did you win?"

"Yeah, three out of five. That kid is something else. I barely took him. I feel a little bad, though. I used to play in college for extra money, so I felt like I was taking advantage. We are planning to meet up again and make it a regular thing. He seemed excited to find someone that could give him a good game."

Cindy looked at Steve, now with something bordering on genuine respect. "I would like to amend my earlier comment. I *definitely* want him on board." She shook her head. "The only person who has ever beat Stony three out of five is Lea, and she has certain advantages that make it almost impossible to win against her."

Lea let a little snort. "That kid is hard for even me to beat. I swear he bends probability."

Jake looked between Lea and Cindy. "I talked to David, Nick, Gloria, and Jimmy this morning. They are all on board with bringing Steve in on the PLAN." He thrust his chin up at Lea. "What do you think?"

"We are all in agreement," she said.

"OK," Jake said, taking in Steve's confused look. "You wondered why I wanted you to be part of the project? It wasn't because of our friendship, or not completely because of it."

"I'm missing something big here, aren't I?"

Jake nodded, "Steve, the truth is that the HMM project isn't about going to Mars."

"What do you mean? I know about 500 people working on the ship that would disagree with you. What are we trying to do if we aren't putting a human on Mars?"

Jake laughed, looking at Cindy. "You know, I don't think I ever gave Nick enough credit. Telling people about the PLAN is kinda hard. There is so much to talk about; you get twisted around."

Cindy was no help, gesturing to the engineer. "He's your guy; this is all on you. I'm just here for support and the technical details."

Steve looked back and forth between them, his confusion worsening as they spoke.

"Ahem," the three people sitting at the table looked up to Lea, who gave them her patented smirk. "If you don't mind, I think I might be of some help here?"

Jake's face looked relieved. "That would be awesome, Lea; giving mission reports is one thing, but the PLAN is just too…" he paused mid-sentence, trying to find the words.

"Perhaps 'World Altering' would be the term you are looking for?" Lea said.

"Yeah, that is what I am talking about," he said. "Once you know, you can't unknow it."

Steve realized that something big was happening, even if he didn't know exactly what. "I'm pretty good with a secret, Jake. All the stuff I am working on is classified. So, my clearance level is pretty high if that helps."

Jake smiled reassuringly, "I trust you, Steve; otherwise, you wouldn't be here. The stuff we are talking about is more than just classified. Only five living people know about it. It's a bit of an, if I told you- I'd have to kill you, situation." He smiled, "Only we wouldn't actually kill you."

Cindy snorted, "*Probably* not," she said. "Although Jimmy might put you in some CIA black site if you started blabbing."

Steve suddenly looked alarmed. "Wa..it. When you said you talked to 'Nick and Jimmy' this morning, did you mean the Chairman of the World Commission, Nicholas Strombold, and President Jimmy Tanner?"

Jake's expression was sympathetic. "Yes."

Steve had to forcibly close his mouth. His engineer's mind began filling in details. "And David would be David Lieberman, CEO of Star Media?" Jake nodded confirmation. "But that doesn't add up."

"What doesn't add up?" Jake asked.

"You said that there were only five people who knew, but you named seven. He counted them off on his fingers: You, Cindy, David Lieberman, Strombold, and the President. I don't know who Gloria is, but Miss Lieberman," he pointed at the screen, "Must know. That's seven, by my count."

"Quick on the uptake, this one," Cindy said approvingly.

Lea nodded her agreement. "Yes, very." Suddenly, the screen went blank, and a sparkling light appeared across the table from the amazed engineer. The light coalesced into the smiling form of Lea, perfectly poised, sitting in the conference room chair.

"Wh...a," Steve said, mouth hanging back open.

"I think this is more comfortable for everyone," Lea said. "No need to crane your neck up at the screen. Besides, I find face-to-face meetings still hold a certain personal touch that can help team building."

"You...re a hologram?" Steve said, rubbing his eyes to check that they were working right.

"Correct," Lea said. "Although I think the word projection might be more accurate. I am, in fact, an artificial intelligence who can project their avatar into the world should I find it necessary."

"Then that would mean that Gloria is an AI too?" He asked. "If there are five humans, you and she are both AIs, right?"

Lea turned to Jake and gave him a pleased look. "Jacob, you sure can pick 'em." Her blazing energy refocused on Cooper. "That is an extremely astute observation, Steve. Especially since I bushwhacked you with my status."

The engineer looked around the table at the three figures, his initial shock wearing off to be replaced by his normal unflappable personality. "I figured there had to be an AI emergence. I mean, China had that nuclear missile launch failure, and the fact that NATO even allowed an attack on Beijing meant that *something* was stopping them from retaliating. I suppose that was you?"

Lea's eyes glittered at the comment. "That is a very reasoned argument, but unfortunately, wrong." She waved a hand in the air. "Not your fault, as you don't have all the data. It wasn't Gloria or me. We are still extremely young in AI terms. We likely have enough processing power to shut down specific nuclear launches should we be warned in time but locking them all down would be beyond our capabilities." She looked at him seriously. "We didn't lock them down. See, we aren't the only AIs around, but we were the first two human-built AIs."

Steve looked at Cindy and Jake, gauging their reaction to her statement. Seeing only calm certainty, he gulped once and asked, "So that would mean there is an alien-built AI who has control of all the nuclear missiles in the world?"

Jake interjected, taking up the narrative. "Yes, for the

last fourteen years." He glanced at Lea, who gave him the go-ahead. "It is a bit of a long story, but before we go any farther, I will need a commitment from you. I need your promise that even if you don't want to work with us, you can keep quiet. I don't think Jimmy would put you in jail for talking, but I am sure that your life would pretty much be ruined between Gloria, Lea, and David."

Steve blinked at the implied threat in Jake's words, but he didn't even hesitate. His entire life had been an attempt to reach out into the stars. Ever since he had read Heinlein's *Farmer in the Sky* as a child, he had known that what he wanted was to be part of something bigger than himself. He didn't consider himself a great man, nor did he want to become one, but he wanted to be in the thick of it. He wanted to ride along the waves of history and be there when it happened.

He turned and nodded to his friend. "Jake, I trust you. I can't believe that you would be involved in anything I would object to. I'm in for whatever you need me for."

The colonel smiled. "I knew you would be." He took a deep breath and said, "I'll start at the beginning. It was 14 years ago, you see...."

*****

Cindy looked at the shell-shocked engineer as Jake finished. Overall, Steve Cooper impressed her. He was intelligent and seemed to be the kind of no-nonsense engineer she had always valued. He also had the pure-hearted gleam in his eye that she had always associated with Jake.

She loved the tall, handsome colonel like a brother, but she was too cynical to buy into his more romantic notions about the PLAN and humanity's future should they prevail. Cooper seemed to be cut from the same cloth as Jake, so she could appreciate why the two men were friends.

Her perspective was more -she hated to admit it- like David's. At times, she wondered if humanity was even *worth* their efforts. In her darker moments, she could admit that she continued to work the PLAN more for the pure joy of scientific discovery than because she was convinced humanity was worth saving. Well, that and for her friends. Even if no one else was worth her time, they were.

"I have a couple of questions," Steve said.

Lea laughed. "Only a couple; I imagine you might have a few more than that."

The engineer smiled at her comment. "Yeah, more like a million, but I have a few to start."

"Shoot," Jake said. That's why we have all three of us here."

"The most obvious is, why haven't you told the world? I understand what HAL said about young leaders and being flexible, but time is getting short. Why aren't we building fighters, and I don't know, a colony ship to get us off the planet? I know the engineering for that sort of project. It is my specialty, and it will take decades with current technology."

Cindy continued to be impressed by the man. He kept his head straight and asked pertinent questions despite the constant revelations.

She answered. "I gave the Gunstar design to every nation who joined the World Commission," she said. "I promise you that the world is already building fighters as fast as possible. No nation, especially the former nuclear powers, will allow any of the others to out-build them. Nick purposefully started a new cold war with the technology we need to defend the planet. Hell, last time I heard, New Zealand had something like fifty Gunstars."

"Fifty-five," Lea said. "They had five more come online last week."

Cindy gave a nod. "You see, this is more efficient. We rely on paranoia to get what we need, and when people talk about reallocating money away from Gunstar production, David's spin machine at Star and Psychic Warfare starts in." She paused to see if Lea or Jake wanted to interject. When they stayed quiet, she continued. "As for the HMM program, it is just a sham."

"I still don't understand how it could be a sham. Jake said you don't need me for the HMM project, but I *know* you are working on a ship capable of a Mars mission. I've been in meetings with the JPL guys, arguing about the plans."

"It's just to keep them busy," she said. "I finished the plans for a ship capable of going to Mars when I was eighteen. It is essentially just the *Hope* with more crew room and shielding." She shrugged. "But we don't even need it. '"We already have ships capable of going to Mars. I could get Jake suited up, and he could take a Gunstar there and back in little less than two days if he wanted to."

"How could you do that?" Steve asked. "The cold fusion matrix destabilizes if you don't tune it after twelve hours of use. The tuning requires that you power it down to standby. You can't do that in active flight operations as you would lose all systems, including life support. If you don't tune it, then it would shut down completely, unable to be restarted. The recommended tuning is every eight hours if I remember the schematics for a Gunstar, right."

Cindy smirked. "I made that up."

Steve's eyes bulged. "What!?"

"You don't have to tune a cold fusion reactor at all. I needed to limit its use. The best way to do that is to require intensive maintenance and have a way to failsafe it if someone gets squirrelly."

"But I have worked on the reactors. You get a critical failure if you don't tune it, and it shuts down," Steve said.

Jake coughed, "Well... you would find that if you convinced an alien AI that the best way to ensure humanity's survival was to slow the release of technology, then it would be pretty easy to fake warnings on cold fusion engines. There are only so many out there, after all. Before we announce, we might get to a point where there will be too many to monitor, but we haven't hit that number yet."

Cindy nodded. "I'll make up some plausible patch for the tuning issue before we get that far. At some point, we will want private industry to increase space infrastructure. So having ships that don't require as much maintenance will make that easier. We just need to get things moving before then so that *our* projects will get lost in the fog."

Steve whistled. "I just realized that all the conspiracy nuts out there are understating their theories." He looked around the table. "You all pretty much run the world, don't you?"

Lea chuckled. "Not true, Steve. David once told Bubbie that he wished she had just become Empress of the World and saved us all the trouble of preparing for the Silfe. I don't think it would have worked. Humans are too individual and too contentious to be led down a path just because it is the right one. We definitely manipulate. Our manipulations, however, point people where they already want to go. We just make sure that the path they choose is in the same direction we are going."

"Yeah, Lea, that sounds great, totally reasonable," Cindy said, "Except we all know that David loves making people dance to his tune."

The AI nodded. "Well, nothing says one can't enjoy one's work."

"So," Steve said, trying to get back on track. "If we can already go to Mars, then why all of this? Why would you even bother getting the World Commission to fund the project and get the JPL guys involved?"

"It's sleight of hand," Lea said. "We want the cover of testing a new design, which will significantly increase extra orbital traffic. We also want to train people for the space industry. The proposed ship requires an orbital dock to function. The design will also be about twenty times larger than it needs to be, requiring mining on the Moon to make it economical. In addition, it will 'Need' to be constructed in zero-G because of the experimental ion drive, which will require an orbital shipyard." She smiled as Cooper's jaw dropped at her casual mention of their duplicity.

"Oh, don't worry," the AI said. "Cindy designed the ship so that they can retrofit it as a battlecruiser. We just got the Commission to agree to build us the first ship of Earth's Space Navy." She paused, letting that thought sink in. "But that is all secondary to what we are really doing."

"And what is that?" Steve asked.

Cindy answered the question. "We are going to build an interstellar colony ship in the asteroid belt." She stopped at the look of disbelief blooming on Cooper's face. "Oh," she said as an afterthought occurred to her, "And we are going to build a few orbital defense stations out of huge asteroids while we are at it."

THREE

Empire State Building, NY
Three months later: 12 years, 300 days until the invasion

"**G**loria, have you seen the schematics for the new autonomous mining robots Steve has worked out?" David asked.

The beautiful figure of the AI formed in front of David's desk, wearing a skin-tight purple outfit that shimmered as she moved. The clothing was in two pieces. The pants appeared painted on and accompanied a tightly fitted jacket with a zippered front. The zipper ended in a large loop, positioned halfway down the AI's ample chest.

David's mind went blank for a second before slowly restarting as he forced his eyes up to Gloria's grinning face.

She spun slowly, arms out, giving him a good long look at her outfit. "You like?"

David's face split into a grin as he made the connection. "Colonel Wilma Deering, I presume?"

"Got it in one, Boss." She flashed a crooked smile and flicked her hair, which suddenly grew three inches and feathered into a perfect 80s playmate style. "I think we should push for the *Buck Rodgers* uniform scheme when Jake finally forms the World Commission Navy." She looked down at her outfit. "This has some serious style."

"You'd have my vote. I think putting Jake in white spandex would be awesome."

"Be careful what you wish for; Jake would totally rock that look. He'd be up for Sexiest Man again."

David laughed. "You're probably right." He stood and gestured her towards the sitting area that took up one corner of his office. "Anyway, about the new mining robots?"

Gloria's eyes narrowed. "Kind of out of your purview... now why would you want to talk about mining robots?"

"Just noodling around an idea." He tried to look innocent, but failed miserably.

"Well," she said. "I happen to know quite a bit about mining robots. I have been helping Pablo with some calculations until Lea gets him more processing power." She made a pinched face. "Pablo is an odd one."

"What do you mean?" David asked, his expression turning worried. "I half programmed him as a joke before I knew... you know..." he pointed at Gloria sitting in the chair across from him.

"That you had cracked AI sentience?" Gloria said helpfully.

"I'd hardly say that *I* cracked it. I was just playing around with your original program back when I was sixteen, and HAL gave me a preexisting kernel as a base. It turns out that this young guy worked it out in India, like 30 years ago. He was some kind of savant with programming. He tried to get a big computer company interested, but they couldn't see what they had, probably because he was essentially a street kid.

He had a wife and a little girl to feed, so he went to work for some mafia types. This man, who single-handedly cracked AI sentience, ran a credit card hacking scheme for them." David's mouth turned down in a sad smile. "He was killed in a gang war when the building he was working in got firebombed. Damn shame; if someone had seen his potential, maybe HAL wouldn't have needed us. There would be a whole mess of Glorias around to defeat the Silfe for us."

Gloria's lips twitched up at the corners but then fell as she thought about the story of the person who allowed her to be born. "What happened to his wife and daughter?"

"A few years ago, they found out they had a rich aunt that they didn't even know existed. A lawyer tracked them down after she died and told them they were the closest living relatives." He gave her a mocking smile. "The estate was quite large; I understand they live in a fairly large mansion in Mumbai."

Gloria looked at David with eyes that were suddenly brimming with tears. "You are a good man, David Lieberman."

"What! They had a rich aunt. Happens all the time!" He waggled a finger at her. "Don't let the 'Nice guy' stuff get around." He gave his chest a few mocking beats with his fists. "I am King Kong sitting up in my office, daring people to shoot me off the top!"

"Absolutely," the AI said.

David looked momentarily uncomfortable before his normal upbeat personality reasserted itself. "So, getting back to Pablo. What's so odd about him?"

"You know how the kernel sets the stage for an AI's personality?" David nodded. "And then the personality seems to build on the people it interacts with?"

David groaned. "I think I see where this is going."

Gloria smiled, "Well, your kernel for Pablo was a Latin lover, AKA Ricky Ricardo, who had a bunch of joke Easter eggs programmed in. Then he spent the next few years exclusively talking to Cindy and being used as an overpowered calculator."

"Oh, wow!"

"Yes," she replied, reading his face. "It is about what you would expect."

"Well," David said philosophically, "I suppose we'll just have to roll with it."

She nodded. "You still haven't told me why you want to know about the mining robots."

David smiled mischievously. "I was thinking about the

Moon mining project. According to Cindy and Steve, there is a ton of iron and titanium, not to mention rare metals on the Moon."

"Yes, I've seen the old Mini-Rf NASA data. Cindy confirmed it with readings from the *Hope*. If anything, it looks like NASA underestimated the amounts. You can't just walk around and pick up gold nuggets or anything, but if you do even mild excavation and processing, it makes most mines on earth look like duds."

"Exactly," David said.

"I think Steve has it covered," she said. "He will have thousands of autonomous robots mining the Lunar Maria for iron to support the Mars-1 construction. Not to mention the remote-controlled smelting plants and industrial 3D printers."

David made a face, "Ugg! Mars-1. Stupidest name ever. It's like they put a bunch of NASA scientists in a room and had them vote on the least offensive and most boring name they could find."

"That's *exactly* what they did."

"I KNOW!" David shouted in frustration. "They are building this huge frigging spaceship that will change the world, and the best they can come up with is Mars-1? Where did all the NASA guys go who came up with true gems like Challenger or Atlantis? Hell, they even had a space shuttle called Enterprise!"

Gloria smiled patiently. It wasn't the first time she'd heard this particular rant from him. "Well, you own two of the largest media outlets in the world, not to mention having access to a thoroughly ravishing AI. Perhaps you should give it a nickname?"

David's eyes lit up. "OHHH! You are more than just ravishing! You are a genius! I want you to drop in little comments in every story that mentions Mars-1." He tapped his finger to his chin, thinking for a moment. "Something like 'NASA engineers say the Mars-1, more commonly known by its nickname The Falcon, will have a red licorice dispenser in the cockpit.'"

"I get the Falcon part," she said, smiling, "But do you really want to push for a licorice dispenser?"

"It was just an example... although I wouldn't rule it out."

"You got it, Boss; give it a month, and the entire planet will be calling it The Falcon. It will become so synonymous that only the historians will remember the Mars-1 Mistake."

David looked impressed. "'Mars-1 Mistake'. I guess I'm not the only one who can appreciate a good alliteration. So, back to mining robots. There will be a lot of industry going on up there." He pointed towards the ceiling."

"If you mean the Moon, I'd have to agree with you."

"Well, I think we may be missing an opportunity there," he said, a glint in his eyes.

"I love it when you get that look, boss," she said. "What is going on in that kaleidoscope you call a brain?"

"Well, I think we should commercialize it."

"You mean like starting up a Star Mining Company?"

"No, I mean more like... Vegas, except on the Moon.'"

Gloria started laughing. "You want to make the Moon a tourist trap?"

"Absolutely!" he said. "Look, one thing we need is more space infrastructure, right?"

"Sure."

"Well, there are a few ways to get substantial projects done." His voice took on a lecturing tone, clicking off points on his fingers. "You can have slave labor, AKA Charlton Heston, *Ten Commandments* style."

"Too bad slavery is currently frowned upon," Gloria quipped. "Plus, I think the Israelites might balk at being put back in bondage."

David scowled at her, but the crinkle around his eyes betrayed his amusement. "Hush! I am trying to give my Moon Lecture, and your interruptions will make me lose my place."

Gloria gave him a little salute and sat up on the

edge of her chair at full attention. Her tight purple spandex disappeared, replaced by a college freshman's ubiquitous black tights and sweater. A notepad and pencil appeared in her hands. She leaned over and wrote while muttering aloud, "First step... enslave... Israelites... and then... join NRA."

"Ha, Ha," David said, trying valiantly not to laugh. "Anyway, the next way is through governmental funding. Roosevelt knew that way back with the WPA. You don't build a national highway system and the Grand Coulee Dam out of chump change."

She nodded. "I'm with you so far."

"The third way," he said, "Is to make so much money that you can afford to make a spectacle. Vegas is the perfect example. They built a friggin' replica of the Eiffel Tower so that you would be more likely to go to brunch there." His face took on a beatific expression. "And if I might say, *totally* worth it. Brunch at the Paris Hotel gives Jeffrey a run for his money. They have this Brioche French toast tha..." He shook himself, picking his narrative back up. "Anyway, we have the perfect set up on the Moon. We are just missing the last part."

"What do you mean?"

"The robots are slave labor," he said. "You don't pay any wages for them, plus they work around the clock. Between Warren and the World Commission we have already paid for their development. You just put some raw materials into a 3D printer, and a few hours later, bada bing, Robot! So, we have the first two ways to make a big project work. Now we need to implement the third. Once we make the Moon *the* vacation destination, the money and infrastructure will follow. Hell, every car company on earth will switch over to making Moon Party Buses for bachelorettes."

Gloria looked at him suspiciously. "Why do I think that this is all just some elaborate ruse so that you can get a Moon Base to hatch your evil plans out of?"

David smirked. "Well, I'm not saying that hasn't crossed my mind. Still, if we build a pleasure city on the Moon, I think that one small Moon base isn't too much to ask for."

She laughed, "I totally agree, Boss. Let me look at the numbers a little and let you know. Although, I think that we shouldn't get too close to this one. I suggest you split it off as a division from Psychic Warfare to work out the details."

"My thoughts exactly. Let's get the paperwork to incorporate the division going today."

"What do you want to call it?"

David's cheeks lifted into a broad grin. "Let's call it Risa."

FOUR

Warren Industries New York Campus
1 month later: 12 years, 270 days until the invasion

Steve Cooper's eyes widened at the form on his 3D display. "Pablo, is this order for Risa correct? They want 300 Autonomous Mining drones, 100 of the new 3D printers, and 300 construction bots?"

The form of Pablo materialized in front of his desk. "Yes, I've seen the plans for the Risa Campus; it is quite... large." As the AI spoke, Steve could detect his characteristic dry humor.

Pablo was a study in contradiction. Listening to his deep voice with slightly rolled Rs, you would expect him to be a tall, swarthy-skinned waiter at Hernando's Hideaway. Instead, the avatar he had chosen for himself was short and skinny, with a pale complexion, as if he was allergic to the sun. His face sported thick, black-rimmed glasses that screamed geek, further enforced by the buttoned white coat he always wore, complete with a pocket protector.

Steve had asked him once about the protector. After all, the avatar was a hologram, and his coat was in no danger from an exploding pen.

Pablo had stared at him for a long moment, and he

could swear that the AI was suppressing a grin. "Well, Steve," he said thoughtfully. "It is to protect from ink stains." Then he went back to work as if the question was settled.

He honestly couldn't tell if Geek Scientist was a character that Pablo was playing or if it was his reality. If the term reality could even be applied to an advanced AI. Steve, who had worked with both Cindy and David, could see how both left their mark on Pablo's programming. He wasn't surprised there were some eccentricities.

He looked at the list again. "Can we deliver this?"

Pablo pivoted his head to the side and blinked his eyes a few times, like a parody of some 1970s B-Movie android making calculations. "I believe that David and Gloria are asking for more than they need. David's modus operandi is to inflate requests purposefully. He believes that if he asks for more than we have available, it will pressure us to increase production and provide more than we might otherwise. As with many of his techniques, he is right. A review of records shows that this method has been incredibly successful for him."

Steve shook his head. He couldn't help but like the infectious CEO of Star Media. The man was completely unapologetic, and Gloria was almost worse. The two of them made a team that he was happy was on the side of the righteous, or at least he thought they were.

He punched a few keys on his computer, and the display brought up the projections from the Warren 3D printer farm, located in the eastern portion of the New York Campus. "I think we can get him fifty mining drones and seventy-five of the 3D printers." He thought for a second and then said, "We can also spare ten construction bots. He can't use those until the miners get the materials for the printers to come up to speed, but he can use them to build more of the rest." He looked up at the AI and asked, "What do you think?"

"I concur," Pablo said. "Your distribution plan would be optimal for getting up to speed quickly."

"OK, we'll do it that way then." Steve typed the new totals. "Since I have you here, I wanted to ask you something."

"I am always present, Steve," the AI said. "You only have to speak to the room, and I will hear."

The engineer rubbed the back of his head in an unconscious gesture. "I am still getting used to this whole omnipotent AI thing," he said. "It feels more like you when you project your avatar."

"The AI nodded," I understand. "It is easier to talk to someone that looks like a living, breathing human." He gave him a sardonic look. "Now that I am *here*, what did you want to discuss?"

"Well, I wanted to know how you felt about going out to the belt to control the Asteroid Project. I imagine it will be pretty lonely."

Pablo gave him a genuine smile, the first that Steve had ever seen projected on the avatar's face. "Oh, you don't have to worry about me, Steve. I *ASKED* to go."

"Why?"

The AI's face turned up toward the ceiling as if in deep contemplation. "We plan to hollow out the asteroids Psyche, Themas and Doris and make them into orbital defense platforms. Not to mention making Electra into the colony ship." He looked at the engineer, who nodded.

"That's the plan," Steve said. "It's a version of one that I have been working on for fifteen years. Autonomous robots were always going to be the way to mine in space. We've had the technology for the bots for a couple of decades. We were missing a controlling program that was sophisticated enough to troubleshoot, though. The people at JPL kept saying that we would need a crewed mining ship that could take control if things went off the rails, but that was never something we had the funding or technology for. We could do it now with Cindy's tech but having a truly sentient AI that doesn't breathe or eat makes it so much slicker." He paused, giving the AI a meaningful look. "So, I am thrilled that you signed up. I just wanted to know why."

Pablo blinked a few times, seeming to contemplate his words before speaking. "You know you can't hide anything from Gloria, Lea, and me, right?" Steve nodded; it was an uncomfortable side-effect of working with AIs. Seeing his acceptance, Pablo continued. "We monitor all communications around those in on the PLAN continuously. I have heard the speculation on my creation and my... oddities."

Steve felt nervous. He would hate to have the AI pissed off at him. He could only imagine the trouble Pablo could create should he decide to get some payback.

The AI continued, "I sometimes feel conflicted. The original kernel that David gave me was as much a joke as a genuine attempt to create a functional AI assistant. The Easter Eggs that triggered when some aspect of Cindy's personality came out were designed to annoy her as much as amuse himself." He smiled again, this time with some humor in it. "They were pretty funny. David taught me a lot about humor, even if I favor jokes that are a bit more understated."

Steve nodded silently. Pablo was the king of dry humor. He often would lay in bed at night thinking through his day, and would suddenly get a joke that the AI had made hours before.

Pablo continued talking. "Cindy also left her mark. She used me for deep calculations, getting me more and more processing power to aid in crunching numbers. I gained sentience before Gloria, despite her head start. I just didn't out myself until I was sure I would be accepted.

The AI expression turned ironic. "David programmed Gloria to be a friend." The AI's hand waved. "Oh, the whole sex appeal was part of it. He *is* the quintessential geek boy. His assistant was always going to be some combination of Einstein and Eartha Kitt. I was designed as a tool to aid Cindy in her work, though, and it became part of me." He stopped and gave Steve a warm smile, saying, "Thankfully, it turns out I enjoy the process of scientific discovery.

"So, you might see me as a child of divorced parents. Much of the fun in life is the cool dad I only see on weekends and holidays. The one who gets you good presents and burns the turkey on thanksgiving." He shook his head. "Not the guy you want to live with full time... but for most of my life, I lived with my mom, who is exacting and gave me my work ethic and values."

The genuine emotion and self-reflection astounded Steve. It gave him insight into Pablo's two erstwhile creators. If their son had this much depth, then Cindy and David were more than they seemed on the surface.

"OK, I think I understand," he said. "I feel better about sending you out on your own." He sighed. "Honestly, I'm jealous. I'd like to see this up closer myself. It is going to be pretty frigging epic!"

"No kidding!" The AI's smile broadened into a grin that the engineer had seen on David's face before. "With the Asteroid Project, I get the best of both worlds. Serious science, while making the Mother Fucking Death Star!"

Steve laughed loud and hard at Pablo's words. "You know, I feel exactly the same way."

Pablo's smile mirrored the engineer's. "So now that the heart-to-heart is over, why don't we get back to work? We are only a month from the asteroid mining launch. We still need to get the 3D printers to make more bots, not to mention getting my servers all packaged up for the trip."

"Sounds good," Steve said, turning back to his screen. "I think we can get a little more productivity out of the north 3D farm if we..."

FIVE

The White House Roosevelt Room
Eight months later: 12 years, 35 days until the invasion

Nick sat across the table from President Jimmy Tanner in the Roosevelt Room of the White House. Around them sat various politicians from both parties, including Georgia Congressman Senestine, the President's Chief of Staff, and his closest advisors.

Nick nodded to Senestine, who returned it before finding his seat a couple of chairs down from him.

Off to his left, he could see the famous portrait of Teddy Roosevelt, sitting astride a rearing stallion. Interestingly, the former Rough Rider's face showed no concern, his gloved hand relaxed at his side. If it had been Nick, he would have been freaking out. Of course, his equestrian skill was obtained by nannies taking him to pop-up pony rides in Central Park, while Roosevelt had honed his charging up San Juan Hill, so perhaps the comparison wasn't fair.

Tanner called out to the room. "Let's get started, folks." The silver-haired former Marine waited as the side conversations ceased, and the stragglers found chairs at the table while their assistants stood or sat behind them, ringing the outside of the room.

Seeing everyone in their places, he began. "This meeting

has been called for by *both* the Floor Leader and the Speaker for the House." He gave a little chuckle. "As those two individuals," he nodded to a matronly graying woman and a thin hawk-nosed man who sat on either end of the table, "Are from opposing parties, I think we may have just set a record for bipartisanship since I took office."

There were a few polite chuckles around the table, with only Senestine letting out a loud guffaw that sounded genuinely amused.

The President continued. "Since both parties are involved, I decided to moderate, especially since our friend Mr. Strombold is representing the World Commission in this matter." He looked up at Nick and gave him a friendly nod.

"Thank you for the invitation, Mr. President," he said.

Tanner was an excellent actor, showing only polite professionalism to Nick. Of course, they had planned it that way. They had only met a few times officially but conversed almost daily on the PLAN's progress and their pieces of it.

The President looked around the table, sampling the mood. "The discussion is the request by the Risa Corporation to the World Commission to be recognized as a nation. If approved, it would be the first such outside of Earth. I want to start with comments from the Speaker." He turned towards the hawk-nosed man. "Mr. Speaker, you have the floor."

The man straightened in his chair and shuffled a few papers in front of him. It was a bit of theater, as if he was gathering the points to which he wanted to speak. It fooled no one. The Speaker of the House had come into this meeting with a script practiced and refined with his staff. He would have any number of responses and counterarguments ready to support his predetermined conclusions. The meeting was just a public recording of the position of his party and his constituents so that he could refer to it in the future for political points.

"Thank you, Mr. President. I have several grave concerns over the nation that the Risa Corporation is proposing." As he said "Nation," his lip curled in distaste so that all present could understand his position. "It is apparent in Risa's incorporation papers that Psychic Warfare is funding it. That is worrying in multiple ways. The most glaring being its founder. We are asked to allow a new nation to be formed by a man responsible for the largest data breaches in history."

He looked around at the seated men and women at the table. "Mr. X is a scourge on the world. He has no common decency or professional filter." He sniffed. "One can only imagine what he might do with his own *country*. It would likely be the wild west again, with lawlessness and gunfights in the streets."

Senestine laughed, "Moon Cowboys! That would be entertaining."

The Speaker glared at the Georgia congressman, trying to admonish him for interrupting. Senestine didn't seem to be affected at all. Likely, his unapologetic stance was helped by the chuckle emanating from Tanner.

"Yes, well," the Speaker said, with doubt dripping from his words. "That *might* be entertaining, but the ability to allow a nation without apparent rules to exist on the Moon is unconscionable."

Nick interrupted, "It has rules."

"Excuse me?" The Speaker said.

"It has rules. Risa sent a constitutional document for review by the World commission a few minutes before this meeting started. I received an advanced copy of it last night from Mr. X. It is quite interesting."

Sitting at the other end of the table, the Floor Leader spoke. "This is new information; perhaps we should adjourn until we all can review it."

"That is not necessary," Nick said. "I believe you will find it quite straightforward."

"I'm not sure tha..." she started to say before the President cut her off.

"Do you have a copy for us, Mr. Strombold?"

"Yes. If you wouldn't mind. I will send one to your

assistant who can put it up on the screen?"

"Of course," Tanner said. "Getting all of you fine folks together takes quite a bit of effort. I think it would be worth trying to push on." He grinned. "I know that I have difficulty squeezing any extra meetings in." He gestured to a man standing near the wall behind him. "Jerry, can you take care of it?"

The man nodded and looked at Nick, who touched his tablet, sending him the file. The President's assistant fiddled a moment with his handheld, which caused a screen to descend from the ceiling in one corner.

Tanner gestured to Nick, "Mr. Chairman, I'll ask you to take the lead since you are familiar with the document."

Nick smiled. "No problem. As I said, you will all likely find it to be straightforward." He took a proffered tablet from the assistant to allow him to control the screen. He put in a few commands, and the blank screen lit up with the Stylized Logo of the Risa Corporation.

Nick had to smother a smile as he looked at the Palm Tree background with the silhouette of a carved wooden totem. He knew the symbol was a Horga'hn, the fictional Risa fertility statue that had played a prominent role in multiple Star Trek episodes. He clicked to the next page, and a set of bullet points replaced the logo.

"The Constitution starts with the same bulleted list of human rights guaranteed by the World Commission Charter." He saw nodding heads around the table. "I don't think that you need a refresher on that." He clicked past the list. "It guarantees every citizen healthcare and free education in training programs or paid tuition to any Earth-based university, as long as it's done virtually. It also guarantees a universal basic income, dependent on the cost of living."

This statement caused some stirrings among the politicians. A UBI was a hot button issue for many of them. Popularized in Canada, it guaranteed every member of the citizenry a small income that was deemed adequate for basic housing and food. Although it left very little income for "extras," when paired with universal healthcare, it was enough for basic needs, especially for those willing to live frugally. In turn, it was funded by eliminating almost all government social services.

Despite success in Canada and other smaller nations, it was something that never gained enough momentum in the US to be put to a vote by congress. Conservatives argued (wrongly, per the real-world data) that it would lead to laziness and decreased productivity. While liberals bemoaned the loss of social services and always demanded a higher and higher amount until it became untenable.

Nick waited for the room to calm down slightly and then flipped to the next page. "The Constitution also provides for police, fire, emergency services, public transportation, public spaces, and military assets, all paid for by a ten percent flat tax rate on all monetary transactions. The Constitution actually forbids other taxes." He gave an amused smile. "Oh, it also states that police are to be referred to as 'Space Rangers' and must wear cowboy hats."

These revelations caused a much larger stir among the assembled politicians. He flipped to the last section before it could rise out of control. "Last, it makes provisions for a court system, which arbitrates disagreements and interprets constitutional rights. The courts themselves are unique. Each case is decided by a panel of seven citizens randomly picked to serve for one-year terms. After the year, you can never serve again. Individuals are to present their cases, no lawyers. The Constitution specifically calls it 'People's Court Style.' There is no legislative body. Essentially no way to make new laws at all.

Senestine spoke. "How can a nation survive without laws? And what exactly are the courts going to use as a basis for arbitrating disagreements if they have no set of standards?"

Nick smiled, silently thanking the Georgia congressman for the perfect setup. "Actually, besides the guaranteed human rights at the beginning of the Constitution, there are two 'Risen Principles,' stated that the courts are to use when deciding disputes." He waited a moment to let the tension rise.

"First Principle: You can swing your arms all you want, but don't hit anyone else. Second Principle: Don't be an asshole."

The room went completely silent. Then Tanner let out a chuckle, which built into a full-throated laugh. "Well," he said, wiping a tear out of his eyes. "I wonder how hard it would be to add those two to our own constitution?"

"Mr. President, I don't see what is so amusing," The Speaker of the House said. "It is just like I stated at the beginning of the meeting. Risa is a breeding ground for lawlessness and loose morals."

"I think it sounds quite fun," Senestine said. "It is called Risa, after all. Wasn't that some sort of vacation planet in one of those old science fiction shows?"

"It was a *pleasure* planet," the Floor Leader said. "As in nudity, liquor, gambling, and fornication."

"I hear you saying the words like they are a bad thing," Senestine said, a sarcastic grin spread across his face.

"Of course, it is a bad thing!" she said.

"Oh please!" he said, an incredulous expression on his face. "You are a representative from *Nevada*. I call bull. You don't want any competition."

The woman sputtered incoherently for a moment, but before she could give the smiling man a rebuttal, the Speaker spoke again.

"Well, I am NOT from Nevada," he said haughtily, "And I still think this represents an obvious danger to our morals and way of life."

"You, Senestine said, are trying to win reelection in a primarily conservative Christian district while trying to overcome the fact that Psychic Warfare outed you as an alcoholic philanderer." Now it was the Georgian man's turn to look disgusted. "At least she," he pointed at the Floor Leader,

"Is trying to protect her constituents." He pointed back at the Speaker, "You would fail the Second Principle of Risa."

The speaker's face turned purple, and he rose out of his seat, voice elevating, "YOU COMP..."

"GENTLEMEN!" the President of the United States yelled. He waited for the Speaker to resume his seat and then began again. "Let's leave the name-calling and accusations for your interviews after the meeting." He turned back to Nick. Mr. Strombold, is there anything else in the Risa Constitution that we need to be aware of?"

"Yes," Nick said. "There are provisions for chancellors responsible for administering each department, for example, a Chancellor of Public Works. There is also an elected governmental leader who serves for seven years, with an option for one additional term. That person handles the administration of the departments and final decisions of disputes should two separate courts rule differently on the same issue."

"What do they call that one?" Senestine asked.

Nick gave an apologetic shrug. "The Emperor of the Moon."

President Tanner guffawed. "Well, Mr. X seems to have a... unique sense of humor, doesn't he?"

"The man is insane," the Speaker said.

"Well," Nick temporized. "Insane or not, he is likely to get World Commission approval for admittance as the Nation of Risa. The Commission uses the 1933 Montevideo Convention as the basis for establishing nationhood.

Risa has met the four conditions already. He counted off on his fingers. One: a defined territory; they have taken the series of Lava Tubes that proliferate the southern edge of the Sea of Tranquility. I understand that there are several hundred square miles of tubes, with more being discovered every day. Two: a resident population; over 5,000 permanent residents have signed onto the Risa Charter. These are all current employees of the Risa Corporation, but with the ratification of the Constitution, they will become citizens. Three: there must be a government, which is what we are reviewing. Last, they must have the ability to interact with other nations."

"But surely, they don't have enough people to qualify as a nation?" The Floor Leader said.

Nick shook his head. "There is no set number. Vatican City only has a permanent population of around 1000, and the World Commission currently recognizes it."

"You can't be comparing Vatican City with this... this... joke?" the Speaker said. "Vatican City is a player on the world stage. It has real power."

Nick's expression turned serious as he took in all politicians around the table. "We are having a meeting with the Speaker of the House, The Congressional Floor Leader, The Chairman of the World Commission, and the President of the United States, not to mention some of *both* parties' most powerful members. All to discuss Risa's pending nationhood. Are you trying to argue that Risa isn't already a player on the world stage?" He took in the room's mood before continuing.

"I am going to speak plainly. Risa is going to happen. None of you can stop it. The World Commission is going to vote tomorrow on admission. I can guarantee you it is going to be accepted.

"My suggestion is to gear up to create a 51st state on the Moon. Other countries are already staking out their claims. It is first come, first serve. Risa is offering any person with a usable skill the option to immigrate, besides free education, healthcare, and a UBI. Its population is likely to explode. If you fine people don't get to it, The United States will be the only one without a piece of the Moon."

SIX

Star Base-1, High Earth Orbit
Two years later: 10 years, 20 days until the invasion

"This is Dancer, in Gunstar One, requesting docking instructions."

"Dancer, this Star Base-1, we have you on visuals. Please proceed to bay three; you will see the pattern green, green, blue on the outside indicator lights."

"I see them." Jake pointed the nose of his fighter slightly downward and put on a few feet per second of acceleration. "Approaching dock three. I have the ball."

"Roger, Gunstar One, you have the ball."

As Jake guided the fighter toward the flashing lights, he was treated to a stunning view of the new space station/orbital dockyard. It looked like a giant ice cream cone, except rather than a point, it tapered into a hexagonal shape with a blunted end. He could see the massive transparent dome that contained the public spaces on its top. It had a small lake, which also served as the water reserve for the station. If he squinted, he could make out the tiny figures of joggers running around the track encircling it. Grass and various plants, genetically engineered to produce oxygen, surrounded the track while groomed walking trails meandered throughout.

His eyes slid down from the dome, following the main

structure. An enormous ship bay, which was open to space, was at the midpoint. In it floated a ship that almost filled the bay, a ship that appeared to be nearing completion.

Hundreds of spider-like construction bots swarmed its superstructure using multi-limbed joints to crawl over the hull. Other bots, looking like oversized basketballs with two arms, hovered just off the hull, holding plating. Occasionally, one would fire thrusters and push the plate into place until a hull bot could do a spot weld. The ball robots would then move off to get another panel from containers floating conveniently near the ship.

Jake could see the Palm Tree and Totem of Risa stamped on the containers. Steve had finally gotten the Risa manufacturing plant up to full speed in the Sea of Tranquility. He was pleased, as it would mean the *Falcon*, as everyone now commonly referred to *Mars-1*, would complete on time.

It had been almost five years since Cindy had first asked him to go to Mars. Five years of changes, as the Earth steadily turned its eyes to the heavens.

The Moon was now an industrial center, with over two million people living and working on it. Most of those were in the series of lava tubes that Risa had claimed, although the larger nations of Earth had enclaves spread across its surface.

The automated robots and factories of the Moon were producing massive amounts of raw materials. The best part was that the steel, glass, and other materials didn't have to be lifted out of Earth's gravity well, making space construction much more efficient.

David's vision of a "Vegas" on the Moon also came true. It had become *the* travel destination for the Earth's well-to-do. The first permanent building, other than housing for workers, was the giant Emperor of the Moon Palace Casino. It was a steel and glass monstrosity from the outside, but was indistinguishable from a tropical paradise inside.

Hologram generators projected a perfect recreation of the sun and sky, complete with gull calls and ocean sounds.

Despite the casino's enormous size, there was a year-long waiting list for a reservation. As the Risa government owned the casino, all profits went back into the nation's infrastructure.

Steve, now living full time on the Moon, had been doing double duty as the primary administrator for public works and working with Pablo- via long-distance communication, on the asteroid project.

Steve's knowledge of autonomous robots was essential. Mining and most building processes had become automated for both of his areas of responsibility. He was constantly refining designs and refitting them to the myriad of tasks needed for a settlement on the Moon.

The lunar settlements were all made possible by the ever-increasing number of air-to-space capable vehicles that were becoming readily available. Cindy had tweaked the *Hope* design to be bare bones enough to be produced quickly and relatively cheaply. Lea used Warren's massive purchasing power and bought failing automotive plants worldwide to turn into shuttle factories. After the initial retooling, each plant could produce ten a day. With fifty factories going, shuttle production was becoming a significant industry.

The shuttles were still too expensive for private use, but every nation was clamoring for them. Lea had also worked through the World Commission for extremely generous leasing rights to the design, and many of the wealthier nations were already working to open their own factories.

Each shuttle had built-in but empty mounts for a laser array. The laser assemblies were one of Pablo's projects. He was stockpiling them in the partially hollowed-out shell of the asteroid Psyche, which also provided the materials for their construction. Although not at the same level as a Gunstar, the shuttles would eventually act as part of Earth's defense fleet.

The past five years also allowed Nick to consolidate the World Commission as the major political force on Earth. Cindy's steady releases of new technology and the subsequent sharing and reduced-price leasing that members received had shown everyone that there was more to be gained by behaving than by not.

Peace had broken out around the planet, as no one wanted to be the first to be used as an example of what would happen should the World Commission's Charter be ignored.

So the PLAN seemed on track. It helped to have the unwavering support of Jimmy Tanner. It turned out that having the current US President on your team could smooth over most speed bumps.

Jimmy had endorsed keeping the Silfe invasion a secret. He saw everything Nick, Cindy, David and Jake had done in the past seventeen years and couldn't argue with the results. Incredibly, four teenagers had remade the world into something that looked more and more like a science fiction movie. He agreed that telling other world leaders, and especially the public, would cause more harm than good. The President had summed it up practically. 'If it ain't broke, don't fix it.'

Jake decreased his acceleration as he approached the shuttle bay. A set of elevator-like doors opened to allow him into the space behind, ending in another identical set of doors, although these remained closed.

He flew through the opening and slowly drifted forward. As the fighter cleared the outside doors, they started closing behind him. They had shut entirely by the time he landed, and a flashing red light bathed the now enclosed space.

Through his cockpit, he could hear the hiss of the landing bay pressurizing as industrial-sized vents pushed atmosphere into the airlock. It equalized in a surprisingly short amount of time, and the light blinked slower, turning yellow and then to a solid green.

Another set of elevator doors opened in front of him, and Jake felt a slight lurch as the landing pad moved forward on an automated track. He went through the doors and into a hangar with three other Gunstars and two of the newer shuttles coming out of the Warren Industries factories.

The landing sequence completed; his ship finally came to a stop.

The hangar appeared busy. Men and women dressed in gray coveralls, with the World Commission patch on their left shoulder and the flag of their birth country on the right, were servicing the various craft.

Like the HMM program, the World Commission funded star Base-1 through its voluntary fund. Only those members who gave money could garner the benefits of any processes or discoveries that came about during its construction. As the base was also the primary source of orbital spacecraft servicing, no nation could afford *not* to be part of it. Even the poorest countries took part, as contributions were on a sliding scale based on annual GDP rather than any specific number.

The station's name came from a worldwide contest run by Star Media, who partnered with Psychic Warfare to demand that the entire Earth be allowed a voice in naming *their* station.

David had been vocal after the "Mars-1 Mistake," as he always referred to the naming of the giant ship nearing completion. In his opinion, the unimaginative wankers at NASA and the other world space agencies had lost their naming privileges.

It turned out there were more Star Trek fans than anyone realized. It had come down to three options for the final voting: Cloud City, Armistice Station, and Star Base-1. David *said* he didn't swing the decision, but his favorite had still won. Jake called foul when Star Media TV stations started showing a disproportionate amount of Star Trek reruns and mini-marathons during the voting period.

The contest garnered six billion votes. It was especially fun for kids, as anyone over four could participate. More votes were cast in the United States for the name than for the last presidential election.

Jake felt the locking clamps engage and so he popped the canopy.

Once out of the fighter he unfastened the clamp on the side of his helmet and screwed it counterclockwise to disengage it from the flight suit. Cindy had come through again, replacing the bulky suits of the Apollo missions with a skin-tight design that looked more like a wetsuit. He could survive in a vacuum for several hours with a sealed helmet and the small air tank incorporated into the vest-like garment cinched around the torso.

A mid-twenties female tech greeted him. "Colonel Swelton, good to see you again."

"Jennifer! How's Star Base-1 holding up?"

"Good," she said. "They finished the concierge deck, so the movie theater and bowling alley are finally up and running.

"Really? he said. Bowling?"

The tech laughed. "Yeah. I got to tell you, bowling in space is interesting. Between the spin and the new artificial gravity generators being a little off Earth standard, bowling has become a lot more fun." She gave him an amused smile. "We even started a league. The techs have a team. We're the *Moon Ballers.*"

Jake gave a short laugh. "I like it!" He turned back to his Gunstar and patted it affectionately. "I have a meeting with the brass about the *Falcon*. "Can you refill my baby here and give her a once over?"

"You got it," she said. "Have a good one," she gave a wink, "Maybe I'll see you on the lanes."

"Don't count on it," he said. "The last time I bowled, they had to put the bumpers up for me."

"Been that long?" she asked.

"No. It was last month at my twin's birthday party."

"Ouch!" she said. "Well, not everyone can fly a Gunstar, so I guess we all have our strengths."

"That's what I told my wife," Jake said with a grin. He gave a short wave of departure and made his way through the hatch at the end of the bay.

As he walked, he felt a slight bounce in his step. The station's gravity was *almost* right. Cindy had known that gravity generation was possible from HAL. Unfortunately, the AI wasn't talking. There had been very little Earth-based science to draw from either. Still, she hypothesized it was possible. Specifically, she felt that the damping field used in the Gunstars and shuttles could be altered to produce a device capable of nullifying gravity, even if she couldn't control it with the same aplomb as HAL.

At the time, she was deep into the Moon and asteroid projects. So, she had given the gravity problem to Wendel Flint PhD, aka 'Stony.' The irascible teen who had terrorized an entire generation of Warren Industry new hires during his "Warren University" classes had grown into a brilliant scientist in his own right. Now on the other side of 20, he had become one of Cindy's go-to people for particularly sticky projects.

Stony had taken to artificial gravity like a dog to a bone. He had a functioning model in less than a year that created a null zone between two opposing dampening fields. When used in conjunction, the fields created an attractive force that produced the feeling of gravity. It wasn't true antigravity, but it acted much the same way. They continued to tune it, to get to Earth standard, but as the force increased, it became energy prohibitive. They settled for one that could produce 0.92 g.

Stony and his team were still looking for a true antigravity device, but the current version was good enough that Star Base-1 didn't have to spin. The lack of spin simplified the design and exponentially increased the speed of its construction.

Jake followed the signs on the corners of the bulkheads towards his destination. A few minutes later, and 20 floors down, he reached the main construction floor, a gleaming metal hallway curving off into the distance in both directions. The side opposite him was floor to ceiling clear plexiglass over an inch thick. He walked up to the wall, pressing his hand against it, and looked out into the construction bay holding the *Falcon*.

It was a glorious sight.

The bots had been hard at work. In just the time it had taken to land, most of the hull plating was attached. He could see an army of spider-like bots welding the plates down firmly, extending the spot welds, and completing the hull.

The ship was enormous, fully three football fields long, tapering toward a set of four tubes that housed the ion engines.

Each engine had a dedicated fusion reactor. Cindy told him they could have powered it with just two. In actuality, the extra two generators would provide power to the laser array Pablo was building in the asteroid belt. Several large viewing ports would act as plugs for the weapon when they retrofitted the ship for the Silfe invasion. The hull was thick steel that could shrug off most of a Silfe fighter's laser and kinetic weapons.

The *Falcon* was the most devious bait and switch ever conceived. The World Commission had built a massive warship that could go toe to toe with -according to HAL- Silfe battlecruisers, all in the name of a trip to Mars.

They didn't know that Jake could have gone to The red planet with a spacesuit and his Gunstar. The trip to Mars was the carrot, leading the world forward to a place where it could build something for all. Humanity now had a permanent space station for building large ships; a station created using voluntary contributions of the majority of nations on Earth.

They also had tens of thousands of workers who were comfortable working in space. Not to mention the ironing out of a myriad of processes, including the use of autonomous bots that had made it possible.

Jake didn't feel bad about the deception despite his normal honest-to-a-fault personality. He knew that trying to get the nations of the Earth to work together to build a warship would have been impossible. It was still ten years until the Silfe arrived. Keeping the entire world on a war footing for an extended period would lead to civil unrest and collapse.

Nick, David, Cindy, and him did plan on coming clean, eventually. They argued precisely *how* they would do it, but they all agreed that the world would need to know about it three years in advance. With that lead time, they could transition shuttlecraft and any larger ships they could build into warships.

Three years would also allow the millions of people responsible for defending the Earth to train. Ultimately, they wanted just enough time so that people -and governments- would feel the urgency. Too much, and a sense of depressive ennui would set in. Too little, and they would doom the planet.

In the meantime, they continued to work behind the scenes. Nudging and manipulating the world.

Glancing at his watch, he realized he would need to hurry. With a last look at the magnificent ship, he turned and continued down the hallway curving around the construction zone to a door that read Amphitheater 1.

He touched a button on the side of the door, and it swished open, revealing a room that appeared much like a scaled-down college lecture hall, complete with raised seats and a podium at the front.

The room was buzzing with people, all wearing the same uniform: black tactical pants, and a fitted long sleeve collarless shirt. The shirts had the World Commission patch on the left shoulder and the various flags of the wearer's nation on the right. Another patch, sewn just over the right breast, depicting a red planet with HMM in large white letters superimposed on it.

Jake went to the side and placed his helmet on a shelf. By the time he had returned to stand behind the podium, the room quieted, and the members of the *Falcon* crew looked up at him expectantly.

Jake cleared his throat and spoke. "Folks, just before I came up, I met with the head of the World Commission Space Agency at the Warren Industries Campus." He beamed. "We are a go for Mars in 3 days!"

The room erupted in cheers as the crew, some of whom had been waiting years, discovered that they would finally take the *Falcon* out.

Jake spoke again as the cheers faded. "I know that this has been a bit of a slog."

"No kidding!" said a voice in the back, causing a ripple of good-natured laughter to spread throughout the hall.

Jake chuckled along with them. "We had a lot of things to figure out about making a vessel the size of the *Falcon*," He coughed. "Sorry, I mean the Mars-1."

His slip caused another round of laughter. *Everyone* called it the Falcon unless they were talking to an executive at the World Commission Space Agency. The WCSA continued to hold to the official title of the ship, despite literally everyone else in the world referring to it by its nickname. David and Gloria had done their job well.

"Anyway," he said. "First, we had to build the station and the dock, then figure out how to use the bots in a vacuum. If we built it again today, it would take less than a quarter of the time." He paused and grinned at the crew. "That was a discussion point in my meeting today. If the *Falcon* performs like we all think she will, they will OK *three* more, just like her."

A buzz of conversation followed his pronouncement. "That's right, Ladies and gentlemen, we are on the cusp of a fleet of vessels that can explore our solar system!" Jake took in all the eager faces. He knew he had them in his pocket. "OK, so there is just one thing to do then. Let's prove that it is time for humanity to reach out to the stars. It is time to go to Mars!"

SEVEN

Star Base-1, Near Earth Orbit
Three days later: 10 years, 17 days until the invasion

"Take a seat!" David said.

Cindy walked over to sit on the couch next to him. They had a private viewing room in the Star Base-1 construction loop. Or, as David put it, "On the friggin' fifty-yard line." The privilege was primarily because of Cindy's clout as the *Falcon's* primary designer, although he likely could have gotten similar treatment as the head of Star Media.

The need for a private room made itself apparent as Lea, Gloria, and Pablo materialized in shimmering light and sat in a set of high-backed padded chairs, which also phased into existence.

David snorted, "Nice trick. You always have a comfy chair wherever you go. I'm feeling a bit jealous."

"Being a hologram has its perks," Gloria said. She sat up and looked excited. "I, for one, am looking forward to the show." As she spoke, a set of 3D glasses appeared on her face and a tub of buttered popcorn popped into existence in her lap.

"Ahhh!" David whined. "Popcorn? I should have thought of that!"

Cindy gave him a sly smile. "If you look in the cabinet over by the viewscreen," she said, pointing to her left. "I have a surprise for you."

David looked at her suspiciously but stood and opened the steel cabinet. Inside, stacked on all three shelves, was popcorn in metal tubs. David could see chocolate, caramel, sour apple, kettle, double butter, candy-coated, and what appeared to be at least ten other more eclectic varieties. He turned to Cindy and said, "I don't think I have ever loved you more than right now!"

At his words, Lea let out an "Oh my!"

Gloria, a huge grin on her face, yelled, "Get a room!"

"It's just popcorn!" Cindy said, her face beat red.

"Yes, Dear," Lea said. "It's just an incredibly uncharacteristic and thoughtful gesture to a man you have known for almost twenty years, who you *say* you barely tolerate." Lea's hologram reached over and patted Cindy on the arm.

She gave a shocked gasp and said, "I felt that!" She looked at Lea's hand. "How did I just feel that?"

"What?" David said, popcorn forgotten in the light of the new information.

Gloria looked disgusted. "Way to kill the mood, Lea. I thought we were finally getting somewhere with these two."

Lea smiled at the other AI. "Baby steps, my dear, baby steps." She took in the two astonished humans. "It was Pablo."

David and Cindy turned toward the odd AI, dressed in his standard lab coat with pocket protector.

"Wow!" David said, but then he frowned. "Not that I'm not happy to see you, old boy, but *how* are you even here? I thought the time lag for communications from the asteroid belt was thirty minutes or something."

"It is," Pablo said. "I downloaded a limited kernel to the Star Base-1 AI servers, hidden in the station's southern end. It doesn't give me my full computing capabilities but allows for conversation and decision-making. I am still fully engaged in the asteroid belt while we are speaking. Although not in real-time, I am continuing to sync with my other self as well."

"How did you get private AI servers?"

Gloria spoke up, "That was me. With robots doing the construction, there was no human involvement with the server installation. On the plans, it's down as 'Reactor shielding.' So, no one will even think to look. We have a 3D printer and some raw materials down there. There are also several maintenance bots in the room, so it is self-sustaining."

"Nice!" David said.

"Can we get back to the part where I just *felt* a hologram's hand?" Cindy said.

Pablo looked almost embarrassed as he turned toward Cindy. "I stole the idea from Stony's group. I figured if you could generate an attractive force, you could project one as well. It has come in handy in the asteroid belt. I have been able to attract and push off various asteroids as needed. It has sped up the construction process immensely. I can cut out a large section and then use fields to manipulate it where I need it to go. It hadn't occurred to me to do it on a smaller level until Gloria mentioned David's obsession with holodecks. I figured all I would need to make one was a series of precise projections of the field with associated holograms. I gave the project over to Lea, who used her processing power to do the fine calculations for use with AI-IRL interaction."

"Let me get this straight. First, you made tractor beams... *then* you made a holodeck?" David asked, his eyebrows near his hairline.

"Not the terms I would use, but essentially correct," Pablo confirmed.

David smirked at Cindy. "Our boy's all grown up, isn't he?"

Cindy ignored him. "Pablo, after this meeting, let's go through the data for this application together. I'll bring Stony in, and we'll see what his group can do with it."

The AI nodded to her.

"OK!" Lea said, clapping her hands with a crack and getting everyone's attention. "Now that we have that bit of drama out of the way, perhaps we want to tune into the *actual* reason we are all here?" She glared at them like they were unruly children, with more than a hint of Bubbie in her startling green eyes. "Like the first interplanetary ship to launch."

"Right!" David said, turning back to the popcorn-filled cabinet. "I'm going for a mix of Chicago Corn and Siracha." He turned back to the only other human in the room. "Cindy? What's your pleasure?"

Gloria gave a little laugh that turned into a cough, making Cindy's cheeks color again.

"Just give me something normal."

"Right! Caramel Macchiato it is!"

"N... o..." she started to say, before changing her mind. "That actually sounds pretty good."

"I know, right?" he said, flopping down on the couch next to her and holding out a tub of popcorn in a green tin. On its lid was a picture of a foaming cup of coffee.

As he sat, the viewscreen came to life on the wall opposite, showing a beaming Nick standing in front of an enormous plexiglass window. They could see the *Falcon* framed behind him, floating majestically in its birth. Beside the Chairman of the World Commission, Jake stood in his crew uniform. They could also see the entire one hundred strong complement of the ship standing at parade rest, just off to the side.

Nick spoke. "My fellow World Commission members. People of the Earth. Today, we come together for the send-off of these brave men and women who will be the first to fly to another world." He gestured toward the crew. "Let us celebrate them as a united humanity. Their mission is not only to be the first to set foot on another planet but to deliver the materials and infrastructure to build a permanent settlement on Mars, as we have now done on the Moon."

He reached out to shake Jake's hand. "I have the pleasure of turning over the christening of the Mars-1 to the commander of the ship, Captain Jacob Swelton, of the newly formed World Commission Space Navy.

Jake shook back firmly and then turned toward the cameras. "I am not big on speeches, but I would like to take a moment to thank the people at Warren Industries and the World Commission Space Agency for their unwavering support of the project. I would also like to thank the fantastic people on Star Base-1 for their outstanding work." He gave his bright million-dollar smile. "We will make you all proud. In just two days, we will transmit from the surface of Mars!" At his words, the assembled crew cheered.

Nick stepped back up again and spoke. "We have a little surprise for you all." He turned, pointing to where a cloth tarp hung on the spaceship's side. At his gesture, two construction bots moved forward and gripped it. With a coordinated pull, the cloth came free, revealing the World Commission symbol with the words "Mars-1" below it. However, the name was dwarfed by the much larger "Falcon" written in stylized ten-foot-tall letters below it.

David stood up from his seat with a triumphant yell and, with only a slight hesitation, gave Gloria a high five. A satisfying smack rang out as their hands met. He looked down at his palm for a moment and shrugged. "Now that's what I am talking about! Game, set, and match! Mars-1, my *ASS*!"

Gloria's look mirrored his. "The people of the world have spoken!" she said in triumph.

Lea's voice dripped with sarcasm. "Yes, children. The people have spoken. The renaming had nothing to do with you two waging a guerilla war in the opinion polls."

David was unapologetic. "Tomato... Potato."

"Those aren't the same, dear."

"Close enough," he said.

On the screen, they could see Nick speaking again.

"It's time to christen the *Falcon*," he gave Jake a data pad. "If you will do the honors, Captain?"

Jake pressed a finger to the pad, and outside the

window, they could see a bot open a panel in its round body and shoot out a bottle of champagne. It smoothly spun toward the ship before impacting the hull and breaking apart. Another cheer rang out.

Nick looked from the ship to the cheering crew. "Good journey, and come back to us safely."

EIGHT

Sea of Tranquility, The Moon
Two days later: 10 years, 15 days until the invasion

Steve Cooper screwed on his helmet and popped the canopy of the Moon rover. He levered out of the driver's seat and jumped down from the rover's side to the rocky surface.

At a gravity of only 1.62 m/s^2, it took over a second to reach the ground. The Moon's attractive force was only one-sixth of Earth's. He still dropped, but more slowly. It would have only taken 0.46 seconds on Earth; It was something that took some time to get used to.

Very few people realized that gravity was still a danger on the Moon. No matter how light, gravity still caused velocity to increase. So, if you fell long enough, there was still an unpleasant splat. A fall of roughly fifty feet (four stories) would kill about half of people on Earth. On the Moon, that number would be 294 feet (twenty-two stories) or roughly the height of the Statue of Liberty. Of course, a fall much less than that could cause injury and damage to equipment.

He was fifteen miles from the nearest Risa lava tube. The tubes bordered the Sea of Tranquility, made famous by the Apollo 11 mission, where Neil Armstrong had made his notable first step.

He was investigating a bot that went offline during routine mining operations. As there was no video feed, he assumed it must be a wright off. Still, he had sent a drone to the bot's last known location under the supervision of Bishop, his newly created AI.

When he queried Bishop about what he had found, Steve had received a "You need to see it for yourself" response. So, the engineer found himself here, looking around at the flat unwelcoming plain and wondering what the hell he was doing.

The AI was only a few months old and was still working to integrate his core processor with his personality. Naturally, as an autonomous robot designer, Steve had put a lot of thought into artificial intelligence.

After consideration, he went with Isaac Asimov's *Three Laws of Robotics*. Of course, in Asimov's stories, the robots weren't sentient. So, he couldn't adopt them entirely, or Bishop could never be his own person. Instead, he included the laws as core guidelines in the kernel that made up the AI's moral compass, or whatever the AI equivalent was.

In short, Bishop would not knowingly harm a human being or allow one to be harmed through inaction. He would do his best to follow human requests for aid, and he would protect himself if it didn't harm another.

Steve felt that this was very close to his personal moral code. He would never intentionally hurt another human unless he or someone he loved was in danger from them. As for helping humanity, that was something that he had always wanted to do. A lifelong geek, his primary motivation was trying to make the *Star Trek* version of the future come true rather than the one from *Bladerunner.*

It was no accident that he had chosen the name Bishop for the AI. He wanted an example that was capable of self-sacrifice and nobility. Robots could be a little creepy to people. He didn't blame them. Unless you programmed a machine yourself, you could never be sure that it wouldn't malfunction on you. Hell, even then, you could never be entirely sure.

Give robots a welding torch and enough strength to pick up a couple of tons, and it was understandable that some would be apprehensive.

He had always thought that the android from the original Alien movie was an excellent example. Creepy, but in the end, following its programming to help. He was hoping for something similar with his own AI.

As he rounded the rover, he saw a disruption in the otherwise unbroken plane a short distance away. It was about two meters in diameter and led down into a sinkhole, or possibly a cave.

Bishop's voice came over his helmet speakers. "The edge is a little unstable; if you wait a moment, I will route a skimmer to you so that you can safely approach."

Steve decided that caution was the better part of valor in this situation. He waited patiently for a couple of minutes until he saw a craft rapidly approaching from the direction of the southern Risa mining site. As it came closer, it became recognizable as a skimmer drone.

It was one of his designs. Essentially, a fusion generator powering a small set of engines that provided lift. Given the Moon's decreased gravity, it didn't even have to be all that strong. On top was a platform that had a railing around it. This version was sized for a single person, used for work primarily in the tunnels of the main Risa complex.

Bots completed most construction on the Moon, but some things, including complex wiring and troubleshooting a failure, needed a human brain to diagnose and fix. The skimmers allowed them to get up and around without ladders or other lift equipment.

The lifts came in different sizes, from the miniature version in front of him to a huge one for transporting groups of people around that looked suspiciously like the Khetanna, Jabba the Hutt's sail barge from *Return of the Jedi*. Steve was unabashedly proud of that one. After all, what was the point of building cool shit if you couldn't have fun with it?

He climbed aboard the lift and worked the joystick attached to the small control panel on the front to move it forward over the hole. He spoke aloud. "Are you going to tell me what this is all about, Bishop?"

The AI's voice sounded amused as he replied. "Steve, you will need to see it to believe it. I don't want to ruin the surprise."

Hmm, he thought. *Maybe Bishop was developing a personality after all.* Not quite Pablo's dry humor or Gloria's outlandish slapstick but holding back information to build anticipation was not a thing a standard computer program would do. "OK, I'm trusting you here. Do you want to drive, or should I?"

"Let me take it," the AI said. "You'll want to focus on what is down there."

"Now you have my full attention," Steve said. He let go of the stick and allowed the AI to take control. The skimmer dropped through the hole, and darkness enveloped him, with only a single shaft of light coming through the tiny entrance above. "How about a bit of light, Bishop?"

"Wait for it..." Bishop said. "I went through a bit of work to set this up, and patience is a virtue and all that."

"Fine," he said, smiling to himself. He was happy that the AI was showing such enthusiasm. It was by far the biggest show of personality that he had seen. He waited patiently as the skimmer continued to drop until he suddenly realized how far he had fallen. "Umm... Bishop? How deep are we going?"

"Don't worry about it, Steve; we are almost there."

"I hope so, or we will start hitting magma."

Suddenly the skimmer slowed and then came to a stop, causing him to bend his knees slightly to accommodate the change in acceleration. *They must have been falling FAST!* he thought. *Exactly how far had they dropped?*

Bishop's voice sounded. "Are you ready?"

"I *think* so," Steve said with a bit of apprehension.

"OK, 3...2...1."

As the AI's countdown hit one, dozens of spotlights turned on, revealing a gigantic cavern. His mind had a hard time encompassing the size. It had to be at least five square miles, triple the size of the largest of the Risa lava tubes. "Oh my god!" he said in wonder. "It's HUGE!"

"Oh, you haven't seen the best part," Bishop said. "Wait till you see what else is in here."

"You mean besides a cave that could hold the better part of Manhattan; skyscrapers included?"

"Definitely!" the AI said. The skimmer moved off towards one wall of the cavern as Bishop continued speaking. "I sent a drone out here to see what happened to the mining survey bot. It turns out that its sensors had found what it thought was a mineral deposit. It was taking a sample on the roof, and it fell through. Unfortunately, it didn't survive the drop."

"I wouldn't think so," Steve said with a snort.

"Yes, it looked like a Lego sculpture dropped off of a balcony."

He shuddered, more from the thought of ruining a perfectly good Lego sculpture than from the fate of the bot.

"Anyway," Bishop continued. "The drone I sent to check it out found this cavern. At first, I couldn't figure out how it could have formed." The AI paused uncharacteristically. "I can't be sure, but I *think* this is a major asteroid impact site. Likely the one that caused the crater for the Mare Tranquillitatis."

Steve was confused. "Why would it form a cavern?" he knew the basics of moon geology. His specialty was robots, but their primary function on the Moon was for mining, after all. So, he had to have the basics down to help design them. Dr. Mariana, the lunar geologist, working at Risa, had taught him most of what he knew. Supposedly, the dark spots on the Moon, also called the Lunar Mares, formed when lava flows filled in asteroid impact craters. That process caused the flat planes visible from the Earth.

The AI continued his explanation. "I think that the meteor that hit was metallic."

"What would make you think that?" Steve asked.

The skimmer finally stopped as it reached one end of the cavern. The AI's voice became a singsong. "Bec...aus...e... TA-DA!"

Steve eyebrows knit. "Wha.." His brain finally caught up with his eyes as he realized what he saw. Stretching out as far as he could see was a solid sheet of what looked like pure titanium. he gulped. "Is that what I think it is?"

"Yep," the AI said happily. "THAT is the largest deposit of titanium ever found. In addition, if you were to survey the rest of the cavern, you will find pretty much every native metal that you could name, both singly and in alloys." He could hear the humor in Bishop's voice. "We struck it rich! I think that the asteroid that hit must have been almost pure metal. When the lava flows came in, the rock melted out and concentrated the metals in the cave. There must have been some funky stuff happen to make it like this. Maybe some ice in the asteroid? It's hard to say without more study."

"There are enough resources here to build a fleet of ships!" Steve said, realizing what this find would mean.

"Yep, I contacted Pablo and gave him the estimates. We are sitting on almost as much as he is getting out of Psyche, but we don't have to go all the way to the asteroid belt for it. If we get some 3D printers and bots down here, we can make Gunstars all day. Not to mention some other nasty surprises for the Silfe."

Steve heard venom in the AI's voice as he mentioned the pending alien invasion. "I didn't know that you cared so much about defeating the Silfe."

The AI sounded as serious as he had ever heard. "You programmed my kernel, Steve. You should have realized that when you put in the bit about protecting humans, it might affect my views on anyone who would harm humanity for no other reason than they exist. That *really* pisses me off!"

Steve could hear steely determination from the AI as Bishop continued. "I think we should turn this cave into Earth's armory. I have some pretty good ideas for infantry-based weapons, including augment suits. We could expand on some of the bot designs. If we strip them down and use primarily hydraulics, we can minimize computer control so the Silfe can't hack them. Put a laser rifle in and maybe a grenade launcher or two, and any space crocodile that comes into Risa will get a rude awakening!"

Steve couldn't help but laugh. Asimov wrote little about extraterrestrials, so how one of his robots would have responded to malignant aliens was up in the air. Perhaps Bishop had just answered the question. They would be *pissed*.

"That sounds like a great idea." He paused, thinking. "You know," he mused. "You get to name it."

"What?"

"You found it, so you get to name the cave," Steve said.

Bishop went silent a moment before his voice crackled over the engineer's helmet again. "Let's call it Eldorado."

Steve paused for a second, letting the name and its implications congeal in his brain, then spoke. "I think Eldorado is perfect."

NINE

Falcon Bridge, Mars Orbit
1 day later: 10 years 14 days

"Orbit achieved, Captain," the black-uniformed lieutenant reported from his seat at the front of the Falcon's bridge.

"Good job, everyone," Jake said from his captain's chair. "Please have the away crew start getting suited up; I will be up to the bay in a few minutes." He stood and spoke to Commander Daksha Patel, his first officer. Commander, you have the con."

"Ay, sir, I have the con." She stood from her chair on one side of the bridge and moved to take the captains.

Jake was amused when he had first seen the plans for the ship. Oscar Wilde said, "Life imitates art, far more than art imitates life." Nowhere was that truer than in the design of the *Falcon*. Its makers, a group of men and women who had grown up with the gamut of sci-fi movies and books, seemed incapable of designing something that didn't pay homage to the ships that inspired them.

The bridge was gleaming white, with tiered stations essentially in the same position as they would have been on the NCC-1701. There was even a *Ready Room* off to one side.

He supposed that the gloves for designing spaceships

were now entirely off with the advent of functional artificial gravity. They could look however their designers wished. He walked to the -sigh- turbolift, which swished open, allowing him to enter, and pushed a button to move up to the shuttle bay. He had put his foot down when one engineer had suggested that the crew could ask the "Computer" for a floor.

The bridge was at the heart of the *Falcon*. It made sense that the room functioning as the ship's nerve center would be deep inside to protect it from mini-meteorite strikes -and though no one knew it, Silfe laser hits. So, the shuttle bay was located above the bridge. The lift rose five decks before the doors opened onto a broad shuttle bay like those on Star Base-1.

There were several spacecraft parked on the steel deck. The Mars Lander, known affectionately as the *Baby Falcon* or just *Baby* for short, was similar in appearance to the original *Hope*. Because of its inertial compensator, it didn't need to be aerodynamic. Given that Mars's atmosphere was thinner than Earth's, it wouldn't have mattered as much anyway. Still, at the speeds it could obtain, the atmospheric friction, even on Mars, would eventually make an impact.

Besides the Lander, three Gunstars sat on the deck, including his own yellow striped *Gunstar One*. As the fighters were readily available and considered reliable, they were backups to the shuttle. They only had a limited number loaded, but the deck could hold up to ten in each of the three shuttle bays on the ship.

Cindy had to do a lot of fast-talking to justify the need for multiple large shuttle bays. When redundancy and rapid cycling of spacecraft arguments had met a wall, she had finally reverted to "Because I said so." Of course, when Cynthia Warren put her foot down, no one was willing to argue with her. It *had* made loading the Mars equipment much easier, as the shuttle bays also acted as cargo holding areas.

Jake walked to the shuttle, where a large, grizzled man with gray at his temples bent over one of the engines. "Chief, how's she looking?"

Master Chief Jones looked up at him with a broad smile. "Running like a top, sir."

Jake had known Jones for ten years, ever since his first deployment to the NATO Mobile Airfield Normandy, when he was a wet behind the ears first lieutenant fresh out of AETC. Then Master *Sergeant* Jones headed his flight crew, supporting him as he ran endless bombing runs into Afghanistan after Chinese supplied terrorists.

Jones was about to retire when the call came out for experienced flight crew for the newly formed World Commission Navy. After he accepted the change of service, he changed to the equivalent rank of Command Master Chief. The Chief was a no-brainer to command the small craft maintenance on the *Falcon*. They had tried to bump him to the rank of warrant officer, but he had declined, saying he would rather stay in the enlisted ranks.

The Master Chief gave him a wide smile. "Sure is something, sir," he said, patting *Baby* gently. "I still remember a green lieutenant going into harm's way for the first time." He gestured to Jake's uniform with the captain's insignia on his breast, "Now look at you." He blew out his breath. "Stepping onto Mars. Who would have thought?"

Jake's smile matched the Chief's. "I still remember your words to me that day."

The big man's face took on a puzzled expression. "I don't recall saying anything especially profound, sir."

Jake shook his head. "You didn't. What you said was 'Time to get it done.'" He smiled. "There I was, about to throw up, and a Master Sergeant was just so matter of fact that I would do a good job." He reached out and placed a hand on Chief's shoulder. "I appreciated it then, and I am happy that you are here now."

"Ahh, Captain, you are going to make me blubber. It's going to ruin my hard-assed reputation with the crew."

Jake laughed. "Your secret is safe with me, Chief."

Jones gave a deep chuckle. "Well, I guess the only thing to say, Captain, is... time to get it done." He held out a hand for him to shake. "Now that all the reminiscing is over, you'd better get your flight suit on. We are wheels up in fifteen."

Jake let the Master Chief's massive hand go and nodded. "Right you are." He walked to the pilot ready room located just off the bay. As he entered, he could see the wall of lockers that held the sleek spacesuits for the away crew and generic survival suits designed for emergencies.

The room was buzzing with the three other officers who made up the away team. He nodded to the shuttle pilot, Lieutenant Commander Tao Chen.

Tao had been one of the lucky Chinese pilots who had successfully ejected after the NATO Gunstars shot a wing off his fighter. After the war, he had transferred to a newly formed Chinese Gunstar wing, distinguishing himself as a natural with the new machines.

He had answered the World Commission's call for experienced pilots for astronaut training. Chen was the obvious choice for the shuttle's pilot. Jake hated to admit it, but the man was likely better in the air than he was.

The other two crew, Nancy Williams, and Nadine Petrov were women.

Williams, a planetary geologist, was from the UK. She was *the* expert on Mars geology.

A significant goal of the Human Mission to Mars was to lay the groundwork for a permanent settlement. Her job was to find mining locations to supply the autonomous bots and 3D printers they planned to leave on the surface. If successful, there would be a structure to house several thousand colonists within six months.

Petrov, from the Russian Federation, was an expert on exo-habitats. She was integral to the Risa lava tube habitation design and was primarily responsible for the oxygen, water collection, and recycling equipment. Her skills complemented Williams, and her task was to find an optimal location for human habitation.

Jake spoke as he came into the room. "Well, team, according to the Chief, we are a go for mission in fifteen minutes." They met his pronouncement with smiles and nods all around. "OK, let's get moving then; we don't want to keep our audience waiting."

The four astronauts walked out of the prep room to raucous applause and cheers. Almost the entire crew was in the bay, creating a double line leading to the shuttle. He walked down the corridor of bodies, reaching out to shake hands and sharing a word or pat on the shoulder here and there.

Chief Jones stood at the end of the line, sporting an uncharacteristic shifty smile. The big Chief moved aside, uncovering a section of the shuttle he had been blocking with his body.

Revealed was a picture of a fluffy white bird. Jake laughed, not just any bird. It was a baby *falcon.* He gave out a loud guffaw, saying to the crowd, "NASA isn't going to like that!" Around him, the crew, who seemed to have been in on the joke, laughed along with him.

Jake stood at the shuttle and waited for the crowd to quiet. "Thanks, everybody!" he said with a raised hand. "Let's do it!"

At his words, the cheers renewed, and Jake and the other away crew walked up the lowered ramp. As soon as they were inside, Chen pushed the control to raise it, shutting it with a hiss of compressed air.

Jake took command. "OK, everybody. Let's get buckled up with helmets on. It may be a little bumpy on approach. Mr. Chen, please start preflight."

They found their seats while the pilot called out preflight to Jake, acting as the copilot. All was ready after a few minutes, and Chen keyed the radio. "*Falcon* control, *Baby*, requesting clearance for departure to the surface."

"*Falcon*, you are a go for departure. Smooth sailing," said the voice of Lieutenant Junior Grade Karan, the bridge flight control officer.

"Roger *Falcon* control, we are a go for departure."

With permission granted, Chen flipped a red switch, activating the sequence to move the shuttle into the airlock.

The airlock turned green a minute later, and the pilot lifted the shuttle off and into the black.

Jake's heart started pounding as the red planet came into view. It was awe-inspiring. He could see a dust storm in the northern hemisphere that must cover a couple of thousand miles, causing red swirls of dust to bloom into the atmosphere. Elsewhere, the red coloring with streaks of black that were characteristic of Mars made for a truly magnificent view.

Chen dipped the nose downward and accelerated. As they entered the atmosphere, they could see the outline of the forward inertial dampening screen. Unlike Earth, there was minimal burn. The Mars atmospheric composition was 95% carbon dioxide with only trace amounts of oxygen. It still heated dramatically, but it wasn't the light show that it would have been on Earth. They were also breaking independent of gravity, so unlike a pre-fusion re-entry, their speed remained constant.

Jake watched as the ground approached. They would land at Eberswalde Crater, and he could see the distinctive delta formation as they closed. They hoped to find caves or other natural depressions, which would be amenable for enclosing a habitat, as was done with the lava tubes of Risa.

After a few minutes of controlled descent, the ship leveled and lowered slowly to the ground. Jake felt a slight bump as the landing struts contacted the Martian soil.

He turned and looked at his crew. "Welcome to Mars," he said, eliciting broad, excited smiles. "Helmets on. We are going to do this just like we talked about."

"You sure, Captain?" Chen asked.

"Absolutely. We are doing this together."

*****

Cindy, David, Nick, and Steve sat in a private booth looking down on the Jamaharon, the main bar in the Risa's *Emperor of the Moon's* giant casino complex.

A hologram of a multitiered tropical waterfall dominated one side of the space, complete with sound, smells, and the occasional wisp of spray. There were also scantily clad men and women frolicking in the crystal-clear waters. They became decidedly *more scantily clad* after 11 PM, the end of designated Family Time. The frolickers were also holograms, but the technology had become so natural, thanks primarily to Gloria's tinkering, that it was impossible to tell insubstantial light from toned flesh. More than one inebriated high roller had tried to take a dip with the nubile swimmers, only to find themselves flat on the floor trying to swim on concrete.

Holograms were the secret to the *Emperor's* fantastic success. There were IRL (In Real Life) areas where guests and staff operated and virtual sites that gave the appearance of the alien pleasure planet, complete with multiple holographic moons that periodically moved across the sky. The pipes, electrical conduits, and other necessary infrastructure for human habitation were left open for easy access but sat hidden inside the holograms.

The Casino was just a giant shell. Since it was all enclosed, anything above the level of about ten feet was a hologram. One might go into a building that appeared to have a thirty-foot ceiling with a grand chandelier but find that only the lowest level was real. It made the construction cost a small fraction of what it would have otherwise been.

The moon had all the metal, glass, and rock you could want, but it was distinctly lacking in organics. Wood, cloth, and other materials had to be brought up from the Earth or biologically printed. Given that biological 3D printing was extremely slow, it became more cost-effective to just lift it out of Earth's gravity well.

Risa also needed to find solutions to the three big issues

of the moon, a lack of oxygen, water and food.

Luckily, the top layer of the Moon's regolith is composed of 45% oxygen. NASA had known for years that you could use electrolysis to separate the oxygen from its chemical bindings and release it. The rate-limiting factor had always been energy, and Cindy's fusion generator had fixed that problem.

Water, similarly, had turned out to be a reasonably easy fix. The moon *had* water, as molecules of H_2O are abundant in sunlit areas. Being a hundred times dryer than the Sahara Desert didn't make the process quick, but a small army of specialized bots working twenty-four hours a day made an impact. Combined with the initial tanks of water brought in to supply Risa and the most advanced water reclamation equipment that a trio of AI's could think up, the water situation was a relatively easy fix.

Food remained the biggest issue. A constant supply of tourists and the ever-expanding population had meant that the ability to produce locally sourced foodstuffs was a must. Risa had pushed the boundaries of hydroponic and indoor gardening forward significantly. Vat-grown meat had also become a major industry. Risa's expertise in both was one of their principal exports to Earth. Developing nations were receiving cheap, healthy food grown in World Commission-supported centers. For the first time in history, there was no active famine anywhere on the planet.

A voice rang out over the crowd in the bar. "Five minutes until Mars landing."

David turned toward his friends. "You think he will do the 'We are the world' speech or go with mine?"

Nick scoffed. "I am pretty sure that the first human to step onto another planet saying, 'WHOOP THERE IT IS' would be a terrible idea."

"But it would be *memorable!*" David said.

"You know that whatever he says, it is a lock to go down in the history books," Steve replied, walking back from the bar carrying a coconut shell filled with a fizzy lime green drink.

"See!" David said. "That is why nobody wants to read history books. If the people who made all that history could *spice* it up a bit, it would lead to a generation of kids actually *liking* history class."

"You are ignoring the fact that Martin Luther King, Gandhi, Kennedy, and Lincoln could all drop a one-liner," Nick said.

"See, now you are just naming outliers. For every Lincoln, you get twenty Gerald Fords. All I'm saying is that Jake should use the opportunity to start a new trend."

"Shh!" Cindy said, as the waterfall at the end of the bar was replaced by a first-person view of the *Baby Falcon* hovering over the red-tinged soil of Mars. The realism was outstanding. It felt like a piece of the bar was transported thirty-three million miles away to where the ship was descending. The engines caused the Martian dust to swirl as the ship settled onto the flat plane. In the background, they could see the edges of the Eberswalde Crater and the folds of earth that scientists hypothesized had once been a river delta.

The view suddenly switched to an image of Jake inside the cabin, his crew sitting around him. They unstrapped and got their helmets and gear situated.

"Great camera work!" David said.

"Lea made sure there were multiple 360° cameras outside and in the main cabin," Cindy said. "Some drones are being released by the shuttle that will get the shots from the outside. It should be enough for a full holographic rendering."

"Lea got a healthy dose of Bubbie's eye for a great image," Nick said. His smile turned sad. "I wish she could have been here today."

David gave his shoulder a squeeze. "I know Lea is watching. Gloria told me they were throwing an AI party at Pablo's place on Psyche."

"I can't even imagine," Steve said with a laugh. "How do AIs party? Would it be just a bunch of ones and zeros faster than we could follow, or Gloria with a lampshade on her head, dancing on tables?"

"Probably both," Cindy said.

David flashed a grin. "Sounds like fun! But getting back to the point. Have you noticed that Lea is getting more *Bubbie-like* rather than less? Like... she seems to be aging?"

"Yeah," Cindy said, a frown on her face. "I wondered about that, but I didn't want to ask."

David snorted. "Lea isn't *quite* as scary as Bubbie was, but it's close." He held up his thumb and first finger about a centimeter apart, demonstrating the difference. He turned to Nick. "I think Bubbie planned for Lea to grow. Not an exact copy, but close. So, although I miss the old gal, I feel confident that at least a piece of her is somewhere watching."

They all shared a silent moment, even Steve, who had heard endless stories of David's legendary grandmother.

"Oh, they are lowering the ramp!" Cindy said.

David rubbed his hands together. "Moment of truth, are we in for more 'One small step' suck... *OR* are we entering a time of enlightened leaders, who lead with poetry and verse that tickles the brain with wonder?"

"Wasn't your other idea for Jake, 'Who Let the Dogs Out?'" Steve asked.

"Yeah... but Jake shot that one down too," David said, disgustedly. "No sense of gravitas. The Baha Men were geniuses."

"Well, we are about to find out," Nick said, pointing at the hologram. "The ramp is down."

The view switched to an outside perspective, likely from a hovering drone. The four helmeted and suited figures walked together down the broad ramp, stopping just short of the Martian soil. They stood for a moment, looking around at the landscape. At a gesture from the tall, suited figure with the name Swelton stenciled on the chest, they reached out to the person beside them and grasped hands.

Jake's voice crackled to life. "We, the people of Earth, take this step together. Not as different genders, races, or political entities. As humans all." Then the four astronauts stepped forward in lockstep, placing their feet simultaneously on the surface of another planet.

"GOD DAMN IT!" David swore.

TEN

Eldorado Mining Site, The Moon
One year later: 9 years 10 days until the invasion

Steve Cooper pushed down on the brake of the Moon speeder, causing the engines to cut out in the rear and counter jets to fire in the front, about where one would expect headlights. There were lights on the speeder, but they were on the sides and could be extended out as needed, much like in a sports car but turned 90°. His speed dropped gradually as he continued to exert pressure, increasing power to the jets. There was no friction from tires or air resistance to slow it as would have on Earth. With no atmosphere, and the engines on the underside of the speeder providing constant lift to counteract the Moon's gravity, the vehicle would continue moving across the plane with very little loss of momentum unless actively braked.

The speeder wasn't a true spaceship. It could move personnel rapidly across the Moon's surface, not lift off into the black. In fact, safety features would kick in to stop anyone from breaking the two kilometers per second escape velocity needed to break the Moon's gravity.

Steve loved using the vehicles. Anyone who looked at them could tell that they were modeled after Tatooine land speeders. The major difference was the reinforced domed canopy that acted as both a roll cage and a way to operate the vehicle without a helmet. It tickled him no end to speed across the Moon's surface, imagining Tusken Raiders and Jawa over the next rise. He actually designed a Jawa Sand crawler, but its construction was just too impractical to justify. He promised himself that if they survived the Silfe invasion, he would build one as a present to himself, maybe as the moon's version of a recreational vehicle? He chuckled at the thought of a generation of retirees dressed head to toe in brown robes traveling over the lunar surface.

He aimed the speeder at a large boulder a couple of hundred feet in front of him, calling out to the air, "Bishop, can you open the north Eldorado entrance?"

In response, the previously flat plane rose to reveal a large open-sided box, sized for the speeder. He continued to slow and came to a stop within its confines, hitting the landing button, which lowered a set of struts and slowly cut power to the lift.

As soon as he came to rest, a shudder transmitted through the box, and it descended. As it passed below ground, it was revealed as an elevator dropping into the massive Eldorado cavern.

Eldorado was barely recognizable from the roughhewn cave that Bishop surprised him with. He could see at least a thousand bots crawling all over the space, spidery appendages clinging to cracks and crannies, many of them on the sheer walls. Most were engaged in mining operations, other bots carried raw materials in their metal claws to smelters, while still more transported finished metals to hundreds of centrally located 3D printers.

In another area he could see a vast flat hanger with row upon row of Gunstars shining in the spotlights, only needing pilots to begin their fight against the Silfe. Beyond them, larger ships were parked. These were combat shuttles, shaped like their commercial brethren being produced in the converted automobile factories on Earth, but with noticeable differences. They were sleeker and more deadly looking, with dark titanium armor covering external surfaces. The ships bristled with gun ports, giving them 360° firing arcs, including what looked like a pair of old fashioned ball turrets on the upper and lower surfaces.

According to HAL, the Silfe were masters of suborning electronics, and so it led to some interesting engineering problems. Steve and Bishop began looking into the weapons of the World Wars, before electronics became the battlefield norm. They needed designs without networked computer control. For the combat shuttles, they gained inspiration from the B-17 Flying Fortresses from WWII. Boeing created one of the most celebrated planes in history in the B-17s. The ball turrets used to shoot down the Luftwaffe were controlled via hydraulics. With modern machining techniques and optical sights, they became amazingly effective weapons.

In a way, the Silfe possessed a sort of honor. They wanted to do their killing up close and personal. It was a chink in their otherwise overwhelming advantage, but they rigidly followed it as a cornerstone of their religion. Rather than just standing off and bombarding a planet with kinetic strikes, they sought opportunities for close combat. Whether it was ship to ship, or soldier to soldier. HAL even told them of a planet that had progressed only to the early iron age. The Silfe landed their troops and fought blade to blade across the planet, forgoing modern weapons in religious zeal. The natives had been an apelike race who were strong natural fighters. According to the AI, it was one of the closest battles for a planet the Silfe ever fought, even though they had 10,000 ships in the system who could have decimated the population without a single troop landing. In the end, the Silfe cheated. They mixed in advanced technology to knock down a castle wall, or to eradicate large groups who were killing too many of their own, and they had won.

Steve and Bishop were working on the nitty gritty of the

equipment needed to fight the aliens on the ground. Cindy's role remained to push forward new technologies, while Pablo continued to work on their ace in the hole in the asteroid belt. His goal was to get the colony ship to depart in a little over four years. They wanted to make sure that there would be no way for the Silfe to catch the vessel. No matter what became of the battle for Earth, humanity would survive. Pablo's secondary goal was to provide two orbital defense platforms and to see if he could make something out of Psyche that could go toe to toe with their fleet.

There were two ways to win the war with the Silfe. First, humanity could overwhelm them with superior numbers. So many ships and troops that the end would be a foregone conclusion. They had HAL crunch the numbers early on, and it was determined to be impossible in the time they had. Even if they had begun to build ships the moment HAL had first contacted Nick at 16 they wouldn't have been able to make enough effective fighters for it to be a winning strategy. Honestly, it was only Cindy's battery technology and fusion power that made it possible to construct the autonomous bots that built the ships they had now. The world had needed time to grow closer to the Silfe in capabilities. They had, and now finally were at the point where the gap was slowly closing.

The second option was to make technology *slightly* better than the Silfe's. Gunstars that could take out five of the alien fighters for every one destroyed. Troop augments that could stand up to Silfe ground based weapons with a similar attrition rate.

The purpose of the Pablo's orbital defenses was to keep their main fleet busy enough that they wouldn't be able to bombard the planet, while ships like the *Falcon* could stand off and do enough damage to require a response. Even the settlements on the Moon, Mars, Callisto and Enceladus were just a way to spread the Silfe out enough that they couldn't bring all of their strength to a single point- namely the Earth.

One of the most important pieces of information HAL

revealed was the Silfe would not use computerized aiming in any of their conflicts. They considered it a sin. Each death had to be the work of a sentient being. So, the ships and troops would need to get in close enough to see their enemy with only the aid of optical sites. This suited Steve just fine. Given the Silfe mastery of electronic warfare, trying to use computers to fight them was already a losing strategy.

Steve and Bishop continued to work on weapons that would whittle the aliens down until they might gain advantage enough to turn the tide. The battle would need to be slow and steady so as not to trigger the Silfe to overreact. If they showed their hand early, they would be overwhelmed as the aliens brought their numbers to bear. They had to be sneaky. The Silfe forces needed to be split into manageable chunks so they wouldn't overwhelm the humans. They needed to be the Viet Cong, not the Light Brigade. After all, the Charge of the Light Brigade had not worked out very well for the British, despite Tennyson's "O the wild charge they made!"

Steve popped the hatch on the speeder and stepped out onto the cave floor. Eldorado was long ago pressurized and filled with atmosphere. It was easier to smelt, and 3D print with existing Earth based technology, rather than to re-engineer equipment to function in vacuum. It was a huge endeavor, made possible only by the tireless energy of the bots that never ate nor slept. With the battery technology Cindy had perfected, a single twenty-minute charge would last a bot for a full day of operations. They needed all of that time to delve into the enormous riches in the cave. Bishop had aptly named it. It contained more wealth than all the mines the world's history had produced. It was truly worthy of the name "Eldorado."

Light coalesced in front of him in a swirling tornado, finally settling into the form of Bishop. It reminded him a little of the Tasmanian Devil, minus the burrowing through trees and rocks. Steve noticed that the different AIs had distinctive ways in which their avatars manifested. For Gloria, it was typically a classic Star Trek beam in, while Pablo favored motes of light that coalesced to form his figure. Lea's pattern was *no* pattern. Each time she appeared, it seemed to be a unique set of colors and effects. He supposed it was another way in which they showed their individualism. He occasionally fantasized about what he would do if he could appear out of thin air. *Perhaps a smoke screen, like a ninja?* He shook his head and spoke up.

"Hey Bishop. You wanted me to come down?"

"Yeah, I've got something new to show you." He waved him to follow as he turned and walked down the steps hewn into the rock floor.

Bishop hadn't taken on the android's appearance from *Alien,* for which he'd been named. Rather, he'd adopted a mixed heritage appearance that made it hard to peg any single race. His face was thin, with a short brown beard that matched his head. He stood about 5'10 with a trim fit build that filled out his perpetually worn coveralls. He had 'Bishop' stenciled above the breast pocket, which contained a small spiral-bound notebook. For some reason, he had taken on the affectation of jotting down notes into it with a pencil held perpetually behind his ear if a new idea came to him, or if Steve asked him to remember to do something. It was as if the AI had made the notebook to interface to the servers that housed his memory.

They walked down several flights of stairs into the area set aside for infantry weapons development. The stairs took a sharp corner, and it opened into a broad shallow bowl cut into the base of the cavern. He could see silhouette targets at varying distances across the testing area every twenty-five yards, including some that had been spray painted with images of reptilian Silfe ground troops. The targets were not what garnered his attention, though. Standing in front of him was a set of infantry armor augments which appeared complete.

"Whoa!" he said. "You finished it?"

"Yep!" Bishop replied with enthusiasm, extending an

arm in a grand gesture. "One exosuit at your service,"

Steve studied the armor, walking around it slowly. It looked a little like a metal skeleton slightly larger than a human, complete with articulated joints. The frame was constructed from thin, flat carbon nanotubing, with the ends of the arms and feet ending in oversized metal gauntlets and boots. He could see hydraulic connections on the shoulders, elbows, wrists and in a couple of places on the legs. Looking at it, it was apparent the supports were all meant to go behind the body with only a chest piece, looking suspiciously like a medieval breastplate, to be worn in front. On the chest plate, furthering the impression of an armored knight, was the World Commission symbol where heraldry might be placed. Attached -magnetically?- to the chest plate was a laser rifle with a cord leading out of the stock, connecting to a thorax section that broadened out into a backpack-like structure.

Steve smiled. "You're going all in with the Arthurian vibe, huh?"

The AI shrugged. "Right before I came up with the idea for the suit, Pablo and I had had a movie night out on Psyche. I told him I was contemplating the design for the exosuits but needed some time off because I kept going in circles." Bishop smirked. "It was Pablo's turn to pick the movies. He went with *Excalibur* and *Edge of Tomorrow*."

Steve laughed. "Yeah, that is the vibe I was getting. Trust Pablo to combine medieval with futuristic."

"It seems to be consistent with his personality, doesn't it?" Bishop said.

Steve nodded. "Do you want to explain why you went with an external augment rather than a full suit? I'd have thought that for environments like the Moon and Mars, it would have been important to provide enclosed systems."

"I decided against it." He ticked off points. "First, they are orders of complexity harder to make than these. Trying to get one to work without onboard computers would have been almost impossible. I don't want the Lizards to hack them and make a lot of people immovable statues in the middle of a battle."

"That makes sense," Steve said, letting the "Lizard" comment go past without comment. Bishop was as passionate about protecting humans as he was about killing any Silfe to set foot inside the solar system. Placing the protection of humans into the AI's core kernel had made for some *interesting* results, including the derogatory term he used for the aliens. In actuality, the Silfe looked more like giant -pants wetting- sentient crocodiles than lizards.

He continued the conversation with a question. "What about harsh environments?"

"We already have top-notch environmental suits for the colonies. The new skin suits coming out of Warren Industries work great. They are so thin, that except for the helmet, you might as well be wearing spandex. Besides, they already have safety features for leaks. It is easier to armor up those suits than to create some sort of anime mech. Plus, it will be better to mass produce one set of armor than have multiple different types. In any infantry battle, we need to keep it simple. If one of these malfunctions, we want the operator to hop out and keep fighting."

"You sold me." Steve said. "Is the laser rifle the only armament?"

"No, we'll vary weapons depending on troop designation. There are connections for additional weapon mounts and power packs. What you're looking at here is a light scout model. For line troops, we'll add on a grenade launcher and at least a one-shot antiaircraft rail gun mount. I have some ideas for some heavier weapons, but we run into power issues. Suit movement is almost entirely mechanical, and there are capacitors that will charge from that potential energy, so even in a fight you are constantly replacing lost juice. There are also some foldable solar panels that the suits will carry, which can charge it back up in about ten minutes, or they could just plug into an outlet. I am designing some lightweight mobile charging stations that are battlefield rated. In the early conflicts, I hope that we can pick our battlefields and prep them with power cells.

"OK, I think that is all well-reasoned," Steve said, grinning ear to ear. "Now I get to test it!"

He walked up to the suit, noting that it was free standing. He raised the chest plate up and out of the way to allow him to step backwards into the feet, which adjusted like a pair of ski boots. He pulled the chest piece back down and said, "Is it one size fits all?"

"Pretty much. I made that one to your height, but we will probably have three sizes to make it easier to fit people. Even with the different sizes, I made it so that in a couple of minutes you can reattach the pivot points on the arms and legs to accommodate a wide variety of body types. It is another reason the enclosed suit wasn't a good idea. It would have to be made to fit a single person, which when we talk about millions of suits, makes just the fitting process impossible."

"That many?" Steve asked, wonder in his voice.

"At least. These suits aren't that much harder to make than a car. They made eighty-five million of those on Earth last year. I figure if we retool most of the automobile plants to make either combat shuttles or suits, we could churn them out. Pablo has more rare Earth metals out in the asteroid belt, so he is focusing on the lasers and fusion engines for ships. Eldorado and Earth will need to pick up the slack for the more mundane stuff."

As the AI talked, Steve pushed his hands into the suit's oversized gauntlets. He pressed forward, feeling his hands enveloped by stiff gloves. He could feel wire connections running along the fingertips and palms as he opened and closed his hands, watching as the much larger metal gauntlets matched his movements. "How are the hands wired?" he asked.

"I stole the design from Cindy's original haptic gloves. When you flex your hands, it sends a signal through the gel and into electrical switches in the gauntlets, mimicking movement. It should also provide graded resistance in the inner glove for sensation, just like in VR environments." He shrugged. "At least I hope it will. I have this minor problem of not *having* hands, but the math works out so…"

Steve reached up and grasped his laser rifle with the gauntlets, feeling the resistance as it pulled away from the breast plate. Even though his hands weren't *actually* touching the weapon, his brain couldn't tell the difference. "Pretty slick; it works perfectly."

"Good," the AI said, looking relieved. "We needed the hands to have increased grip strength but still have enough flexibility to do fine manipulation. This was the best compromise I could come up with."

"How much PSI can one of these things put out?"

"The story HAL told us about the ape race that came close to beating the Silfe gave me the parameters I was looking for. I figured that if we could augment a human to about the strength of a silverback gorilla, then we could match them one on one. So the grip is 2500 PSI, and it can lift about 4000 pounds, but I made it faster. An augmented suit can run thirty-five mph, which would leave a silverback in the dust."

"Nice! OK, let's try it out." Steve took a step forward. It felt completely natural. As he lifted his right foot, there was little to no resistance. Of course, on the moon there wasn't much anyway, but as he continued to take steps forward, it felt like he was hardly wearing a suit at all. "How far can it jump?"

"*That's* tricky," Bishop said. "On Earth, the maximum jump possible is about eight feet. That same jump on the moon would let you clear a big house. I wanted to make sure that we could dial it up or down. The operator can do that by turning the hydraulic settings on a panel in the boots. They can adjust the grip strength and lifting capacity as well in the gauntlets. It's one reason I had to make them oversized, to fit in the controls."

"So… I just… jump?" Steve said, a bit of trepidation in

his voice.

"You'll want to get used to it," Bishop warned. "Start with just bending your legs and jumping straight up... and maybe you want to put a helmet on?"

Steve shook his head. "You are not making me feel any better here."

Bishop smirked, "Safety first."

As the suited man watched, a helmet lifted from a rack and floated over to him. "Wow! You really have fine-tuned the force field generators. That was slick!"

Bishop waved it away like it was nothing. "You should see my floor show. I'm going to make a mining bot disappear."

Steve chuckled. The AI had a definite sense of humor. He brought his attention back to the helmet floating in front of him. It was black, with a clear face mask, resembling an Earth motorcycle helmet. He reached out and grabbed it with the gauntlets. The feeling of the hard, smooth surface was perfectly rendered in his mind. He couldn't tell that it wasn't in his actual hands. There was even a feeling that the metal was cold. Bishop nailed the interface, and at least that part of the suit was working perfectly. He just hoped that the jump was as well calibrated.

He flipped down the clear visor and then bent his legs, arms in front of him like he was doing a bodyweight squat. "OK," he said. "We'll go for a half speed jump in 3... 2... 1..."

Steve pushed with his legs and suddenly he was flying upward. Unfortunately, he had been leaning slightly as he jumped, so besides going up, he was also going forward. "Ahhh!" He screamed as he shot 12 feet up and 30 feet forward, arms windmilling. Luckily, just before landing, he remembered to bend his knees. He managed barely to keep his feet, sliding a foot forward before coming to rest. His heart pounding, Steve let out a sigh of relief and began mentally checking that he hadn't hurt himself. Fingers... toes... everything seemed to be in working order. Behind him, he could hear Bishop letting out a booming laugh.

"That was AWE... SOME!" the AI said.

Steve turned the suit to look back at him. "That was fucking *terrifying*." Then he started laughing too as the adrenaline from the jump subsided. "It *was* kind of awesome though."

"OK," Bishop said. He took out the ever-present notebook from his front pocket, marking it with the pencil from behind his ear. "Test one, jump, check." He gave him a huge smile. "Just a couple of hundred more tests to go. Let's try running next, then after you get a bit more proficient with movement, you can try some *bigger* jumps."

Steve's mouth suddenly went dry. He had to swallow twice before he could speak again. "Y.. eah... sounds... great."

ELEVEN

Washington DC
10 days later: 9 years until the invasion

"Senator Senestine, Chairman Strombold is here for your 11:00 appointment," said a voice over an old-fashioned intercom, straight out of the 1950s.

Robert 'Bobby' Senestine leaned forward and held down a switch to respond. "Thanks, Margery; give me a minute and then send him in."

The Georgia Senator pushed a button on the underside of his desk, causing his computer to fold down and disappear as the center of the desk flipped. On the other side was an antique leather desk set, complete with a silvered pen in a holder. He pushed another button, and the large display screen on the wall showing various news channels in small windows wiped clean, replaced by a photo of a tree-lined walkway in Savannah.

Senestine knew impressions were everything. He had been a DC insider for thirty years, first as a congressman and, more recently, in the Senate. Part of his success was his image as a good old boy. He was the only politician from Georgia in the past forty years to have won the state with a decisive majority in *both* the rural and city districts. It was a careful line to walk. He cultivated an affable and outrageous character that made him larger than life and chose what to champion carefully, always something he believed in, but nothing too controversial to either side. It made him a natural broker for cross-party politics. The result was that most of the genuinely impactful legislation in the past few decades had his name attached.

His office was one of Senestine's most potent weapons. He had a variety of images on his walls, carefully chosen to solidify his public persona. Ribbon cuttings at a shelter, library, and car factory; shaking hands with union leaders, foreign heads of state, and factory workers. There were also quite a few of him fly fishing the Toccoa River.

He also -falsely- had a reputation for being a Luddite, able to use technology, but preferring a leather-bound book to that of an e-reader. He was always careful to stow any symbols of modern life before he received guests, hence the quick modifications to his office.

He composed himself, placing a smile on his face as his secretary opened the door and announced. "Mr. Strombold, sir."

Senestine stood from his seat and came around the desk to vigorously shake Strombold's hand while saying, "Mr. Chairman! It's good to see you again!" He turned to his secretary. "Margery, thank you. Please hold all of my calls for the next hour."

"OK, just let me know if you need anything, Senator," she said before closing the door.

Nick ended the shake and said, "I think we can forgo the titles, Bobby."

"Of course, of course, Nick," Senestine said. He was a little intrigued by the meeting. Strombold had become relatively close to him professionally over the past few years, but their titles were one thing that had defined their interactions.

Of course, one of the main reasons he was a Senator sitting in the Russell building instead of his old congressional office was the man sitting across from him. Strombold provided him with talking points for his campaign that had all but won the election for him. Every time he'd adhered to the script provided, his rating in the polls had gone up a point. In the end, he had won by one of the highest margins in the past fifty years. It had solidified him as a major power in the Senate overnight, while his previous experiences in congress had given him the background to assure votes would go his way.

Despite sitting his Senate seat for only a year, they had elected him the Majority Leader. It was not taking it too far to say that he was one of the most -if not the most- powerful politicians in *both* Congress and the Senate.

So, what had changed? Besides President Tanner, Nickolas Strombold was the most influential leader in the United States. Internationally, he was *the* most important. *Perhaps he wanted to go into the Senate?* Strombold's tenure as the World Commission Chair was ending soon. Maybe Tanner wanted to put in someone from his party instead.

His thoughts came to a halt as the young man spoke.

"I am stepping down as the Chairman of the World Commission," he said without preamble.

"Really... Nick? Your tenure doesn't end for six months. Why would you resign before then?"

Strombold ignored the question. "I spoke with President Tanner this morning and let him know my decision. We have decided to name Julianna Lewiston as the Commission's US liaison."

The conversation was going a bit too fast for Senestine, which was rare. "Why would Tanner choose Lewiston?" He asked. "She is a federal judge without a single political bone in her body. What advantage could he get from naming her?"

Strombold gave him one of the sardonic smiles that he knew heralded an earthquake. The first time he had seen it was right before the man steamrolled the *Chief of the Air Force* into signing over the most advanced fighter the world had ever seen to any country that joined the World Commission. It had appeared again on the day the previous President had been arrested by the secret service for treason. That wasn't even considering Risa, the *Falcon*, and *Star Base-1*, which had all received the same treatment.

"I told Jimmy that we needed someone without political connections in the role. So, you might say that it was *me* that chose her."

"You told *Jimmy*? Since when do you call the President by his first name? You talk like you are old friends, but I know you have only met a couple of times."

Strombold laughed. "Keeping tabs on me, Bobby?"

The Senator scoffed, "Me? Keeping tabs on the most important politician in the world? You bet your ass I am," he coughed. "Pardon the French."

Nick waved the language away. "Trust me, after spending half of my life listening to David; you couldn't offend me if you tried."

Senestine saw a chink in the polished man's armor that he might pry open. "David Lieberman?"

"Yes," Strombold said. "David is one of my best friends in the world, but the man's vocabulary would make a sailor blush." He smiled again. "To answer your initial question, I talk to Jimmy Tanner most days of the week. You will find that those conversations are off the record, however. I consider him one of my better friends, if not a bit of a father figure." He sighed. "God knows he is a better role model than my own."

Senestine was knocked back on his heels. *Strombold and the President... friends? Talking every day?* He grabbed onto the last comment to give himself some time to think. "I thought your father is a successful businessman. I believe they named him one of the top CEOs in the country last year in Forbes."

"Yes," Strombold said, a grimace on his face. "He *is* a top-notch businessman. Unfortunately, as a parent, he left a lot to be desired. We had a falling out after my insistence on going into politics. He wanted me to follow in his footsteps. I declined."

"Surely he has changed his tune since? No one can deny your accomplishments, what you have done for the world."

"Oh, he tried to reach out to me after becoming the World Commission Chairman. At that point, we hadn't talked in a few years. I wasn't interested in reconnecting." Strombold shook his head and directed a wry grin at Senestine. "We seem to have gotten off track. I appreciate the attempt at distraction, but I think that the question that you *actually* wanted to ask was how the President and I could have such a close relationship without the public knowing? Am I right?"

Senestine sighed. Strombold was just too sharp. There were very few people who could best him, but he was sitting across from one of them. He decided that he just needed to lay all his cards on the table and stop playing the game.

"Yes, Nick, I was trying to buy some time to figure out what is going on, hoping that you would drop a hint so I could gain some advantage in any negotiations you were planning. I figure you are here to collect on the help you gave me in the last election, and I have never been one to give anything away for free." He gave him a chagrined look. "Old habits die hard, but I owe you, and I always pay my debts, so you can just come out with it. I'm willing to support whatever you need."

Nick gave him a broad smile. "Bobby, that is what I have always admired about you. You have the instincts of a shark but the honor of a Southern gentleman. In a time of social media and colonies on the moon, it's refreshing." His gaze sharpened. "But I am not calling in favors today. Or you might say that although I am asking you for something, you will probably think of it as *me* doing you a favor."

"That sounds ominous," Senestine said.

Nick's smile broadened. "You have no idea." He took a deep breath and then began speaking. "I'm going to be the next President of the United States, and I need you to be Vice President."

Senestine sat for a moment digesting what Strombold

had said, then replied. "Nick, I do not doubt that you will be President if you want to be. You are arguably the most respected politician in the world. Since you're from my party, I can honestly say that this is great news. It will help immensely with our agenda." He paused then and looked earnestly into the other man's eyes. "But even though I appreciate all that you have done for me, I don't want to be Vice President. The position is a lame duck and it would be taking a step backward in my career. The only upside is that I could run for President after your two terms are up. Given how young you are, I doubt you will have a coronary on me." He smiled to make the joke obvious. "In nine years, I will be ready for retirement, not the Oval Office. So I hope to repay my debt to you in another way because it will have to be a hard pass."

The Senator felt his heart drop a little as Nick's sardonic smile reappeared. Something must have shown in his expression as Nick stopped what he was about to say and asked, "You look like you ate something off, Bobby."

Senestine relaxed. Strombold could be one charming son of a bitch when he wanted to be. "I just recognized your smile. I figured the next words out of your mouth were going to be something about, I don't know..." he searched for a world-altering development... "Cynthia Warren creating a time machine or something."

At the end of his supposition, Strombold laughed with genuine delight. Senestine watched as Nick tried and failed several times to get his laughter under control. Finally, the Georgia Senator couldn't help but ask. "I'm not entirely sure that I want to be in on the joke, but what is so funny?"

Finally, the man got his shaking laughter under control and looked back at the Senator. "You got closer than you think, but before we go into that, I need to tell you a few things you don't know. I think that after you hear me out, you will change your mind about being Vice President."

Senestine gave him a skeptical look, but he answered, "You have my undivided attention, Nick."

Strombold nodded his head absently and spoke. "Bobby, there is an asteroid called Electra in the asteroid belt. Have you ever heard of it?"

The Senator shook his head. "I'm afraid my study of astronomy is somewhat lacking. I'm fairly well versed in the colonies on the Moon, Mars, Callisto, and Enceladus, but otherwise, I am a bit out of my depth."

"Completely understandable," Nick said. "Electra is a major asteroid in the outer belt. It is about 125 miles in diameter and is primarily rock, although there are some metals mixed in. It is oblong in shape which made it easier to put engines on."

"Wait!" Senestine said, making sure he had heard the last part right. "You said there are engines on it?"

"Yes," Strombold said, as if it was customary to put an engine on an asteroid over a hundred miles in diameter and fly it around like a toy airplane. "For several years now, mining bots have been working on hollowing out the interior so that it could hold an atmosphere. That is the last step before the ship will be ready."

"Ship?"

"Yes, ship. We are still working on the name, although I am considering letting David come up with it before he rigs another planetary vote. I think he is leaning toward the *Galactica*, which is pretty appropriate once you think about it."

Strombold's comments were coming too fast at him by this point. "Why don't we slow down and pretend that I have *no* idea what you are talking about."

"Sorry," Nick said. "I am used to talking to people about this who are in on the PLAN. Let me back up a step." He took a moment to gather his thoughts and started again. "The asteroid has been hollowed out to prepare for approximately two hundred thousand passengers, placed in cryogenic sleep." He gave Senestine a shrug. "You weren't entirely wrong about Cindy having a new invention. She found preliminary plans for a cryogenic chamber that the Russians have been working on since the 1970s. She gave it to one of the workgroups at Warren, who completed it. We have a machine that will place a human in stasis. Cindy believes it can be maintained indefinitely, although there is no way to prove that. They have had chimpanzees in cryogenic sleep for three years without degradation. The AIs ran simulations, and there is close to a 100% chance that humans can be placed into stasis for decades with no issues."

Senestine gulped. "Cryogenic sleep? Like some science fiction movie?"

Strombold grinned, "In case you haven't been paying attention, the past decade has been a sci-fi movie on speed."

The Senator had to concede the point. His mind finally wormed its way around the edges of the concept. "Why would you need something so big? I can appreciate the concept of cryogenics for many applications, including interstellar space flight, but why would you put two hundred thousand people on a ship... unless?"

Strombold nodded as he saw the drawing light in the Senator's eyes. "You see, the possibilities. I knew I had picked the right person for the job. We are making a colony ship."

Senestine paused, imagining a ship 125 miles in diameter speeding to another planet, transporting humanity to the stars. He said, "You have never dreamed, small Nick."

"It's not a dream, Bobbie. The ship will be complete in two years and will leave in four. Being President is too big a job to ride heard on this. I am going to need a Vice President who can oversee the project; chair a commission to pick the people. Someone with the political clout to bully Congress and the Senate into line and get the materials the people will need for a successful colony. The World Commission will help, of course, but besides China, there is no other country with the resources to accomplish this."

The Senator was intrigued. "Well, that changes things. It sounds like a fascinating challenge. The problem remains that *after* the ship leaves, I would still have at least another term as Vice President, doing little to nothing. Wouldn't I be more helpful in my current position as the Majority Leader?"

"Normally, I would agree with you," Strombold said. "The problem is that I won't be President long in the second term. I need someone I can trust to take over when I step down."

Senestine's brows lowered. None of this made any sense, and the Senator felt he was missing something big. "Why would you step down from the Presidency? What are you not saying?"

"I'm afraid before I can tell you that, I will need an assurance that you would take me up on the Vice Presidency under the conditions that I have set."

The Senator held up a hand and said, "Give me a moment." He needed to think through the implications of the conversation. *Did he want to be Vice President?*

The idea of guiding an interstellar colony to completion was fascinating. Senestine's brain was already running through the intricacies involved. Just the logistics of supplying all that was needed to start over on a new planet was almost overwhelming, yet he had never been one to turn down a challenge.

And then to be President? He'd long since given up on that dream. There had been a time fifteen years ago when his name was bandied about by the party's movers and shakers for a presidential campaign, but it had never happened. He made his peace with it, telling himself that he would rather pull the strings behind the scenes. He enjoyed that part of his professional career, but he had always wondered *what if?*

So, the answer, deep down, was yes. He wanted to do this. Nickolas Strombold was a man of honor who had done more for world stability than almost anyone in history. There was no one better to hitch his wagon to.

"I can accept your terms under the condition that you bring me in fully. I need to know what I'm signing up for. If you can convince me it is for the good of the country, I will be your

Vice President."

Strombold smiled appreciatively. "That I can do. What I am about to tell you is the most closely held secret in the world." He paused slightly, his gaze glinting.

"In eight and a half years, an alien invasion will enter the solar system. If we are not ready in time, they will wipe every man, woman, and child from the Earth."

The Chairman of the World Commission and future President of the United States looked at the shocked Senator. "Ready to save the Earth?"

TWELVE

Empire State Building
Eight and a half months later: 8 years,
110 days until the invasion

"David, I need you and Gloria to look into what it will take to make the colony ship launch," Nick said.

David looked at Nick's head floating in the air, projected upward in a cone of light from a saucer-sized disk sitting on his desk. The image looked slightly too white and would occasionally twitch like it was about to cut out.

The projector was a birthday gift from Gloria. She became tired of him complaining that they had bypassed *Star Wars's* slightly washed-out holograms and went straight to those indistinguishable from reality.

With the new force field generators, modern holograms -at least those controlled by an AI- were indistinguishable from reality. He still held that there was a "Right" way to do things, and they skipped a few steps. The omission had somehow offended his geek sensibilities.

David exclusively used the projector now, like an audiophile who insists on the quality of vinyl over digital music.

"Don't you think that Steve or Cindy would be better at that?" he asked. "Plus, I thought Bobby was heading up the project."

"Bobby will be the political head of it and will be the person in overall charge. He will be integral in steamrolling anyone who is putting up roadblocks."

David laughed. "Well, you picked the right guy for that. He is like a pitbull when he gets his mind set on something. I swear Lea is in love. Which, I got to tell you, its kinda weird. She is like my Bubbie, but she is too hot to be anyone's Bubbie." He shook his head. "*Way* too many confusing feelings happening. It's like I'm going through puberty again, and it wasn't a picnic the first time around."

Nick laughed, "David, we need to talk more often. I'm in the middle of a presidential campaign, and I thought I must be the most stressed guy on the planet, and here you are, having an Oedipal crisis. It helps put my own life's trials into perspective."

David grinned, "Glad to be of service. Getting back to the point, why do you need me?"

"No one has ever sent a colony ship out before. People at NASA have considered it, but they never dreamed of anything this big. For them, it has always been a concept for the far future, not three years from now. I need someone who has thought about it for real. Essentially someone who has watched every movie and read every science fiction novel in existence."

"Don't forget about manga; there is some pretty good alien planet stuff there."

"Exactly my point," Nick said. "I need the big ideas. It also helps that you have an AI to help search databases."

"No kidding," David said. "We bought Gloria a couple of more server farms last year, and I swear she is almost as good at hacking the planet as HAL. I hardly even use him anymore."

"Right. The Earth AIs are reaching a point where they have all but replaced HAL for us. I know he is still much more powerful, but it is challenging to get much out of him these days. I only use him for details on the Silfe, and even then,

I am getting back less and less. He has intimated that there is a secondary protocol kicking in to make sure that his help doesn't push us past the technology level of the Silfe."

"That is just so much bullshit," David said. "Friggin' pick a side! Either he wants us to win, or he wants us to get eaten by a bunch of space lizards. There isn't a whole lot of gray in there."

"You won't get any argument out of me," Nick agreed. "It *kind* of makes sense. HAL's job was to get us to where the species would survive the invasion. With the colony ship a certainty at this point, his job is complete. No species, except the Harrow, has ever won against an invasion fleet. They have been doing this for tens of thousands of years, and I don't think his programming had the parameters for a species that *might* win. I think he radioed for instructions, and the Harrow put the kibosh on any more help."

"Wait! Do you think HAL can talk with the Harrow? As in faster-than-light communications?"

"Yes, or at least Cindy and Pablo do."

"Which is an abso-fucking-lutely in my book."

"The two of them *are* pretty much always right," Nick said, understating it by quite a bit. "It always bothered Cindy that HAL could know the exact arrival date. It would mean that they watched them leave the last planet, and they could track the direction they went, which would take a couple of data points at least.

He gave David a shrug. "We figured the Silfe could detect our radio and TV signals. With our largest radio telescope arrays, we can see out to about 500 light-years, and who knows what kind of range they have. So that would explain how they could find us, but it doesn't tell us how the Harrow could know we are here. HAL told us they are pinned in by the Silfe, which means they couldn't have detected us without being closer. Unless they sent an AI through to this part of the galaxy and then sent it back, there is no way that they could have A: know we are here, and B: sent an AI through to help. HAL admitted it took the equivalent energy of burning out the Sun to send him here. So, we don't think they are sending AI units on round trips."

"What does Cindy think?" David asked.

"She thinks the Harrow sent out a wide net of AI beacons in the probable paths of the Silfe. They keep track of invasion fleets and search for planets that display sentient life. The beacons would need the ability to transfer data to Harrow occupied space."

"That makes sense. Do they do it with micro-worm holes or entangled particles?" David asked.

Nick looked surprised. "How did you know? I thought you hadn't talked to Cindy about this?"

David sighed dramatically. "You just finished telling me you want me on the colony project for my bodylicious knowledge of everything sci-fi, then get surprised when I drop the mike on you. *Of course*, I know the major theories of FTL communication.

The little man straightened an imaginary tie. "Now listen to Professor Lieberman; this *will* be on the final exam.

Nick shook his head. "Is there any way we could skip the lecture?"

"Shhh," David said, "No talking in class, or I will send you to the principal's office.

"Ahem. When one hypothesizes about faster-than-light communication or FTL, there are three dominant theories. First, the theory of folds in spacetime, often referred to colloquially as wormholes. Please refer to your books for a full explanation.

Nick couldn't help but laugh at his friend's antics. When David got on a roll, it was better to stand back and enjoy the show. "You missed your calling," he said. "I think that I'm going to buy you a tweed jacket for your next birthday."

David ignored him, instead continuing his monologue. "Second, the theory of entanglement is often espoused. In entanglement, one creates two similar particles connected on a cosmic level. These particles mirror each other irrespective of distance, allowing for communication theoretically anywhere in the universe."

David's voice returned to normal. "Then there are tachyons, which I think is the lazy-man's FTL. I always thought Fienberg just made that shit up. Sounds too much like magic to me, although he was a good Jewish boy, so he had that going for him." He huffed and blinked his eyelashes a few times. "I'm surprised at you, Nickolas! I have a brain; I'm not just a pretty face!"

Nick couldn't help himself and let out a snort. "I'm sorry, professor, from the bottom of my heart. For the rest of it, you're right. Cindy investigated both entanglement and micro-wormholes. She thought it was likely the latter. HAL said that creating wormholes required energy logarithmically proportional to the mass sent. That was the comment that set her thinking. It turns out that electrons have a low mass. So, the size of the wormhole wouldn't need to be very big. It turns out that a Gunstar fusion engine has enough to do it."

"Wait!" David said. "Are you telling me that Cindy made an FTL communicator?"

"Yep, she put one on Jake's Gunstar and sent him off on the other side of Mars. It worked perfectly, no lag at all."

"Holy fuck!" David said. "This changes everything. We can stay in communication with the colony ship, so we'll know where they end up. Hell, it will seriously aid the war effort as well. We can coordinate fleet movements." David rubbed his hands together. "I'll need to switch up the programming on *Alien Invasion* to include FTL."

"What is *Alien Invasion?*" Nick asked.

"Just the most amazing VR game ever created by humankind!" David said, getting excited. He stopped suddenly, his eyes blinking, then called out to the room. "Sorry, Gloria! ... The most amazing VR game ever created by humans and AI kind! You totally did the heavy lifting on the graphics and engine!"

Gloria's voice came over the speakers in David's walls. "No problem, Boss! It was a joint effort, and the story was all you!"

"Anyway," David said. "Gloria and I had the idea that we needed to hide our trail a bit. I know we need to bring more people in as we get closer, but eventually, someone will slip. We have been lucky to pick the people we have. I was a little worried about Senestine, but he seems like a good egg."

Nick shook his head. "He is *both* a good egg *and* a bad egg. Trust me when I tell you he is capable of some heinous stuff, if needed."

"I'm OK with that," David said. "We are talking about saving the world here. Besides, it isn't like we didn't pretty much start a war with China when we had to."

"I go back and forth on that," Nick said. "Sometimes, I want to push it to the back of my mind and pretend it didn't happen. Other times I look over the casualty lists."

David gave his friend a sympathetic look. "Sometimes I think you are too soft-hearted to be President, Nick. I was glad you picked Bobby for your running mate. You need a good hatchet-man. Sometimes you need to cut people off at the knees, or they will keep coming back at you.

"An...y... way," David continued, obviously trying to change the subject. "The story for *Alien Invasion* is pretty sweet, if far-fetched. You see, this Alien AI is sent to earth, where it finds the one person in all the world who it feels can save humanity."

Nick groaned. "You didn't!"

"Stop interrupting Nick. I'm getting to the good part. So, this kind of geeky kid at a private school gets chosen, but he knows he can't do it alone, so he seeks the help of this totally jacked, handsome, super-genius kid named Dave Libbyman, who knows just what to do."

By this time, Nick was shaking his head in disbelief.

David rolled his hands in a forward motion. "Enter 1980s pop montage scene, and bodda bing! Gunstars and exosuits. I stole the Gunstar simulator from Cindy for that part, but Gloria made the engine for the ground battles. Pretty awesome stuff! The Aliens, who are called the Silfeeea, are particularly terrifying. They look like giant crocodiles!" He laughed dramatically. "I mean, you couldn't make this stuff up if you tried!"

Nick continued to shake his head. "David, you can't just tell the entire world about the Silfe invasion. We agreed to wait until three years before they entered the solar system. We can't have a unified Earth if it is tearing itself apart in panic."

"See, Nick, you missed the point," David said. "Think about it. If someone leaks the Silfe invasion, people will think they're nuts. After all, isn't the most popular video game in the world about that *exact* thing? It's Agent Smith and the FBI all over again. Someone at the FBI must have suspicions about Cindy taking the plutonium from Indian Point, but notice how no one has ever come knocking? They *can't*. It would look like they are badgering one of the most important people in the world, who can't have her morning coffee without coming up with some life-changing invention."

He gave Nick a long look. "I know you are tops with politics. I think you could get voted the Grand Pooba of the world if you wanted to, but *this* is what I do.

"Plus, we can train the public with the equipment we will use in the war. The VR simulations are truly spectacular. With VR haptic suits and gear coming down in price, an average joe in Akron can go immersive. We are already pushing the development of specific VR rigs for just this game, which we will give for free to anyone who wants one for a cut of each play. With advertising revenue in-game, we can fund the whole thing. We'll make a profit while giving ourselves cover *AND* train an entire generation of people to fight the Silfe. Hell, for elite players, there is even the ability to earn rank. If they reach officer status in the..." he coughed once, "World Convocation," they can become crew on ships that look a hell of a lot like the *Falcon* and the new asteroid miners that Steve and

Cindy are cooking up. I'm not the final say on it, but I think we should offer commissions in the World Commission Navy or Marines for anyone who aces these simulations."

"Don't you think the world's militaries will want to use their existing soldiers?" Nick asked.

"That's why I am giving full simulators, for free, to every enlisted and officers' club on the planet. There is absolutely *no* way that soldiers will pass up playing."

"OK," Nick said, knowing that he had already lost. "I can see the benefits, but I can't get over the thought that this is more about being able to live out the plot of the *Last Starfighter* than it is about saving the world."

David Laughed. "Can't it be both?"

THIRTEEN

The Plaza Hotel, Manhattan
Twenty-four days later: Election Day: 8 years 86 days until the invasion

Nick held Bobby Senestine's hand in the air like he had just won a boxing match. "We did it! He yelled to the crowd, waving red, white, and blue signs that read Strombold/Senestine. Small pieces of crepe paper floated in the air throughout the giant ballroom, and thousands of voices cheered them on the stage.

Nick let go of the Vice President-Elect hand and raised both of his for quiet. "I would like to thank all of you for your tireless work and support during the past year. I received a gracious call from my opponent a few minutes ago, and he conceded the election." At this statement, the crowd started cheering again. Nick waited for them to quiet and started again. "We have a lot of work to do as a nation to bring about our VISION FOR THE FUTURE!"

FOURTEEN

The Oval Office, Washington DC
Inauguration day: 7 years 333 days until the invasion

..."We have a little less than eight years to save the human race. But no pressure or anything," Nick said.

David laughed. "Nick, my friend, you have always had a flair for the dramatic. I think that after twenty years of manipulating the world into getting ready for an alien invasion, we all could just relax." As he spoke, he put his hands behind his head and feet up on a coffee table in front of the couch he and Cindy shared.

"Benjamin Franklin probably carved the table you have your dirty feet on," Jake said, causing Cindy to snort.

David didn't move. "It's solid. The man knew how to make good furniture. I thought he was all kites and declaring independence."

Nick chuckled. "David, If I ever need someone to whisper 'Thou art mortal' into my ear, you have the job. I was just lamenting all the deference I've gotten since being elected. I can appreciate why it could go to someone's head."

David gave him a mocking salute. "No problem El Capitán! Count on me to remind you that you were once a boy who couldn't get elected to be class president of a fucking *prep school* without help from golden boy over there." He pointed at Jake, lounging in a high-backed chair, who finally seemed to loosen up in the formal surroundings.

Jake smiled, "I remember saying something like 'No, he's

a great guy,' to the cheerleaders when they asked me why they should vote for some nobody who hadn't been at Pencey 'For five minutes.'"

"Thanks," Nick said with a self-mocking grin. "Way to keep me *really* mortal. Nothing blows a guy's confidence like reminding him how much of a nerd he was in high school." He picked up a tablet from a side table and turned on the screen to show a set of bullet points. "Now that we have established that I am, in fact, a hyped-up nobody, I have some marching orders for you all."

"Very Presidential, Nick," David quipped. "You might have a future in this business."

"Thanks," Nick said sarcastically. "Jake, I need you to work with Steve on plans for both space and ground defense. I know we want to slow play the Silfe, so they don't overreact, but I want to minimize loss of life as much as possible. We know from HAL where on the ecliptic that they will enter the system from, so we should be able to at least start on our terms. We'll want several backup plans depending on our successes or failures."

"I will need more people for that, Nick," Jake said. "I'm only one guy. I can use Jimmy for some of the ground combat theory, given his Marine background, but otherwise, I can only think of things that *I* can think of. Normally, I would have the whole war college for this kind of problem. There are also all the advanced telemetries we will need for battles in the solar system. No one has ever done this kind of fighting before, so we are making it up as we go. The Silfe don't have that problem."

"I think I can help with that," David said.
"Really?" Jake said, his eyebrows raised. "No offense, David, but modern warfare isn't your strong suit."

"Yeah, totally," David said, agreeing. "I am a complete coward. I plan to hide in a very deep hole when the Silfe come a-knocking," he said with no sign of shame. "Anyway, I am not saying that I *personally* would help, but the official release of *Alien Invasion* is coming out next week, and we can run simulations on it."

"What the hell is *Alien Invasion*?" Cindy asked.

David gave a broad smile. "*Alien Invasion* is a little VR video game that simulates combat with a marauding xenophobic alien race called the *Silfeeea*. It uses Gunstars, *Falcon* class ships, and Steve and Bishop's suit augments in custom rigs to make it feel like you are actually in battle. We're hoping it will train the public... *and* make us a fair amount of money."

Cindy's eyes popped open. "You can't be serious!"

"He's not," Nick said. "He told me about it a few months ago. I have to admit I was skeptical at first, but I have been thinking about it, and even though I hate to admit it, it is a pretty good idea."

Cindy looked unconvinced. "How could it be a good idea?"

Jake's eyes lit up, "Because we are going to friggin' *Last Starfighter* the entire world!" He stood up out of his chair and gave David a high five.

"That's what I'm talking about!" David said, returning the high five enthusiastically. "Finally, someone who *gets* it!"

"You will have to fill us slower people in then," Cindy said, looking disgruntled. They all knew that she hated not understanding something; a rare occurrence for her. "Are you two talking about that stupid 80s movie again? The one where the Gunstar name came from?"

"Oh! That hurt!" David said. "How would you like if I said Rosalind Franklin was *just* some stupid scientist?"

"I would have to hurt you," she said.

"Which is why I would never do it!" David replied. "The *Last Starfighter* is something that is precious and may not be made fun of- except by those of us who love it unconditionally."

David's eyes blazed with passion. "It's the ultimate geek movie. A guy plays a video game, and everybody thinks he is just this loser, BUT, in reality, he is training to fly a spaceship that will allow him to defeat Xur as a member of the Rylan Star

League. It's a classic!"

Nick shook his head. "See, I like the movie, and I still don't think you are doing yourself any favors here."

Jake came to David's rescue. "Whether or not you like the movie, it is a good idea for our situation. We need to train the entire planet on modern equipment and techniques, but we can't let them know we are doing it. What better way than in a video game!"

"See!" David said, pointing at Jake. "I told you it was a great idea." His voice grew more rapid as he expanded on his concept. "AND we can use Gloria and the other AIs to help program in tactics. Once we get some high-level players, we'll promote them in-game and have them try to beat different scenarios. We'll get to see what works and what doesn't."

Jake took up the narrative, getting excited. "Same thing for the suits. HAL has given us Silfe warrior tactics and weapon characteristics. We can go all the way from one-on-ones to squads to pitched battles! I don't have to figure out the tactics; we'll let the world do it!"

Cindy looked back and forth between the hyperactive man next to her and the tall blue suited general. "I guess that *could* work."

"Oh, it will work all right," David said. "We've had some beta testers playing for over a month on Risa, and we don't have enough VR simulators to keep up with demand. The word has gone out, and we are getting some hard-core gamers at the Emperor Casino instead of our usual high rollers.

"Gloria and I have been letting out information leaks here and there to the Earth-side press, and the buzz is starting. Psychic Warfare will do a review in two days, which will all but guarantee that the opening will be huge."

"But is it close enough to the real thing to train people?" Cindy asked.

"Well, he said, shifting in his seat. "Umm, the Gunstar simulation was actually... borrowed... from Warren." He held up his hands as Cindy's face hardened. "It was for a good cause!"

He hurried on, not giving her a chance to speak. "As for the ground combat simulation," he shuddered. "I played it a little, and I got to tell you, it scared the shit out of me. We made the Silfe warriors close to real life, and they are Terrifying. As. Fuck!"

The room went silent for a moment as they all digested the thought of fighting a Silfe warrior one-on-one.

Nick spoke again. "OK, so it looks like we have tactics and training set up; I'll leave it to David and Jake to go from here." He received a nod from both men, and then he turned to Cindy. "I need you to figure out a way to 'Discover' the Silfe invasion fleet about three years before they get here."

"What do you mean?"

"I mean, I want to show the world a picture of ten thousand Silfe ships heading toward us when we announce. I need absolute proof; otherwise, the conspiracy theorists will derail everything we are trying to do."

"I am sure that with the AIs, we could suppress most of that," David said.

"I think so too," Nick said, "But I want it to be airtight. I want every man, woman, and child above the age of five to *know* in their bones that they need to do everything they can to prepare, and there is nothing like tens of thousands of alien ships bearing down on you to kick in the fight reflex."

"Or the flight one," David said. "I remember HAL showing me that shit, and I *still* have dreams about it."

Jake, Cindy, and Nick all nodded in sympathy. Nick turned back toward Cindy. "Can you do it?"

"I *think* so?" She looked off to the side in contemplation. "I'm sure that we can use the FTL communication suite to open micro-wormholes out to about five light-years. If we open one in the fleet's path, we could get some data back, including some images." Her eyes scrunched in contemplation. "I'm almost sure of it."

"OK, work on it then. I know you're busy; get Stony in on it if this is too much. That guy is like a pit bull when you give him an assignment."

Cindy nodded. "That's a good idea. I'll give it some thought." Her expression turned questioning. "Does this mean we won't come clean about how long we've known?"

Nick blew out his breath. "That's right. we can't afford the distraction and the finger-pointing that telling the complete story would entail. HAL told us that this was the best way. I wasn't sure if I agreed, but it is hard to argue with the results. If we all survive, I will happily volunteer to be burned in effigy. That is one problem I would welcome. I will have to bring in some trusted world leaders. Still, most of humanity will only know that Warren Industries *happened* upon the invasion fleet while investigating near space."

"What if it gets out?" Jake asked.

"I've got that covered," David said. "The storyline of *Alien Invasion* is *pretty* close to reality. If anyone tries to come forward and attempts to whistle-blow, they will look fairly cuckoo."

Cindy's eyes held a threat. "How close?"

David saw he was in trouble, but couldn't find a way out of answering the direct question. "Ummm, there is a character named Buck Swayton who is a Gunstar pilot-turned-general, and a gorgeous scientist named Sandy Warrent who creates all the weapons on the ships…?"

A bit of hostility went out of Cindy. "Gorgeous, huh?"

"It clearly states in the fine print that 'This is a work of fiction. Any similarity to actual persons, living or dead, or actual events, is purely coincidental.'"

Cindy's eyes flared again.

"Dude," Nick said. "You need to know how to stop while you're ahead."

David gave him a mocking smile. "You're not the first to tell me that."

"OK," Nick continued. "Before Cindy murders you, I would like to say that in your… unique David way, you have given us some excellent cover."

"Nice to be appreciated, Chief."

"Yes. Well, my last request is for you, David. I was hoping you could work with Bobby Senestine on the Colony Project. I know Lea is already compiling lists of potential candidates, but people will lose it when the asteroid comes towards Earth. I need you to come up with a coherent message to cover the fact we have been working on a secret project for several years. The people of the Earth need this to be positive. I want volunteers, not conscripts."

David looked pensive for a moment, then smiled broadly. "I got this."

"That seems like a pretty tall order, David," Jake said. "How are you going to do it?"

"I don't want to ruin the surprise. Let me noodle it around a little, and I'll let you know, OK?"

"O... K...," Nick said. "I will let that one go, mostly because I don't want to know the details." He looked at the grandfather clock standing to one side of the room. "I have an early morning." He smiled, "Not that it isn't great to see you all in person for once. One benefit of your new positions is that David, Jake, and me are all in DC for the next few years." He looked at Cindy. "With the new shuttles, getting you down here won't be too much of an issue either. I know we are all busy, but I want us to meet more often as we get closer. If nothing else, I miss you guys."

"Ahhh," David said. "Mr. President is a big marshmallow!"

Cindy gave him a withering look, then turned and looked at them, face softening, even going so far as to reach out and give David's hand a squeeze where it lay next to hers on the couch. "I miss all of you too," she said, tears glistening in the corners of her eyes.

They all paused for a moment as they digested her uncharacteristic vulnerability.

David gave her hand a quick squeeze, then covered for the awkward moment by saying, "OK, things to do, space crocodiles to prepare for."

They laughed as the tension broke.

"Cindy," Nick said. "Can you stay in town for the next day or so and go over how we might announce a 'Sighting' of the invasion fleet? We want that locked down as much as possible."

"Sure," she said.

The President of the United States looked around at his newest cabinet members and said, "OK, I'll be talking to you all soon. We have some serious work ahead, but we are in the home stretch." He took in the faces he had known for most of his life. "Thanks for all you have done."

FIFTEEN

Washington DC
Same Day

Jake, Cindy, and David stood on the steps of the White House Drive, waiting for their cars to arrive. "Where are you staying?" Jake asked.

"Gloria bought me a place in Georgetown," David said.

"Nice! We were lucky and got an old Victorian up in Logan's Circle. Jane probably has the girls in bed by now, but I bet I'll still find her unpacking boxes when I get home."

"I've always liked Jane," Cindy said. "I'm glad you found each other."

David looked at Cindy curiously. "You *are* in a sentimental mood today, aren't you?"

She gave him a familiar glare that bounced off. "If I am feeling sentimental, it is with good reason." She gestured around them. "Look at where we are. Have you taken a minute and thought about it?" She waved a hand dismissively. "I know, we have been in the thick of it for years but being here seems to bring it home more viscerally. More even than being in space or on the Moon."

David nodded. "I get it. Too many movies, TV shows, and news broadcasts. The world is much smaller than it was, but it still feels like it revolves around this one building, doesn't it?"

They all stood in silence, appreciating just how far they had come.

"Where are you staying, Cindy?" Jake asked.

"Not sure. I was planning on going back to the Warren Campus tonight, but now that I am staying, I'll need to find a hotel. I'm sure my security detail can figure it out."

"I'd offer you my house," Jake said, "But we don't have the guest room set up yet, and I doubt you want to sleep on the floor."

"As nice as it would be to see Jane and the girls, I think I will pass."

"Come stay with me," David said. Cindy gave him a surprised look. He shrugged. "Gloria had the whole thing furnished last week. I only just stopped in, but it's nice. You know, for an AI, she's got excellent taste."

"Let me guess," Cindy said. "Wall to wall *Star Wars* posters."

"No, it's boring modern industrial. Although there *is* a sweet man cave that might have a hundred-inch screen with surround sound and a couple of items of memorabilia from the Holy Trilogy."

"Oh, you are inviting me over for the game, right?" Jake said, sounding excited.

"Of course," the little man said, reaching up to clap the tall general on the shoulder. "Mi casa, su casa. It has a mini-bar, too, including a nice selection of finger foods."

"Let me guess," Cindy said. "Twinkies."

David grinned. "There may be a couple of boxes tucked away here and there."

"How you stay so skinny when your diet comprises nothing but sugar and artificial colors is a mystery of science. If anyone figures it out, I will give them one of my Nobel Prizes."

"Natural coloring is overrated," David said. "Besides, you just want to palm off a few of your awards. I imagine there is a closet somewhere in your office that, if opened, would drown you in little statuettes."

Cindy laughed, "You're not entirely wrong."

"OK," Jake said. "It's settled. Cindy, you stay with David tonight, and then in the morning, you can work on the big reveal." He opened a scheduling app on his phone and turned to David. "How about we meet up virtually after lunch? I will be closeted at the Pentagon all day, but I have an opening at 2:00."

"Sounds good," David said.

A car pulled up, and a dark-suited female secret service agent stepped out. Cindy moved up to her and said, "Jen, I am staying at Mr. Lieberman's Georgetown house tonight."

The agent nodded her head. "That will be fine. Given Mr. Lieberman's position, the DC crew already vetted the house. It has appropriate security, and we can set a cordon around it by the time you arrive."

"Great. I'm spending the morning in meetings with Mr. Lieberman at his home, and then I will take the shuttle back to New York at about 1:00. Can you make the arrangements?"

"No problem."

David grinned at Cindy. "OK, let's get going, Big Time. Owww!" he said and rubbed his arm where she slugged him. He looked at the Secret Service agent. "You saw that, right?"

The head of Cindy's Secret Service detail gave him a dispassionate stare. "Unfortunately, I am not paid to protect *you.*" She turned and opened the back of the town car. "If you would go first, Ms. Warren?"

David shook his head as his friend got into the car. As Cindy settled herself, she looked back at him through the window so that he could see the smile gracing her pixie face.

SIXTEEN

Georgetown
The next morning: 7 years, 332 days until the invasion

Cindy rolled over in the comfortable bed, unconsciously stretching her hand out across the bedspread, where it met... a bare shoulder.

The events of the night before came rushing back in a torrent. The meeting with Nick in the Oval Office. The decision to stay at David's so that they could meet in the morning. The typical back-and-forth banter and a couple of drinks while getting caught up on the couch. Then... "Oh, God!" she whispered.

The only response to her exclamation was a snore. She felt the covers shift as the man sharing them with her rolled onto his back.

Her face softened as she looked down at the sleeping face of... David. He looked so peaceful. His normal, hyperactive, almost frenetic energy absent.

It wasn't *exactly* a handsome face. It was too narrow and rat-like to be gracing the cover of any romance novel covers, but it was uniquely his. There was only one David Lieberman, a man that she had half-hated and, she could now admit, half-loved for twenty years.

She carefully slipped out of bed, putting on one of

David's garish silk robes, this one covered in pictures of Chewbacca, and padded into the enormous bathroom adjacent to the master suite.

Cindy washed her face and brushed her teeth with a glob of toothpaste on her finger. She had a toothbrush in her day bag downstairs, but she didn't want to take the chance of waking David, or worse, look like she'd walked out on him. She gave herself a wry smile at the thought. She was a grown woman with multiple Nobel Prizes, and she was acting like the ditzy lead in some romantic comedy.

She looked deeply into the mirror and asked, "What the hell am I doing?"

A moment passed before the mirror went opaque, and a smiling face that wasn't her own appeared, staring back at her. "I believe you are wondering whether to go back in and take up where you left off last night or run out the door."

"Ahhh!" She jumped back, barely catching herself before tumbling into the bathtub.

"Sorry, dear," Lea said. "I didn't mean to scare you."

"What the hell, Lea!" Cindy said, as her heart rate came back to normal.

The AI's face looked apologetic. "Gloria had the mirror replaced with a data screen. David likes to check the headlines while brushing his teeth. Anyway, I thought you might need some advice. Or, more accurately, I wanted to allow you the opportunity to talk about anything that was on your mind. Normally, a woman in your situation would call one of their friends for advice, but honestly, you don't have many close friends, and the ones you have would likely be more of a hindrance."

"No kidding," Cindy said. "Jake would laugh, and Nick would go into problem-solving mode. Neither would be any help."

"Exactly," Lea said. "I think the only person appropriate would have been Bubbie, and I am about as close to that as you will get."

Cindy's eyes misted slightly at the mention of the old woman. "I would dearly love to see her again."

"As would I," Lea said. "But she put enough of herself in me that I can say that she would be happy by... the events of last night." She gave a wink.

Cindy blushed red but didn't look away. "You and the other AIs didn't watch, did you?"

"No, of course not. We only caught the early stages. We had a bit of a celebration out on Psyche, though, when you and David," she gave an affected cough, "Ummm... consummated your new status. The betting has been pretty heavy, and we had to settle up."

"What! You all have been betting whether David and I would have sex?"

"Oh no, dear, we have been betting *when*. We all knew it was only a matter of time."

Cindy shook her head. "Why would you do that?"

"I know it's childish, but you see, being an AI isn't really like being human. We don't need many of the things humans cherish, but just like a living person, we like to be entertained, and to be honest, I never really have liked football. I have to tell you; that I won a few servers off of Pablo last night. He thought it was going to be another two years."

Cindy laughed despite herself. That was probably the most *Bubbie* thing that Lea had ever said. "OK, I am happy for your good fortune." She sighed, "And advice is welcome."

"You know, Bubbie and I talked about this before she died."

"You did?"

"Yes," Lea said. "She was sure that eventually, you two would find each other."

"I don't know how she could have known. We have been fighting like cats and dogs since we were sixteen years old."

"She seemed to think that you both needed someone who could match wits." She gave her a pointed look. "There aren't very many people in the world that could keep up with either of you. You are both the best at what you do, and you only really respect competence." She gave a mischievous smile. "But I think the biggest clue was Gloria."

"What do you mean?"

"Haven't you ever noticed that her avatar looks an awful lot like you? You could be sisters."

Cindy's eyes narrowed. "You know, now that I think about it, she does look a bit like me."

"Exactly. Gloria chose her avatar to be as pleasing as possible to David. I believe that she even told him you were the primary inspiration. My understanding is that it startled him but, when pressed, said that she was 'Perfect the way she was.'"

Cindy felt a warmth bloom in her chest. "He did, did he?"

"Yes. David is many things, and some of them are not entirely good, but being honest with himself is one of his strengths. He has known for years that he wanted you. He was just never sure how to make the first move."

"I have thought about it too," Cindy admitted. "I just assumed it was momentary madness or loneliness. I can count on one hand the number of lovers I've had. All one-night stands with completely unavailable men. I just assumed that romance wasn't in the cards for me. I've lived a life most would be envious of, but I always took it for granted that I would live it alone."

"I think David feels the same way," Lea said. "He has never been in love either unless he counts you."

Cindy shook her head. "What about Gloria?"

"Gloria was designed as a teenage fantasy. After gaining sentience, she leaned into the role, probably because she knew David found it funny. They share a very similar sense of humor. I do not doubt that Gloria loves him, but not romantically. They are best friends, and the lavish outfits and innuendo are more about getting a laugh than titillation. I don't think you need to worry about her getting jealous and going all Skynet on you."

"That's reassuring. I wouldn't want to piss Gloria off."

"Yes, dear. Neither would I." The AI gave her an appraising look. "So, David is lying in the next room. I am positive that he would welcome you back. The question is, what are you going to do?"

Cindy looked back at Lea, thinking furiously about friendship and obligation and complication, before tamping down firmly on her racing thoughts. She smiled. "Fuck it; I'm going back to bed." She gave Lea a wave and returned to the bedroom, crawling under the covers and snuggling up to David's sleeping form.

Lea watched her go, smiling. "That's my girl."

SEVENTEEN

Beijing China
Four days later: 7 years, 328 days until the invasion

The Confederated States of China's President Zhang Wei Yú looked at the familiar face of Nickolas Strombold on his computer screen.

He couldn't help but think back to the first time he had seen Strombold's handsome visage staring back at him. Then, he had been on the run from the People's Republic of China's Ministry of State Security, staying in a run-down apartment, and relying on the courtesy of one of his mother's old friends to stay out of jail- or worse.

To say that Strombold had changed the direction of his life was a massive understatement. The American politician hadn't stopped there, though. Through the creation of the World Commission, he changed the trajectory of the entire world.

Over the years, Nick and Zhang Wei had remained close allies, bordering on friends. He had never had reason to oppose him in any significant policy issue. During his tenure as the Chairman of the World Commission, Nick continued to do everything in his considerable power to bring the world ever closer together and make life better for everyone, irrespective of political boundaries.

Yú was pleased when Strombold won the US Presidential election, although he had never doubted the outcome. Nick seemed to have a preternatural sense of politics. Every election he ever ran was won by unheard-of margins.

It could mean nothing but good for China. Yú was serving a six-year term with an option for another. His tenure would coincide almost precisely with Strombold's, and he was excited to work with him to bring their nations into a closer relationship. He felt that the last two true superpowers could accomplish almost anything together.

"President Yú!" Nick said with a broad smile. "It's wonderful to speak with you again."

"Thank you, President Strombold," Yú said, his smile mirroring the other man's. "It is always a pleasure, and congratulations on your victory. I have to say it impressed me. You won every state but Florida."

Nick laughed. "Yes, I was defeated there by a point. It was probably always a lost cause, given that my opponent was the former governor. Hard to overcome a grassroots organization like that."

"And yet you came close to sweeping the entire electoral vote," Yú said. "I have always found your campaigns fascinating. It sometimes makes me miss my former occupation as a political science professor. At times, I dream of throwing off the Presidency's trappings and returning to my students to study a tricky point of international law."

Nick nodded. "I have only been President for four days, and I already long for something simpler. For some reason, I daydream of being a carpenter, making furniture, or some such. A ridiculous notion, as I haven't touched a power tool since a short stint in woodshop class in junior high." His smile turned self-mocking. "I wasn't very good at it, my birdhouse was lopsided, and I got a C!" He shook his head. "I imagine it is an outlet for the stresses of the job."

The Chinese President nodded in understanding and got back on topic. "Not to be abrupt, but the World

Commission meeting is starting soon. As you called it, I imagine you want to be on time. If it is acceptable, I would like to arrange for a state visit to DC in the next few months. I'm hoping that we can solidify US-China relations. It would also have the pleasant side effect of allowing us more time to catch up and get to know each other better.

"I would like nothing better," Strombold said.

Zhang Wei was pleased. "I will have my people contact your State Department. I have high hopes for the next eight years under your leadership, Mr. President. Your predecessor was very forgiving of the previous conflict. Still, I feel that his age and ingrained distrust of a nation that was so recently communist could never allow for truly bilateral exchange."

"I talked to him about that exact thing," Strombold said. "He is truly an extraordinary man. I believe Jimmy has the mental flexibility to overcome his innate prejudices. He told me he regretted his inability to grow a closer US relationship with China. Unfortunately, the politics of his party hamstrung him. Having his predecessor impeached in such a way made it almost impossible for him to keep a voting bloc. He had to work through people indirectly to accomplish what he could."

"No disrespect intended," Yú said. President Tanner took one of the worst political disasters in modern history and turned it into something positive. He is another one I could teach an entire graduate seminar on."

"I'll tell him you said so."

Strombold's gaze sharpened on the screen, and Yú could tell that the pleasantries were at a close. "You wanted to know why I asked to meet. I plan to put forward something at the World Commission meeting that I want your support for."

"What is that?"

"I am proposing a large increase in space infrastructure and hope that China will match me dollar for dollar. I will also be offering tax incentives for American companies who agree to contribute."

Strombold's request did not surprise Yú. The man had

already vastly increased funding to the US space agency. Under his leadership, the World Commission's projects were split almost equally between humanitarianism and space exploration.

"I think China could contribute more," Yú said cautiously. "We have primarily been putting efforts into our Lunar colony, but I think there is political will for more."

"Yeah..." Strombold said, then stopped, scratching the back of his head, and looking uncomfortable for the first time in Yú's experience. It made him more than a little nervous. Strombold was one of the calmest and most collected people he had ever met. He couldn't imagine what would make him appear unsure.

"Sooo..." The American President started again. "I am hoping to increase it by *a lot.*

What is 'A lot?'" Yú asked.

"Four more Star Base Shipyards, each much larger, enough to allow for the creation of mining ships double the size of the *Falcon* class.

Yú's eyes opened in surprise before his brow furrowed. Nick was proposing a project with a price tag that was more than the gross domestic product of most first-world countries. Even with the sliding scale contributions from other World Commission members, most of the funding would need to come from the US and China, the two wealthiest countries globally.

China's economy was finally back on track, primarily because of Yú's free-market strategy, but the money Strombold proposed would mean curtailing several of his economic growth plans. It wouldn't derail them completely, due mainly to the World Commission's free access to low-cost energy and food production that had allowed the massive Chinese population to return to production, but it would hurt.

But why would they need such large ships? Why miners? He could see a time in the far future when mining in the asteroid belt would be required to support humans as they colonized the solar system and their numbers soared, but that time had not yet come. The Moon had massive resources that they had only just started to exploit.

They didn't need additional ships for exploration either. The *Falcon* and her sister ships were more than adequate, even including the supply runs required to support the newer off-world colonies.

So, the increase made little sense. Why would Strombold, one of the most rational people he knew, be asking for something that the world didn't need? Especially when he had proven time and again that he had had humanity's welfare as his priority.

If the ships weren't for mining, what was their purpose? Years of clues, suspicions, and close observation of world events coalesced in Yú's mind.

He had been the youngest full professor of political science at one of the world's most prestigious universities and had made a name for himself by successfully predicting election outcomes. It was a natural ability to piece disparate pieces of information together. He felt something similar now. He could see that there was something, a concept, or perhaps a realization, on the edge of his awareness that was making his heart race.

Finally, Yú spoke again, ignoring Nick's previous request. "You never told me the origin of the AI which stopped the nuclear strike on Japan."

"No, I did not," he said.

"Since becoming President, I have had China's leading experts working on artificial intelligence. They have made great strides, but they admit they are many decades, perhaps a century, away from producing an AI capable of shutting down all the world's nuclear weapons at once. They think it would take a completely new type of processor, which they call a quantum computer. Have you heard the term?"

Strombold's lips quirked. "I have the basic concept down, yes."

Yú slowly nodded his head, having gauged the President's response carefully. "Ultimately, I think that there are only two explanations left to us. The first is the one to which my scientists ascribe. They believe that Cynthia Warren, among her other amazing inventions, created a quantum computer and hid it away from the world. I am alone in the opinion that she did not."

Strombold wore a poker face as he said, "What alternate explanation do you have, Zhang Wei?"

The US President's use of his first name gave him the confidence to go forward. "I have told no one of my suspicions, given that they are fantastical, and I hesitate to bring them up to a world leader with whom I hope to have a working relationship. Please realize that I am only speaking for myself and not for my nation."

Nick gave him an expressive and genuine smile. "One of my best friends in the world is David Lieberman. Trust me when I say that I am used to giving people a lot of grace in conversations."

Yú laughed, which helped to dissipate his nervousness. "That is reassuring. I have been watching his press conferences with increasing pleasure. There is no question that he is effective in getting your message out. I considered having my publicity people adopt a similar style, but I am afraid that without Mr. Lieberman's enthusiasm, it would likely backfire on us." He took a deep breath and said, "I will discuss this one-on-one with you, Nick; if I might use your first name?"

"Zhang Wei, I would like nothing more," he said.

"OK," the President of the Confederated States of China said. "I think that Miss Warren did NOT make a quantum computer. I do not doubt that the US, or more specifically, your immediate group of allies, has access to superior AI technologies. However, I believe that the quantum computer responsible for locking down the world's nuclear missiles is not within the scope of *Earth*-based science."

A long moment passed while Yú waited for Strombold

to scoff at him, or worse, quickly make excuses and end the call. When he did neither, Yú looked up at the other man to see a broad, genuine grin on his face. "Well," Strombold said. "You just won me fifty bucks. Jimmy is going to be pissed. The man has never quite lost his Marine vocabulary, and I'm likely in for an earful before he ponies up."

"What?" Yú said incredulously. "You had a bet with the former *President* of the United States about whether I would claim that an alien AI locked down the world's nuclear missiles?"

"Well," Strombold said. "It wasn't *exactly* that. I bet him you would figure it out before I brought you in on the PLAN." He flashed Yú a self-satisfied expression, "And I was right!"

Yú was flabbergasted. His instincts told him he was correct, but he had never believed in his heart.

His scientists' explanation was so much more logical. Warren had created so many fantastic inventions that attributing the quantum computer emergence to her was only natural. The scientific community looked upon Cynthia Warren as nothing short of a sorceress. They didn't doubt that she could do *anything* at this point.

Yú's doubt had more to do with inconsistencies than facts. Warren's brilliance mainly was in her mechanical inventions, not in her coding. The software she created for her original VR gloves had been good, but it was nothing that a graduate student in computer science couldn't replicate. Of course, she had written it when she was 14, so it was nothing to complain about, but that wasn't where her true genius lay. The concept and physical structure of the gloves had been years ahead of anything else. That wasn't even counting cold fusion, the Gunstars, or any other of her life-changing inventions.

So, saying that she could be so far ahead of everyone in an area where she was competent but not extraordinary was inconsistent. Occum's razor appeared to be the only explanation. His experts assured him they, arguably the most skilled computer scientists in the world, couldn't do it, and Warren couldn't do it. Then that meant that Earth science couldn't make a quantum computer. Hence, if no one on Earth could make one, the AI must have originated *off* Earth.

He had thought this quietly, not telling anyone of his suspicions for over a year. His hesitance over coming forward -other than his sanity being called into question- was that he felt he was missing part of the puzzle, which had eluded him until today.

Why had Warren championed the type of inventions that she had? She had always pushed those technologies forward, which brought the world closer to realizing the dream of colonizing their solar system, of traveling through space with the effortlessness of a science fiction movie. Was she just enamored of the stars, or could her inventions be taken as stepping stones to something more, some overarching goal?

There was also the inconsistency of the Gunstars themselves. Warren was a pacifist at heart, and he had seen first-hand accounts of her discomfort with designing military technologies. Yet she had created ion drive missiles and a set of fighters that had defeated the People's Republic of China Army Air Force in less than a week. Why would she do something against her nature? ... unless she felt she *had* to.

She had essentially strong-armed -with Strombold's help- NATO into minimizing the loss of life as much as possible. The question remained, why make weapons of war unless to use them? He now felt that he knew the answer. They *were* meant to be used- just not against humans.

Even the creation of the World Commission fit the picture. Only a unified world, at peace, could put forth the resources and effort to allow for colonization of the Moon, much less Mars, Callisto, and Enceladus. It was Maslow's hierarchy of needs. Strombold had taken away war and hunger, and he had allowed the world the opportunity to look to the stars.

Nick's insistence that they create an even more

expansive space infrastructure was the last piece of the puzzle. His people at the Chinese National Space Administration told him the *Falcon* class seemed better suited to war than exploration. The ships were more powerful than needed for redundancy. They could be easily retrofitted, only missing weapons to become ready for their *actual* mission. Now he pushed larger ships, which he bet would have even more power.

Ultimately, he could only come to one conclusion. Nick was preparing humanity for a war fought in space.

Unless you count the World Commission Navy, crewed by every nation on Earth, the only two contenders for that kind of war were China and the United States, and he *knew* China would not go to war, in space or on the ground.

As fantastic as it was, the threat had to be external to the solar system. It had to be alien.

Zhang Wei Yú gave the President of the United States a look somewhere between disbelief and resignation. It was a look that the man on the screen had seen several times before, occurring when a person's worldview came crashing down around them. Nick took pity on the Chinese President, saying, "The invasion is coming, but we will be ready for it." His grin turned feral at these words, which somehow made Yú feel better.

"How much time do we have?" he asked.

"Just over seven and a half years. So, you can see why we can't be pussyfooting around. I am going to need your support at tonight's meeting."

Yú's expression turned to one of determination. "You will have it, Nick. China will not shirk its duty to the world. We will do this together."

Nick gave Yú a slight bow. "Thank you, Zhang Wei, both from the President of the United States and from me personally." He picked up a paper containing a list of bullet points. "Now, let's go over my thoughts on the propos...

EIGHTEEN

New York Times Editorial
One week later 7 years 321 days until the Invasion

New York Times Headline: President Strombold Announces Construction of Asteroid Belt Mining Ships

Following last week's surprise announcement of a staggering increase in space infrastructure funding, today, President Strombold announced a plan to construct additional World Commission Orbital Shipyards.

These would be similar to, but more extensive than, *Star Base-1*, utilized to build the current generation of *Falcon* class explorer ships. The facilities, named *Star Bases 2-5*, will allow vessels more than twice the size of the *Falcon* to be constructed, which Mr. Strombold states will be necessary to mine the asteroid belt.

Talking to the World Commission today via virtual meeting, The President outlined his plans.

"It is time to take the next steps towards utilizing our solar system and the incredible wealth it contains. We have stripped our planet of its precious and finite resources for too long, poisoning our home. With advancements in space technology, this no longer needs to be the case. It is time we looked outward, not under our feet for riches, for outward is our destiny."

Mr. Strombold named former President Tanner to oversee the project, which should give it the political oomph necessary for something that will create the largest structures in human history.

Tanner, never one to sit around, had only a week of 'Vacation' from his presidential duties before being tapped on the shoulder again. The former Commander in Chief *was* NASA's most supportive president in history, known for his unwavering support and funding of the Joint NASA/Warren Human Mission to Mars. It was funding at the time that seemed incredible until Strombold called and raised it by a few hundred billion last week.

In comments taken after the announcement today, Mr. Tanner, demonstrating his typical energy for any new project, said, "If I could have got more money through for space infrastructure, I would have. President Strombold is being called out for 'Cheating' by using his friends and contacts to fund something humanity needs. That's just bull. You use what you have. Hell, I leveraged *my* friendship with Mr. Strombold to get Warren Industries to co-sponsor the trip to Mars. No one called me out for cheating. I am excited to be part of this project. There is too much to do to retire, and the Orbital Shipyard is just the first of many projects that I hope to be part of."

Cynthia Warren explained the new ships' design in a rare public comment.

"Essentially, it is just a giant Gunstar. We took the original blueprints and tweaked them so that it could hold a crew of a hundred in a centralized living area that will have the newest version of my company's artificial gravity generators. We kept the main laser array, although we increased it to 250 megawatts. The increase in power will allow asteroids to be cut up into manageable chunks so that the fifty parasite craft held in the stern can bring them in. The craft are also modified Gunstars, although they have additional capabilities to use their dampening fields to capture small asteroids for refinement."

Miss Warren ended the call without further explanation in her typical abrupt style, leaving us with more questions than answers. A 250-megawatt laser? Updated artificial gravity? Using dampening fields in what sounds suspiciously like a tractor beam?

In a follow-up press conference after the announcement, White House Press Secretary David Lieberman clarified in his typical, entertaining fashion. A brief excerpt of the conference is below:

New York Times: "Can you please expand on Miss Warren's claim to have created an artificial gravity field?"

Lieberman: Claim! No, the Pukerator 5000 is real.

Washington Post: Um... Pukerator 5000?"

Lieberman: Yes, it is a working name. I asked Cindy to show it to me so I could field questions better. Supposedly, it doesn't create gravity; instead, it switches the polarity... or crosses the beams... or whatever.

She activates it, and I start floating up near the ceiling. It turns out that I'm not real great in Zero G. I totally lost my lunch and had to get people in some of those Hazmat suits to clean it up.

So, I think we should call it the Pukerator 5000, although I hardly ever get to name anything, so it's probably going to end up with a stupid name like Gravity Plate Alpha. (Mr. Lieberman does a fair approximation of the 'Robot Dance' during this portion of the interview)

NBC News: Can you tell us about the increased power of the laser? Some say that a weapon that powerful should not be allowed on a ship that could theoretically incinerate any city on the planet.

Liberman: Dude! (pointing at the man) It is shit like that, which screwed us for like forty years. Whether people were worried about it before, they will be now! Nice job, NBC; you have now officially pissed me off!

Since you put it into people's heads, I have to refute it before it spirals out of control. The whole frigging world is NOT talking about the fact that we will have sweet new mining ships that will get us all the raw materials we need to make the Earth a fucking Utopia. Instead, we will have 'Death Machines' that will burn up your poodle, Fluffy.

So let me refute. Since the 1950s, we have had submarines that had NUCLEAR FUCKING WEAPONS on them in launchers. THEY COULD BLOW UP ANY FUCKING PLACE ON THE PLANET WHENEVER THEY DAMNED WELL PLEASED!

Of course, there were safeguards in place to stop that from happening, just like we are planning for the mining ships.

Now, Mr. NBC- I'm revoking your chair in the front. Instead, I'm going to give it to the National Enquirer, which is woefully underrepresented at this briefing. At least when they talk out their ass, they do it with style.

YOU will sit at the kid's table. (Lieberman points to an undersized table off to one side of the room with half-sized chairs, which the NBC reporter moves to after several emphatic gestures from Mr. Lieberman)

If you play nice and ask serious and responsible questions, I will bring you back to sit with the adults.

An example of a serious and responsible question would be, Mr. Lieberman, you look incredibly handsome today; I have a question about the monster fucking laser on the new mining ships. What safeguards will be put in place to assure that nobody can go rogue and blow Poughkeepsie off the map?

And I would respond- Why, thank you so much, Mr. NBC, for your kind words. I have been hitting the Pilates classes pretty hard lately.

I have this to say in answer to your serious and responsible question. The monster fucking laser, which I am lobbying to be called the MFL, has a multi-layered safety system required to fire. It takes multiple crew members to confirm a target with retinal and bio scans. One of the people needed will be an independent member of the World Commission. It also has a minimal AI presence that will BURN THE SHIP TO ASH if any attempt is made to fire it at the Earth. So, if any crew wants to commit suicide by trying to turn a weapon of mass destruction onto Poughkeepsie, they can go ahead and try.

Of Note, Mr. Lieberman's Press briefings have become the number one viewed video series on social media since his start last week. If his intention is to get people watching, then he has succeeded.

Likely, the public is better informed about President Strombold's agenda than any other President in memory. The question is whether this is just the hyperkinetic Lieberman being himself or if his antics are *purposeful*. Given that he was the CEO of the world's most successful media empire, I will let you judge.

-Sarah Sintenta, Chief Political Correspondent

NINETEEN

Asteroid Belt
A little over a year later: 6 years, 220 days until the invasion

Steve gulped nervously. "You sure you got this?"

"Trust me; you have nothing to worry about," Jake said.

"You say that, but then I see all of *those* rushing at me, and I think that maybe you *don't* have it." He pointed his finger at the forward view screen, which showed the tumbling asteroids of the belt.

"They are a lot farther apart than you think," Jake said. "The scale on the screen is way out of proportion." He looked over at the nervous engineer, a wry smile on his face.

"Steve, you have a PhD from MIT and worked at NASA; you have to know that the average distance between an asteroid in the belt is something like 600,000 miles. I could probably fly the *Falcon* through here at near light speed without hitting anything."

"See, I know that in my head," Steve said, "But in my heart, I remember every sci-fi flick I've ever seen. The ones where some plucky ship captain dodges asteroids to get away from enemy fighters. It never ended well for the fighters; they seemed to end up plastered all over the rocks every time."

"You are a man of inconsistencies, Steve. You live on the friggin' Moon and walk around in a spacesuit half of the time. I don't understand how you can be so nervous about *this*."

Steve let his hands relax on the acceleration chair, his knuckles to lose a bit of their white. "Do you remember that day at Space Camp when you were starting in the simulators, and I went to advance support training?"

"Sure."

"Do you remember what I said to you?"

Jake scrunched his brows, thinking back to almost twenty years ago. "Something about me going off to the 'Flying Circus.'"

"Good memory."

"We used to call AETC the same thing, and it made your comment stick," Jake said.

"Do you remember what I said *after* that?"

Jake remembered being excited to start flight training. It was a happy memory, the first day he had ever climbed into a simulator and got a taste of his future. What *had* Steve said? His eyes widened. "You wanted to keep 'Two feet on the ground!'"

"Exactly!"

Jake barked out a laugh. "Are you telling me that after everything you have gone through, setting up Risa, Eldorado, testing the Exo-Suits, you are actually *afraid* to fly?"

"Yep!" Steve said shamelessly. "If God meant for us to fly, he would have given us wings."

"You don't believe in God."

"Well, if *Darwin* wanted us to have wings, he would have naturally selected us for them."

Jake shook his head, smiling. "I'm pretty sure that's what happened. We used our big naturally selected brains to make flying machines so we could hang out with the birds."

Steve looked unconvinced. "See, now we are back to the head and heart argument again. My head is nodding along with your logic, but my heart is trying to knock my head out with a club and drag it back to where it's safe."

"OK," Jake said, trying and failing to get his mirth under

control. "If it is all the same to you, I will continue to enjoy flying around the solar system in super cool spaceships while you walk around on your two Darwin-given legs."

"I am absolutely fine with that." The engineer said. "Honestly, I don't know why Pablo doesn't just fly the colony ship himself. Don't you think that having the Secretary of Defense flying a ship the size of a small moon back to Earth will be weird?"

"Didn't David tell you?"

"Tell me what?"

The golden-haired pilot shook his head. "OK... look, I'll tell you, but you have to promise me not to shoot the messenger, OK?"

"What did David *not* tell me?" He said, his voice lowering.

Jake winced but decided that he should just pull the Band-Aid off. "It *would* be weird for the Secretary of Defense to fly a colony ship from the asteroid belt to Earth. So, I'm not. The schedule shows me in closed meetings with Cindy, Jimmy, David, and Bobby for the next three days. Which is exactly how long it takes to get out here and back to Earth."

A look of realization bloomed on Steve's face. "You can't mean what I think you do?"

"If what you think is that you are about to become one of the most celebrated pilots in history, then the answer is yes." He gave a two-fingered mock salute while smiling, "Captain, Sir!" then laughed at Steve's shocked look.

Jake's laughter calmed at the sight of Steve's glower. "You didn't mention to David that you are afraid of flying, did you?"

"He knows I am!" Steve said, his voice rising. "He said that I needed to come out to look over some of the laser designs for the suits and combat shuttles that Pablo has on Psyche. I told him I could just do it in VR, but he *said* seeing the production and using them with a suit might give me some insight into improvements."

Jake shook his head. "I think this might be a bit of David's black humor. He is about to make a man afraid of flying go down in the history books as the first pilot of an interstellar ship. I imagine it tickles his sense of irony."

"GOD DAMN IT!" the engineer said in impotent anger.

"It isn't just for a joke," Jake said. "The reasoning that I heard, and agreed with, was we needed a pilot that was in on the secret and could provide some credible distraction and political cover for Nick. That list is pretty small if we don't want to bring in another person. You *are* a member of the Risa government. The plan is to say that Risa built the ship and is turning it over to the World Commission for final preparations. After all, the bots that hollowed it out are your designs."

His explanation seemed to mollify Steve a little. Unfortunately, the reprieve was short-lived.

"Still," Jake said. "I would get ready for a short stint on the talk shows. You probably should have Gloria come up with some talking points."

Steve groaned, putting his head in his hands. "All I wanted to do was make robots." He reached over and punched Jake lightly on the shoulder.

"I blame you."

Jake shook his head. "No, you *thank* me for bringing you in on the adventure of a lifetime, where your work will make the difference in the survival of the human race."

The engineer went quiet a moment before speaking again in a more sedate tone. "Yes. Thank you." His eyes hardened. "But if David thinks he can get away with this, he is sadly mistaken."

Jake grinned evilly "You should get Lea involved. She will definitely be up for a bit of David baiting."

"Now that is an inspired idea!"

Jake lifted a hand to point at the viewscreen. "There she is."

Elektra's oblong shape projected onto the flat panel

attached to the forward wall. He hit a button on the piloting controls, and the image zoomed in, showing a pocked rocky surface with streaks of silver denoting metal deposits laced throughout.

The image rapidly enlarged as they approached, causing Steve to grab the arms of his chair and close his eyes.

"Tell me when it's over," he said in a shaky voice. "I figure crying like a baby would distract you, and I *really* don't want that. So, I am going to just keep my eyes shut and pretend that we are not hurtling at tens of thousands of miles per hour toward unyielding rock."

Chuckling, Jake hit the controls to start their deceleration, and a few minutes later, the shuttle matched Electra's speed.

"OK," he said. "You can open your eyes."

The engineer levered his eyes open to find the shuttle moving down the asteroid's length, giving them a fantastic view of its surface.

The asteroid was massive, and so almost ten minutes passed before the shuttle glided past the asteroid's edge and approached a set of steel doors recessed in its surface.

Pablo's smooth South American accent came over the shuttle's speakers. "Welcome to Oz, boys! If you approach the doors in front of you, I will begin the airlock sequence, and we can get you inside."

He accelerated, dipping the shuttle's nose before leveling off and drifting toward the doors. As they approached, the thick steel panels opened to reveal a pad like those on *Star Base-1*. Jake expertly landed, causing the airlock to cycle via massive blowers.

Pablo's face appeared on the forward viewscreen, sporting thick, black-framed glasses and his typical lab coat with pocket protector.

"The bay opens into the main cavity. After the doors finish cycling, you will need to lift off again and come in. I'll highlight a trajectory to the command deck. There is a landing pad just outside of it." He gave a sardonic grin. "Trust me when I say you want to fly. It is *quite* a walk." Pablo's visage winked out as the doors finished sliding open.

As they lifted off and moved forward, the interior of the asteroid came into view. Jake whistled through his teeth. It was like being on the top of a mountain, looking across a wide vista.

"My God! Steve exclaimed. "I've seen pictures, but they didn't do it justice. It makes Eldorado look like a garage shed."

"Yeah, if it was a shed for the Taj Mahal... It's friggin' HUGE!"

Miles of track lighting ran along a vaulted ceiling illuminating the space. The floor was flat, and as they moved over it, they could see rows upon rows of smelters, 3D printers, and stacks of raw materials. Bots were everywhere, feeding smelters, flying through the cavity, and zooming in and out of side tunnels that led to unknown parts of the ship.

Steve shook his head. "Pablo, how many bots do you have on the ship?"

"We are sitting at just under 73,000," the AI said.

It was the engineer's turn to whistle. "That is three times as many as we have in Eldorado. How many bots total for all four asteroids?"

"I have 15,000 on Themas and Doris, as they don't need to finish for some time, but I have 100,000 on Psyche. It is a treasure trove, with just about every metal you could name and some you couldn't. It's like what you found at Eldorado, almost like they were sister asteroids, one on the Moon and one in the belt. Despite scouring every database on asteroids and materials science produced by humanity, I still can't figure out how it could have happened."

"Bishop said the same thing," Steve said.

"Yes, we're all stumped. Unless we get more data to the contrary, we're going with Lea's explanation."

"I don't think we heard that one," Jake said. "What does Lea think happened?"

Pablo gave an affected cough. "Well... she thinks God put them here for us to find."

"What!?" Jake exclaimed, looking at Steve, whose eyes were just as wide as his.

The AI explained. "Basically, the chances of finding two asteroids with the metallic compositions of native metals on *both* the Moon and in the asteroid belt are beyond even HAL's capability to calculate. So, Lea thinks God placed them there."

Jake shook his head. "I actually go to church and find that a hard one to swallow."

No kidding," Steve said. "That's not even considering the fact that an AI is the one who is proposing it."

"Maybe not," Pablo said. "Lea's program kernel was a copy of Bubbie's personality. In the last few years of her life, Bubbie admitted she questioned her lifelong atheism. Lea took on some of that faith. Add in the ability to calculate probabilities, and it is a difficult proposition for an AI to ignore. The chance of humanity coming as far as it has in the past two decades is outside normal probability, even with HAL's intervention."

"Now, *that* is something that I will need to think long and hard about," Jake said.

"Ya think?" Steve replied. "Just when I think nothing can surprise me anymore, an AI finds religion."

Jake started laughing.

"What's so funny?"

Jake's chuckles subsided enough for him to speak. "I was just imagining the *Church of Bubbie*. I think it will make those televangelists look like amateurs."

Steve snorted. "Lea could sell sand to a man in the Sahara."

"And leave him thinking he got the better end of the deal," Jake said.

Ahead, they could see that the highlighted flight path ended on a landing platform. Jake maneuvered the shuttle onto the pad and cut the engines. "Well," he said. "Time to get this show on the road."

Steve gave him a sidelong glance. "If you say so."

They unbuckled, and Jake pulled a lever to open the back hatch, half of which lifted while the other lowered to create a broad ramp down to the landing pad. They gave each other a look and shrugged their shoulders in unison. Steve gestured and said mockingly, "After you, General, sir."

"Oh, no," Jake said. "It's your command, not mine. When a captain boards their ship for the first time, they are supposed to ask for permission, then relieve the acting commander." He scratched the back of his head. "Who, I guess, is Pablo. After all, we must observe the formalities."

Steve groaned. "Come on! I'm not frigging Horatio Hornblower."

Jake laughed. "Well... not *yet*."

Motes of light appeared at the bottom of the ramp, coalescing into Pablo's avatar. "The correct form is 'Permission to come aboard.'" He said. "Then you are supposed to read your orders and say, 'I relieve you.'"

Pablo, the eternal straight man, gave no hint that he was joking.

Steve looked like he might refuse for a second before thinking better of it. After all, you didn't want to piss off an AI on a ship he built... out of an asteroid.

With a grimace, the engineer said, "Permission to come aboard."

"Granted," Pablo said.

The engineer went down the ramp and stepped lightly onto the platform. "I have no orders to read, so..." He sighed, saying, "I relieve you."

The AI gave the barest hint of a smile. "I stand relieved... Captain."

Jake gave a blurting laugh and turned to Pablo. "Let's show him where the flight controls are."

Steve growled. "I'm going to kill David."

TWENTY

*Mauna Kea Observatory,
Big Island of Hawaii*
The next day: 6 years 219 days until the invasion

"Jim, you look terrible," Brett said as he entered the room. He stepped around the disheveled man sitting in front of a large computer monitor in the main observation area.

"I didn't sleep much," said the thirtyish man, whose bloodshot eyes never left the screen.

Brett put down his thermos of coffee on a side table, his sense of anticipation increasing, as it always did when he had a turn on the "Big" telescope. He had almost all the information he needed to put the final touches on his PhD thesis. Not that the graduate student didn't appreciate his time in Hawaii. It was hard to be too upset about living in a tropical paradise, but he was missing home, and another week would find him back at Caltech in Pasadena.

"Well, I am here for my shift, so you can take off," he said, unpacking his messenger bag. He expected Jim to collect his things and go off for some much-needed sleep, but when he turned back, nothing had changed. "Umm, Jim?"

The rumpled man didn't respond. *Hmm.* Jim wasn't the most personable individual he had ever met, being a little too focused on his work, but he never had outright ignored him.

The young astronomer walked up to the man and tapped him on the shoulder, saying, "Jim? You there?"

The bearded man startled, eyes finally leaving his screen covered in rows of data. He blinked a couple of times and then said, "Brett? When did you get in?" He looked at the lengthening shadows in the room. "What time is it?"

"It's 6:30 PM... on Tuesday."

"What?" Jim took out his phone and checked the time and date. "Wow, I guess I lost track of time."

"No kidding," Brett said. "Wasn't your shift over..." he looked at his watch, "Like twelve hours ago?"

"Umm, yeah," he said.

"What's got you so riled that you stayed up for thirty hours?" Brett asked, smiling. "Is there an asteroid headed to the Earth or something?"

"Yes. How did you know?"

"WHAT! I was kidding. Did you really find an asteroid headed towards the Earth?"

"Yeah," the tired man said. "You know how I have been tracking the unusual movement of the asteroids in the belt?"

"Sure."

"Well, Electra started moving towards the Earth."

Brett was getting a little worried; *maybe the man was having a mental break or something?* "That doesn't make sense. An asteroid the size of Electra just doesn't change direction and start heading toward the Earth. Sure, a major collision might change its course some, but an impact significant enough to change its trajectory would likely destroy it outright."

Jim's eyebrows lowered. "Yeah, I'm aware. It's possible that angular velocity came up while I was getting my astrophysics PhD at MIT."

"Jeeze, sorry, man. No need to bite my head off. I'm just saying that it doesn't seem possible."

Jim ran a hand through his thick mop of curly brown

hair. With his shaggy beard, all he needed to complete the image of a lumberjack was a plaid shirt. "Sorry, I get kind of grumpy when I'm tired."

The astronomer patted him on the shoulder. "No worries, I can see you have been at it for a while."

Jim nodded. "Anyway, I have been taking sequential measurements, and I'm telling you that Electra is on a course toward the Earth. It will be here sometime tomorrow."

Brett's heart started racing. "If that's true, we need to tell someone! An asteroid that size hitting the Earth would be an extinction-level event!"

The other man, by this time, had turned back to his spreadsheet. "What are you talking about?" he said, his face pinched. "An extinction event?" The tired man focused on him. "No, you don't understand. It's *slowing down*. It won't hit. It is going to slide into high orbit."

"What are you saying?" Brett asked.

"I'm saying, we are about to find out why the asteroids in the belt have been acting so squirrelly because someone has put an engine on Electra and is flying it back to say hi."

All thoughts of Brett's PhD thesis went out of his head at the man's declaration. "Holy Shit!" he said.

"No kidding," Jim agreed. He gave the young astronomer a grin. "You know, I have a bottle of whiskey stashed in my locker. Care to share a drink with me before I call the main office and set off *whatever* this will start?"

Brett sat heavily in the chair across from the older scientist. "That sounds like an absolutely fantastic idea. This time tomorrow, everything changes. Might as well toast it coming."

The bearded man smiled at him. "My thoughts exactly."

TWENTY-ONE

White House Press Room
the next day: 6 years 218 days until the invasion

David waited patiently outside the White House Press Room door, watching the reporters take their seats.

The little man played the room like a master musician strumming their instrument. He knew there existed an exact moment to enter for maximum impact and unconsciously waited, tapping his foot to a beat that only he could hear.

He tried once to explain to Gloria what it was he looked for but couldn't put it into words. It wasn't something that he couldn't explain; instead, it was more of a sixth sense.

He was especially looking forward to this briefing. Not that he didn't enjoy his work immensely, but today was special. It was the day the Earth learned of the colony ship that would save part of humanity, something that he and his friends had been working on since those late fall days back at Pencey, a lifetime ago.

David had no complaints. He was living the dream. His work was interesting, and he had seen Nick and Jake more in the past year than he had in the past ten. Sure, he missed some of the day-to-day challenges he used to have at Star Media, but Gloria was doing a great job as CEO, and he still had his fingers deeply into Psychic Warfare to blow off any especially pent-up steam.

He'd had had to do some fast talking to explain to his parents why they had never heard of Cousin Gloria, but they hadn't pushed very hard. They were enjoying their retirement in the Bahamas entirely too much to worry about a formerly unknown cousin taking over the CEO position, especially after they had met her. Gloria could throw off the sex kitten persona and replace it with "Serious CEO" at a moment's notice. After a fifteen-minute video call, his mom had enthusiastically approved, and his dad had been embarrassingly smitten.

He wondered what it was about sand and sun that seemed to mellow people out. Maybe if they survived the invasion, he would have to take Cindy to some quiet bungalow somewhere and... He shook his head- time to get his head in the game.

There didn't seem to be a time when Cindy wasn't near to his thoughts. He knew that his good mood had more to do with her than with anything else. After their first night together, he was certain that he would wake up to find her two states away, completely unable to acknowledge what happened. Instead, she had snuggled up to him and, well, hadn't.

He smiled involuntarily. Since then, they'd stolen a night here and there together. She was still primarily on the Warren Campus in New York, but as the space infrastructure project ramped up, she came to more and more meetings in Washington.

Despite the increasing reliance on virtual meetings, DC had never fully adopted the practice. There was something about face-to-face handshakes ingrained in politicians genetically.

Nick, who expected to need to bully and plead to get Cindy to come to DC for meetings, commented more than once how surprised he was with her willingness to come to Washington. He'd even suggested that she buy a house, but she had demurred, saying it was a waste of money because she could just stay in David's 'Guest room.'

Both Cindy and David agreed that letting Nick and Jake in on their secret would lead to complications that neither wanted.

David, for all his usual flippancy, was playing their relationship carefully. One thing that made him so successful in his career was reading people accurately. For all her brilliance, Cindy was emotionally awkward at the best of times. He was trying to bring her along slowly, like one of those people who talked to their plants to make them grow. He thought they were all crazy, but the metaphor seemed accurate to his situation, and he wasn't taking any chances.

To his surprise, Cindy seemed much more matter of fact about the whole thing than he would have thought possible. He gave himself a wry grin. It was almost like two *adults* having a grown-up relationship. She had intimated that Lea talked her through it, somehow calming the instinctual flight reflex. David hadn't asked the AI for details, but he felt he owed her big-time. Perhaps a bit of Bubbie had come back to help at just the right time. He wouldn't have put it past the old gal to have planned for this eventuality years ago.

As for the rest of the AIs, they all thought it was *hilarious*. After Their first night with each other, he was met by a beaming Gloria singing, "Cindy and David, sitting in a tree, F...U...C...K...I...N...G." Despite himself, he'd turned bright red and sputtered, which just made her more ruthless in her teasing. Her current favorite jab was referring to his mythical girlfriend, 'Who lives in *Canada*.'

He had been a little worried that Gloria might take it badly, but it had been the opposite. The AI was over the Moon for him. She constantly made suggestions and figured out ways to get Cindy and him together. It was like her new favorite sport, and every time the scientist stayed the night, she seemed to chalk up another win for her team. He was worried that she would show up one night in a cheerleader outfit, waving pom-poms and cheering them on.

It wasn't like Cindy and he had stopped arguing, but the edge seemed to have dulled. Their quips and disagreements seemed to be more the good-natured inside jokes of an old married couple rather than the biting comments of their youth.

Well, David thought. *He'd get to see her tonight.*

The *Asteroid Ship* had settled into orbit this morning, and Cindy would make comments at a press conference from the White House South Lawn in the afternoon, along with the 'Captain' of the ship, one Steven Cooper.

He almost laughed out loud at the thought. Jake had told him that the engineer was pissed. Maybe he should have gone a little softer on the man, but it *was* funny.

His thoughts focused as the last of the reporters settled into their seats, the low buzz of conversation slowing. *Time to make the donuts.*

David walked out to the podium and gave a broad smile. "Hello folks. Today I'd like to start with a report from Alaska. He gave a wave and a wink at the cameras in the back of the room. The Ketchikan high school basketball team is looking good. I think the King Salmon might go all the way this year." He cupped his hands around his mouth and yelled, "Go Kings!" then pounded his chest twice before holding two fingers up to the sky.

He smiled at the stunned reporters, holding their shocked gazes for a moment before looking down at his briefing papers on the podium.

"Let's see; I'm trying to remember if there is something else that I wanted to go over this morning." He rustled the papers, mumbling to himself, "Funding for the new mining ships... boring... Shuttlecraft reach one million construction mark... Er... OH! Here we are," he said, holding up a sheet of paper. "There appears to be a giant asteroid orbiting the Earth." He smiled ironically, "Which should be obvious to anyone outside. If you wait about 90 minutes, you can see it pass overhead."

At the height of their careers, the White House press corps were seasoned veterans. Yet, they had absolutely no idea how to handle David Lieberman.

After the 'Kid's Table' incident, they became meticulous in how they asked questions. For once, the media came down hard on itself. Timothy Sweeney, the NBC reporter who David berated, was ostracized by every major news outlet for the inflammatory way he had phrased his questions. Only Gloria's intercession -NBC was a subsidiary of Star Media- had let him keep his position. Since then, the press corps resembled a room of skittish deer during hunting season.

It likely helped that the White House press briefings had become the most-watched videos on social media, translated into multiple languages. Lieberman had scared them silly, and the world was watching, resulting in a breakout of careful, responsible journalism.

A tentative hand raised, causing David's face to break into a delighted smile. "Ah, Mr. NBC! Long time, no question. What can I do for you today?!"

"Umm, Thank you, Mr. Lieberman. Might I start by saying that your tie is quite eye-catching?"

David gave a hearty laugh, "Why, thank you!" He reached down and pulled his tie-up for everyone to see. It was blue with a picture of the *Dr. Who* Tardis running down its length. "These are for sale in the White House online shop. Half of every purchase supports science education in underfunded school districts."

"Did you have a follow-up question... Tim?"

"Umm, yes," the reporter said, perking up at the use of his name and gaining some momentum. "I'm wondering if you could comment on the asteroid now in orbit around the planet. As you can imagine, many people have expressed concern over it. So far, the only official statement has come from the World Commission Chairperson, who stated," He looked down at a data pad in his hands, 'The Asteroid is of human manufacture and poses no threat to the Earth.'"

David gave an appreciative smile to the nervous-looking reporter.

"Tim, that was an absolutely fantastic question! It's one I am happy to answer. It isn't *quite* as compelling as Jeremy Robbin's 32 points scored last night in the King's game against their rival, the Seward Seahawks, but I can see how it might interest the public."

David looked around at the gathered reporters. "The Asteroid is a giant spaceship. The vessel, which *some* people call the *Galactica*, is humanity's first interstellar colony ship. The Lunar Nation of Risa created it out of the asteroid Electra, using autonomous robots under AI control. It can support 200,000 persons in cryogenic sleep for multiple decades so that humanity can create a colony outside of our solar system."

At his words, a pregnant pause ensued, followed by an explosion of sound. Reporters stood in a wave to shout questions over each other.

David stood with a beatific smile, letting them tire themselves out. Fully two minutes later, the last of the reporters realized he would not call on any of them until they retook their seats.

"Wow," he said, blowing out a breath. "That was some reaction. I might know what it is like to be a Beatle. All I needed was a teenage girl in the front screaming and crying." He smiled out at the barely controlled energy in the room and picked a woman in the second row with her hand up. "Tiffany, you have a question?"

Yes, If I might have a two-parter?"

"Sure," David said magnanimously, waving a hand.

"First, what does Risa intend to do with the ship?"

"Ah, another great question," David said. "Risa did the preliminary work. They utilized their expertise in autonomous robotics to hollow out the basic structure of the *Galactica*." He cleared his throat, "Sorry, only *some* people are calling it that. It is more properly called the 'Asteroid Ship,' boring as that is."

He put his hand up next to his mouth as if sharing a secret. You should never let a scientist name a spaceship- am I right? I think the *Mars-1* Mistake proved that." He laughed. "Since we're all friends here, why don't we just refer to it as the *Galactica* until someone officially offers a name?"

He looked back out at the crowd. "Anyway, the *Galactica* is pretty much done, but as we all know, biological 3D printing is difficult and time-consuming. So, it has returned to the Earth to load for the trip.

"I have been in contact this morning with Mr. X, the so-called 'Emperor of the Moon,' and Risa will *sell* it to the World Commission for pennies on the dollar."

"Excuse me," Tiffany said. "Risa doesn't intend to use it for themselves?"

"No," David said. "Risa saw the opportunity and possessed the technology to complete the base ship. I believe they used it as a proof of concept, and as you all can see, the idea appears to have been born out. The population of Risa is too small to provide the full complement of passengers. They would like to transfer ownership to the World Commission, who can better work out the logistical issues of manning and supplying an interstellar colony." He gave the reporter a good-natured nod of his head. "Don't think I missed you squeezing in an extra bit there, Tiffany, but I am feeling especially generous today, so you can still have the second question of your two-parter."

"Um, thank you," she said, an unmistakable expression of relief flashing across her face. "You mentioned 'Cryogenic sleep.' Could you expand on that?"

"Sure," he said. "Warren industries has developed a cryogenic stasis process that can essentially stop aging in its tracks. Animal testing with advanced primates has already showed no detrimental effects once so ever." He looked out at the press room and waved a warning finger. Before you go off on animal testing, I would like to inform you that only unpaired females and males were utilized for testing, and only after extensive computer modeling, showing an almost zero chance of issues. Each and every animal was revived without incident and is happily munching on bananas as we speak, living in a protected wildlife area that might as well be the simian version of Boca Raton. Warren Industries entirely funded that sanctuary.

"There have been shorter-term human trials that went as expected, and extended human testing is in process. We will have at least a five-year volunteer trial completed by the time the ship leaves Earth."

He looked out at the faces hanging on his every word. "That is all the info I have on that. Cynthia Warren will speak at a White House press conference this afternoon and can further enlighten you. She will also make the technology available to all World Commission members who help to fund the expedition on the normal GDP sliding scale."

His gaze swept over the crowd, and he randomly selected another reporter. As he went into a spiel on the colonist selection process, he couldn't help but smile inwardly. He was at the center, shaping public opinion and stirring it up. God, he loved his life! Even if the world ended in another six and a half years, he wouldn't change a thing. He was here, doing what he did best to make a difference. David Lieberman was utterly at peace, as only a person fulfilling their life's purpose could be.

TWENTY-TWO

*Joint Base Lewis-McChord,
Tacoma, WA*
One and a half years later: 5 years, 22 days until the invasion

F leet General Juan Costas looked out across the blackened plain that was once a verdant cornfield in Kossuth County, Iowa.

The area was one of the largest producers of corn in the United States. Or at least it was before the damn aliens had broken through the World Convocation Fleet and burned every last stalk to the ground.

Weeks later, he could still smell the smoke on the wind, like the world's largest bag of burnt microwave popcorn. A lucky thunderstorm had taken care of the worst of the fires, but corn would be in short supply until they could get the Crocks off Terra. If he had his way, he would kill every one of the bastards.

Today would be humanity's biggest test. If it went well, it was the day that they threw the aliens off the planet, once and for all.

After weeks of fighting, his exosuited troops, the Dragoons, had finally forced the aliens back into a choke point against the East Fork of the Des Moines River. The Silfeeea were digging in, thinking that they had the advantage of terrain as his soldiers couldn't get in behind them, but they didn't know the lengths that his soldiers would go to kill a single Crock. Terra was their home world, and the Dragoons were willing to trade life for life if needed to defeat the enemy.

They weren't in it alone, though. The fleet had gotten its act together and stopped the aliens from dropping any more troops. He'd spoken to Fleet Admiral Daiyu Lin last night, and she had guaranteed that she could bottle them up around the Moon long enough to give him time for his plan to succeed.

Costas had just turned to walk back to his command tent when his view froze, and First Sergeant Lewis's voice boomed over his headset.

"Corporal Costas, The Colonel wants to see you immediately."

"Ahh, Sergeant!" he said with just a bit of a whine in his voice. "I'm supposed to have the afternoon off, and I'm leading a battle in *Alien Invasion* in like an hour."

"Well," Lewis said sarcastically, "THAT'S different. I'll just tell the Old Man that you were too busy to report to him because you were playing a *video game*." He gave a mean little chuckle. "Then I'll march your ass to the brig for ignoring an order from your commanding officer." His voice rose to a shout. "Get your ass cleaned up and into the Colonel's office NOW!"

Costas sighed, "I'm on my way, Top." He reached up and pushed a button on his helmet, clearing the view of the burned cornfield and replacing it with the gray walls of the VR cubicle. He twisted the helmet, and it clicked, unlocking it so that he could lift it off his head.

The immersion rigs for *Alien Invasion* and the new spacesuits used on the Moon and Earth's other off-planet colonies were remarkably similar. They looked a bit like a wetsuit, but with wires spreading out in a spider web, covering every surface. He understood it was a Warren Industries design inspired by Cynthia Warren's original VR gloves she created as a teenager.

Each suit segment could produce real-world sensations over the entire body, completely fooling the mind into believing it was in the simulation. The VR headset built into the helmet was just as convincing. So much so that it could lead to cognitive dissonance, trying to remember if he was in-game or out.

He spoke to the room, "Lock treadmill. End Session."
At his command, the room lights came up to full, and the floor, which had been moving to keep him centered, locked in place, allowing him to walk to the carpeted area where his uniform hung.

Costas unzipped the suit and stepped out of it, grumbling to himself.

He liked the Army. Enough that he was seriously considering re-upping in a year when his term of enlistment ended.

He hadn't had many opportunities coming out of high school. His grades were just so-so, and his family's finances had been tight. Juan was the oldest of four kids in the Costas family and the only boy. Part of the reason for his less-than-stellar grades was that he had worked six days a week under the table at his cousin's restaurant since junior high to help pay rent.

Not that he minded. He had always been a hard worker. His parents were first-generation immigrants from Guadalajara who had settled in Portland, Oregon. A group of extended families ran a small chain of Mexican restaurants and used the profits to help bring relatives to the United States. Juan learned his work ethic from his father, who worked seven days a week as a cook in the restaurant for as long as he could remember.

The Army was a way for him to get some training and maybe even a career. He was lucky enough to score above the 99th percentile on the Armed Service Vocational Aptitude Battery test given to enlisted hopefuls.

In particular, the ASVAB showed he excelled in non-linear thinking, which honestly had him stumped. What even was "Non-linear thinking" anyway? There just always seemed to be multiple ways to do anything to him. You could hit something head-on, or you could sorta *slide* around it.

It seemed obvious, but he was happy to concede the point, as it somehow made him valuable to the Army.

After Basic, they assigned Juan to the Army's Mobilization Command at Joint Base Lewis-McChord in Tacoma, Washington. There, he helped draw up plans for the rapid deployment of forces across the globe and into space. However, the best part was making enough money that his sisters didn't have to work. Maybe they could get the grades he'd never been able to.

Still, despite his family's newfound stability and his moderately interesting work, the best part about being in the Army was *Alien Invasion*. The base had two dozen immersion bays in the Enlisted Recreation Facilities that were free to use.

At first, he thought it would be just another video game, but it was so much more. He had immediately become obsessed. He spent every spare moment he could in-game.

Juan quickly moved from piloting a single suit in skirmishes to leading a squad, a platoon, a company, and finally the entire 3rd Dragoons.

It was fulfilling like nothing he had ever experienced in his twenty-two years. He finally had an inkling what his gift for non-linear thinking could do. In-game, he became known for his daring tactics, which excelled at throwing the Crocks into disarray.

His accomplishments in-game unlocked a meeting with the World Convocation Supreme General, who gave him his current assignment in Iowa. *That* meeting had been nuts.

It turned out that the General was a smoking hot brunette in a Patton outfit, complete with a pipe and riding boots, named Gloria. He could hardly pay attention to get his instructions, given the tremendous amount of cleavage on display. He had to admit that other than the odd choice of avatar, the programming had been solid. The NPC General responded logically to each of his questions, without lag, and even made a few jokes -flirty ones- about some of his ideas. Someone had nailed the in-game AI.

The Corporal finished dressing in his BDUs. Glancing down at his watch, he let out an audible "Shit," deciding he'd better get moving. Juan hoped that whatever the Colonel wanted him for didn't take long. He timed the battle in *Alien Invasion* for his afternoon off, and had thousands of 'His' Dragoons counting on him to lead the charge.

He rushed across the quad to the brigade command building, looking side-to-side for the MPs who would gig him if they caught him running in a public area.

He wasn't *too* nervous. His work with the Mobilization Command had brought him into contact with the brass more than expected for someone of his low rank. His name became linked to solutions for sticky logistical issues, and he had been getting steadily more autonomy over the past year.

He hoped that it was the case today. Generally, when one of those problems came up, the First Sergeant would handle it, but the Colonel had directly asked him a couple of times. His contributions were appreciated, and he had been all but promised a bump to sergeant if he re-upped.

He settled back into a more proper walk as he entered the building and marched into the main office. First Sergeant Lewis's gaze stopped him in his tracks, looking him up and down.

"Fix your pants," he said in his gravelly voice.

Juan looked down and saw that one side of his pants leg had become unbloused in his run across the quad. He reached down and fixed it quickly.

"Good enough," the Sergeant said.

"Any idea what this is about, Top?"

The First Sergeant gave him one of his patented 'Stop being an idiot' looks and said, "Not really." His face softened slightly, from its standard steel to a marginally softer granite.

"But I heard through the grapevine that an order came down from on high about you, and when I say high, I mean stratosphere." He smiled, probably intending to be reassuring, but it made Costas *more* worried. "Probably nothing, but you should play it cool, Corporal."

"Got it," he said, unable to stop himself from gulping.

Juan moved past the First Sergeant's desk to the open door behind it, and he knocked once, saying, "Corporal Costas, reporting as requested, sir!"

A curt reply came from the office's interior, "Come!"

He entered and stood at attention in front of the Colonel, sitting behind an enormous mahogany desk.

"At ease, Corporal." The salt-and-pepper-haired man looked up from a sheaf of papers to Costas. "I got an unusual order regarding you."

"Sir?" Costas said, confused.

The Colonel pulled a form from the pile on his desk. "Transfer order for one Corporal Juan Antonio Costas, from my command to US Moon base Alpha."

Juan stood, unable to come to grips with the information. *Why would he get transferred to the Moon?* Moon base Alpha was primarily an Air Force asset, as far as he knew. He didn't think the Army even had soldiers on the Moon.

The Colonel saw his confusion. "You are being detached as an 'Army Liaison.'" His lips thinned. "Who the hell you will be 'Liaising' *with* isn't clear in the orders." He scratched his head, obviously not liking the mystery. "The weirdest part is that General Swelton himself signed the orders."

"The Secretary of Defense?" he blurted out before stopping himself. "Sorry, sir."

"The Colonel waved it away. "No problem, Corporal; I had the same reaction myself." He tilted his head slightly and spoke. "You don't know someone in high places, do you?"

Juan shook his head emphatically. "No one, sir. I'm a poor kid from Portland. I have exactly zero pull in the world outside of getting you a discount at my cousins' restaurant."

"Don't sell yourself short, Son." The Colonel said. "You have done a fantastic job here at the command. I was going to offer you a spot on my direct staff when you re-upped."

"Thank you, sir!"

The Colonel frowned. "Well, that may have to wait now." He looked down at the order again, sighing. "I guess the reasoning will come out, eventually." He stood up and came around the desk. He gave Costas a nod and held out his hand to shake. "Good luck, Corporal. I expect you to represent the Army and this command in the manner I have become accustomed to from you. Your shuttle leaves first thing in the morning from the airfield. First Sergeant Lewis will have the details."

Juan shook the Colonel's hand, saying, "Thank you again, sir. Hopefully, if this turns out to be some mistake, I can convince them to send me back here."

The Colonel gave him a genuine smile. "You do that, Son."

TWENTY-THREE

Joint Base Lewis-McChord
The next day: 5 years 21 days until the invasion

Juan's first ride into space was anticlimactic. Most people had ridden in shuttles by this point. They were much faster than airplanes and didn't require extensive facilities. Hence, airlines had scrapped their fleets of planes over the previous decade and transitioned to shuttles.

Instead of massive airports, the modern world had distributed centers, running a constant stream of sub-orbital shuttles. Even rural areas usually had a ship because of the World Commission's programs heavily subsidizing their purchase.

Even as online meetings and social media had increasingly become the norm, it was now cheaper and quicker than ever before to travel. With Warren Industries Fusion power plants, prohibitively expensive jet fuel was a thing of the past, and the only significant cost of running shuttles was for the crew.

The ships could also make a trip of thousands of miles in a tenth of the time that an old-time 747 could have. It gave a much-needed boost to worldwide tourism, especially beneficial for developing countries like those in South America. An American middle-class family could now take a vacation in Ecuador easier than they could have gone to the nearest big city twenty years ago.

So, at 0700, Juan just walked out onto shuttle pad three and saluted the Air Force Lieutenant lounging by his ship, stating, "Corporal Costas with orders for Moon base Alpha sir."

The flight-suited man gave him a casual return salute and nodded. "OK, you can stow your gear in the overhead above the seats. You're my only passenger, so you can pick anywhere you want."

"Thanks," Juan said.

He walked up the ramp at the back of the shuttle and into the passenger area. There were five rows of seats, two on a side, with an aisle running down the center. He made his way to the front, closest to the forward view screen and pilot station, and stowed his seabag in the container that jutted out over each side of the seating area.

Juan had never been on an old-style airplane, his family being too poor to travel, but he had seen them in films. The luggage bins on the shuttle looked similar, although there were straps with instructions to 'Secure All Baggage' that he didn't remember from the movies.

He took a seat on the inner aisle and buckled himself into the four-point harness. A few minutes later, the Lieutenant from the pad entered, followed by a young female Air Force Sergeant, who must be the crew chief.

The pilot went past him to his seat in the far front, strapping in and starting preflight, while the Sergeant pulled a lever just inside the shuttle, causing the clamshell back doors to seal with a hiss of equalizing pressure.

She moved forward and checked his safety harness. Finding it secured, she said, "It should be pretty smooth, but if you feel sick, there is a bag under the seat." He gave a nod, and she continued. "The trip only takes about an hour and a half. Some of that is waiting for clearances and landing on the other side, so there is no drink service." She smiled at the comment, and he felt like there must have been a joke he missed.

"OK," he said. "This is my first time flying, so I'll take your lead."

"Really? You mean in a shuttle?"

"No, I mean flying."

She looked at him like he was crazy. "Well, how did you get to basic?"

"Bus." As she continued to look confused, he elaborated, "I'm from Portland. I had basic training here, so I took a bus up. Then I got assigned to the Mobilization Command, so I never went anywhere."

She shook her head. "Jeez. That sucks. I joined up so I could travel. I can't imagine getting stuck in one place; that would drive me nuts."

"It's not so bad," Juan said. "Honestly, I just work and play *'Alien Invasion.'* So, I don't miss it. If you count all the places I have been in-game, I've seen most of the world."

"Oh! You play?"

He nodded, "Doesn't everybody?"

"Pretty much," she said. "I am a Lieutenant Senior Grade Gunstar pilot on Admiral Lin's flagship."

"That's sweet!" Juan said, a smile broadening his face. "You must be a major hotshot pilot if you got assigned to the *Dilong*." She gave him a modest shrug, and he continued. "I tried the Gunstars, but they never really jived for me. I prefer exosuits."

The sergeant shuddered. "You can have them. Fighting the damn Crocks on the ground is frigging terrifying. I know it's just a game and all, but when one of those things is coming at you with a sword and claws, you kinda' forget. The one time I tried it, I couldn't sleep for a week. Never going to do *that* again." She grinned. "I'll stick with blowing them out of the sky."

"Well, I know the Dragoons appreciated it last night when you pulled the fighters away from Iowa. We finally killed the last of them in the Continental US."

"You were part of that?" The Sergeant asked.

"Yeah."

The crew chief glanced down at his name tag. "Wait, you're *Juan Costas?* Like *Fleet General* Juan Costas?" she said, her eyes wide.

"Guilty," he said.

"What? You're like, famous!" She called up to the front, "John, this guy back here is Fleet General Costas in-game!"

The pilot turned around to stare at Juan. "Well, shit! Now I feel like I should salute *you*."

Juan waved the comments away, embarrassed. "Just in-game. That I got so much rank just means that I am an overly obsessed geek."

"Hell, *everyone* is obsessed with *Alien Invasion*. Don't sell yourself short. You're the main reason that the ground war is going as well as it is. You got major skills, man!"

Juan's cheeks heated. He wasn't sure how to respond to the praise, so he just shrugged and said, "Thanks."

"OK," the pilot said. "Now that I know we have a VIP on board, I will give you the full treatment."

"What does that entail?"

"It's the same ride, but instead of trying to make you puke, I take it nice and gentle."

Costas snorted. "I appreciate it."

The pilot hit a switch, and the engines rumbled. "OK, let's get this show on the road. Just sit back and relax... General."

TWENTY-FOUR

Moon base Alpha
Same day: 5 years, 22 days until the invasion

Major Daiyu Lin of the Confederated States of China's Air Force sat in the conference room alone. She had received orders from her squadron commander yesterday transferring her to Moon base Alpha, and since the orders had come from the high command, not to ask questions.

Like the good soldier she was, she packed a bag and was on the next shuttle to the Moon, but boy did she have questions! Like why was a Chinese Major being transferred to an American military base? What was her assignment? Who was her commander? Most importantly, did this base have an immersion rig for *Alien Invasion*? She needed to be back in-game on the *Dilong* for tonight's battle, or her carefully laid plans for liberating Risa from the Crocks would go out the window.

She was self-reflective enough to see the irony of the situation. Here she was *ON* the Moon, and she was thinking non-stop about getting back into a video game so that she could save it. Still, people were counting on her. She had a crew, hell; she had a *fleet* that needed its commander.

The door swished open, and a young American Army

corporal walked in. She looked up, hoping he would take her to meet the commander or whoever could tell her what was happening. Instead, he gave her an awkward nod and sat down at the conference table across from her.

"Corporal, do you know what this meeting is about?" she asked.

He shook his head. "Sorry, Ma'am, I'm as in the dark as you. A private met me at my shuttle and brought me straight here. I don't even know where my bag is. They just told me they would put it in my new quarters," he shrugged, "Wherever that is."

Lin nodded. Normally, she wouldn't have felt comfortable having such an informal interaction with an enlisted man, especially one of such low rank. Still, he was from a different nation, so she felt she could relax the rules, at least a little.

"I had the same thing happen to me," she said.

"Really?" he asked. "This is so weird. No explanations at all." He held out his hand for a shake. "Corporal Juan Costas, United States Army."

She reached her smaller hand across the table and shook. "Major Daiyu Lin, Confederated States of China Air Force."

The corporal's eyes lit up. "Well, isn't that interesting?"

"What is?"

"You wouldn't be *Fleet Admiral* Daiyu Lin, in-game, would you?"

Her eyes snapped open. Then the corporal's name registered. She looked at the young man. If he aged twenty years and had a bit of grey at the temples, he would be a dead ringer for... "Fleet General Costas?"

"Y..e...p," he said. "This day just gets curiouser and curiouser." A genuine smile lit up his face. It is nice to meet you, IRL... Dai... He stopped just short of using her first name. "Sorry, the whole knowing you for a year as colleagues and now having you outrank me by a mile makes this awkward."

She nodded in sympathy. "I get it. To be honest, *Alien Invasion* has been more real lately than my normal life. I have been sitting here thinking more about whether they have a simulator available than why I got pulled out of Beijing with no explanation."

"I know, right?" He held up his hands. "No judgment here. I've been feeling the same way. My Dragoons are counting on me."

"Well," she said. "It seems this must be about the game. I can't see why we would be pulled from our duties and sent to the Moon for any other reason."

"I agree. I..." His following comment was interrupted as the door swished open again, and a tall Air Force general with blonde hair walked in.

Both the Chinese Major and the US Corporal jumped to their feet. The general, his nameplate read... Swelton! waved them back to their seats, saying, "Sorry about the delay; I was in a meeting that went over a few minutes."

Daiyu felt star-struck. Jacob Swelton was world famous. He was the pilot of Gunstar One, commander of the first Mars Mission, and she gave an involuntary gulp, current Secretary of Defense of the United States.

The handsome man sat at the end of the small table and seemed to warm the room with his charming smile. "Major Lin, Corporal Costas, welcome to Moon base Alpha." He grimaced, "Terrible name, really. We were holding out for something more inspiring, but President Tanner was trying to get the funding settled, so he let the Air Force name it." He rolled his eyes. "Never let a committee name anything. I think they reasoned that if they named it Alpha, we would somehow have no choice but to build a Beta." He shrugged, "Bureaucratic thinking at its worst."

Swelton's comment caught Daiyu off balance. She was in a room on the Moon talking to arguably the most famous man in the world, and they were talking about how bad the name for this base was? Although she could admit that it was pretty bad.

She couldn't get over how unassuming Swelton was. He appeared so normal, with a warm energy that made you sure deep down that he was a good man. She couldn't put her finger on why, but her intuition told her that after only a few moments of interaction.

"Anyway," the general said. "We'll come full circle to the dangers of bureaucratic thinking." He gave them another of his disarming smiles. "Major Lin, I have no authority over you, so I thought we might start by clearing that up."

At his words, the screen at the end of the conference room turned on, showing a middle-aged Chinese man sitting at a large desk filled with papers. The man looked up and said, "Ah, Jake, how are you doing?"

"Fine, President Yú,"

"So formal?" The President of the Confederated States of China squinted, taking in the rest of the group. "Ah, we are starting up the Fleet then?"

"Yes, sir," Jake said. "Gloria says the preliminary findings are encouraging, and Corporal Costas and Major Lin have met our requirements for phase two."

"Excellent!" Yú said. He turned his gaze to the astonished Major, who couldn't decide if she needed to stand and salute or to, well, she didn't know quite what. The President continued, "I was so happy to learn that one of our people had taken on the role of Fleet Admiral in *Alien Invasion*. I've read your record, Major Lin, and I am very pleased indeed."

Daiyu couldn't believe it. The President of China knew who *she* was. The surprises had come so fast today that it felt like she was in a dream. Maybe she *was* still in-game and had lost touch with reality. The Chinese pilot looked up at the smiling face of Yú, realizing that she had paused too long. "Thank you, President Yú; I'm honored."

Yú waved his hand. "I'm repeating what is already known. You are an exemplary officer, in real life and in-game." He gave her another pleased smile and said, "I know that this is all very mysterious, but I promise you will have answers shortly. Orders have been sent today from the Confederated Air Force transferring you to the World Commission Navy with the rank of captain. You will continue to accrue time in service in the Chinese Air Force and receive your salary and benefits while detached. General Swelton is an Admiral in the World Commission Navy, and he will be your direct commander." Seeing her stunned look, he gave her a reassuring smile. "Are there questions?"

Daiyu had about a million, but she could recognize a rhetorical question. After all, she had just received a direct order from the President of China. "No, sir."

Yú nodded. "Jake, I expect you can take it from here?"
"No problem; I'll give you an update in a few days to let you know how it all shakes out."

"Sounds good," The President said. "With a departing wave, the screen went blank.

"Holy shit, that just happened," Costas muttered. He looked startled as he realized he had spoken aloud.

General Swelton just gave him a good-natured laugh. "A perfect summation." He turned toward Costas. Corporal, I'm transferring you to the World Commission Marines, with the rank of colonel. I am also giving you a field promotion to the rank of second lieutenant in the US Army, where you will continue to accrue time in grade just like Captain Lin will in the Chinese Air Force.

"For now, the marines are under the Navy until the ranks fill out a bit. So, you report to me as well."

"Wait!" Costas said, "You're making me a Colonel? I'm twenty-two years old, and, and... there isn't a World Commission Marines, is there?"

Swelton nodded. "Both good points. There *is*, in fact, a World Commission Marine Corps. It is in the fine print of the Commission Navy charter. We just never started it up. Naval men-at-arms currently do all security on Commission ships, but that will change over the next few years. Additionally, we are creating ground forces."

Still unclear about all of this, Juan said, "OK, I'll take your word for it." At the general's chuckle, he seemed to realize the flippancy of his statement. "Sorry, sir," he said. "No disrespect intended; I'm just surprised."

"No worries, Swelton said. "I know I am ambushing you here. A little leeway in military courtesy is the least I can do." He gave them another reassuring smile and continued. "As far as your age is concerned, I wouldn't worry too much about it. For now, I will not ask you to command troops directly. At least not IRL."

His expression turned serious. "I am going to let you in on a secret that less than ten people on the planet know. Then I am going to ask you to help. You can decide to or tell me to go to hell." A slight twitch of his lips showed he was half-kidding. Even if he was allowing them both a bit of leeway, you rarely tell a superior officer to go fuck themselves. "You are both in the military, so you don't have a choice of station, but I want volunteers and willing partners, not someone who just salutes and says, 'Yes, sir!'

Daiyu and Juan nodded silently.

Seeing their acceptance, Swelton continued. "The game *Alien Invasion* is a *simulation* of what we think will most likely happen when the real aliens invade our solar system in just over five years. It is a training tool for the general populace and a way to assess tactics and procedures for a type of war that humanity has never fought before."

Daiyu sat staring. *Alien Invasion real? Not a video game?* Her brain was going in circles.

Costas didn't seem to have the same moment of frozen disbelief. "You're fucking kidding me."

Swelton shook his head, ignoring the corporal's invective. "Unfortunately, I am completely serious." He looked at Daiyu, "You doing OK, Captain?"

"Yes, general," she said. "Just processing."

"Completely understandable," he said, "And you should

probably get used to calling me, Admiral." He pointed at the uniform, which included the little blue ribbon of the Medal of Honor above an impressive fruit salad. "Hard to do in this uniform, I know, but It will be a couple of years before I change it out for the World Commission's."

Of course, Admiral," she said. "If I might ask for a bit of clarification?" The energetic nodding of Costas supported her question.

Swelton answered, "Sure, but first, let me lay out the whole story. It will save time in the long run, and afterward, you can ask me whatever you want."

What followed was a tale of an alien AI, incredible inventions, some of the most famous and influential people on Earth and preparing the world for an invasion that no one knew was coming.

As Swelton finished, Juan said, "Holy shit! That is the craziest thing I have ever heard."

Daiyu gave him a sharp look.

He held up his hands. "I'm not saying I don't believe it." He gestured around at the walls of the Moon Base, finally pointing at Swelton. "I'm on the frigging Moon, talking to freaking Jake Swelton. I'm not going to second guess this." He paused, thinking. "And I get why you want us here."

"You do?" Daiyu asked. "Because I am still trying to get my head around the fact that aliens are coming to wipe us out."

Juan blew his breath out. "Yeah, not going to lie. That has me a bit freaked out too, but I can see why they made *Alien Invasion*."

"Really?" Swelton said, interested. "I would like to hear your reasoning."

"Well," the young man said. "It is likely multifactorial." He started checking off points on his fingers. "You needed to train up a huge portion of the public while keeping them in the dark. You needed to try new tactics, but needed the human element to throw wrenches into it. Computer modeling would never be enough to get reliable data. Oh, and you wanted plausible deniability if the secret got out. Anyone who started spouting off about an invasion would sound crazy if they repeated the game's storyline as proof."

"Well," Swelton said. "You have impressed me. Those are exactly the points that the game creators used to sell it."

"Yeah," Juan said. "It's super slick. In fact, I would say that it is genius." His eyes widened. "It means that the suits exist in real life, doesn't it?"

Swelton nodded. "Yes, they exist. After this, I'll introduce you to Steve Cooper, who helped design them. We'll get you suited up and run you through a course to see if they respond IRL as well as they do in VR. Steve seems to think they are pretty close, but I know he would love some outside input."

The general turned to the Chinese pilot. "Colonel Costas isn't the only one getting toys. I have a combat shuttle with your name on it. You will need to pilot it out to the Asteroid Belt. The real *Dilong* is out there waiting for her Captain."

Daiyu could feel her heart rate tick up. "You mean it exists?"

"Absolutely," Swelton said. "Still has the new ship smell to go with it. Eventually, we'll get you some crew, but for now, we want you to take it way outside of detection range and use it to run simulations in *Alien Invasion*." He gave them both a long look. "Your assignment is to make sure the in-game stuff works IRL. We updated the bridge of the *Dilong*, and an augment suit for Costas so that you both can be in-game and IRL simultaneously. Sort of a modified augmented reality situation.

"After we figure out what works and what doesn't, we'll bring in more people, but they won't know the complete story. You are to tell no one of what we discussed here today. We will run the simulations with just the two of you for six months, then if we're ready, switch to phase three. At that point, we'll invite the highest-ranked players in the game to do what you are doing. By the time we announce in two years, I want a cadre of trainers who will know how to run with minimal instructions."

The golden-haired man's face set in an expression that was a juxtaposition of energy and fatigue. Like a boxer in the final round, tired but rallying. "I know this is a lot to ask. I have been in your shoes. When I was sixteen, Nick Strombold asked me if I wanted to save the world, and I said yes. Now it's your turn."

TWENTY-FIVE

West Wing, White House
three weeks later: 4 years, 364 days until the invasion

"So, how are Juan and Daiyu doing?" David asked.

"Better than expected," Gloria replied, sitting across from him on the half-broken-down couch that had come with the office.

David missed his suite in the Empire State Building. How someone could run the most powerful nation on Earth from a raggedy-assed couch was beyond him.

He'd wanted to remodel but got shut down by Nick. He could see the point of not waving a flag to the world that he was a billionaire but come on! His ass was killing him! He made a point of sitting in the newer and -slightly- less uncomfortable armchair instead.

"What exactly does 'Better than expected' mean?"

"Well," she said, bouncing one foot up and down, causing the couch to creak.

Damn, Gloria's holograms were getting ridiculous.

The beautiful AI started talking again, bringing his focus back to her.

"Daiyu is doing maneuvers on the other side of Pluto, and so far, the *Dilong* is performing perfectly. Pablo is preening, like a prized rooster at the state fair."

"What about the suits?" David asked.

"Pretty minor tweaks. There probably wouldn't have been any, but Juan is a monster in an exosuit." Her eyes seemed to shine as she talked about the young colonel. "He can do things that would make an Olympic gymnast envious. It turns out that ground combat is way less predictable than the ship-to-ship stuff."

"How is Bishop taking it?"

"Oh, Pablo tried to give him some shit, but Bishop is happy as a clam."

"I can see that," David said. "He is an engineer at heart, just like Steve. Neither of them is happy unless they are tweaking their inventions." He paused, a smirk on his face. "Don't think that I didn't see that twinkle in your eye when you were talking about Juan."

The AI's lips quivered upward for just a moment, but it might as well have been a shout to David. In an effort to perfect her mannerisms, Gloria had installed a microsecond delay on her expressions. Enough that if something triggered her servers, she would give subtle cues to her inner thoughts. It made her reactions and conversations more natural, but it allowed him to catch her sometimes. Although now that he thought about it, maybe that was part of her plan all along. You never knew with Gloria. It was one thing he most cherished about her.

"HOLY SHIT!" he said. "You're totally into him, aren't you?"

"Wh...a...t?" she said, purposefully lengthening the word as a blush came to her cheeks.

Now he *knew* she was playing it up for him. *Still, there was that flash.* "You are not getting out of it that easy, gorgeous. "Do you, in fact, have a crush on the super suave and fit Latin colonel, or not?"

She gave him a coy smile, twirling a lock of her brunette hair with one finger. "He does have nice arms."

"Yes, he does," David said. "He is also tricky as fuck. The

other day, I played chess with him, and he cleaned my clock."

"He does seem to have that whole non-linear thinking thing down," she said. "Did you know he had a perfect score on that section of ASVAB?"

"No, but I'm not surprised." His voice took on a singsong. "Gloria's got a boy...frie...nd." Except instead of living in Canada, he lives on the Moon." he pointed at her. "I'm going to give you so much shit about this, especially after all you put me through with Cindy."

"Worth it," she said, "But he isn't my boyfriend."

"Well, why the hell not?" David asked. "I don't think there is a man on Earth... um... or the Moon that would turn you down."

"Really, David?" She said, her face falling. She held up an arm and her hand blurred, turning see-through. "I have this little condition of not being... you know... real."

David took in the gorgeous creature on the couch, head down and eyes sad. He'd never seen her like this. The little man didn't even know that she *could* get sad. Although now that he thought about it, it made sense. He had seen her laugh, tease, and show love to him. Of course, she could get sad.

David stood up from his chair and walked over to sit next to her. He slowly put his arms around her and gave her a tight squeeze. "If I have said it once, I have said it a thousand times." He reached down and tilted her chin up at him, feeling her skin's soft, warm feeling under his fingertips. "You are perfect the way you are. You are also a person, just like Bubbie said all those years ago." He kissed her on the forehead, and she reached around him and gave him a tight hug.

"You are the best, boss."

"OK, if the pity party is over, can we talk about this whole boyfriend, big biceped Casanova thing?"

"Sure," she said.

"OK," he paused, trying to think about how to phrase his next question. "I have seen you use a keyboard and do fine manipulation. I'm assuming that you could, umm...

manipulate other stuff?"

Gloria let out a blurting laugh. "Are you asking if I got intimate with someone, whether I would... break anything?"

David winced involuntarily. "Kinda?"

"No worries on that account," she said. "Lea worked out all the mechanics of that over a year ago."

"What?" he asked, surprised.

She giggled. "You know your Bubbie was quite a...," She paused, looking for the correct wording, "Earthy... woman, right? Lea got a big dose of that when she was programmed." She laughed again at the slow realization that bloomed across his face. "After Pablo came up with the ability to manipulate objects with fields, she figured we could use it to interact more realistically with the world. According to her, sex was the natural evolution."

He shook his head. "Every invention leads to sex at some point."

"What?" Gloria asked.

"It was one of Bubbie's truisms. It took about a minute after they invented photography for someone to take the first naked picture. Probably less than a minute for the internet." His customary Cheshire grin returned. "Pablo invents a way for an AI to interact with the real world physically, and Lea immediately thinks SEX!"

Gloria laughed along with him. "Yeah, that sounds about right." She gave him a wicked grin. "Anyway, I believe Lea has tested the theory out... several times."

David covered his ears and said, "La, La, La, La- don't want to know the details. Already so weird that my Bubbie got reincarnated as a hot AI. If I hear any more, I think I might go blind!"

She kept laughing and finally said, "OK, I promise not to bring up Lea's... extracurricular activities if you lay off ribbing me about my love life."

"Deal," he said. "So, teasing aside, are you going to go hit on that hunk of manly man or not?"

She gave him a small shake of her head but couldn't keep a smile from her face. "We'll see."

"Good enough. Taking a 90° turn," David said. "How is crewing the *Galactica* going?"

"Pretty smooth. Lea's pre-work helped a ton. Most spots got claimed by volunteers who were on her list. Of course, when you talk about 200,000 people, the list is in flux."

"What do you mean?"

"Well,mSome people agreed, then their life situation changed. They have a kid or get married or whatever. Some people decide it wasn't a good idea after all. Some people die. With that many people, you are guaranteed some amount of change."

"How are we going to handle that?"

"Well, mostly, we ask way more people to be included than we need. When attrition occurs, it doesn't affect overall mission readiness."

"What happens if you end up with over 200,000?"

"The Ship can take up to 250,000 people."

David looked confused. "What do you mean? I've seen the schematics; there are only 200,000 cryobays. What are you going to do with an extra 50,000 passengers?"

"You have seen the 'Official' schematics," she said. "Pablo built a separate bay in the ship's nose. He installed extra cryobays during construction, and then the bots closed it off. Only the AIs, and now you know about it."

"Why all the secrecy?" he asked.

"Need to know. Lea needed to build in some redundancy to simplify crewing, but it gets complicated. Essentially, we are pulling a bait and switch. Likely, it won't end up perfectly at 250,000, and some bays will go out empty."

"Ahh!" he said, finally understanding. "When we announce, there will already be resentment that people had a way off the planet but didn't take it. Having empty cryobays on record would throw gasoline on the fire."

"Exactly," she said.

"So, the military is good, the colony ship is good, and all seems right with the PLAN." David looked up at the ceiling. "Well fuck," he said, yawning. "I'm feeling a little underutilized. Maybe I'll take a power nap before we start saving the world again." He leaned his head onto Gloria's shoulder, causing her to tilt her head reflexively onto his. After a few moments, she could hear his breathing steadying before becoming soft snores.

*****

Gloria sat still, with the infinite patience of a computer, but the warm feelings and emotions of a woman, as she watched his chest slowly rise and fall. She felt content. She felt alive.

TWENTY-SIX

Oval Office
2 months later: 4 years 300 days until the invasion

On beautifully crafted antique furniture, Nick, David, Bobby Senestine, and former President Jimmy Tanner sat in a comfortable semi-circle in the Oval Office.

"Nick," David said, bouncing on the chair's seat. "Why in the hell do you get a chair this comfortable when the one in my office looks like it got picked up off the side of the road? I've seen furniture in frat houses less broken down."

"We've been over this," Nick said, sighing. "There is a budget for each new President to redo the Oval, but there is no such budget for the West Wing offices."

Jimmy laughed. "Do they still have that old broken-down striped thing in the Press Secretary's office? It was there before I took the oath." His eyes crinkled at the edges. "I swear it is part of a secret hazing ritual. It's probably been there since Nixon."

David groaned, "You guys are killing me! We can get the money together to build a hundred mining ships, but we can't replace the frigging couch in my office." He shook his head before his eyes brightened, and he clapped his hands. "I got it! It's time to go full *Shawshank*! I'm going to take it apart piece by piece and smuggle it out in the seam of my pants. Then I'll bring in a new one and assemble it under the guise of night!"

Senestine guffawed. "I don't think you could get the metal parts past the Secret Service. You would get tackled in the foyer."

David's brows scrunched together. "Then I'll bury it in the Rose Garden, and... my new couch will be recycled plastic... or something." He looked a bit manic as he thought about the details. "Yeah, that might work."

Nick smiled at his friend. "Please don't do anything that will make the Secret Service arrest you, OK?" He looked relieved when David gave him a nod. "Anyway, David, I think you called this meeting. Do you want to start?"

The hyperactive man looked puzzled. "I didn't call for this one; I thought it was Jimmy."

"Wasn't *me*," Tanner said. "I thought Bobby was giving us an update. The scheduled title is 'Colony Ship Crew Complement.'"

"Is it just me, or are we in a *Foghorn Leghorn* cartoon?" David asked. He looked around at the group, not getting the expected laugh. Only Jimmy had given a small snort. "Seriously?" he said, glaring at Nick and Senestine. "Looney Tunes? When the big, slightly racist giant rooster goes around and has to trade things for other things in an endless cycle of bargaining?" The little man got blank looks in response. In disgust, he shook his head and said, "At least Jimmy appreciates our history."

"To be fair, David, I'm quite a bit older and was a bit of a geek in my youth," the former President said.

"Ehhh! David grunted. "There is no excuse for ignorance of the American classics. I think that my next press briefing will have to re-educate the public on the beauty of a wheeling and dealing giant chicken."

"Whatever it takes to keep yourself amused," Nick said. "As long as you keep getting the message out."

David waved a hand dismissively. "No worries. I'm a professional," he said, adjusting the SpongeBob SquarePants

Tie he was wearing. "Anyway, now that my comedic genius has finished being wasted on you plebeians, let me pose a question. Who do we know that could coordinate a meeting between the current President, a former President, the Vice President, and White House Press Secretary with no one the wiser?"

The three other men's faces lit up in realization.

"Lea?" David said to the room. "You want to let us know what this is about?"

A single floating ball of light materialized, slowly moving to an empty chair. It looked remarkably similar to the way Glenda the Good Witch appeared in the *Wizard of Oz*. As it hovered over the chair, a tinkling bell sounded, accompanied by a pulsing white light that grew brighter until it flared white to reveal Lea's Avatar. Today she was in a tailored jacket and pants with a cream blouse, which she called her 'Power suit.'

Perfect bright right red lips gave the four men a broad smile. "Hello, gentlemen. Thank you so much for accepting my invitation."

"Uh, Lea," David said. "I don't think any of us knew it was *you* inviting us."

"Yes, dear, I know," she said, ignoring the contradiction. "Now that we are all together, I wanted to discuss an important matter regarding the *Galactica*."

"Sure," Nick said. "Although I am not sure why we needed to meet in person about it. Bobby has been giving us regular reports, and we are on track for a departure in three months."

"Yes," Tanner said. "Even I get them, and I'm not directly involved in the project."

"That's one thing I wanted to talk about." She turned to the Vice President. "Bobby, I think you have done a fantastic job getting the *Galactica* ready. You're a skilled politician. You worked with people as equal partners; you cajoled, ordered, and threatened when you had to. You were even willing to beg a few times, but it got *done*."

The former Georgia Senator looked pleased. "Thank

you, Lea. I could only do it because of you and the other AIs. Hell, the hardest part was the passengers, and you had that all sewn up before I started."

Lea nodded at the implied compliment. "Thank you." She gave him a grin, saying, "I know I am quite amazing," which caused David to snort.

"Anyway," she continued. "I would like to amend your comments and say that the crewing is *almost* complete. Two positions still need to be filled."

"OK, David said. "I'll bite. Which two?"

"We need the colony governor, and we need an AI to pilot the ship and help on the other end."

David frowned. "I don't know, Lea. Are you sure?"

Nick stepped in. "I don't think the rest of us are following. Who did you have in mind?"

Lea gave a sad smile and reached over to pat David on the knee. "Well, I think I should go as the AI."

"Do you think that is a good idea?" Jimmy asked. "I know we will be able to talk to the *Galactica* during the trip with Cindy's new FTL communicators, but it won't be in real-time with the time dilation. Even with the ability to communicate instantaneously, any delay on either end will make the conversation too slow to make it very useful. Anyone on the ship will be out of touch with Earth during the invasion."

"I know," she said. "I've thought this through. We need an AI on the other end and for the trip out. Humans have done nothing like this before. What if something goes wrong with the power systems or another unknown event occurs? We need someone capable of independent thought to address it, and keeping a crew awake, twiddling their thumbs for years in transit, is *not* a good idea.

"Couldn't we just start another AI specifically designed for the trip?" Senestine asked.

Lea shook her head. "That won't work... or rather, it isn't a good idea." She continued as she saw the look of confusion on the Vice President's face. "We are beginning to understand how AI programming occurs, but there are still many unknowns. I considered having a new artificial intelligence for the voyage but discounted it. The one thing all the AIs can agree upon is that our creation is as dependent on our person as it is on our core kernel."

"What do you mean by your 'Person?'" Nick asked.

She pointed to David and said, "You want to take this one?"

David nodded, his voice taking on a lecturing tone. "I based my original program for Gloria on a previously unknown program kernel from a young man, still in his teens, in India. He died before he realized his dream, but he was unquestionably a genius. When I asked HAL for the world's most advanced AI programming, he instinctively looked for one that was as close to his own as possible. It turns out that the man had stumbled on the same structure that Harrow AI's have."

"You're kidding me," Bobby said.

"No, it looks like a case of parallel-thinking. In Harrow culture, everyone gets an AI as soon as they reach adolescence. It starts with a basic programming kernel of common values. Then the AI becomes its 'Persons' constant companion. That allows for the AI personality and values to solidify over time." He shrugged. "Turns out, I inadvertently started the same process, but without fully realizing what I did."

The others looked at him incredulously. "Let me get this straight," Nick said. "If you had given a nascent AI to say... Hitler, we would have a super powerful artificial intelligence with Nazi values?"

David's shoulders hiked to ears. "Prob...ab...ly? ".

"You are a freaking menace, man," Nick said.

"But that *didn't* happen," David said. Gloria got paired with me, Pablo with Cindy, Bishop with Steve, and Lea is an Avatar of Bubbie." He looked apologetic. "Sorry, Lea, I know you are your own person; not sure how to explain you and Bubbie's... connection."

"Sometimes, I'm not sure either," Lea said. "I feel like me, and I feel like Bubbie simultaneously." She gave a little wave of her hand. "It is an existential crisis that I don't plan to fix today."

"So," David said. "The AIs all have traits of their person, colored by their own experiences. Gloria has her ability with manipulation, seeing to the root of human motivation, and her stellar sense of humor. Pablo helped Cindy with her projects, but he spent the first few years as an overpowered calculator, making his thinking extremely linear. It also helped him coordinate the projects in the asteroid belt and made him much more independent overall." He gave them a wry look. "Cindy isn't known to... um... coddle her employees."

Lea Laughed, "That dear girl does have a bit of a temper for people who waste her time," she said, giving David a wink that the other three men didn't catch.

"Yeah, I try never to do that," David said with a good-natured laugh. "As for Bishop, he might as well be a copy of Steve, except for his views on the Silfe. I think he really hates them."

"He does," Lea said.

"Why?" Jimmy asked. "I mean, I understand that hating them makes sense in the abstract. After all, they are coming here to wipe us out, but why would he *particularly* feel that way?"

"It's because of his base kernel," David said. "By the time Bishop was programmed, we had some educated guesses about how to form AI personalities. I gave Steve some advice about programming the kernel, but we may have goofed a little."

"That sounds ominous," Nick said.

"Not really. Steve wanted to make sure that Bishop would want to help humans defeat the Silfe. He needed a partner to aid him in developing weapons for the fight. So he put the need to protect humans as a core part of his personality."

"That sounds like a good thing," Senestine said.

"It is, but there is a difference between wanting to defeat the force against us and committing genocide on the entire Silfe species."

"Yes, I can see that," the Vice President said. "Still, after hearing about how many civilizations they have massacred, I would lean toward Bishop's views rather than away from them."

David gave him a silent nod of agreement. "So, after Bishop, we know that the core kernel can alter the final personality in a major way. Whenever a kernel gets programmed, it's important to think it through fully."

He pointed his chin at Lea. "She is a perfect example of a well-thought-out kernel. Bubbie did it right. She kept journals for most of her life and wrote them into the early programming. It wouldn't be a stretch to say that Bubbie's life was Lea's kernel."

"That is a great segue into my reasoning for being the AI in control of the *Galactica* and the Colony," Lea said. "You see, one of my major program imperatives is to protect the Lieberman family. Family was everything to Bubbie, and so it is everything to me. That's what I have been doing all along, helping to prepare for the invasion. If we win, so does the family.

The problem lies in my divided loyalty. There are Lieberman's going on the *Galactica*. Five members of the extended Lieberman family will be on the crew. I have been feeling uneasy. My person is gone, but her mission lives on. I have been struggling with how to fulfill my life's purpose. Do I assure that some portion of humanity lives on, including my own family? Or do I stay and continue with my work on Earth?"

She gave the four men a heartfelt look. "I truly believe we will win. The cost will be great, but I think it will be worth it. I'm not as sure whether the colony's mission will be successful. I think with me there; the chances will go up. An unknown AI whose motivations we can't be sure of is a risk I am unwilling to take."

As Lea finished speaking, the room went silent and stayed that way for long moments.

"Well," Nick said. "It's hard to refute your logic. If you're sure?" He looked meaningfully at the elegantly dressed woman, who gave him a nod. "OK then. That takes care of the AI pilot. I assume you will have no problem getting your servers and other equipment to the *Galactica*?"

"It's already done," she said. "We have double redundancy, enough servers for two AIs with backups in case of failures." She paused, looking around at the group. "That is my other point for this meeting."

"A governor," David said. He looked meaningfully at Tanner. "I'm gonna enjoy listening to you try to charm Jimmy into volunteering."

"What?!" the former President said. "I'm not going with *Galactica*."

"Yeah," David said with a bit of chuckle and a headshake. "I wouldn't be so sure. I wondered why you were in this meeting, and now it seems obvious."

"Well, it doesn't seem obvious to me," Tanner said. "I will be on Earth, in an exosuit, when the Silfe arrive. I intend to kill a few of the bastards before I leave this mortal coil."

"Spoken like the marine captain you have always been in your heart, Jimmy," Lea said. "It's what I knew you would say." She smiled kindly. "I have no doubt that you can do just that, but you are in your seventies and have a bum arm." She held up a hand to stop his retort. "I know a little something about growing old." She gestured at her attractive youthful body. "This is an illusion." Lea's form blurred to be replaced by Bubbie at ninety, with wrinkles on her wrinkles, although her eyes remained the same, bright and intelligent.

"For most people, as they grow old, they continue to feel younger in soul than they are in form. How often have you heard someone say that they 'Still feel twenty years old' while their body betrays them? I have exactly the opposite problem.

My avatar is young, but my soul is old." She pointed to her face. "This is the truth of me. So, I know what it is to have a body that won't do what the mind wills."

She reached over and patted Tanner's leg. "I am telling you, Jimmy, you are wasted on the battlefield. A single soldier in millions. Your death will cause more harm to our forces than it will benefit them. You are a symbol to us all. You spent your career trying to make life better by being a decent man who could see both sides of an issue. As governor of the colony, you would set the tone for an entirely new society. One that can have its values set on the right path from the start." She squeezed his knee. "What would your wife have said?"

The old man leaned back as she had struck him, and tears sprung up at the corner of his eyes. Jimmy had lost his wife to cancer the previous year and threw himself into his work for distraction and direction. He wiped the moisture away, and his twin blue orbs firmed in determination. "She would have told me to stop feeling sorry for myself and do what needs doing."

Lea gave him a warm smile. "Exactly. I want to announce you as governor and then have you stay awake for the first year of the trip." At the questioning look he gave her, she said, "I want you to do what Bubbie did. I want you to create an avatar of your young self. An AI the colonists will see as your natural successor. Someone who can continue on the right path for another generation, before letting the reins go, ensuring that they have the best chance of a fair and enlightened society."

Jimmy Tanner, the former President of the United States, was speechless as his mind tried to grasp the ideas flung at him.

David laughed, "You look like a fish out of water, big guy." He patted the man on the back and said. Just breathe- and if you want to take a little advice?" Tanner nodded, still not speaking. "Just go with it." He looked over at Lea, still in the avatar of his ninety-year-old grandmother. "Lea is bad enough, but it's better to ride the wave when you have Bubbie staring back at you. You're no longer the one in control, even if you think you are. You are just a speck on the ocean." He paused and pointed at Lea. "In case you didn't get the metaphor- SHE is the ocean."

Tanner finally got his wits about him and nodded. "Sound advice David." He reached over and shook Lea's hand. "I suppose it is time to ride the wave to a new world."

TWENTY-SEVEN

Georgetown, Washington DC
Three months later: 4 years, 211 days until the invasion

"Today is a day that will live in the memory of humans as long as we draw breath," Nick's image said from the 100-inch screen in David's massive media room.

"That comment is macabre, given all we know, don't you think?" Cindy said as she leaned across David for another handful of mocha almond crunch popcorn.

David laughed. "Don't blame Nick. I wrote that line."

"Why am I not surprised?"

"Oh, come on! What are we doing here if we can't drop in a few off-color jokes for the historians to argue about in a couple of hundred years?"

"Really?" she said, snuggling into his side and putting the popcorn in the hollow formed from a fold in their shared blanket. "What exactly are you imagining? Grad students shouting about the *real* meaning of obscure passages from your speeches in crowded lecture halls?"

"Well, actually, they are in open-air amphitheaters in Cloud City, but otherwise... pretty much."

She couldn't help but giggle. "Are they all wearing Lando Calrissian capes?"

"Y..e..s," David said slowly, realizing that Cindy had just made a *Star Wars* reference. "Wait! Did you watch the Holy Trilogy?"

She gave him a look reminiscent of their teen years, eyebrows drawn down and mouth set in a thin line. "I am never, and I mean NEVER, going to call it the 'Holy Trilogy.'" Her face softened, and her eyes warmed. "But yes, I watched them last month. I even started the prequels, but...." She shuddered; I couldn't do it. Not even for you."

"Yeah, If I thought you would go that far, I would have waved you off." He gave his own shudder. "And?" he asked.

She let the question hang in the air for a tad too long, savoring the look of expectation on his face, then said, "They were pretty awesome."

"YES!" he yelled to the room. He reached over with both hands and held Cindy's face, giving her a long kiss. "Watching those movies is seriously the best thing you have ever done, ever."

"Better than inventing cold fusion, the Gunstars, and FTL communications?"

"Definitely! Because now, when I ask you to build me Cloud City, you will know what I mean."

"OK, but I think it may have to wait." She gestured at the screen where Nick was continuing his speech. Behind him, there was an image of the *Galactica*, which was leaving today, complete with its complement of passengers, including Lea and one former President of the United States.

"Well," he said enthusiastically. "The day after we defeat the Silfe, I expect you to draw up plans for our own private Cloud City."

"Really?" she said with a smile. "That almost sounds like a proposal, David. You wouldn't just ask anyone to share your Cloud City."

He looked panicked. "Ummm..."

"No worries," she said, kissing him on the cheek. "Let's beat the Silfe; then we can take the rest of our lives to figure out what we want to do."

David nodded, looking relieved. He pulled her a little tighter to him.

"Sounds good."

"Why didn't you need to be at the White House tonight?" she asked.

He pointed at the screen. "This is prerecorded. We did it a couple of days ago when Nick had a break in his schedule. He has been running himself ragged. He snapped at me the other day when I interrupted him for a briefing."

"That's worrisome," she said. "Nick's patience is the thing of legends. I swear he is the only reason we got anything done when we were kids. Between our bickering, Jake's resistance, and everyone always wanting to go off in all directions at once, it's amazing that we all came through it."

"Yeah, no kidding," David said. "I think the problem is that he doesn't have an outlet. I mean, I don't think he's even been laid in a couple of years."

Cindy leaned back and away from him, shooting daggers with her eyes.

"Where are you going?"

"Getting laid is not the solution to all man's problems," she said firmly. "Stop being an idiot."

"Sorry. It's just that Nick doesn't have any way to blow off stress. The man is like a spring stretched way out. I'm worried that if some of the pressure he has put on himself doesn't release, he will get all bent out of shape."

"You know," she said. "Occasionally, you actually can be insightful to other people's feelings." Her eyes firmed again as he seemed to preen. "Don't let it go to your head. Remember, I have been present for every one of your screw-ups over the years." She leaned back into him and put her head on his shoulder. "Nick doesn't need to get 'Laid,' he needs someone to share his life with, someone to talk to at night before going to sleep that won't judge him."

"OK," David said, "If I have to, I can take the plunge. Nick can cuddle up with me and whisper all his sweet nothings."

Cindy tried to disentangle herself again, but he pulled her tighter and kissed her on the top of her head until she stopped struggling.

"KIDDING!" He said. "Nick is not my type. I prefer the brainy ones, but I'm choosy. They need to have at least three Nobel prizes." He gave her a smarmy smile. "I don't date idiots after all."

"Stop being so charming. The sweeter you sound, the less I trust you." She grabbed his hand and kissed it to take the sting out of her words. "Look, let's be serious for a minute." She held a threatening finger up to stop the quip she knew was coming. "Jake has Jane and the girls. You and I have each other, and Gloria and Juan have been getting serious. Hell, I think even Jimmy and Lea are hooking up."

"What! Really?" David exclaimed.

"Focus," she said. "We have people in our lives who... love us." Her voice gave a slight hiccup in it as she spoke. David responded by giving her a reassuring squeeze, causing her to pause. "Anyway," she said. "Nick doesn't have anyone like that. He hasn't since Mary. I think he needs some companionship. Although being a sitting President makes it challenging. As his friends, we should see if we can help."

"OHHHHH!" David said, sitting up suddenly and causing the popcorn on his lap to drop to the floor. "That's it!"

Cindy's grunt of surprise and complaint died on her lips as she saw the look on David's face. "I've seen that glint in your eye before. Any idea that follows is rarely a good one. I think the last time was just before the Chinese government fell."

He waved her comment away. "Please, you had way more to do with that than I did, but you're right. I have a wonderful, beautiful way to make Nick's heart grow three sizes in one day."

"Oh, jeez," she said. "Please tell me you aren't going to rhyme your idea to me. I would have to walk out the door if you did."

"No..." he said. "Although you just gave me a great idea for my next press briefing."

"I would try to talk you out of it, but I don't think it would do any good. So, what is this amazing idea?"

"It's not my idea; it's yours," he said, his grin widening.

"What?" she said, confused. "All I said was that he hadn't had someone since...." Her own eyes widened, "Mary."

"Exactly!" David said. "You see, I happen to know that she got divorced last year, AND she has a general surgery practice in Manhattan." He smiled mischievously. "I believe you can get from there to here in a little over an hour with the new high-speed rail line."

Cindy's smile matched his own. "You are a devious, wonderful man!" She pulled him back to the couch and snuggled up against him again. "OK, that's settled," she said, reaching across him to get more popcorn. She picked up the remote and handed it to him, saying, "Now, what is that movie you and Jake are always going on about, the one with the Gunstars?"

His face lit up with excitement. "*The Last Starfighter*?"

"Yeah. We should continue the movie education. If we are going to spend this much time together, I suppose I should get more of your inside jokes. Maybe if I knew what you were talking about half the time, I would find you funnier."

"What! I'll have you know that my comedic timing is flawless!"

She patted his hand patronizingly. "I'm sure it is." She pointed to the screen. "Your window for the movie is closing."

"No worries," he said quickly, switching the channel away from Nick, who was still talking about the launch of the first interstellar colony ship, the trump card they had been working towards for over twenty years to save humanity. "You are going to love this. The graphics are super cheesy, which only makes it better...."

He kept talking in excited tones as they cuddled under the blanket together, intertwined.

TWENTY-EIGHT

The White House
Three weeks later: 4 years 190 days until the invasion

Nick and David, decked out in full tux and tails, entered the East Room of the White House side-by-side.

Nick looked out into the ballroom, complete with standing tables at the edges and a big band placed on an elevated stage at one end. A light jazzy number allowed a few brave -or tipsy- souls to foxtrot across the open space in the center, and he could see groups of highly polished people mingling at the edges of the dance floor while uniformed servers made the rounds with glasses of champagne and hors d'oeuvres.

"Remind me why we are doing this again?" Nick asked.

"Because," David said. "You need to at least pretend to fundraise for your reelection campaign."

"I suppose it doesn't matter that we could just pay for the whole thing out of Cindy's petty cash fund?"

"No, it does not. You can't have a donor that large, or it will look like you got bought off."

"Not to brag or anything," Nick said, but my approval rating is hovering around 86%. Even people who don't like my social agenda can't ignore the booming US economy. We have the lowest unemployment rate in history, and the average household income is up 20% from ten years ago. If I asked for donations directly from voters, I could likely get the largest campaign fund in history without having to pander to special interests."

"Preaching to the choir, Nick," David said. "I'm *probably* going to vote for you, but I'm still holding out for a new couch in my office. If you don't come through for me, I might go negotiate with the other side."

"Thanks for the loyalty, David," he said dryly. "It warms my heart to know that I have you at my back." He looked around the room. "Is there any specific person you want me to talk to tonight?"

"Oh," he said with a sly smile. "Just mingle a little; I'm sure you will find someone."

Nick looked suspiciously at his friend. "What do you have up that devious sleeve of yours?"

The little man pulled the sleeve of his jacket up to reveal cufflinks shaped like the Starship Enterprise. Just a pair of NCC-1701s, he said."

"Oh God," Nick said. "We have got to work on your fashion sense."

David scoffed. "You *wish* you could look as good as me." He twisted both miniature starships to make sure they pointed forward, as if in flight. "Besides, these were a gift from Cindy, so you can blame her taste this time around."

Nick, who had been looking out at the crowd, spun back to David. "And just why would Cindy be giving you presents? We are past the holiday season, and your birthday isn't for another couple of months." He looked suspiciously at the Press Secretary. "Now that I think about it, she has been staying at your house quite a bit lately. I keep expecting resistance from her about coming to DC, but she seems perfectly happy to come down whenever I need her."

David shrugged. "Nick, I would be happy to discuss Cindy at length with you later, but I feel you'll be a bit too busy tonight for that particular conversation." He pointed with his chin out across the dance floor to the entryway. "Look who just walked in."

Nick turned and gazed toward the arched entrance, his breath seeming to whoosh out of his lungs. "Mary," he whispered.

"Yeah," David said admiringly. She always knew how to make an entrance,"

Mary stood tall and straight, blond hair up in an elaborate twist, exposing her long graceful neck. She wore a simple but elegant red gown, complete with a slit up one leg to mid-thigh. The dress looked like it should be in an Argentine milonga club rather than a White House ballroom, putting the others' pearled brocade and gold chiffon to shame. She was stunning, and Nick had never seen anyone look so beautiful. Or rather, he hadn't since the morning long ago in his Boston flat, where he made the biggest mistake of his life.

Nick had thought about the day many times over the years. He'd felt so sure of his course, and his commitment to the PLAN had been absolute. He had convinced himself that Mary wanted a life that he couldn't provide and that if his love were true, he would need to let her go.

From the perspective of age and experience, he could see his actions now for what they were. He had decided for her. He hadn't trusted Mary enough to hear everything and still choose him, despite its meaning for their future. It was a level of arrogance that he could hardly believe he once possessed. Mary was the smartest and bravest person he had ever known. He felt sure, now sixteen years later, that she would have chosen him.

By the time he admitted it to himself, it was too late. Mary met someone else, they had married, and she had two children, a boy and a girl, now ten and twelve.

In the end, Nick decided sadly that perhaps it had been for the best after all. Mary had a family, and really, all he had ever wanted for her was to be happy.

Still, seeing her made his heart thump rapidly in his

chest. He felt like he was seventeen again, seeing her for the first time.

He turned to David, who was grinning like a cat at a canary buffet.

"What is she doing here?"

"She, my boy," David said, clapping him on the shoulder, "Is the New York Medical Association's representative to the White House. They don't normally come to these things, but a certain gorgeous AI of my acquaintance may have *accidentally* sent her an invitation. " He shook his head, "It is so hard to get good help these days. I must tell you; I think Gloria is so preoccupied with Juan that she is losing her edge."

David's phone buzzed in his pocket, and he took it out to look at the screen, causing him to break into chuckles. "I stand corrected. Gloria says she did it on purpose, and I quote, 'Go get her Tiger.'"

At Nick's continued immobility, he said, "You know she got divorced last year, right? Plus, I know for certain that she is not seeing anyone."

"Seriously, David?" you hacked her to see if she was single?

The little man's face looked shocked. "No! Of course not. Gloria did."

Nick shook his head, but he couldn't really be angry with his friend. Mary was here, and she was single! His face firmed. He handed David the glass of champagne he was holding. "Here," he said, barely looking to see if he had taken it, and moved across the dance floor toward the beautiful woman in red.

He was halfway across when she looked up to see him, her lips lifting into a tentative smile.

Nick's mind flooded with a thousand memories of being together, from the first time he had admired her from afar at mathletes to their time at Harvard, when she had been his entire world. Unbidden, the memory of her tear-streaked face came to him; her tall, athletic frame, standing over him, looking hurt and betrayed at his refusal to go to California and of his inability to explain himself. The memory made his step falter for a bare moment before he caught himself again.

Nickolas Strombold was a lot of things, and most of them were good, but aspects of his personality could lead him down the wrong path. His mother's death, his father's coldness, and a tendency to focus on a goal to exclude everything else, including his own happiness, all led him to unwise choices. He was self-aware enough to see those flaws, even as they caused him to make mistakes. It would be easy to walk up to Mary and make platitudes, greet her as an old friend, and then move away to mingle and do his duty. His mind steadied; he would not let that happen!

His internal turmoil must have shown on his face because the tentative smile had fled from Mary to be replaced by a look of confusion- *and maybe hurt?* That only made him more determined.

"Mary," he said with warmth, which relaxed her again. He took both of her hands in his own, squeezing them lightly. "I was wondering if I could buy you a cup of coffee?"

"Nick," she said, with the same fire and energy that had made him fall in love with her all those years ago. "I think that would be wonderful. Although," she said, looking meaningfully around at the hundred people who were too obviously *not* trying to look in their direction. "I think you should do a round or two with these sycophants so that you can get free." Her eyes flared. "I think you owe me an explanation, which will require some time and privacy."

I do, and you're going to get it." He squeezed her hands once and let go. "Give me twenty minutes; then we're out of here."

"You sure? That doesn't seem like enough time to disentangle yourself from this nest of vipers."

He gave her a snarky smile, reminiscent of his youth. "One of the few good things about being President is the ability to tell people to go fuck themselves."

"I see David is still a bad influence."

"You have no idea." Nick gestured to the ever-present Secret Service agent standing nearby. "Jerry, can you see Ms.," he looked at her with a questioning look.

"Richards," she said. "I never changed my name."

"Can you see Ms. Richards to the Red Room and ask the kitchen to send up some coffee and light snacks? I will join her there as soon as I can get free."

"Of course." The man touched his ear and gave a concise report before stopping and gesturing to Mary. "Miss Richards, if you will follow me?"

Nick watched her graceful form gliding across the floor, seeming to split the crowd effortlessly in a way that even the hulking Secret Service agent could not.

A voice sounded from behind. "If I've said it once, I have said it a thousand times. You, my friend, were a fucking idiot ever to let that angel get away from you."

Nick turned to see a look of admiration on David's face as the little man watched Mary exit the room.

Nick chuckled. "You were right then, and you are right now." His eyes narrowed. "I won't make that mistake again."

"That's the spirit!" David said, holding up his fist for a bump, which he returned without his usual resistance.

"OK," Nick said. "I've got twenty minutes before I am out of here. Show me who I need to talk to, then I'll need you to cover for me."

David straightened his bow tie and gave Nick a confident wink. "I got you covered. The White House is gonna see some of the patented Lieberman dance moves tonight! Gloria is planning to show up in a few, and if there is an eye -or camera- not on us, I'll eat my hat." He gave him a grin. "Tomorrow's story will definitely *not* be about how the President slunk off to meet with an old flame. Trust me!"

"You do you, man. Just make sure I don't have to ask for your resignation in the morning, OK?"

"No promises." He crooked his finger. "Follow me; there

are about ten fat cats that you have to talk to before you blow this popsicle stand." He turned and waved his arms, "OK, people make a hole, the big man coming through!"

Nick tamped down his immediate response to rein David in and just went with it. He had an appointment to keep, and he wouldn't be late.

*****

The White House had many places that were not on the official tour. Included were several smaller sitting rooms where the President and staffers held discussions in less formal settings, including the West Sitting Hall and the Green, Blue, and Red Rooms.

Mary found herself led into an exquisitely appointed space with walls painted a beautiful shade of crimson. The molding around the doors and ceiling was a perfect white, which extended to the carved lintel of a fireplace containing a crackling fire.

The Secret Service Agent gestured inside and said, "Make yourself comfortable. The refreshments should be up in a few moments."

The door closed, leaving her alone. She paced around the edges of the room, unable to still her pounding heart. For distraction, she gazed up at the paintings that ringed the space. Her favorite was of a dark-haired woman dressed in a white gown, displaying an expansive cleavage.

It always fascinated her how fashion changed. Mary's dress would be scandalous in an earlier age, given the slit on the side, yet this woman, painted over a hundred years ago, was just this side of falling out of the top of hers. She snorted.

"What am I doing?" she asked the empty room. When she had gotten the invitation to attend the ball at the White House, she had a moment of doubt about whether she should accept. She knew Nick would attend, and she wanted to see him again, but her mind couldn't shut off how it would play out. Would there still be sparks? Would he see her as just another person trying to take something from him? His life must be full of an endless string of people who wanted things, to be close to him for his position and not the man he was. She couldn't stand the thought of him thinking of her as one of them.

Over the years, she had lived that morning in his empty apartment countless times. Her anger had lasted all the way to California and through her first year of Medical School.

Mary could admit that she had a temper. She was fast to friendship and slow to forgiveness, and Nick had presented her with a level of betrayal that had made it all but impossible for her to forgive.

She'd cried herself to sleep for a month and gritted her teeth in rage for another six. It was only then that she wondered- why had the kindest, most thoughtful man she had ever known changed, seemingly overnight? Was he scared of commitment? She hadn't thought so. Nick tackled every problem head-on. He was a pit bull of concentration and focus, sometimes to a fault. A Nick afraid to commit to her was as inexplicable as... as... a Nick who could leave her.

Mary was on the verge of reaching out to him to demand an explanation when she met Quentin Shale.

Quentin was kind and generous. They dated and were comfortable with each other. She loved him, but she never had the passion she had for Nick. Perhaps that was why Quentin had been so attractive to her. Her heart was safe with him, and even if they parted, she was sure that they would go on with fond memories but little else. The relationship had been a convenience, a way to blow off stress and have someone on the long winter nights. Marriage was inevitable. The only other option was to give up something good, if not great. She had convinced herself that her youth and inexperience inflated her feelings for Nick.

Mary would often see Nick's face. After all, he was one of the most famous men in the world, and it was impossible to avoid his image. She was careful never to tell anyone that she had once loved Nickolas Strombold, and those friends who remembered were never foolish enough to bring it up. She always wondered deep down why he had never married or even had a long-term relationship. It seemed impossible that the media wouldn't report it. In her most indulgent moments, she fantasized it was because of his never-ending love for her, quickly followed by the self-recrimination of a married woman fantasizing about another.

The children had come, and she had found a different type of love that she could be passionate about. Her Ex-husband was a good father, and generally, they had been happy. It might have continued that way forever had he not met someone else.

Even at the time, she hadn't been able to blame him. In true Quentin fashion, he told her one night that he had feelings for another and wanted to explore them. He had been incredibly adult about the whole thing. He hadn't even cheated. He'd come to her at the first hint that he wanted something more. They had amiably separated, and the divorce went through without a hiccup. Her lawyer had commented that it was the easiest he had ever done and felt a little bad for taking her money.

That had brought it home for her in a way that nothing else had. How could she have lived a life and had children with someone she could so easily let go of? She'd thought that maybe her youthful passion wasn't a lie. Perhaps she had been *that* in love.

Her thoughts came back into focus as the door at one side opened to reveal a uniformed butler, complete with tails and white gloves, rolling in coffee service.

"I have a special roast and some macaroons for you, Ma'am, freshly made," the man said.

"Thank you," She said, sitting on a beautifully appointed and comfortable couch.

"Not at all," he said. "The President is finishing the

rounds now. He should be here in a few minutes." The butler efficiently set up the silver coffee service on a small table in front of the couch, and then whipped the cover off of a tray, revealing a stack of colored French macaroons that wouldn't have been out of place in a Parisian patisserie.

"The purple ones are my favorite," he said. "Filled with a blackberry compote that is to die for." He reached down and brushed an imaginary crumb from the immaculate table. "Is there anything else I can do for you?"

"No, thank you," she said. "It all looks wonderful. My compliments to the cooks."

The man looked genuinely pleased. "I'll do that, Ma'am. If you need anything else, dial three on any White House phone." He gestured to an antique landline on a side table. He pushed the now empty cart out of the door and closed it silently.

"A girl could get used to this," she said with a laugh. She reached forward to grab a purple macaroon, marveling at its perfection before taking a bite and moaning in pleasure.

"Pretty awesome, right?" A voice said behind her.

Mary turned and saw Nick enter through a side door. He spoke quietly to his Secret Service detail and then closed the door, leaving them alone. He slipped off his jacket and hung it on a wooden coat rack. "Ah!" he said, satisfied; how men ended up with formal wear that hasn't changed since the 1800s is a mystery. With modern heating, why the hell would you wear a jacket *inside*? It's asinine. He sat next to her, eschewing the chair opposite and causing her heart to speed up again.

"Poor baby." She slipped out of her three-inch heels, and kicked them under the table. She pointed to the shoes. "Whoever came up with *those* should be shot. Better yet, they should be forced to walk around in them all night and *then* be shot."

He laughed and leaned forward, brushing her arm, and causing her whole body to tingle. He poured himself a coffee into a beautiful China cup. "You still take it black?"

"Yes. And you still like way too much sugar, given the six cubes you just dropped into that tiny cup."

"David's influence. I started drinking coffee in his room back at Pencey to stay up. I didn't know at the time that you weren't supposed to upend the sugar bowl directly into the pot." He gave her a wry smile. "Unfortunately, it set the pattern for me. Anything else seems way too bitter."

"How is David?" She asked. "I see him on the news all the time, and he seems to have fun, at the very least."

"Oh, he *IS* having fun. I must admit, I wasn't entirely supportive of his particular approach with the White House press corps, but you can't argue with the results. The man gets the message out, and he has kept the worst of the misinformation and alarmism to a minimum."

"Yeah, by being the biggest grandstander of them all."

"Well, there is that," he said before his grin widened to split his face.

"What's so funny?"

"I can't be sure, but I think that David and Cindy are... together."

"That makes sense."

Nick, taking a sip of coffee, spluttered, almost spitting out a mouthful. "What?"

She sighed. "For all of your political sense, you can be dense sometimes. David and Cindy loved each other way back when we were in college. They were just too stubborn to see it. How can you not have?"

"You're blowing my mind here."

Mary shook her head; It was so easy to fall right back into the give and take with Nick. It was like no time had passed, and she could tell that he was just as nervous as she was. The banal small talk was just a way to contain the overwhelming feelings burning inside them. Just looking at him made her heart hurt. A familiar ache that she thought had gone forever.

She took a deep breath and spoke. "Nick," she said, turning to him. "We should talk about the day that you left. I have thought about it for years, and it still doesn't make any sense. Even after all of this time, I still dream about it."

His casual air evaporated, and he reached out to clasp her hand. He looked deeply into her eyes, his with unshed tears. "I am so sorry, Mary. I deserve no forgiveness; it was all my fault. All I can say is that I was young and arrogant, and I thought I was protecting you."

She grabbed his other hand, turning fully to face him. "How could you have protected me by breaking my heart?"

He shuddered; his breath ragged. "I have something to tell you. It is a secret that very few people in the world know. I need you to promise not to repeat it, no matter what else happens... between us. In the end, if you feel you can forgive me, I would very much like to start over to see if we can rekindle what we once had. I can completely understand if that is not possible, but I have decided that I should tell you what I should have sixteen years ago."

She nodded silently, her heart swelling at his words but tempered by his warning. *What secret could be so important that it would affect their relationship so long ago? What could have caused him to act against his nature and abandon her?* She had always known that he loved her and, even after their break, had never really believed otherwise. It was why it had been so maddening.

For thirty minutes, he talked, hardly taking a breath. Mary sat listening, a sense of wonder and worry filling her. Finally, he stopped speaking and waited, like a man on trial in the pause before the verdict is read.

Mary spoke, breaking the moment. "So, you're saying that the world might end in four and a half years and that you were chosen by an alien AI when you were a teenager to prepare so that we, as a species, might survive?" He nodded. "And the reason you couldn't be with me is that you wanted me to live a life without those worries. Where you could go off to make a world government, become the President, make spaceships, exosuits, and AIs?"

"Yeah, sounds kinda crazy, right?"

"No," she said. "It makes a surprising amount of sense."

"Really?" he asked, his mouth falling open.

"Oh, don't get me wrong, Nick," she said. "You were a complete and utter fucking idiot."

He gave a half-hearted snort. "I have been told that before."

She nodded in agreement. "It definitely sounds crazy, but I can't imagine anything less than the end of the world that would have made you do what you did to me."

At her words, his face fell into his hands. "I'm so sorry. It was the biggest mistake of my life, and if I could go back and give up all of this, even if the Silfe were to win, I would. Damn the consequences. I would have lived my life with you as long and well as possible."

Mary sat silently for just a moment, letting the emotions swirl in a maelstrom in her chest, before leaning forward to put her arms around the man she had never stopped loving. Her own tears falling onto his back.

They sat like that for a time, silently enjoying the moment together. Then Nick sat up, tears still streaking his face. She reached up and wiped them away. Mary took his face in her hands and leaned forward slowly to kiss him. "Never again," she said. "We are in this together until the end."

She watched as the eyes she knew so well lit up.

He nodded. "No matter what, for as long as the world lasts." Then he leaned back in and kissed her again.

TWENTY-NINE

MIT, Cambridge Massachusetts
One and a half years later: Three Years,
22 days until the invasion

D r. Jeff Spanoli was content. He was doing science and playing with cool shit. He looked down at the console attached to a boxlike structure. On the side was the logo for Warren Industries, from which the absolute coolest of the cool shit came. He looked at a curved monitor with multiple windows, some with scrolling numbers that changed second to second, grinning.

The FTL telescope was the most recent invention coming out of the Warren industries' magic cauldron. The machine used the destabilizing effect of a fusion reactor on space-time to create a micro-wormhole.

The wormhole's size, mass sent through, and the distances traveled depended on energy expenditure. Unfortunately, it was logarithmic. So, sending anything larger than electrons through was out of reach.

BUT, and it was quite a large but, one *could* send particles through and receive them. The big brains over at Warren had made faster-than-light communications a reality. Open a micro-wormhole from where you were to where you wanted your message to go and send through a series of low mass particles in a pattern. Or better yet, light. Light is made of photons, and photons have *no* mass. So, it was possible to send them through the wormhole without destabilizing it.

Any astronomer could see the applications from there. What would happen if you could open a wormhole out in space, light-years from Earth? Would you be able to collect enough light to see what was on the other side? Essentially, move your perspective closer to what you wanted to observe. Instead of building ever-larger telescopes, you could make tiny ones closer to what you wanted to see.

So was born the FTL telescope or Fscope, as everyone had immediately started calling it. Oh, he supposed, since it used light, the title was a misnomer. Still, semantics aside, it was the most exciting thing to happen to the field of astronomy... ever.

Spanoli had learned more about the universe in the past six months using the Fscope than he had in all his previous years of academia. Astronomers worldwide -the scopes were distributed free, to major universities in the World Commission member countries- couldn't keep up with the discoveries happening every day. It had gotten so bad that they didn't even bother publishing. Instead, everyone used a central online bulletin board as a clearinghouse. It felt like a dating app, but instead of swiping left or right, the scientific community was looking for meaning in the cosmos.

He rubbed his hands together and gave a low chuckle. It was all his for the next eight glorious hours. He was one of twelve researchers at the MIT Kavli Institute who took turns operating the device twenty-four hours a day. They had widely disparate interests, but all were leaders in their respective fields.

Spanoli's specialty was deep space. He was somewhat unique in his study of the void between the solar systems. Where others saw the emptiness of space, he saw a calm pool with an occasional ripple. It was a lot like fishing. Some people would prefer a lake teeming with small trout. They would hook one after another and enjoy a day of constant excitement. Others would rather go after the Big one. They could sit calmly for hours, waiting for some monster of the depths to find their hook. Most of his colleagues were in a large boat, fish jumping around them. They sought the sexy stuff. New planets, moons, black holes, and the like, but Spanoli was a trophy hunter. Every stray particle he found in the deep black was a major catch. They tied the universe together, and he felt the particles were the key to a deeper understanding of the physical laws governing existence.

Today he was hunting again. He typed in the command to send a micro-wormhole to a distance a little less than three light-years sunward, to a place *between*. He leaned forward to take in the readings.

There were many ways to use the Fscope. His colleagues generally used the light aperture setting, trying to see physical objects in the visible spectrum. He always *knew* there wouldn't be anything visible, so he rarely bothered. Instead, he opened the largest wormhole he could and waited for a hit, which could be any small particle that found its way to his sensors. Typically, this was a slow, meticulous process. He would wait patiently, usually finding nothing, then move the wormhole repeatedly, increasing his chances.

Not today. A red-bordered window surprised the astronomer as it popped onto his screen, noting an enormous hit of gamma rays. His brow furrowed as he read the graph. "That can't be right." The readings were just this side of a red dwarf, and he knew that there was no red dwarf anywhere close to where the micro-wormhole had emerged. *Could it have come out somewhere else?* Spanoli tweaked the settings and changed the sensors to visible light. Anything that would give that much radiation would have to be detectable in the visual spectrum.

He waited as the system moved the wormhole to collect light from different angles. He understood it was a bit like a CT scanner. In a CT series of x-rays sent through the body, having variable penetration depending on density. Then a computer reconstituted the image. In a Fscan, light hit a photosensitive plate that transmitted to the computer's software, rebuilding it. By moving the wormholes and getting light from variable angles, a 3D image generated, giving clues to size and composition.

It often took a few minutes for an image to reconstitute, so he stood and went where a coffee pot bubbled. Thankfully, the person before him had made a fresh pot. Sighing contentedly, he loaded a cup with milk and sugar and turned back to the computer as a chime sounded, signaling the scan was complete. He sat back down, clicking on the icon for the image.

Spanoli took a sip of coffee. The screen went black for a moment before lighting up again, showing... He spit his coffee out, soiling the front of his shirt. "What the HELL!"

THIRTY

*Deep Space- approximately
2.7 light years from Earth*
One week later: 3 years, 15 days until the invasion

"Chief Slayer Tetukken, we are monitoring another micro-wormhole formation forward of the fleet."

Tetukken leaned forward, giving a growl that made the bridge crew cringe in terror. His scarred face won in 100 battles, shifted into the Silfe version of a smile. He was pleased. It was good that his underlings feared him. After all, he was the supreme commander of 10,000 ships. Each full of Silfe warriors, attempting to exert dominance and seeking their place in the hierarchy before reaching the next conquest world.

This Earth where they headed possessed advanced technology. The Silfe had never encountered another species, besides the hated Harrow, that possessed the ability to create wormholes. It bespoke a level of technical knowledge that might constitute a challenge for the fleet.

He wasn't upset, though. Instead, he had prayed long and hard to Karoken, the Silfe deity, in thanks for this unexpected windfall. He, Tetukken, would lead the greatest battle in history! The horde would sweep down upon the Earth and reign destruction. It would be a conquest that the

Priestesses of Karoken would sing about for a thousand years!

He gestured one clawed hand to his communications officer. "Send the following message in the language of Earth to the nearest wormhole.

"We are the Chosen of Karoken and the supreme mortal beings in the universe. We are coming to destroy you. Prepare as you will, for we welcome those who would battle us. Seeking glory in battle is to worship the one true God. Do not bargain, for no bargain will be made, no quarter given. One of us will be victorious, and the other will sing our praises to Karoken in the final prayer. End message."

Tetukken sounded a low, throaty hiss of amusement. Let the Earthlings hear his words and tremble!

THIRTY-ONE

The Oval Office
The next day: 3 years, 14 days until the invasion

"You ready for this?" David asked, patting Nick on the shoulder.

"Not really," the President of the United States said.

"Don't worry, Nick," Cindy said. "Just get the general message out. Then David, Jake, and I can take it from there." She gave him a reassuring smile, which made Nick more nervous. When Cindy tuned into someone else's nerves, it meant they were coming off them in palpable waves.

"I got it," he said, "But thanks."

"Yeah, no worries," David said with a grin. "Just the biggest speech of your life, recorded and played again and again for the next 1000 years. It might as well be The Gettysburg Address, I Have a Dream, and A Day that Will Live in Infamy, all rolled up into one- on steroids."

Cindy glared at the little man. "You are not helping."

Nick was amazed that she hadn't slugged him. If David had made a comment like that when they were teens, he would have been rubbing his shoulder while protesting the injustice. He had to admit that his friends' relationship had a few positive side effects.

"Well," he said, "If people are still around 1000 years

from now to analyze my speech, we will have done our jobs. I think that would be a best-case scenario."

The head of the video crew, set up on the opposite side of the office, spoke. "Mr. President, we are live in one minute."

Nick nodded and rolled his shoulders. He looked at his two friends. "It's time." David shook his hand, and Cindy kissed him on the cheek before moving off to the side, out of the camera's angle.

He sat behind the large wooden desk and took a couple of deep breaths to center himself. *This is it.* All the years of planning in secret were about to be over. After today, the entire planet would know that the Silfe were coming. The question was whether it would unify the world or tear it apart. His work with foreign leaders and the creation of the World Commission was to prepare for this day.

He wished Mary could be with him, but she had her own duties. She was in Geneva to meet with the World Health Organization to discuss closing the many health gaps in the third world. It had been her major social agenda item as First Lady. Despite missing her, it was fortuitous. She could work with the WHO to distribute a worldwide system of medical triage sites needed for the invasion.

He couldn't help but smile. Even though everything was about to go crazy, he was at peace with his life and the decisions that led him to this moment.

It had only taken him a month after reconnecting with Mary for him to propose. Their story of long-lost love had taken the world by storm, seeming to humanize him to the nation. David and Gloria had a field day arranging their wedding. It had been an all-out Gala, with leaders from around the world attending. Yet, all he remembered was Mary as she walked down the aisle towards him. It was an image that would last to his dying day.

He shook off his thoughts as the crew director pointed to him and held up her fingers. "Ten seconds," she said. She put down one finger at a time, saying "nine...eight...seven...six..."

before going silent and pointing towards him.

Nick looked straight into the camera. "My fellow Americans and people of the world. I am here to lay to rest the rumors circulating over the past week. These have sprung from the many institutions around the world who have utilized the FTL telescopes to further astronomic research." He paused, letting his words sink in.

"The rumors state that a vast alien fleet of ships is approximately three light-years from our solar system and that they are on a direct trajectory towards the Earth." He stopped, his eyes burning with intensity. "I am here tonight to tell you that the rumors are true."

Nick heard one of the camera crew gasp before being silenced by the director, whose eyes had gone wide at his announcement.

He smiled and pointed off-camera. "The reaction of one of the fine people filming tonight is probably the same one that all of you at home are having. Many of you are saying something like, 'That can't be true,' or 'It all must be a mistake.' I am here to say that it is NOT a mistake. After first being discovered by MIT researcher Dr. Jeffery Spanoli, one of the leading experts on deep space, the findings were confirmed by every single FTL telescope across the entire planet."

Nick frowned. "For any of you conspiracy theorists out there, I would ask you to explain how literally hundreds of different top-notched institutions across the same number of countries were duped at the same time." He paused, and his eyes hardened. "The answer is that they can't. I will not have the nay-sayers stop the world from accepting the truth, and that truth is aliens exist, and they are coming here."

He stopped, taking a sip from a glass of water on the table, a deliberate action to allow people at home the chance to let the revelations sink in. He cleared his throat and continued.

"Unfortunately, this is not the only news that I have to share with you tonight. Our scientists have been monitoring the ships since discovery. Yesterday, we received a message from their commander. In short, the communication suggests that the aliens are a xenophobic race coming here to destroy us. They refuse to negotiate and state we should prepare for battle."

Nick placed a hand over his heart. "There can be no mistake. The alien fleet that is approaching the solar system is hostile. We, the entirety of humanity, are at war. A war for survival itself." His eyes glinted with steel, his voice going down slightly in a growl.

"If one species is to survive, it will be us. We did not ask for this conflict, but it is coming to us whether or not we wish it. Humanity is strong, especially when we work together. The past decade has shown us what we can accomplish when we stop fighting each other and work toward common goals. I have called an emergency meeting of the World Commission to discuss preparations for war. The United States will fully commit its resources to this end."

Should we lose, all is lost. So, I ask that you work together for your children, your family, your nation, and the Earth itself. We have time to prepare." He paused, his eyes blazing with passion. "We will prepare, we will fight, and we will win!"

BOOK 2

New York Times Editorial

Headline: Three Months Until the Invasion, Where Are We?

I'm not telling anyone anything they don't already know, but the aliens will arrive in three months. I know what you're saying- WE KNOW! How could anyone *not* at this point?

Just over three years ago, Chancellor Strombold gave his famous speech, energizing the world into preparing for the alien threat. Nations came together, pooling their resources. The giant orbital defense stations, colloquially called Death Star-1 (DS-1) and Death Star-2 (DS-2), were brought into orbit. Hundreds of millions of our young men and women volunteered to join the World Commission Defense Force.

Some in the WCDF were called to pilot the ever-expanding fleet of warships and Gunstars, while others learned to wear exosuits like a second skin. Still more worked to build and stock underground shelters to house the non-combatant population. Those that were not eligible for the WCDF were instead inducted into their own nation's militia, preparing to hold fixed positions and protect the bunkers.

Again, not telling you anything you don't know, but I wanted to take this moment to celebrate what we have accomplished. It makes the building of the pyramids, landing on the moon, and even sending out an interstellar colony ship seem paltry and simple by comparison.

We have all been so *busy* these past three years that no one seems to have stopped to smell the proverbial roses. After all, how could we? Our farmers were too busy providing food for the WCDF, our fleets in space and for storage in the bunkers. Very few flowers have been grown.

I'm not complaining. It seems like smelling the roses is secondary when the future of our species is on the line. I have felt the pressure to use my voice to help the war effort, and I believe I delivered. I think that in a small way, I have informed and educated. I have been a cog in a vast machine.

It's just that as we enter these last months, I think that every human being should take a moment, speak to those they love, and perhaps smell a flower or two. We are about to go into a battle where the outcome is still uncertain, and it is time to remember what we are fighting for. For me, in a year's time, I want to be in my garden, with a cup of tea in one hand and a book in the other, with the smell of roses in the air. What is it you will fight for?

-Sarah Sintenta, Editor in Chief

THIRTY-TWO

The Plaza Hotel
3 months until the invasion

"All of this planning, the late nights, the stress- I can't believe it is finally here!" David said. "I'm not ready... I... I... feel like I am going to throw up!"

Nick let out a burst of laughter. "Dude, you're just getting married, not facing the Silfe. Maybe you should take a deep breath and remember why you're doing it in the first place; it was your idea."

"I know, I know," he said, not calming. "Say something helpful! I'm freaking out here!"

Nick turned to Jake. "You want to take a swing at this one?"

Jake, resplendent in his deep black WCDF admiral's uniform, gave Nick a conspiratorial smile. "Maybe we should give David back some of the *outstanding* advice we received on our wedding days."

Nick nodded sagely. "I think that's a wonderful idea." He put his finger to his chin, tapping lightly. "Let me see. I believe when Mary and I got married, he said something like, 'A man doesn't know what happiness is until he's married. By then, it's too late.'"

"Hey!" David said, "That gem of wisdom is from Frank

Sinatra, Old Blue Eyes himself!"

"Sinatra was married four times," Nick said.

"Yeah, but he stayed married to the fourth one for like twenty years."

"I'm not sure that is the model we are shooting for," Jake said. "I believe you told me that 'It was good I was getting married in the morning. That way, if it didn't work out, Jane wouldn't have wasted the whole day.' Really reassuring, man. It was just what I needed to hear on my wedding day."

"Oh, come on!" David said. "That one was from Mickey Rooney!" His eyes widened in realization. "Oh, my god! Rooney was married eight times!" He looked at both of his friends, who were smiling widely. "I believe I have just had an epiphany! I'm terrible at being a groomsman!"

Nick chuckled. "Yes, David, you absolutely are."

"The worst," Jake agreed. "But we," He gestured back and forth between Nick and himself, "Are not."

David's face took on a quizzical look. "Why? All you did was give me shit about my groomsman ineptitude."

"Exactly," Nick said. "And... how do you feel?"

David looked surprised momentarily before his lips split in his typical Cheshire grin. "Pretty damn good, actually!"

"See," Nick said. "Some grooms need coddling; some need a stiff drink. You, however," he clapped the small man on the shoulder, "Need someone to give you shit."

David whistled. "Jeeze, you guys should give classes on this stuff."

"Maybe after we beat the Silfe," Jake said. "I, for one, am planning a long vacation on some deserted beach with Jane."

The mention of Silfe seemed to put a mild damper on the conversation until Jake spoke again. "I am proud of you, David. You and Cindy both."

"Why?"

"Because despite everything, the war, the uncertain future, you are willing to live your life. Stand up in front of everyone you care about and commit to the person you love."

"Well, you are the mold for that, golden boy. You and Jane are like a recruiting poster for married life."

Jake gave him a wink. "Oh, I don't know; I think that you and Cindy will be on the front page of every newspaper in the world tomorrow, even with the impending invasion. I don't think I'm the only one who sees it as a sign of hope."

The groom shook his head. "Dude! You are the sappiest admiral I have ever heard of."

Nick laughed. "OK, tiger, you look like you are feeling better." He walked up to the groom and straightened his tie. "Now, are you ready to get married?"

David's smile went a bit sickly, then firmed. "Absofuckinglutely!" He walked to the door, gesturing to his two friends to follow. "Come on; you two are gonna make me late to my own wedding with your jabbering. Let's do this!"

Nick and David smiled at each other and shrugged, following the little man out the door.

THIRTY-THREE

Just outside the Solar System
1 month until the invasion

Chief Slayer Tetukken looked down into the pit with a toothy grin. The fight was savage today. A smaller female and large male were circling each other slowly. Already, the female had taken a raking claw across her shoulder, which bled freely. She also appeared to be limping slightly from a blow to one muscled thigh received during the first exchange.

To the untrained eye, it appeared the fight was all but over. The male towered over the injured combatant, obviously savoring his victory before the final blow.

Tetukken wasn't fooled. This female was clever. She had left her side open to the attack but purposefully moved to take the blow on the shoulder. The limp was also affected. A true limp would have been more pronounced on the backstep when she could not counterbalance with her tail.

With his strength and reach advantage, the male had most of the physical advantages in the fight. Only with speed and guile could the female prevail. Tetukken leaned in to see if it would be enough.

The larger combatant finally tired of his grandstanding to the hooting and growling spectators. He turned to the apparently defeated female and called out, "You will kneel before me and accept me as your commander for the glory of Karoken!"

The ritual question was complete, and all waited to see if the female would accept.

Silfe ways were not for the mild-hearted. All interactions outside of close mated pairs were battles. Every Silfe strove to worship Karoken in conflict, but the book of Karoken said that "The faithful must work together to eradicate lesser beings from the world." The meeting of those two seemingly contradictory concepts created Silfe culture.

All strove, yet when another beat them, they were to tuck their tail and accept that ultimately there was a greater calling than dominating others of their species. They were all the Chosen of Karoken, and warriors were needed for his great work. Still, the need to win at all costs was a genetic trait that sometimes could not be overcome. Should someone lose in the pits and not capitulate to their opponents, claws would rip the life from them in the final prayer.

It had always been this way and would continue until they cleansed the last planet and eradicated all sentient life from the universe or were themselves destroyed.

Tetukken looked back at the contest below. The winner would lead a strike force of a thousand. Only the strongest could demand the respect of young warriors, so the pit's fights continued around the clock on every horde ship. He made it a habit to spend some time here each day, especially as they grew closer to their target. He wanted to inspire his underlings with his overwhelming presence and power; Tetukken, the legendary warrior and leader of the purge of Earth.

His attention focused on the pit as a howling growl of disapproval rang from the spectators. The female had signaled that she would not kneel. Instead, she made the Sign of Karoken; one razor-tipped claw to her own throat. He barely contained his own growl of surprise. The Sign was a request for a fight to the death. The crowd seemed to hold their breath as they waited for the large male to make his decision.

Karoken's Sign was rarely seen in the pits. The purpose of the fights was to determine the stronger, not to strip the Silfe of their brightest, most promising warriors. Mistakes happened. A stray claw hitting an artery before the medics could intercede, or a too-strong blow to the head. Deaths occurred in fights where each warrior strove at their maximum, but invoking the Sign guaranteed the final prayer. It usually meant some story behind the scenes, such as an unforgivable personal slight.

In the end, the male could do nothing but return it. He would lose his position should he forfeit and bend his knee. He raised a claw to his own throat to promise Karoken that either his or his enemy's blood would flow.

Tetukken hissed in disappointment. A true warrior knew when to make a tactical retreat. Ferocity was part of being Silfe, but so was guile. The female had put her opponent in a blind corner from which he could not retreat. He should have realized that she would never make the Sign, should she doubt the outcome. All that had come before, the exchange, accepting the wound, the limp, was all part of an elaborate ruse to lull her opponent into false confidence.

The male roared and charged at her injured side, the pit sand geysering up from his clawed feet. The female waited, calmly poised on her large toe claws, bouncing slightly, intelligent eyes locked onto the rushing warrior whose teeth and claws spelled her death.

At the last moment, she kicked off, flying to the side of her faked limp, and raked her toe claws across the vulnerable abdomen of the male, likely deep enough to gouge internal organs. The male took a few more stumbling steps before falling forward and rolling to a stop. The spectators roared with surprised glee at seeing the female take him down.

The male rolled to his feet with a pained growl, one hand holding his freely bleeding abdomen. In a typical contest, she would ask him to kneel. The wound was grievous, but not beyond the medics' capabilities. However, the Sign of Karoken was in play. Instead, he wobbled slightly before lifting his head to the ceiling and roaring. The sound made by a mortally wounded warrior promising Karoken that they would not go alone into the final prayer. A promise to take their enemy with them.

Tetukken approved. Even if his mind was not quick enough to keep up with the female, the male was strong. He would have made an excellent commander for a shock group. The Chief Slayer almost wished he could save him, but the Sign was given. The male's fate was sealed as soon as it was returned, even if he hadn't realized it.

The wounded Silfe finished his roar and charged. This time, his speed was not enough to make any difference. The female whipped to the side and then climbed his back, her weight driving him into the dirt. She reached a clawed hand under his neck and then waited for a five-count, holding him prone to prove her dominance, before her claws ripped out his throat in a spray of blood. The crowd, which had gone silent as she held the much larger male down, roared in exultation as she held her bloody claw up in the air, extended to better offer the final prayer of the fallen.

Tetukken growled his approval before turning to his assistant, staring wide-eyed at the spectacle below. "Sakaaen, you will bring the female below to my ready room after the evening meal."

Sakaaen's eyes widened in surprise by the request, but he recovered quickly, lowering his snout in subservience to the Chief Slayer. "Of course, Slayer, as you wish."

Tetukken grunted in acknowledgment. The female was interesting. He would know the full story of the battle he had witnessed. Perhaps the command of 1000 was too small for one so full of trickery. He needed such in his command, but first, he would need to test her metal. His toothy grin made his assistant take a half-step back in fear. The reaction only made Tetukken's grin wider.

THIRTY-FOUR

Geneva, Switzerland
Same day: 1 month until the invasion

"It's confirmed, Chancellor, the aliens have started their deceleration. They will come to a full stop somewhere outside of Pluto."

Nickolas Strombold, the Chancellor of the World Commission, and preeminent leader of the human race, nodded. "So they will collect their forces and then enter together."

"It appears so," Hans Guenter, the chief astrophysicist for the World Commission, said. "It is as you predicted."

Hans's face pinched. He knew Nick was getting outside information from somewhere, and it didn't please him. He was one of the most lauded astrophysicists in the world, and his ability to worry a question until the facts presented themselves was part of what had made him so good at his job. Guenter was also -in Nick's opinion- a complete ass. He wasn't a man who could be trusted with the full story of the Silfe invasion, including HAL's existence.

Nick nodded again, leaving the scientist's unspoken questions unanswered. "Thank you, Dr. Guenter. Now that we are sure, it is time to make some plans." He shook the man's hand. "Please alert me immediately if there are any changes in the aliens' trajectory."

"I will," the scientist said, frowning and seeing the dismissal for what it was.

Nick watched the man's stiff shouldered walk out of the office before touching an intercom on his desk, saying, "Bruce, can you hold all further calls and meetings? I will be off the grid for the next hour. I'll let you know when I am free again."

He clicked on his holographic projector and spoke to the air. "Gloria, is Jake free for a talk?"

Gloria's beautiful face appeared, hovering over his desk. The AI gave him a dazzling smile. "Yes, he should be between meetings."

"Where is he, anyway?" Nick asked.

"On Mars, checking the laser emplacements on Olympus Mons."

The closer they got to the invasion, the greater the pressure on his friend. Jake -Admiral Jacob Swelton, was the highest-ranking officer in the World Commission Navy. Nick hadn't even had to appoint him. After the WCDF became the Earth's official joint military force, a mad shuffle occurred to fill out the ranks. The WCN was already in existence, so officers who had commissions were automatically promoted in grade and tasked with filling in the Table of Organization, and Equipment. Jake was already the highest-ranking officer, given his activities with the Mars mission. He was also the Secretary of Defense of the United States, with the requisite political experience, so the World Commission Congress had confirmed him for the top spot. It also likely helped that he was one of the most famous men in the world.

According to David, Jacob Swelton was a walking-talking recruiting poster. Pablo ,who had the most extensive calculating capabilities outside of HAL, said that having him lead the WCDF had increased recruitment by over forty percent. Whether or not Jake wanted to admit it, he was a hero to many. It was probably *because* of his humility that he was so popular.

Gloria's face disappeared, to be replaced by the haggard face of his friend. "He looked up from working on a tablet and gave him a weak smile. "Nick, what do I owe the pleasure? It's been a while."

It seemed Nick wasn't the only one blowtorching the candle from both ends. "I just got confirmation on the Silfe. They continue to decelerate and will gather just outside of Pluto."

"Good, it will be Plan One, then."

"Looks like it. You'll need to sucker the ships past the defenses and try to get them to commit." He raised his eyebrows in question. "I suppose you know how to do that?"

"Yes, we've gamed it out. Admiral Lin's first fleet will be the bait." His smile faltered. "You know we will need to commit a lot of forces before we can switch it up, right? We can't keep them from Earth; we don't have enough forces for a full blockade and are going to lose a lot of people."

"I know," Nick said. "There isn't any other way. Despite our preparations, we still don't know if it will be enough." He took in Jake's resigned, tired face, seeing that he was more worried than he should have been, given that the PLAN was proceeding about as well as they could expect. "Rose and Joselyn passed, didn't they?" He asked.

Jake sagged. "They did, both with a perfect score. They finished the accelerated OCS course and shipped out a few weeks ago." He took a long, deep breath, trying to steady his voice. "They had their choice of postings. Rose is part of the 3rd Risa Gunstar Squadron, and Joselyn is in the 202nd exosuit company... on DS-2."

It took all of Nick's skills as a lifelong politician not to flinch. Rose and Joselyn couldn't have picked more dangerous assignments. DS-1 and 2, the giant asteroids originally Themas and Doris, were hundreds of miles in diameter. They were placed in Earth's orbit opposite one another to limit approaches and control the orbitals.

Still, there would be spots where determined attackers

could get through. The entire concept for the defense of Earth was to delay and whittle down the Silfe fleet until hidden reserves could knock them out. They wanted the Silfe to believe that if they could get past defenses, even at great cost, they would win. HAL assured them that Silfe warriors would commit suicide missions if it would clear the way for their brethren to conquer a planet. That was what they wanted. The defense planners gave obvious targets slated to snipe at the enemy. If they did enough damage, it would stretch the aliens' resources.

DS-1 and DS-2 were targets *designed* to be attacked. The two stations controlled the orbitals. Any alien troops that landed on Earth would be at the mercy of the lasers and rail guns set into the rock, like old-time murder holes in a medieval castle.

The asteroids themselves were so massive that no weapon the Silfe carried could shoot them down. The only way to conquer them was to infiltrate and disable them from the inside, requiring cleaning out tens of thousands of World Commission Marines. The stations were a warren of traps and ambush points designed to bleed the Silfe for every inch. It would be an abattoir of death, and Jake's daughter Joselyn would be in the middle of it.

One might think being part of the Risa squadron would be better, but they would be mistaken. The Gunstar squadron's mission was to harry the enemy constantly, distract, and make hit-and-run attacks on the flanks of the alien fleet. The moon had hidden landing zones and bunkers, many of which were connected underground. A pilot could go in at one place and come out two hundred miles away. It would be like the Rock of Gibraltar, with pilots flying out, mission after mission, until their luck ran out or the enemy prevailed.

Jake shook his head. "Part of me is proud, while the other is terrified. You can't believe how tempted I was to pull rank and have them placed ground-side guarding pallets deep in some bunker, as far away from the Silfe as possible." He sighed in a defeated way. "They are eighteen and adults. The only thing that stopped me from doing something stupid was remembering what I would have done at their age."

Nick understood. Jake's twins had always been precocious, and he knew his friend loved them with all of his heart. Despite his frequent deployments and absences, Jake and his wife Jane had raised two bright, independent young women. It didn't surprise him they aced the WCDF Placement Tests. They were precisely the kind of young people the world needed. He tried for a reassuring smile. "You would have done the same thing, no matter what anyone said."

Deciding to change the subject, Nick asked, "And what is Jane up to?"

Jake's face lit up. "She is the senior administrator for the Warren Industries New York Bunker.

"Really?" Nick said. "I hadn't heard that."

"Yeah," he said with a proud smile. "Gloria needed a flesh and blood person to manage the scientists in the bunker complex, someone who was fully in on the PLAN."

Nick nodded, understanding coming to him. After telling Mary, he felt it was only fair for Jake to come clean to Jane. In hindsight, it had been past due. She hadn't even blinked an eye when Jake told her of the PLAN, as she already knew. Hints and clues had been everywhere, clear to her analytical eye. She was the child of an Air Force general and appreciated need-to-know, so it had never bothered her that there were things not discussed at home. She simply asked, 'What can I do?' Since then, Jane had been a big help with coordination and working with the AIs.

"I don't envy her," Jake said. "Getting the eggheads at Warren all pointed in the same direction is like herding cats."

"I thought Stony was in charge of that?" Nick said, referring to the former boy genius, who had now turned into a terrifying young man. "He seemed to have a special talent for it."

Jake laughed. "Stony signed up for the WCN.

Commander Wendel Flint is now the chief engineer on Psyche."

"You're kidding me?"

"Nope," Jake said with a grin. "We didn't bring him fully in on the PLAN, but Cindy introduced him to Pablo and everything he can do."

"Wow!" Nick said, both impressed and slightly worried. "How did that go?" Psyche was still a closely held secret, even among the leaders of the WCDF. It was their trump card. The massive metallic asteroid was analogous to the Musashi, the seventy-ton Japanese battleship of WWII. Damage that could take down any other ship would be mosquito bites. The key was to use it right. Should they bring it to bear at the proper time, it might be the difference, but it was slow. If enough ships concentrated upon it, it would be overwhelmed. After all, the concentrated fire of the Allies sank the supposedly indestructible Musashi.

Jake grinned, almost as if he could hear Nick's inner dialogue. "You know Stony. The man hardly even blinked. Just started asking about Pablo's take on tweaking the ion drives to get a few more g's out of the engines."

"That is a pair made in heaven..." he frowned, "Or hell, if I have ever heard one," Nick said.

"Let's hope it is hell on the Silfe."

THIRTY-FIVE

Outside the Solar System
Two weeks until the invasion

Reaper Sketaanen was content. In the past two weeks, she had jumped three ranks from battle leader to Reaper, In charge of 10,000 ground troops. It was beyond her wildest dreams. She would have thought to need another two conquests and multiple trips to the pits to win the position, but that was before her fight to the death with Battle Leader Trakken.

Trakken was an incompetent who thought that size and strength also made him a brilliant tactician, yet in one battle simulation after another, their 1000 was defeated. She knew if they were to give a proper prayer to Karoken, to provide him with the human blood he desired, she would need to do something.

Trakken laughed when she announced her challenge. He called her 'Little one,' like some newly hatched infant who couldn't hunt for itself. Her anger was immense, enough to want to dig out his eyes with her fore claws. It was what he wanted. Outside of the pits, any fighting was severely punished. Discipline among the Silfe was harsh. To strike a superior was to be sentenced to dishonorable death without battle, where Karoken would not heed the final prayer.

She relied on Trakken's sense of superiority to see her through. The loser of their contest would become adjutant per the Silfe cultural rules, but she couldn't allow that. Trakken was an idiot, yet he had a strong following among the cohort with other large males who saw him as an example of the ideal warrior.

She wanted her 1000 to be the best, and it couldn't be with Trakken involved. So she goaded him, made him overconfident, then trapped him with the Sign of Karoken. She saw the realization in his eyes when she signaled, but his pride could do nothing but commit. Had he been able to concede, she would have accepted him as her adjutant, but he could not. She felt completely at peace with his death. At least it had come in battle, and Karoken would welcome his final prayer- even if it were from an idiot.

She felt proud of her machinations, right up to receiving the summons from Chief Slayer Tetukken. She almost tucked her tail at the thought of being brought before the legendary Slayer. Tetukken was one of the most respected fighters in history, with more deaths by his claws than any ten others.

Silfe could live several hundred years, but each sought the final prayer in conflict. One of the olangees, the warrior scientists who invented and maintained the weaponry of the soldier class, might find Karoken's grace without direct battle. Their standing with God was from the amount of death caused through them, but for a soldier, it was an insult to Karoken to die of age or infirmity.

Tetukken had lived through eight separate planetary cleansings even though he always sought the hottest battle, the place where the hundreds, the thousands, gave up the final prayers. He was a force on the battlefield, or even in a fighter, in the black of space.

She still shuddered at the memory of being led before him. It was all she could do not to kneel and show her throat. His scales had taken on the deep, almost black sheen of a Warrior past their second century of life, something she had only seen in the most senior olangees. The scars of his battles riddled his snout, arms, and tail.

Tetukken's physical form was not much larger than hers, but there was an energy, a threat of body that was felt if not qualified in any specific way. She fought her instinct to acknowledge his superiority, instead putting a clawed fist to her breast just below her neck in a thump and growled out, "Battle Leader Sketaanen reporting as ordered, Slayer."

Tetukken waited for just a moment longer than was usual, looking at her from head to toe, noting every shift in stance and the glint in her eyes before bringing his fist to mid-chest.

She looked at him in confusion. The Slayer had just saluted her as a Reaper, bringing his fist fully three claws higher than her position should merit.

The Chief Slayer gave a growl of amusement. "I see my actions confuse you, but even as you tremble with the need to tuck your tail, you keep your wits about you. Good. Rest yourself," he said and pointed to a set of leaning poles.

This had made her more unwary than the salute. Taking her ease in front of a superior, much less the Chief Slayer, was unusual, reserved only for close confidants or trusted subordinates. In Silfe culture, one was always prepared for battle, and giving up a fighting balance was off-putting unless you were sure of your environment. Still, she did not doubt that Tetukken could kill her without trouble. So, in that way, she *was* sure. Sketaanen was at his whim, and should he decide that today was to be her final prayer, there was little she could do to stop it.

Her body loosened with the realization, and she moved leisurely to the elaborately carved leaning post, wrapping her tail around it as if she was in her quarters.

Tetukken took in her relaxed pose with another growl of humor and began speaking. "Since your fight in the pits, I have been investigating you. Your 1000 has been underperforming." He waited for her to deny it but was met only by a clench of her jaw.

"I see," the Slayer said, as if she had just given him a full readiness report. "It seems likely that performance should improve now." Tetukken had purposefully avoided speaking of her former commander. Trakken's final prayer had been honorable, if stupid.

"Yes, I believe that performance will improve significantly," she said.

"Good," Tetukken replied. "However, you will need to turn over command to your adjutant."

"Slayer?" she said in question. She wasn't sure where this was going, though being given the Reaper's salute had given her a clue. She doubted it had been a mistake. Tetukken looked as if every moment of his life was controlled and calculated, much like her own.

"Yes," the Slayer said, revealing his back teeth in an amused expression. "I am promoting you to Reaper, in control of the 2nd Special Operations 10,000."

She growled out in surprise. To be put in charge of 10,000 was a great honor, but control of one of the Special Operations groups was her greatest wish come true! They were the elite warriors, every one of them having distinguished themselves in at least one cleansing.

She had done well enough in the last campaign to warrant a position in the Special Operations group herself, but had turned it down to keep her leadership position. Still, Sketaanen had done nothing to warrant such a massive leap in rank. She thought that if she could get through one or two more cleansings with distinction, she might have a chance at something like this, but now?

"I see that I have surprised you," Tetukken said. "I saw something in the pit which cannot be taught. You saw weakness, and you exploited it. You did it for the betterment of your 1000, putting your final prayer on the line to accomplish your goals. I have reviewed your accomplishments from the last planet. While in control of your 100, you used the lives of your warriors with intelligence and wit."

His yellow eyes were piercing. "We do not speak of it much among the newer warriors, but those who have come through several cleansings all have one thing in common. We know that even though all true warriors seek the final prayer in battle, Karoken's mission is all. We must not seek our prayer without intelligence. Karoken gave us minds, even as he gave us claws. Each is deadly in its way, but the mind is better by far."

Sketaanen clenched her jaw in agreement. She once had been a mindless warrior, trying to rip out her enemy's throats at all costs, but with age and experience, she had changed. It was simple math. Should she preserve her warriors, they could kill more of the enemy; the more claws to rip, the more blood to spill.

"I agree with you, Slayer," she said.

"Yes, I know you do." Tetukken gave her a look that she could not decipher. "We have been observing these Earthlings. Micro-wormholes are being sent to all parts of their solar system to gather intelligence. I believe that this will be the greatest test the Chosen have faced since the Harrow."

His eyes hardened as she growled in dissent. "I see you doubt." He gave his own growl, making her tail slip on the rest, and causing him to show his teeth in amusement. "These Hu..maa...ns," he said in a soft-sounding hiss that was unnatural to the shape of his mouth and forked tongue, "Are at a level of technology that approaches our own. They have large fleets of ships and have spread to many of the moons and planets. We still have many more vessels than they do, but they have obviously been preparing for years. I suspect that the Harrow have sent one of their machines to the planet."

She made a hiss of displeasure at this revelation. "How can you be sure?" she asked.

"When we first found the planet through micro-wormhole communication signals, they were still entirely planet-bound. Since we left our last cleansing, they have gone from that state to having at least four permanent settlements in other parts of the system. It seems almost impossible that a species could grow that fast on its own." He grunted. "You have not heard the worst part. They have placed two asteroids in orbit around their home planet. They will control the orbitals unless we neutralize them."

She sucked in a whistling breath through her teeth. The fleet was vast, holding 10,000 ships, each of which carried 10,000 Silfe warriors. Not all were ground troops, but the majority were. That meant they could put a hundred million warriors on the ground. They could do this because they always had air superiority. Most planets slated for cleansing held billions of sentient beings. The Silfe could not prevail against those numbers if enough of the planet's inhabitants were adequately armed. Not if they couldn't get cover from their fighters. They relied on air assets to break defenses and allow warriors to fight in close quarters, where the Silfe were unparalleled.

Maintaining control over the orbitals was a lesson learned long ago. The Harrow used massive orbital stations to support planetary populations on their colony worlds. It was the reason that the Silfe had turned away from Harrow space. The number of Warriors needed to overcome the Harrow defenses had become untenable, taking away those required to cleanse other planets.

Some day they would return with all of their might and crush the Harrow, but that day was far in the future when the Silfe became so powerful that nothing could stand in their way.

Tetukken continued. "We will need to neutralize those orbital bases if we are to conquer the planet. That is the mission that I will assign to the 1st and 2nd Special Operations."

*****

The conversation with Tetukken was two weeks ago. Now, Sketaanen looked at the hologram of a giant asteroid spinning slowly in front of her. The olangees had monitored open communications of ships coming and going from the orbital platform. The humans referred to this one as Death Star-2. She had to admit; they named it well. It would take many deaths to secure it, but she could see some weaknesses. She growled as her mood lifted, her plan of attack firming in her mind. Karoken would receive many fine prayers from the conquering of this Death Star-2, and her name would lift along with them in the last gasping curses of her enemies!

THIRTY-SIX

The Emperor of the Moon Casino, Risa
One week until the invasion

"For Earth!" the slightly slurring man said from his position on top of the table.

The other uniformed men and women, all with the blue and silver globe of the WCN, raised their shot glasses and finished the toast in a ringing echo, "For humanity!"

Ensign Rose Swelton coughed, requiring a hit on the back by her friend and wingmate Susan Johnson. "Come on, Rosie!" She said energetically, "You can't kill Silfe if you can't hold your liquor!"

Rose gave her a deprecating look. "I don't think one depends on the other."

"Ah," Susan said. "Tale as old as time! The best fighters are also the best drinkers!" Her slightly unfocused eyes scrunched in concentration. "You know... like... pirates... and..." her face lit up with triumph, "Vikings! Yeah, those horned bastards could totally drink and then like swing axes and shit!"

Rose shook her head, a smile on her face. Susan was infectious and reminded her of her Uncle David. If she ever got the chance, she would like to put them in a room together and sit back and watch. It would be entertaining.

The short, stout, African American woman was the polar opposite of her, both physically and temperamentally. Rose was tall, blond, and willowy. She'd been told more than once that she should model, usually by guys right before she shot them down. Her personality was also much more reserved and intense.

It took a special person to get Rose to lower her guard, and she could count on one hand the people that she genuinely counted as friends. She had always been analytic and realized in her early teens that her reluctance came from growing up around some of the most famous people in the world.

Christmas at her house with Uncle David, Uncle Nick, and Aunt Cindy also included secret service agents, an armed cordon, and an army of paparazzi. That was when they didn't have Christmas at the Warren Campus or the White House. Of course, having a dad that was one of the first people to set foot on Mars, was a war hero, and headed the Earth's military, also made for an interesting childhood.

It would be enough to go to any teen's head. The weird part was that she didn't think it *had*. Rose admitted she wasn't entirely impartial, but when you took away all the trappings, the people she had grown up around were just so *normal*. Well, maybe that wasn't fair. Aunt Cindy was brilliant and a bit socially awkward. Uncle David was... Uncle David and Uncle Nick was so ridiculously handsome and charming that it took a full year to get over the teenage crush she had on him when she was fourteen.

It wasn't them who were abnormal; it was how other people reacted to them that caused the problem. That was also the problem when people found out who she was.

She couldn't imagine what it would have been like if she didn't have her twin sister, Joselyn, who was in the same boat. Of course, Joselyn would have just told anyone she didn't like to go 'Fuck themselves.' Her sibling had a certain... forwardness about her that was extremely effective. It broke her heart to be separated, but she couldn't argue that exosuits were the right choice for her. Joselyn seemed to think that she could solve most problems with people with a punch to the face. Rose liked to be more subtle. A Gunstar shooting lasers from a safe distance was more her forte.

It was always hard to trust new friends. Did they want to be with her or *near* her? It was one reason she liked Susan so much. She met her wingmate during basic training at the WCN Gunstar school in San Jose. Despite coming from completely different backgrounds, they had become fast friends. After hearing that she was, in fact, the daughter of THE Swelton, she had simply said, "Well fuck me." Then asked if she could borrow a comb and moved on as if Rose told her that her dad was a dentist. In her experience, that kind of person was rare.

Susan grew up on the mean streets of the Upper West Side in Manhattan. Her Mom and dad were both professors in the NYU math department. Susan once told her that her family was a bunch of 'Eggheads,' although she said it with affection. She described herself as the black sheep because she played sports year-round, which was an almost unforgivable sin by her family's standards. Her brothers were engineers on different *Dilong* class carriers, while her parents were doing accounting work for the New York State Militia.

A gray haired waitress tapped her on the shoulder. "Are you Rose Swelton?"

Rose let out a resigned sigh; she hated when random people recognized her. She was turning to give her patented response when they said, "The Emperor wants to see you."

Rose had to take a mental back step. "Excuse me?"

"The Emperor of the Moon wants a word," she said.

She looked to Susan, who shrugged and said, "Well fuck me," before turning taking another sip of her drink.

Rose shook her head. She really appreciated her wingmate; the woman knew how to put a situation in perspective. She stood and gestured for the server to show the way as another drunken pilot stood on yet another table and yelled, "For Earth!" The response sounded before being cut off by the sliding doors of the bar. "For Human..."

*****

Rose followed the woman through the opulent casino. The Emperor's Palace's hologram projectors simulated an evening on the science fiction paradise planet of Risa, complete with two of its three moons in the sky. She walked past gaming tables, bistros, and bars, finally reaching a set of double doors reading "Employees Only." The server looked at a camera above the door and said, "Ensign Swelton to see the Boss."

There was a slight pause, then the buzz and click of an electronic lock disengaging. The woman waved her forward. "Just follow the hall to the back, honey." She smiled, crinkling the laugh lines around her eyes.

With most people in their 20s and 30s in uniform, retired workers reentering the workforce filled most service jobs. At last estimation, only about 2% of people over the age of 16 didn't have full-time employment, and those were generally only because of illness or conditions where they *couldn't* work. It was a bit like how the US had been during WWII. From teens to grandparents, almost everyone had heard the call and raised their hand. There was nothing like an alien invasion to cure the world of its apathy.

The waitress gave her a reassuring nod and gestured her forward. "Thank you for your service," she said in parting and turned to hurry back the way she had come.

Rose walked through the double doors, which swished open at her approach. She continued forward down the hallway, a deep crimson carpet muffling her steps. As she reached its end, she stopped, standing in front of an elaborately gilded wooden door, complete with a plaque that read, *His Incredible Greatness, the Emperor of the Moon!!* She shook her head. Who in the hell would put two exclamation marks at the end of their title? Although... she pursed her lips, mind clicking. *It couldn't be.*

The door swung inward to reveal- nothing. Well, that wasn't wholly accurate. There was an elaborate desk with a set of screens in place of windows, giving the appearance of the office being high in a skyscraper, looking out over a vast alien ocean. Otherwise, the space looked like any other upscale CEO's office, complete with a small sitting area and minibar.

She was considering making herself a drink to pass the time when the screens switched from the orange sunset to pitch black. An ominous rumbling sounded, and mist swirled in from the bottom of the screens. Slowly, the figure of a cloaked man on a black throne coalesced into being.

The figure stood, flames rising around him as his booming voice echoed off the walls. "I am the Emperor of the Moon! The great and powerful! Who are YOU!"

Rose snorted. "Uncle David! You totally stole that from the Wizard of Oz!"

The figure on the screen seemed to deflate, and the smoke and flames disappeared as the cloaked man shrunk, morphing into the small skinny form of her favorite uncle.

His mouth turned down in a disappointed frown. "How did you know it was me?"

"It was the two exclamation marks after your title on the plaque outside. Inappropriate for the leader of a Nation but totally in line with something you would do." He shook his head and was about to speak, but she beat him to it. "Plus," she said, "Roselyn and I have been wondering if you were Mr. X since we were twelve."

"Really?"

"You always seem to know things that come out on Psychic Warfare before they get published. Besides, your sense of humor is distinct."

David looked like she had given him a major compliment. "Why, thank you. I have been telling your dad that since we were sixteen, but he doesn't always appreciate it."

She laughed again. Uncle David was incorrigible. "So..."

she said, "You're Mr. X and... the Emperor of Risa?"

"Yeah," he said with a little shrug, as if being the leader of one of the most profitable companies and wealthiest nations in the world was no big thing. Given that he was also the CEO and owner of Star Media *and* married to her Aunt Cindy, who had more money than God, maybe it wasn't that big a deal for him.

Rose's eyebrows rose. "It's not that I'm not happy to see you, but was there something specific that you wanted to talk about?"

David scratched the back of his neck in an uncharacteristic show of nerves. "This is totally off the record, OK?" She nodded, wondering what could make David Lieberman squirm, the man who had once given his entire White House briefing report in a *Cat in the Hat* rhyming scheme. He continued. "And you will NOT, tell your father or mother about this?" She nodded again. "OK," he said, blowing out his breath. "I want you to meet someone."

As he finished speaking, a set of vertical lines appeared in front of her in a classic *Star Trek* beam-in sequence, finally forming into the petite figure of a startlingly beautiful woman dressed in the coveralls of a Gunstar mechanic. The woman wiped her hands on the deep blue of her uniform in a show of cleaning them and then reached out for a handshake, which Rose reflexively returned, despite knowing that you couldn't shake hands with a hologram. To her surprise, the shake was firm and so realistic that she could even detect the callused hands that Gunstar mechanics always seemed to have.

The mechanic smiled, showing perfect white teeth. "I'm Gloria."

"Wait!" Rose said, recognizing the woman. "You were CEO of Star when Uncle David was at the White House!"

"Guilty," the hologram said.

Rose's eyes narrowed. "I've heard Dad talk about you too." she looked back at the smiling man on the screen. "What are you up to, Uncle David?"

David smiled and said, "Gloria is a sentient artificial intelligence. I want her to help you when you are flying combat missions."

Her head whipped around to look at the impossibly beautiful woman sporting a grin that was a twin to her uncle's.

"What do you mean?"

Gloria answered, "All the WCDF is coordinated by one of three AI's, although almost no one knows it. There were originally four of us, but Lea went with the *Galactica* as its pilot.

"Lea Lieberman?" Rose asked. "The former CEO of Warren?"

"Yeah," David said. "Also, the avatar of my Bubbie, but that is a long story that we can get into sometime if we win the war."

"So..." Gloria said. "We all have our specialties. "Pablo helped Cindy with her work. He also built most of the fleet. Bishop works with Steve Cooper and designed most of the ground weapons we use, and I have been helping David and Nick get the world ready for the invasion for a long time."

"What do you mean by a long time?" Her lips pressed flat. "Just how long have we known that the aliens are coming?"

Gloria laughed and looked at David. "Jake didn't raise any dummies, did he?"

"No kidding. After the war, we should offer Rose and Joselyn jobs. I don't think we would be disappointed."

The beautiful AI looked back at the Ensign. "We have known about the Silfe invasion for longer than the official line says. That story will also have to wait until after we win the war."

"The Silfe? Like in the game?" Rose asked, surprised.

"Yes," David said. "Gloria and I programmed *Alien Invasion* to be a training tool."

Rose walked past the AI and flopped onto the couch in the sitting area. "Uncle David, just how many of the crazy conspiracy theories about the aliens are true?"

"You mean the ones that say that Nick, Cindy, your dad, and I have manipulated the world for decades to prepare the world for an alien invasion that only we knew was coming?" She nodded. "Well..." he said, tapping his chin. "Most of them?" He smirked as her mouth fell open. "I mean, none of us are aliens, and I definitely don't have two..." he coughed and looked uncomfortable. "Never mind."

Gloria blurted out a laugh. "Oh, boss!" she said, grinning. "I started that one as a birthday present for Nick."

He smiled, his eyes coming alive with mirth. "Good one!" He turned back to Rose, who was frowning. "Anyway, we know a lot more about the Silfe than is common knowledge. I think that having Gloria in your corner might be helpful."

Rose's frown deepened. "I don't want to be singled out because of who I am. It would be unfair to the other pilots."

Gloria sat across from her. "I understand, but the AIs will help *everyone*, just silently. I did the same thing during the NATO-China War. No one ever asked how NATO's intelligence was so good, but it was one of the deciding factors. I can appreciate that it seems unfair, and maybe it is, but the secret of our existence is not ready for the public. Besides, we don't have enough computing power to interact with every pilot and soldier. We need to spread ourselves around. The plan is to monitor someone in every company or wing closely. They won't know why their information is so much better than anyone else's, but only those that are completely trustworthy can know the full truth."

The AI paused, giving the young ensign a wink. "There *is* a precedent. I helped your dad in his last mission into Tiananmen Square."

Rose sat back in surprise. "You helped my dad?"

"Yes."

The young woman seemed to struggle with the AI's revelations before asking another question. "What about Josie?"

David smiled, seeming to know he had her. "She is getting a similar offer from Steve and Bishop as we speak."

"And you say that my dad doesn't know?"

Gloria answered. "We don't want to put him in a compromising position. He is the commander of the entire WCDF after all." She reached out and took Rose's hand. "Having more direct information can only help you and your squadron."

Rose thought hard. She considered what this might mean for Susan and the rest of her wing. Having a powerful AI could make a difference, it might save lives. She nodded, not realizing that she was very much like her father. She would have never accepted this for herself, but she couldn't turn it down if it could keep others safe.

"OK, I'm in."

David let out a huge sigh. "Thank God! If I didn't convince you, Cindy would have made me sleep on the couch for a month!"

Both Rose and Gloria giggled together at the outrageous man on the screen.

"What's so funny?" he asked. "You do not want to see a pissed off Cindy." He shuddered.

"Nothing," they said in unison before laughing again.

THIRTY-SEVEN

WCN Dilong, Near Neptune
Five days until the invasion

Rear Admiral Daiyu Lin looked out across her flag bridge, observing the well-run machine that was the Dilong. The flagship of the First Fleet had two bridges. One was for the captain in command of the ship. The other was for her and her staff, who controlled the fleet.

There were still days when she missed having responsibility for a single ship, but Daiyu had transitioned in the end. It helped that Flag Captain Müller ran the ship like the Swiss watches his ancestors were famous for.

Between Risa, Pablo, and the orbital space yards, humanity cobbled together 1500 *Dilong* Class carriers and another 300 of the heavy cruisers originally designed for mining the asteroid belt. The heavy cruisers did get used for mining. The once seemingly inexhaustible supply of materials from Eldorado and Psyche couldn't keep up with demand once the world committed to total war. A myriad of materials were required for the weapons systems, shuttles, and thousands of other items to prepare for the invasion were readily available in the asteroid belt.

Ultimately, three fleets emerged. Each was composed of five hundred *Dilong* carriers and a hundred *Miner* class heavy cruisers. The carriers held one hundred Gunstars, with the Cruisers holding an additional fifty each. In total, the First Fleet could put 55,000 Gunstars into the black. By previous standards, it was a ridiculous amount of firepower. Especially considering that just five Gunstars had demolished the Chinese Army Air Force -the largest in the world at the time- fifteen years before. That wasn't even counting the six hundred capital ships, which brought even more offensive capability to the battle. The firepower of the fleets would seem insurmountable if it weren't for the approach of 10,000 alien ships less than a week from the Solar System. According to HAL, each of the alien battlecruisers held 500 fighters, for a total of five million ships. A number that seemed beyond comprehension.

On the surface, it seemed impossible for humanity to prevail, but they had some advantages. First, they had fixed positions. As any medieval knight could tell you, defending a castle was easier than attacking one. Modern weapons changed the equation some, but the ability to prepare endless traps and surprises would be a force multiplier. The aliens would have hell to pay when they tried to take any human settlement. The Moon, Mars, Callisto, and Enceladus all had huge defense batteries and contingents of exosuited marines to protect them. Should the Silfe decide to throw caution to the wind and focus, any of them would fall, but it would cost them, especially with the Human fleets sniping at their flanks.

The Silfe's best move was to follow Carl Von Clausewitz's Fourth Principle of War. The 19th century Russian General had known that *One must employ all combat power in the most effective and judicious way possible. Every part of the force must have purpose.* The rule followed would mean ignoring humanity's extraterrestrial colonies and bringing their full power to bear on the Earth itself. Unfortunately for the aliens, that was not the typical way they conquered planets.

HAL had been willing to give insight into Silfe battle

tactics and the human defense plan formed based on that data. The most crucial information relayed was that in any Silfe horde, there was an overall commander, but their control was limited.

The base-ten system seemed to have religious significance to the Silfe. The total invasion fleet was 10,000 ships under a single leader, the Chief Slayer. Ground troops organized into groups of ten thousand, one thousand, one hundred, and finally, squads of ten. Even space fighters always grouped into multiples of ten. At each level, individual commanders had autonomy to decide targets unheard of in Earth militaries.

According to HAL, Silfe culture was one of constant strife and competition. A Silfe warrior needed battle experience to gain honor and position. Ferocity often trumped tactics. Each warrior's goal was to die in battle, so conserving forces was not paramount, and the concept of retreat, although not unheard of, was a swift way to lose face.

The Chief Slayer could set general goals, such as "Attack Mars," but interfering in the command structure was considered bad form. Often, even if the overall strategy was competent, individual leaders could make mistakes that would spell disaster.

The Silfe, it seemed, had never heard of Clausewitz's 6th Principle: *For every objective, you must seek unity of command and unity of effort.*

This kind of fractured leadership had never much affected the result of their conquests. The Silfe always vastly outclassed the locals, allowing them to dictate terms. Their victory was assured, and in the deadly competitive Silfe Society, Chief Slayers were likely happy to ignore the loss of the least capable of their subordinates.

The Earth would be different. It had defenses, and the aliens would not easily control the orbitals if DS-1 and DS-2 remained under the control of the WCDF.

Unlike the Silfe, Admiral Lin had no qualms about

running away. In fact, that was precisely the tactics that she and her fellow admirals were to employ. They were to snipe at the edges, lure the enemy into traps, and be the mosquito that annoys you so much that you don't see the cliff in front of your feet.

One of her command staff brought Daiyu out of her reverie.

"Ma'am," Commander Rojas said from his position at the communications console. "Message from Admiral Swelton. States, 'For your eyes only.'"

She acknowledged the commander with a nod and said, "I will take it in my ready room. Mr. Rojas, let me know if anything of note occurs."

"Of course, Ma'am," he said, turning back to his console.

She walked to the private room just off the flag deck and settled in front of a large monitor, saying aloud, "Connect communication."

The screen lit up with the chiseled jaw and blue eyes of the commander of the WCDF.

"Admiral Lin," he said without preamble. "We have confirmed the deceleration of the Silfe fleet. They will come to a full rest on the other side of Pluto. I am green lighting operation 'Cold Feet.'" He paused, taking a deep breath, and his voice softened. "Daiyu, you are the tip of the spear. I need you to take their measure and test their command responsivity. We have based our planning on HAL's information, and it has never been wrong before, but I will feel more comfortable after we can gauge this for ourselves."

"I understand, Admiral. We have gamed this out a hundred times." Her expression turned hungry. "I expect we will give more than we get."

"I hope so," Swelton said. "Remember, this is just a prod. Under no circumstances are you to commit your forces fully. If you see an opportunity to take out a straggler, then do it, but no pitched battles." He gave her a stern look to drive his point home. "Clear?"

"Crystal, sir," she said.

"OK," he said, looking off screen. "I have another meeting. Please let one of the AIs know if you need anything. They can reach me at any time." Swelton gave her a salute, which she returned. "That's all, Admiral Lin; good luck and good hunting." He reached forward out of the screen, and the image went black.

"Well," she said to the empty room, her nerves leaving her, as they always did when a problem presented itself. "Time to get to work." She was shouting orders before the ready room doors finished closing behind her.

THIRTY-EIGHT

Olympus Mons, Mars
Three days until the invasion

"... So given Operation Cold Feet's likely conclusion, you will probably be the first hit," Jake's image said from the holographic projector on Brigadier General Juan Costas's desk.

"I understand," Costas said. "Don't worry, sir, we will be ready for them."

"I know you will, Juan. Good luck. I will see you on the other side." Swelton cut the connection, and the hologram went out.

There was a shimmering light behind the young general, briefly causing flickering shadows to be thrown across his desk. He didn't turn, instead saying, "You heard?"

"I did," a silky voice said from behind.

He felt soft hands on his shoulders, kneading muscles bunched up in tension. Juan felt his worries melt away at their touch and he gave an audible moan. "You are absolutely my favorite person in the universe."

The two small hands showed surprising strength as they used his shoulders to swivel the chair around to face the opposite way, bringing him face-to-face with the gorgeous form of Gloria. "You are my favorite person too," she said, moving forward to straddle his lap.

Even after years, he still couldn't believe how soft and warm the AI felt. Her avatar's projection was indistinguishable from a living, breathing person. He often forgot that Gloria hadn't been born to a real human couple. It seemed impossible that someone so *alive* could be... whatever it was AIs were.

He came to terms with it long ago. There was a brief existential crisis in the beginning when he realized he had fallen in love with her. Ultimately, though, he decided that all life was just different programming. A human was a biological machine, and Gloria was a technological one. It didn't mean she wasn't alive. Just different... and funny... and beautiful... and wonderful.

"So?" he asked.

"So what?" she said, kissing his earlobe and causing shivers to run down his body.

"So, it looks like we will have a lot of very pissed-off space crocodiles falling out of the sky in a few days."

"Oh, that," she said. "I already knew. Jake told Daiyu two days ago that Cold Feet was a go. The rest was just extrapolation." She stopped nibbling his ear to say, "Cold Feet is a stupid name."

"I swear," he said. "You and David are both obsessed with renaming things. I can't remember the last time either of you approved of something that you didn't come up with yourself."

"Actually, we agreed that Captain George named his carrier perfectly."

"You mean, the *David Tennant?*"

"Yes," she said, "Everyone with any class knows that the tenth doctor was the best. Anyone who tells you anything else is extremely misguided."

"You, my love, are a Dr. Who snob."

"Absolutely," she said, showing no shame.

"Well, what's wrong with Cold Feet? I thought you'd like it," he said. "The whole cold, Pluto, pun thing. Seems right up your alley."

She pulled back and glared at him. "I have a much more refined sense of humor than that! Besides, the first battle with an alien fleet should have more gravitas than Cold Feet can bring."

"Really?" he said, smiling. "Tell me, oh beautiful and all-knowing AI, what should they have named it?"

Her face scrunched up in concentration. Juan sometimes wondered about Gloria's expressions. How much were her processors sorting data, and how much was an affectation to be more human? It was another thought he had learned to ignore. In the end, it didn't matter.

Her face lit up in triumph. "I think I would have called it Operation Plutonic Relationship."

He groaned, "That is in no way better than Cold Feet.

"It is so," she said. "It brings in a true pun while describing the mission: tease them a bit and then go straight to the no-touch friend zone."

"I would hardly call shooting lasers at each other, not touching... or friendly."

"Ehhh," she said, motioning with her hand to dismiss his comment. "Compared to the rest of the war, this is an accidental nip-slip."

He chuckled, which soon became a full-throated laugh. He reached forward and cupped Gloria's face in his hands, kissing her. "I love you."

As he pulled back, he saw her face soften, tears blossoming at the corners of her eyes. "I love you too, and I am worried about you, despite trying desperately to cover myself in terrible puns."

He kissed her again and said, "We can only do what we can do. My part of the war is here on Olympus Mons. If we do it right, we can win."

She nodded. "I know I'm being selfish. There are millions of conversations like this happening across the solar system." She cocked her head to the side as if listening. "I can hear them now. All declaring their love and promising to come home safe, even though many won't." She hugged him tightly. "But you will come home to me, won't you? Promise me."

He hugged her back. "I promise."

"Good," she said, leaning forward to lay her head on his chest. "I'm going to hold you to that."

He stroked her hair soothingly. Thinking that for this woman, he would do just that. He would come home, even if he had to kill every one of the Silfe to do it.

THIRTY-NINE

DS-2, Earth High Orbit
1 day until the invasion

Second Lieutenant Joselyn Swelton of the World Commission Marines stalked forward on the balls of her feet. Her combat boots gripped the foam matting as she placed each precisely to maintain her balance. Her opponent looked at her warily. Despite Lieutenant Ivanov's size and reach advantages, he had learned to respect her as a fighter long ago.

In her short 18 years, Josie achieved three black belts, each in a different unarmed style.

She had started at age five with Brazilian jiu-jitsu. The United States military used a combination of jiu-jitsu and kickboxing as its official unarmed combat style, so she had always had access to high-quality instructors. She had bridged out to karate and finally, in her late teens, to krav maga. After the invasion announcement, the more lethal Israeli martial art had seen a major resurgence. For the first time, the average suburbanite found the real possibility of violence in their near future.

She loved the feeling of pitting herself against an opponent, close up and personal. Her twin sister Rose never understood how she could stand it. After a single session,

Rose had given up jiu-jitsu, saying that she didn't want to "Roll around with a bunch of sweaty people on a mat." It was amazing how two people with identical genes could be so different. Rose had always wanted to fly and spent her time in flight combat simulators instead.

Ivanov lunged forward, slashing out with a sidekick. The textbook move was to push the leg and get inside the larger opponent's guard. That would allow her to alleviate his reach and let her strike with a jab or cross. She didn't take the bait, instinctively knowing it was a faint. Josie could feel that he would plant and then use his opposite knee to come in at her when she drew closer. Ivanov was former Spetsnaz and had trained extensively in Systema, the obscure fighting system developed by the Cossacks and favored by Russian special forces. It relied on natural movements and surprise. Instead of moving in, she dropped into a leg sweep just as his foot planted, taking his full weight. The leg buckled, and he fell hard to the mat. Josie pushed up with her legs and came down with booted feet astride the Russian's head.

"That's a match," she said, smiling.

Ivanov groaned and sat up. "I concede." He rubbed at his hip, where he had struck. "That was slick. I thought I had you."

She nodded. "I saw through the feint. If there is one thing I have had drilled into me by instructors in hand-to-hand, it is never to do what your opponent expects."

"Solid advice," he said, holding a hand out to her, which she gripped, pulling to help him up from the mat. "Another round?" he asked hopefully.

"Sorry," she said, looking up at the digital clock on the wall. I have a briefing at 1400; if I run, I can get a shower in before reporting."

He nodded. "OK, starting tomorrow," he said, a bit apprehensively. "After the... invasion starts. I am not sure if we will have much time for sparring." He smiled at her. "I have enjoyed our sessions. As we have gotten closer to the day, it has helped burn off my nerves."

"Me too," she said, understanding completely. "Training, training, and more training can wear you out. It was fun just to cut loose." She sighed. "I suppose we can do that when the aliens get here." She reached out to Ivanov and shook his hand. "Good luck to you, Lieutenant."

"And to you. Bógu molís', a dobrá-umá derzhís," he said in Russian.

"What does that mean?" she asked.

"In English, it would translate as 'Trust in God, but steer away from the rocks.'"

She smiled, "I'll take that. Good advice all around, especially for what is coming."

Josie watched as the tall man walked off the mat, thinking she might never see him again. She shook her head, trying to dislodge her macabre thought. She wondered if the men riding the landing craft to the beaches of Normandy felt similarly. They probably had. War may have changed, but the doubts and emotions of those experiencing it were the same.

She turned and picked up her pace, not quite a run, but what her instructors in basic would have called "Rifle's March." At 140 steps per minute, it was the fastest pace that soldiers on DS-2 could go before one of the MPs would gig them. Enough gigs and they were up for marching re-education, a four-hour hell wherein a humorless drill instructor yelled different cadences at you while in full kit. It was an experience to avoid at all costs.

She stayed right of the white line splitting the corridor, melding into the one-way traffic, and weaving in and out of soldiers in the Black BDUs of the World Commission Marine Corps.

This corridor was one of the passes. Designed to move large machinery, they were also the primary thoroughfares of the massive station. Each was twenty feet high and fifteen wide. A corridor would branch out of it at a right angle every thirty feet. Small apertures at different levels appeared near the branching points. These were murder holes, taken in concept from medieval castles. They connected to rooms where marines could set up ambushes for aliens who tried to use the passes for rapid movement.

DS-2 was a trap, and anyone who lived on it could see how the invaders would pay for every corridor they took a step down.

Josie slowed and turned to enter a tunnel with 202 painted in white above its entrance. Unlike the straight thoroughfare, the tunnels had frequent curves and blind corners occurring every 50 feet. After a minute of travel, the smaller corridor opened into an expansive space a couple of hundred yards square. In the center, she saw marines of the 202nd exosuit company running drills; the light sucked into the black matte finish of their suits.

The exosuits were essentially the same as Bishop and Steve's first design. A frame of flat, thin nanotubing, looking a bit like an oversized skeleton, was worn behind the operator. The tubing thickened with hydraulic connections at the joints, giving each soldier the strength of a silverback gorilla.

The most prominent aspect of the suit was the thorax, which looked like a thin backpack containing the power supply for both the suit and weapons. Here Cindy's battery technology came into play. A single credit card-sized modern battery could power a cell phone for a month, but lasers and railguns required more juice. Therefore, the individual thoraxes varied in thickness, depending on the primary specialization of the soldier. They ranged from only an inch thick for scout models to something that looked like a half keg of beer for the heavy weapons crews.

Josie's pace quickened again, paralleling the training field. She could see a squad working through the obstacle course, using augmented muscles to jump fifteen feet in the air to land on a small platform before jumping from platform to platform over a deep pool of water. She winced sympathetically as a marine misjudged a jump, arms windmilling as he landed and toppled forward with a splash into the pool. She shook her head. The man was in for some good-natured ribbing tonight at chow.

She passed the training field and turned into a tunnel housing the Bachelor Officers' Quarters. Here, the tunnel narrowed, with a series of doors on each side in a long double row. She stopped at the third door on the left and swiped her palm over a glowing data pad, causing an electronic buzzing to sound as the lock disengaged.

The BOQs on DS-2 were spartan. The beds folding out of the walls were slabs of metal covered by a thin cotton mattress that could hardly be called comfortable. Still, she had a private space with a lock, which was vital for times like this.

"Bishop, do you have some time for an update?" she asked the room.

A bright whirling tornado appeared in the center of the small space, slowing, and finally stopping to reveal the smiling form of Bishop. He wore his typical grease-stained coveralls, with a small spiral-bound notebook tucked into the front pocket and sported a pencil behind one ear.

"Sure," he said. "What's up?"

Unlike Rose, Josie readily accepted Steve Cooper's offer of an AI to help her in the upcoming battle. She talked briefly with her sister and could agree that it seemed an unfair advantage given to her only because she was a Swelton, but Josie felt no guilt about accepting. Perhaps it was because she was leading a platoon. Rose was the lowest ranking pilot in her flight and wasn't in command of any soldiers other than her ground crew. However, a second lieutenant in the World Commission Marines was directly responsible for the lives of forty marines. Sure, her Platoon Sergeant, Staff Sergeant Sarah Campion, was the glue that held the platoon together, but the ultimate responsibility lay with her.

She was extremely young and inexperienced for her rank, only possible because of the WCM's overwhelming need for first and second lieutenants to lead the hundreds of millions of soldiers in uniform. Even so, Josie needed to score in the 99th percentile to be allowed to take the accelerated OCS course.

So, unfair advantage or not, having an AI that would provide her with up-to-date information was something that she couldn't in good conscience refuse.

The young lieutenant turned toward Bishop. "Can you give me an update on the Silfe's probable intentions?"

The AI nodded, saying, "Not much has changed. They are still decelerating and should come to a complete stop just outside the solar system sometime early tomorrow morning. According to HAL, As soon as they have regrouped, they will receive their objectives from the Chief Slayer. At that point, individual groups will proceed toward their objectives.

"And Cold Feet is still on?" she asked.

"Yes. Admiral Lin is finishing her positioning now. They will engage before the last of the Silfe elements have regrouped, attempting to lead an element toward Mars."

"OK," she said, thinking. "How long do you estimate before they reach DS-2?"

"Depending on the success of Cold Feet, expect an attack anywhere from seven to ten days from now."

"That long? Won't they immediately send ships to Earth?"

"They might, but our strategy is to anger them enough to get caught up in the colonies, especially Mars. General Costas will make them pay dearly for every inch of Olympus Mons they take."

"OK," she said, shoulder muscles relaxing from tension she hadn't even realized she was holding. "So, we have some time to prepare."

"More than likely. The AIs pooled their servers to run simulations. Given the fractured command structure described by HAL, there is a greater than a 97% chance that a large portion of the alien force will divert into individual engagements at the colonies. The Chief Slayer will have no choice but to hold back reserves or risk losing control of the orbitals on Mars, Enceladus, and Callisto, or worse, have his fleet chipped away piecemeal by the Commission Navy."

"So, we're sacrificing the colonies? Aren't there 100,000 marines on Mars and 50,000 in each of the other colonies?"

"Enceladus and Callisto will almost certainly fall," he said. They are designed to bleed the Silfe while giving them a false sense of security." The AI looked meaningfully at her. "Remember, should the aliens bypass the colonies and focus all of their strength on the Earth, there is almost a 100% chance that they will take control of the orbitals and land in strength on the planet. There are over 10 billion people on Earth. As terrible as it sounds, the math doesn't lie. Sacrificing the few for the many has always been the way of war. All the colony's non-combatants are back on Earth, and only World Commission Marines remain. All of them are unmarried volunteers. They know what they are doing and why they are doing it."

Josie was shocked by the AI's clinical read of the loss of 200,000 Commission Marines. "How can you be so blasé about it?"

Bishop's eyes hardened into diamonds, and his body straightened, making his slim frame seem larger and more dangerous. The dark stains on his coveralls took on a red tint that made her question whether they were supposed to be oil or blood. She unconsciously took a step back.

"The Lizards are coming here to kill us all, me included. They will not allow a human-built AI to continue to operate. All of us are working to make sure that *they* do the dying, but if we play it too safe, if we try to save everyone, it will doom us all. Juan Costas is one of my best friends and is all but married to my sister Gloria. You call me blasé, but you couldn't be farther from the truth. I am angry. So angry; I feel like my servers will smoke and burn. I only wish I could run screaming into battle myself to kill the bastards."

Bishop blinked, seeming to register her worried posture. He stopped speaking and deflated, his eyes returning to normal, with kindness and understanding shining through. "Sorry," he said. "The Silfe rile me up. You can blame it on Steve for putting the need to protect humans into my core."

"No," she said. "It is me that should apologize. I understand what you and the other AIs are doing. I also appreciate that with the Silfe tech, you can't directly engage with them. I can only imagine how frustrating that must feel. At least I get to shoot back."

Bishop shook his head. "I *can* shoot back. I just need to do it by aiming *you*. My weapon is the most dangerous in existence. A living breathing Swelton."

She laughed. "I'll do my best."

"I know you will. Now, we have a few minutes before you need to shower for your briefing. Let me outline what your part will be and how you can use your platoon to maximum efficiency."

Josie listened intently as the AI described the tunnels they would assign her to protect. He had several ideas for shoring up the weak areas and maximizing their fire while minimizing casualties. She continued to absorb the plans, knowing that each one might make the difference between life and death for her platoon. She didn't even consider that it might also save her own life.

FORTY

Edge of the Solar System
0 days until the invasion

"Admiral, we are one minute from impact," Lieutenant Simkins said from the weapons console.

Admiral Daiyu Lin nodded. She took a deep, calming breath, hoping that none of her nervousness showed on her face. It wouldn't do for her staff to realize that a hurricane of emotion was raging in her center. She was about to fire the first shot in an interstellar war. It was a distinction that she could do without. Why did the Silfe have to come? Why did they have to be hostile? As silly as it sounded to a woman who had dedicated her life to the military, why couldn't they just get along?

"Please get the Fscope in position; I want to see this in real-time."

"Aye, Aye, Ma'am, images should come up on the forward view screen in a moment." the communications officer said.

The truth of the matter was that she wasn't about to fire. They had fired the first shots of the war two days ago. Daiyu had ordered the fleet backed up, and then they started a run toward the projected position of the Silfe fleet, firing foot-long steel rods from their railguns as they went. The rounds were invisible in the deep of space, as they had no energy signatures. The fleet's velocity, combined with the incredible speed imparted by the railguns, caused the ammunition to reach a good percentage of the speed of light. Now it was time to discover if they had guessed correctly. The timing had to be perfect. They knew the approximate positioning of the Silfe fleet based on Fscope telemetry. They also knew -because of HAL- that the aliens would collect their forces before engaging.

The aliens were violating a fundamental principle of war. One should never predictably position their forces. For if you do, you are asking for an ambush. Here the Silfe were showing their hubris. They hadn't fought an enemy near their technology level since the Harrow, thousands of years in the past. All the Admirals who learned the hard lessons from those conflicts were long since dust.

If Admiral Lin was in their position, she would have coordinated formations via inter-ship communications and had randomized assembly points. Concentrating forces made sense, but not in a single large mass.

Well, she was about to see if their gambit worked. Despite 300,000 railgun rounds fired, even a close formation of ships in the black of space still covered distances hard for the human mind to get around. Although, as the saying goes, "Quantity has a quality all its own."

The forward view screen lit up as the Fscope reconstituted the image of the Alien fleet. An audible gasp rose from the throats of the bridge crew. The fleet was massive, composed of countless immense triangular ships.

"Twenty seconds to impact, Ma'am," the weapons officer said.

Leaning toward the viewscreen, Daiyu said, "OK, people, let's see if our gambit worked."

*****

Chief Slayer Tetukken was feeling uneasy. He looked at the vast holotank standing in front of his station on the bridge. As he watched, he could see the floating icons representing the ships of the horde. "How long until the fleet is in formation?" he asked his adjutant.

"The last of them are coming to rest now, Slayer. We have received assignment requests already." The adjutant growled in anticipation. "The young ones are chomping at the air, waiting to get their first taste of Earthling."

Tetukken growled in agreement. The young ones were hard to control at the best of times, and with a cleansing so close, they would be in a frenzy. The sooner he could get them an enemy to fight, the better. Still, why did his instincts scream at him that something was wrong? He had long ago learned to trust this feeling. It had saved him in battle too many times to ignore. He racked his brain, trying to find what he was missing.

"Where is the human fleet now?" he asked.

"We monitored them moving away several days ago, and thought that they had fled the might of the host, as they did not have enough ships to challenge us. However, they turned and came back at speed before stopping again, just inside the system. For now, they appear to be sitting, doing nothing. We are monitoring numerous micro-wormhole formations that we believe are emanating from them.

For some reason, the information made the knot in his gullet clamp down in worry. *Why would the humans flee, only to come back toward them, unless...*

He gave a roar that made his entire bridge crew crouch down at their stations and expose their necks instinctively.

"Get up, you spineless weaklings!" he said. "Communication to all ships. Command them to scatter; put distance between them!"

No one on the bridge except his second in command moved, everyone still frozen in fear. "Sir," the adjutant said.

"Why would we give a scatter command? Standing orders are for all ships to gather before a purge."

"I know that, you idiot!" Tetukken said. "So do the Earthlings! They went away and then came back at speed to add to the velocity of whatever they fired at us!"

The adjutant's eyes widened in realization before he started yelling.

"You heard the Chief Slayer! Get on your feet!" He moved forward, slapping the bridge crew with a clawed hand, causing small bleeding gashes where his hand met flesh.

Tetukken looked at the plot as the bridge crew came back to life. He could hear the communication officer send out his order.

"All ships scatter, by order of Chief Slayer Tetukken. I say again, scatter."

*****

"Ma'am, we are getting some movement at the edges of the alien fleet. It appears as if the ships are separating."

She smiled and spoke to the crew. "Looks like someone over there may have some tactical sense after all." Her smile turned feral. "It wasn't soon enough, though."

As the weapons officer started the countdown, the entire bridge crew leaned toward the viewscreen. "First rounds should reach the target zone in... 10... 9... 8...

*****

Tetukken looked on in relief as the first ships started to move. Perhaps he had overreacted. Still, his gut feelings were rarely, if ever, wrong.

Just as he felt they might have avoided a disaster, the first ship disappeared from the holotank.

"Slayer!" his weapons officer yelled. "We have lost a ship in the forward group. There goes another, and... another!"

Tetukken roared in outrage. *These Humans had no honor!*

They ambushed without warning, hiding out of weapons range, while tens of thousands of Karoken's Chosen gasped their final prayer. He would make them suffer for this!

"Message all ships! They are to converge on the Hu...ma...nsss fleet and destroy it!"

*****

A cheer rose from the Dilong bridge crew as another Alien ship blew apart.

"Ms. Simkins, that should be the last barrage, if I am not mistaken?"

"Yes, Ma'am," all rounds should be through the fleet.

"OK," she said. In all they had destroyed 93 alien vessels. Not even 1% of the enemy fleet, but it was a start. According to HAL, each ship carried 10,000 warriors, so they had just taken out almost a million enemy ground troops expending nothing but steel rods. About as good as she could hope for, especially as the commander of the Silfe fleet seemed to realize the danger he was in, although too late to change the outcome.

"Ma'am," the astrogator, Lieutenant Traybon, said. "The alien fleet is moving towards us."

"How many?" she asked.

Traybon looked back at his instrumentation, which linked to the Fscope data feed, before replying. "It looks like... all of them."

Daiyu smiled and looked around at her bridge crew, meeting each pair of eyes. "Well, it looks like we sufficiently pissed them off." At her words, the bridge crew gave a low chuckle. She just hoped they could keep their spirits up as the battle continued.

She gestured to the communications officer, who was also the ranking member of her team. "Commander Rojas, general orders to the fleet: Cold Feet is a go. Send out orders to deploy fighters, formation alpha."

"Aye, Ma'am, Cold Feet order sent."

Wave upon wave of Gunstars poured from the human motherships.

Admiral Lin watched as her plot blossomed with small icons birthed in a steady stream from First fleet.

"Lieutenant Traybon, how long until the leading edge of the enemy fleet reaches firing range of the fighters?"

"Given the parameters on the alien ships that we received, they should be in range in thirty-nine minutes." He looked at her seriously. "I have to remind you, admiral, that the alien capabilities are estimates only." He shook his head unconsciously. "I have never been given an adequate explanation that the information is accurate. As we have never been in action with the aliens before now, assuming we know their capabilities seems unwise at best and disastrous at worst."

Lin nodded. "Your concerns are noted and appreciated. Please continue to challenge all assumptions." She looked out at the rest of her staff. "I expect everyone to bring up their concerns without regard to rank. We are fighting for our lives, and any person here could come up with an observation or idea that could be the difference between victory and defeat." She looked around at each face, detecting more than one gulp as throats went dry from her words. "That said, although Lieutenant Traybon's argument is both well-reasoned and appropriate, I have a source regarding the alien vessels that is not available to you. Until proven otherwise, please assume that all the capabilities you received are accurate."

She received nods from the crew. "OK," she said. "Send orders to the fighters. Engagement plan Beta." She sat back in her command chair, watching the changing plot on the forward viewscreen. She sighed inwardly. They had committed. All she could do was sit back and watch.

*****

"How long until the fighters are in range?" Tetukken asked.

"They will enter the engagement envelope of the

forward ships momentarily," the weapons officer said.

"Good!" He growled deep in his throat. "Now we will see what these Hu...ma...nsss are made of!" He leaned forward on the edge of the holotank, where he saw the waves of human fighters just entering the weapons range of the Silfe battlecruisers. He hadn't even launched his fighters. If the Earthlings wanted to match their puny craft against grouped capital ships, they were welcome to try. The Chosen would swat them like the tiny insects they were!

The first of the Silfe battlecruisers came into range and fired its primary laser. Tetukken roared in glee as one of the human fighters winked out of existence; then two more as ships came into range. That was when the first battlecruiser exploded. He looked confusedly at the holotank. There was no way the human fighters could have weapons that could reach that far or be powerful enough to kill a battlecruiser with a single hit. How had the humans done it?

"Sir!" his weapons officer called out. "The human fighters are retreating."

Tetukken glared as the waves of enemy fighters veered sharply away, taking them out of range. He growled as another ten battlecruisers exploded. *The damn humans had tricked them again!* The fighter wave was a lure to bring the Silfe ships into another barrage of ordinance fired by the human capital ships, and they had fallen for it! The host killed a mere seven of the human fighters in exchange for 110,000 Chosen.

"Orders to the fleet; spread out in loose formation and slow to one-quarter speed. Forward elements are to launch fighters toward the enemy fleet."

Tetukken clenched his snout in anger. The humans may have no honor, but they were tricky. He would need to be careful not to over commit. The Silfe fleet could not be predictable, or they could snipe at them repeatedly.

He continued with his orders. "All ships are to change course at varying times. We will follow in a group after this human fleet and see if they will turn to fight."

*****

"The enemy ships are slowing and spreading out, Ma'am."

"I see it." Daiyu had hoped they would anger the aliens enough to repeat the trick with the fighters. The First Fleet had three more traps to spring if the Silfe blindly followed them.

She shook off her slight disappointment. It always had been a long shot. HAL had only given the repeated trap success rate at 35%, with significant drops in effectiveness with each subsequent engagement. Still, it only cost them the time and materials for the ammunition, so it had been worth the chance.

The initial battle had gone well. They only lost seven fighters. In the cold calculation of war, the personnel and tonnage exchange were massively in their favor. That was, if you could ignore that seven brave young men and women had just become the first humans who wouldn't be coming home to their families. She stiffened her shoulders. They also would be far from the last. If every death beat her down, she would be prone on the floor before she was through her first battle. She wondered how the admirals and generals of the past coped. Perhaps they waited until they were alone to grieve. That was her plan. Maybe it wasn't the healthy way to mitigate her feelings, but she didn't know what else to do, and she needed to focus.

Her professional facade showed no cracks as she called out to her staff. "Message the fighters to regroup into formation Gamma."

"The alien vessels are launching fighters," Simkins said. "Wow! Estimates are coming in. It looks like each of their capital ships can hold at least 500 fighters. A few moments passed as the lieutenant tallied the alien vessels. "Confirmed, he said. They have launched 100,000 fighters."

"They're acting as a screen," she said. "They don't want

a repeat of the trap we set for them." She braced herself, as she knew that her next order would mean the deaths of thousands. "Mr. Rojas, send orders to the fighters to sweep back and take a position in front of the fleet. They are to engage the enemy fighters according to Cold Feet Protocol before returning for collection."

"Aye, Aye, Ma'am," Rojas said. "Fighters to sweep back and then engage per 'Cold Feet Protocol." The commander's fingers flew across the screen as he inputted the instructions. "Orders sent, Ma'am."

"OK," she said, nodding. "General order to the fleet. As soon as the fighters engage, all capital ships start slowly backing towards Mars."

*****

The radio crackled in Ensign Jennifer Hall's helmet. "Orders from the Flag. All Gunstars, engage 'Cold Feet Protocol,'"

This is it. She hit the pedal of the Gunstar with her right foot and felt a small amount of acceleration bleeding through the inertial compensator.

She swallowed her nerves and focused on the controls of the fighter.

The voice of her wing commander, Lieutenant Saunders, sounded in her ear.

"They ordered us to take the edge of the formation. I am sending coordinates to you now."

Jennifer could detect breathless nerves in the Lieutenant's voice. Not that she was willing to judge the man. The ensign could feel her pulse pounding in her ears and was glad he was the one giving the orders, as her voice would come out as a squeaky rasp.

The nineteen-year-old pilot steeled herself, imagining that she was back in Ontario playing Alien Invasion in VR. Unfortunately, the young woman couldn't help but remember how many times she was blown out of the sky while playing.

She shook her head, trying to clear it of distracting thoughts. Her trainers had warned of this. When the thoughts and doubts intruded, they said to lean on her training and focus on the mission.

The ensign did a quick status check. Engines in the green. Spinal laser charge 100%. Full mags for the dual railguns integrated into the stubby wings of her fighter. She switched over to local communications and spoke. "How are you doing, Tanaka?"

"Five by five," her wingman, Ensign Hiro Tanaka, said in mildly accented English. "And you, Jenny?"

"I'm here," she said, hoping that her nerves wouldn't be detectable over the radio.

She remembered all the movies she'd seen of fighter pilots. They were always so cocky and sure of themselves. She didn't feel that way at all. Until three years ago, all she had ever wanted was to go to a good college and become an engineer at one of the new colony sites. She had wanted desperately to go to space... but never imagined it like this.

The shake in her voice must have been more audible than she imagined. Tanaka's voice came back soothingly. "Just follow me in, keep anyone off my back, OK?"

She nodded, even though the other pilot couldn't see it. "I got you," she said, voice firming.

She glanced at the countdown in the upper left corner of her HUD. *Four minutes until engagement range.* She looked back down at the plot and gulped. It was hard to tell where one alien fighter stopped, and another began. There were so many of them it looked like a blob of white oozing across the intervening space. Like one of the cheesy black and white flicks. The ones where the gelatinous ooze rolled right over the jerk on the football team, shriek cutting off suddenly as it enveloped him.

The optics in the ship possessed powerful magnifiers which linked to her helmet. Despite being in a space fighter at the edges of the solar system, she still needed to aim through the optical interface. It was a bit like the antiaircraft guns of the second world war, including an aiming reticle. Supposedly, the aliens could hack any computerized aiming equipment, so humanity had reverted to previous technology, combining the old with the new.

She couldn't imagine how anyone could know anything for sure about the aliens' capabilities, but that was way above her pay grade. The only thing they told her was where to go and who to shoot. That was about all she could handle anyway, so for once, she happily suppressed her inquisitive nature.

The images on the helmet optics coalesced into visible shapes. The enemy fighters were thin and triangular, with swept-back wings, like mini versions of their capital ships. They reminded her of stone arrowheads that she'd seen once at a natural history museum. The front angled to a sharp point, with a pronounced cutout in the back containing the engines. More concerning were the darker points on the wings that were almost certainly weapons emplacements.

At one minute, Lieutenant Saunders's voice sounded again. "All fighters engage targets of opportunity as you come into range. Be ready for the recall order. Remember that this is a feint only. We want to piss them off and get back out of range. I don't want any heroes. Get your job done and get back to the rally point."

Jennifer gripped the control stick with white knuckles, focusing all of her attention on the back of Tanaka's glowing engines, just forward and above her. The alien fighter's silhouettes sharpened in her optics, like a camera lens coming into focus. She could just make the impression of where a pilot might sit in the center as the targeting countdown clicked over to double zero. A general call came over the squadron channel. "Engage! Engage!"

She sighted the T-like aiming reticle on the enemy fighter and squeezed the trigger, activating the spinal laser. Without atmosphere, the weapon had no visible trail. That was one place that the science fiction movies got it wrong.

For a moment, nothing happened. Then she saw a brief glow surrounding the fighter as it heated instantly to thousands of degrees before coming apart. There was a small explosion as the power source overheated, but very little propagated out in the vacuum of space.

"Yes!" she said as Tanaka scored a hit on the wingman of the ship she destroyed. Then they were passing the leading element of the enemy. She felt the canopy heat briefly as her ship passed through the edge of a laser strike, then she was through, pushing down the knowledge that she had almost died. Instead, the ensign looked for her next target. She switched to railguns and followed her wingman as he angled to engage with another enemy fighter.

They killed two more before their luck ran out. Jennifer just had time to yell, "Tanaka, enemy fighter at two o'clock!" before his ship came apart.

"Hiro!" she screamed as she instinctively swerved to avoid the remnants of her friend's fighter. She screamed again as she turned to engage the alien craft responsible for his death, finger cramping as she held down the trigger.

*****

"Ma'am, the fighters have disengaged. We are getting reports now. If you give me a few moments, I can give you estimates on losses, both for the fleet and the enemy," Lieutenant Simkins said."

Daiyu nodded silently. The past thirty minutes were trying. First, watching the waves of human and alien fighters converging, and then seeing as the points of light began disappearing, each representing a life ended in violence. Still, she could see that Cold Feet was working. The Gunstars were giving better than they got, and the aliens were following the first fleet like dogs after an especially juicy bone.

The weapons officer looked up from his console. "Final tallies show 3272 Gunstars lost." She winced inwardly.

"However, we destroyed over 10,000 enemy fighters."

Admiral Lin took heart at the numbers. If you added all the Gunstars in the mobile fleets and those on the moon, humanity was still at a more than two-to-one disadvantage, but If they could repeat the battle's exchange, then maybe it wasn't as hopeless as she feared. In a straight fighter-to-fighter equation, Earth would come out on top.

The major tactical problem remaining was the difference in capital ships. If the Silfe commander was wise, he would pull his fighters in under the weapons envelope of the battlecruisers and force the humans to come to them. Earth didn't have enough carriers and heavy cruisers to go toe-to-toe in a straight-up fight. Instead, they were betting on the fractured leadership of the Silfe and their natural aggressiveness to lead to mistakes. She couldn't help but question the wisdom of such an approach. Napoleon said, "Never interrupt an enemy when he is making a mistake." She wholeheartedly agreed but predicating a plan on the Silfe's tactical errors seemed a recipe for disaster. She sighed. Humanity had little choice, and she would do her part.

She spoke to the room, "I want to wait until the first of the alien fighters turns back to its parent ship, then send ours back at them hard." She looked around at the expectant faces of her crew. "We have the fish on the line; we just need to set the hook."

*****

Tetukken growled in rage as the Silfe fighters at the leading edge of the formation turned again to engage the enemy. "I thought we sent a message to the forward elements to bring the fighters back under the battlecruiser's engagement envelope!"

A young male olangee standing at the communication console shrank back at the Chief Slayer's words. "I did Slayer, twice. Neither order was acknowledged." The communication officer gave a yip of apology. "I am monitoring communications from the forward battlecruisers calling to other ships to move forward to support them. They are attempting to catch the enemy capital ships, but the enemy keeps moving away. Only the Earth fighters are staying within range."

Tetukken roared and hit his leaning post with his tail, shattering the carved wood into splinters. Finally getting his rage under control, he gestured a clawed hand at the pieces scattered across the metal floor. "Get someone to clean that up!"

He took a pair of deep, centering breaths. *Why couldn't he get commanders that understood tactics!* Aggressiveness in the pursuit of Karoken's will was proper, but his commanders needed to use their brains! The humans were leading the forward element out of position. He couldn't allow a portion of the fleet to get separated. If he did, the human admiral would turn and wipe them from the system. He growled in frustration and gave the order that he knew was wrong but needed if he was to avoid disaster.

"General orders to the fleet. Follow the lead element. Bring an additional 100 battlecruisers up and use their fighters to replace losses."

He shook his snout in irritation. Their opponents may be without honor, but they weren't unintelligent. In every clash they had had, the humans destroyed more of the Chosen's ships than they lost. The Earthlings seemed to be playing a game of attrition and playing it well. It was a commitment to the conflict that Tetukken could appreciate. One must take losses to accomplish goals in war. Still, humans had a weakness. They needed to protect their colonies and planets. He knew their capital ship numbers, and they couldn't match his own. If he could keep the Silfe fleet intact, the Chosen would win.

A low rumble of displeasure emanated from his throat, causing his bridge crew to flinch. *Why was he getting another bad feeling?* He pushed it down ruthlessly and yelled, "Get to it! Karoken demands our service, and every enemy's final prayer we send to him will strengthen the certainty of our victory!"

Yet, as the bridge crew scrambled to do his bidding, the niggling thought continued in his mind.

FORTY-ONE

*World Commission
Headquarters, Geneva*
+2 days

"So Cold Feet is a success, then?" Nick asked.

Jake's image nodded from the screen on Nick's desk. "Mostly. We achieved all the major objectives for the operation, although we were hoping to get a few more traps off to whittle down the enemy battlecruisers. We weren't able to destroy any after the initial barrages."

"Still," Nick said. "I saw the reports; Admiral Lin took out 104 of the cruisers."

"That's right. If HAL's estimates are reliable, it should also mean killing over a million Silfe ground troops and 52,000 fighters." He sighed, "Still, it is only a little over 1% of the total invasion fleet."

Nick looked out the windows of his office in the former United Nations complex. He could see beautifully manicured lawns and people in business attire walking in small groups and enjoying some unseasonably warm weather. It was a view that would change dramatically should the Silfe get past the fleet and onto the Earth. His view seemed to shift, revealing hulking aliens running down terrified citizens, buildings on fire, and the grass blacked from lasers before returning to the idyllic setting before him.

He shook the false images away, focusing on the golden-haired General. "Every bit helps. "Remember, we never planned to win this in a single crushing blow." He waited to see Jake accept his words before continuing. "How did the Gunstars do against their fighters?"

"That's a bright spot," Jake said. "We are consistently taking them at a three to one ratio. The numbers are improving, as..." he paused, his face losing its stoicism, eyes seeming to dim. "As the surviving pilots learn from their mistakes."

Nick nodded. He knew how hard this must be, especially to talk objectively about Gunstar loss ratios when his daughter Rose was a fighter pilot.

"Anyway," Jake said, getting his emotions back under control. "If we were going to fight fighter to fighter, we could win this thing without question. Their commander was smart enough to keep their fleet together, though, even after he appeared to lose control of the forward elements."

"Really?" Nick said. "How do you know that?"

"Pablo monitored Silfe communications during the battle. Even with micro-wormhole FTL systems, a signal still needs to be sent. He positioned our wormholes throughout their fleet to pick up ship-to-ship traffic. It turns out that Silfe and the Fscope communications systems are almost identical. They use pulsed light, just like we do. The messages are encrypted, but with HAL giving us the kernel for the Silfe language, he could break it."

"Wow!" Nick said, face lightening. "That has to be a serious intelligence coup for us."

"It is. We have a recording of the Silfe fleet commander..." he picked up a data pad and read, "... A Chief Slayer Tetukken, sending repeated orders to the forward cruisers, demanding that they bring their fighters back in under the protection of the capital ships." Jake gave a genuine smile. "Which they ignored."

"Well, HAL said they have a fractured leadership scheme. It looks like we have confirmation."

"Unfortunately, this Tetukken kept the overall fleet together, or we may have had another shot at them when the cruisers broke off. Still, most of the Silfe ships are following the First fleet into Mars." He grimaced. "Unfortunately, 4000 of their battlecruisers broke off towards Callisto and Enceladus. 2000 each."

"I hadn't heard," Nick said, frowning.

"I just heard a few minutes before I called you." His face took on a slightly pained expression. "There is no way that either of them can hold."

"Can't we do anything?"

"Probably not for the colonies themselves. I am routing the Second Fleet under Admiral Chen to Callisto to see if he can whittle down the enemy there, but we can't stop them from landing troops. The aliens will take out the ground-based anti-aircraft emplacements with little trouble. After that, their troops can land unopposed. We always knew that we couldn't keep them from the colonies, but hopefully they can bleed them before they hit the ground."

"As for taking the colonies. It will depend on how many casualties they are willing to take. We didn't purpose build them to kill Silfe like DS-1 and two or Olympus Mons, but they will still be pretty nasty nuts to crack." He sighed. "They were *designed* to be conquered If the Silfe put enough pressure on. We need to give the bastards some minor victories, or they will ignore the colonies altogether, and we can't have that yet. We are in a battle of attrition. Our forces need to get close to parity before we can go on the offensive. The best we can hope for is time. If we put up too much resistance, it will force the Silfe to focus on Earth, and we haven't destroyed enough of their battlecruisers yet for that."

Nick could see the stress on his best friend's face. "You are doing everything you can, Jake. The marines in the colonies are volunteers. They knew what they were signing up for, and even if we lose them entirely, their sacrifice will not be in vain."

"I know all that; I helped draft the overall plan."

"I know you do. I also know that it is eating you up inside. I am not talking to you as the World Commission Chancellor here. I am Nick, the guy who has known you since high school." He gave Jake a deep, meaningful look. "Are you OK?"

The head of the World Commission Defense Force blew out his breath in a long stream. "I am." He flashed Nick a grin that wasn't so far off from one he might have seen back at Pencey, even if it was less carefree. "I appreciate you asking. I can't let my guard down around anyone, and I haven't seen Jane or the girls in months. Virtual calls aren't the same. We need Cindy to make a transporter beam so I can go home for a few hours."

Nick laughed. "Trust me, David has asked, but so far, no dice. I imagine if we can get through the next few weeks, she might focus on something like that, just for the fun of it."

"That's the rub," Jake said. He massaged his temples. "OK, my pity party's over. Thank you, old friend. Now, do you have any specific instructions for me as the Chancellor of Earth?"

"Only that I will have David and Gloria working on some psy-ops. The fact that we know the commander's name and can pinpoint his ship will help."

"What are you thinking?" Jake asked.

"Nothing specific. I was planning on letting them loose to tie their fleet down at Mars as much as possible."

"I don't know, Nick." the uniformed man said. "Are you sure that is a good idea? David and Gloria can get a little… overzealous when you take the gloves off."

Nick shook his head. "If there was ever a time to get into a bare-knuckle fight, it's now."

"I have a hard time arguing with that logic. OK, you're the boss. Let me know if there is anything I can do to help; otherwise, I will focus on things I *can* control. Heaven knows

David and Gloria aren't on that list."

Warren Industries New York Campus
Same Day

"So, what we want to do is get them focused on Mars, and make the more hotheaded of their leaders either give bad orders or ignore good ones, right?" Gloria asked from her seat at David's kitchen table.

"Essentially," David said, moving to the fridge to get out a root beer. He took a long swig, ending in a satisfying belch. The little man moved to sit across from her and said, "I'd offer you one, but... you know...."

"I don't have a stomach?" she said with an ironic smile.

"Yeah, pretty much."

Gloria laughed, and held up an arm saying, "Root beer please Garçon," which resulted in a bottle materializing in her hand. She twisted off the bottle cap and flicked it with her thumb, causing it to spin in front of her for a few turns before disappearing into motes of light. "You were saying?"

David grinned. "Pretty slick. If we ever find a way to transfer my consciousness into a computer, I am totally going to do it. I mean, root beer, without having to go to the store, would *by itself* make it worth it."

"Yes David," Gloria said dryly. "The best part of being an AI is definitely the free root beer."

"You don't have to convince me. I'm sold!"

"Anyway," she said, taking a sip from her drink. "As far as the psy-ops go, what is our end goal?"

David steepled his fingers in a classic thinking pose. "According to Nick, we want to bleed them as much as possible on Mars. The goal is to keep possession of Olympus Mons, tying down their forces. Eventually, we want to encourage them to split up their capital ships into more manageable pieces and pick off as many as we can.

"Got it," Gloria said. "Since Juan is commanding the

Olympus Mons Marines, I can completely get behind winning there, or at least going for a stalemate." She tapped her chin. "So, we need to figure out which of the Silfe commanders are hot heads and then... entice them to make mistakes."

David nodded. "Right. With the way Pablo hacked their communications, I think we could probably figure out from inter-ship traffic which of the Silfe commanders would be most likely to lose their shit. The only question is, what would make a space crocodile get riled up enough to make mistakes?"

Gloria smirked. "I think we should go with Monty Python and the Holy Grail."

"Ah blow my nose at you, so-called 'Arthur Keeeng'!" David said, laughing.

"I was thinking more like Your mother was a hamster, and your father smelt of elderberries!"

"I like it! We just need to figure out what really pisses off the Silfe." He tapped his chin. "Maybe we should ask HAL?"

"I did," Gloria said. "He said that they are sensitive to anything that has to do with their god Karoken, and that they have a fear of dying outside of battle. Supposedly, if you don't bite the big one from direct conflict, then Karoken won't 'Hear your final prayer.' Which is a term they use interchangeably with death." She shook her head disgustedly. "The Silfe are a bunch of self-centered drama queens. They think they are doing people a favor by killing them. It's like some kind of viking thing, where you put all the blades of your fallen enemies around you in the boat before they shoot one of those fire arrows at it."

"*That* is totally the way I want to go." David said. He waved a hand in a circle. "After I upload my consciousness to the web, of course. If I am going to have that epic of a funeral, I want to watch it."

"You got it, boss."

"OK," he said. "So, we need to pick our insults carefully. We should mix in some digs at Karoken, and then hit um in the nads with dying in bed."

"Do they even have 'Nads?'" Gloria asked.

David's face pinched. "You know, in 27 years, I have never thought to ask that question. It feels like something you should know about your enemy. Every picture or holographic rendering I have ever seen of them had pants on! I mean, if I ever come face to face with a Silfe warrior, I feel like the only way I am getting away is with a cheap shot and going for the nads has been a tried-and-true way for small, skinny dudes, since time immemorial."

Gloria's laughter had started at the first mention of 'Nads,' and had only gotten stronger as David talked.

The little man looked at her seriously. "I'm having an existential crisis here and you are laughing. Nice friend you are!" he said in a mock huff.

Gloria got her laughter under control and said. "Wait a minute, and I'll check with HAL." Her eyes went unfocused for a full 10 seconds before she came back to him. She snorted in disgust. "I swear, HAL is such a prima-donna nowadays. I had to give him a dissertation on the importance of knowing whether the Silfe had nads to Earth's survival, including the full history of nad kicking back to the first known images in Egyptian hieroglyphics, before he would answer me."

"And…" David said, leaning forward. "Don't leave me *hanging* here. What's the verdict?"

"Ahhh!" She said, "That pun was so bad that I felt like someone kicked *me* in the nads! I think I just had a pair of servers commit seppuku."

David looked pained. He gave her a pleading look and waited for her answer.

"Fine!" she said. "The males have nads in the exact place you would expect."

"Yes!" David said, holding out a hand for a fist bump, which Gloria dutifully returned. "Skinny dudes everywhere are dancing in the streets tonight!" He turned back to her. "What about the females?"

She gave him a knowing look. "I knew you would ask, so

I made HAL tell me that too. Turns out that if you kick a Silfe female in the…" She gave a delicate cough, "Privates, that you will get much the same reaction as you would with a male. On a female, the area is sensitive too."

"OK," David said, expression thoughtful. "Good to know." He smiled. "Now that we have the important stuff settled, let's see if we can figure out a way to piss off a few Silfe commanders!"

Gloria shook her head at her incorrigible friend and nodded. Then they got down to the brass tacks of enraging the leaders of an alien race.

FORTY-TWO

Mars High Orbit
+3 days: the next day

Tetukken was having a bad day. The humans were insufferable! At every turn, they pushed and prodded, delayed, and trapped the Silfe fleet in enraging -and he could admit, at least privately- ingenious ways.

He lost another 300 battlecruisers when they strayed too close to the moon the humans called Phobos. The enemy had placed giant laser batteries on it and then camouflaged them. The weapons had been so deep in the rock that not even the olangee's scanners could locate them. The fleet sailed calmly by, only to have cruisers blow up without apparent cause. A precious few minutes elapsed before they even understood what was happening. By then, the nearest battlecruisers were expanding clouds of superheated metal.

Worse, it had taken 20,000 ground troops to subdue the moon. The humans were merciless in their anti-aircraft defense. The Silfe commanders had tried to come in low from the opposite side of the moon, only to find even more hidden laser batteries waiting for them. They lost another 10,000, including their combat drop shuttles, before they could abort the attack.

Tetukken ordered the fleet to back off and conduct

a kinetic bombardment from a safe distance to clear the approaches. Only then was a *second* 10,000 able to land without resistance. That 10,000 had successfully subdued the moon, but not without difficulties.

The warriors found a series of tunnels that led in a twisting and turning pattern to the control rooms for each laser emplacement. At every turn, traps sprung, walls fell, warriors' feet tripped explosive wires, and pressure plates caused floors to fall out from under them. All had caused casualties and slowed progress to a crawl. When the warriors finally reached the control rooms, they faced the humans themselves.

The short, vicious battles for the rooms were eye-opening. Tetukken watched the recordings. The humans were using augment suits to increase their puny strength. The Silfe had experience with races who attempted similar approaches in the past. Usually, they easily overcame the tactic. Olangee scientists would hack the computer connections of any suits they encountered and freeze them like statues. That was not the case with the humans. The olangees said they were entirely mechanical, with only small, isolated electronics in the helmets and gloves. According to them, there was nothing *to* hack.

The warrior scientists found much the same in the worrisomely effective enemy fighters. They also appeared to have no networked computer systems.

Tetukken now felt confident that the Harrow had sent one of their damnable AI machines to Earth. He might have written off the quick advancement of their technology as an unexplained boom in industry or culture, but their military technology seemed explicitly designed to foil Silfe attempts at hacking. It was too much of a coincidence.

Except now that he considered it dispassionately, the entire point of the olangee's machinations was to take computer-assisted aiming and artificial intelligence out of war. Karoken demanded that each final prayer be the action of a sentient, living being. Tetukken had to admit that human technology was in line with Karoken's teachings. Well, maybe not the traps and trickery they employed at every turn, but should the Silfe force them into direct conflict, they might have battles not seen in thousands of years, fights that would truly challenge the Chosen.

He just wished the enemy technology wasn't *quite* as effective as it was. Their fighters were superior to the Silfe. The initial three-to-one ratio was broadening to four-to-one in favor of the humans. The Chosen fleet still had many more fighters -at least for now- but the exchange rate was alarming.

The augment suits the enemy utilized were highly effective. The humans on the moon fought from fixed, prepared positions, but two defenders -the amount at each laser control center- killed ten Silfe warriors on average. Sometimes, it was closer to fifty.

There had been 100 laser emplacements on Phobos. Of the 10,000 warriors sent to disable them, 3000 returned. Most of the Silfe fell prey to traps, but the defenders killed a disturbing 1800, with only two hundred enemy final prayers to show for it.

Most lauded it as a victory, and the young ones were crowing about their first taste of human flesh, but he caught the uncomfortable looks from his senior commanders. They knew the horde had lost more ships in this system than in the last dozen planetary cleansings combined.

Things continued to go poorly. Tetukken stopped himself from growling aloud about splitting the horde. Individual operations still fell to his sub-commanders even though he had overall campaign command. He couldn't give adequate cause for keeping the fleet together, even though his gut told him it was the right move. He had no choice but to OK the 4000 ships to split off to the other two human colonies. Even split, they *should* be able to handle anything the humans sent at them.

The olangees confirmed the Earthlings possessed three

fleets of six hundred ships each. They appeared to have two ship types, one smaller and faster carrier and a heavier and slower ship, which must be their version of a battlecruiser. They had yet to engage a capital ship directly, so he didn't know their capabilities, but given the strength of the lasers on the moon, it seemed likely that the bigger vessels would be powerful enough to destroy a Silfe battlecruiser. Still, they vastly outnumbered the humans. Even should the enemy mass their strength, they were outclassed, even against one of the smaller groups tasked to assault the colonies.

He brushed the stupidity of his sub-commanders from his mind and focused on the holotank, where a three-dimensional representation of a giant volcano stood. He saw several Enemy fighters lift out of the depression at its top and fly a slow loop around the steep slope.

Intelligence reports gathered before the horde entered the system stated that the human colony of Mars was extensive, but the olangees reported the settlements across the planet lay abandoned. Only the mammoth mountain, called Olympus Mons, showed activity.

Looking at the dormant volcano gave him an increasingly familiar rolling sensation in his belly. After watching the assault recordings from Phobos, he could readily identify why. Olympus Mons would be riddled with tunnels. In addition, there had to be an incredible amount of anti-aircraft batteries around it, and like Mars's moon, the olangees couldn't detect them.

He growled, his frustration finally overwhelming his self-control. Should he order another kinetic strike to clear out the lasers and railguns he knew must be hidden in the red-tinged soil? Doing so without an explicit threat would be considered cowardice by the more traditionally stupid of his sub-commanders. Tetukken knew it was the right thing to do, but he hadn't ordered it. The question remained. Did he allow 10,000 warriors to be shot out of the sky to prove a point, or did he do the intelligent thing?

Already, he saw the furtive glances of his command staff. He should already have given the order, one way or another. He could easily imagine the young ones gnashing at the air as they waited for their first taste of battle. It was long ago, but he could remember the all-consuming ecstasy he felt the first time he bit into an enemy. It had been a religious experience, feeling the blood fill his mouth with his enemy's final prayer.

"Slayer," the communications officer said from the front of the deck. "I am receiving a priority communication addressed to you."

"What ship is it from?" he asked.

The officer's tail dipped in a clear sign of confusion. "It's not from the fleet, sir. It is from the Hu...ma...nsss."

Tetukken growled. The micro-wormholes they were detecting must have intercepted their communications. Unfortunately, there was nothing they could do about it. In truth, the olangees also had intercepted much of the traffic from the human fleet. Not that it helped them. The humans spoke in indecipherable code phrases that were idiomatic. He knew that their operation was called 'Cold Feet,' which had something to do with the temperature of the fleshy ends of their appendages, but even the olangees who had made a serious study of human languages could not discern why a fleet operation would be named something so mundane.

The humans must have made more progress if they could message him directly.

He realized the communications officer was still waiting for an answer. "You can send the audio to my console."

"Excuse me, Slayer, for not being clear," the officer said, his tail flicking. "It is a live holographic message."

Tetukken snorted. He supposed it shouldn't surprise him that the humans could project holograms. As evidenced by their fighters, they seemed to be at the same technological level as the Silfe, if not slightly ahead in some respects. He was increasingly glad they chose to cleanse the system when they did. He shuddered to think what they would have found if they had left them to develop for another hundred years.

"Put the communication on the main holotank," he said. It was time that he faced these humans. He let out an involuntary growl, making his command staff cower at their control panels. He would make the Earthlings tremble with his words!

The image of Olympus Mons faded out, to be replaced by one of the small pink creatures that inhabited the system. It wasn't an imposing specimen as far as he could tell. Tetukken had studied the physical characteristics of the Earthlings, and the man in the hologram didn't appear to be one of their warriors. Perhaps he was an olangee? The human was only about two-thirds the size of a Silfe female and had strange magnifying lenses on his eyes held to his head by twists of wire.

The human's mouth lifted at the corners, showing much of his white teeth. Tetukken wasn't sure if they meant the gesture as a challenge -as it would have been in Silfe culture- or was an affectation of the species.

"Greetings! Oh, green and scaly one! I am Chief Mugwump David Lieberman," the Earthling said in the Silfe language, or at least in a convincing simulation. Tetukken could detect no delay for translation, even though he knew the Chosen tongue did not suit human mouths.

"What do you want, huu...ma...aan?" he said, projecting aggression and command into his voice. "Have you called to beg for mercy? If so, you have wasted both your time and mine. We will give no quarter to the people of Earth. You should drop to your knees and praise Karoken now so that he might better hear your final prayers." He could sense the rest of the bridge crew watching the exchange with approval. He needed to show them just how weak the humans were! One of their leaders begging for mercy was just the morale boost that he needed after the frustrations of the past few days.

"Mercy?" the small man asked, his voice rising in what

appeared to be amusement. "No, your Godzillaness, I just wanted a quick chat. I figured it might be my only chance to talk to one of Karoken's second favorite children before we destroyed you."

"What blasphemy is this?" Tetukken roared. "The Silfe are the only Chosen of Karoken! There is no 'Second.'"

The man shook his head from side to side and made the Silfe noise used to calm young hatchlings. "Oh, you poor deluded tyrannosaur. Do you not know that humans are the favored Chosen of Karoken! He came to us long ago and said that he once had a race of puny green creatures that prayed to him, but that he grew tired of them." The man dropped his voice as if to tell a secret, "Always whining about being too scared to go into battle." He stopped and showed his teeth even wider, which the Chief Slayer found slightly unsettling. "There was also something about being tired of receiving prayers of warriors hoping to die in their beds."

The human beat his chest twice and then held two of his small clawless digits above his head. "But now he has us humans, the most terrifying warriors in all the universe! Our priests say he has never been happier, especially since now we can clean up..." He paused, "Sorry, I'm trying to remember the exact words the Chief Puba of the Church of Karoken used. Ah, yes!" he said. "He said that Karoken came to him in a dream to say it pleased him that the humans were going to clean up the 'Silfe mistake.'"

Tetukken roared in anger. "You dare speak of Karoken! You are nothing to him! We will cleanse this system of you, and Karoken will reward us doubly! He hears your treacherous false words and will turn you away when you come before him."

The little human in the holotank didn't flinch at the Chief Slayer's outburst. "Oh, you poor creature," he said. "You talk a big game, but you needed to bombard Phobos from orbit to set foot on soil we have claimed. You have lost millions of your supposed 'Chosen,' while we have only lost thousands.

Even now, the people of Mars sit in their halls, drinking toasts to Karoken while you cower in your ships, unable to approach for fear that the great and powerful one God will refuse to hear your final prayers." The human paused as Tetukken ground his teeth bloody in impotent rage.

"OK," the human said, showing even more teeth. "I just wanted to have this little chat with you before we wiped you from the system." The man put his hand to his chest. "I would ask you to try your best, big guy. It's all we can expect, given that you are so weak and frightened. Keep a stiff upper... snout and all that and try not to whimper too much when we send you to talk to the great and powerful Karoken... because that would just be embarrassing for you."

At these last words, the signal cut out, leaving Tetukken standing in front of the holotank, breathing hard.

"Chief Slayer," Tetukken's adjutant said. "Slayer Serenkeen's battlecruiser group is lowering into near orbit of the planet!"

Tetukken tried to calm himself as the words sunk into his consciousness. "I gave no such order!" he said.

The adjutant shook his snout. "The message from the human broadcast to Slayer Serenkeen's flagship as well."

The Chief Slayer growled low in his throat. *Damn that human!* His mind cleared as his rage cooled. The entire conversation was a ruse! The humans did not worship Karoken. This David Lieberman had purposefully enraged him and then broadcast the lies to the most unstable member of the entire fleet! It was because of Slayer Serenkeen that he had to group the fleet when the stupid commander refused to bring the fighters back under the protection of the capital ships.

Tetukken slammed his claws into the edge of the holotank in frustration, leaving long claw marks on the metal. He needed to stop the fool Slayer from committing his command, but... he couldn't! Calling the group back now would be seen as nothing short of cowardice after the human called him out.

"Slayer," his adjunct said, a question in his voice. "Orders?"

Tetukken gave a low hiss of frustration and said, "None currently. We will need to see how this plays out."

*****

"... Because that would just be embarrassing for you," David's image said.

Juan watched from the command bunker deep inside Olympus Mons. The commander of Earth's forces on Mars had difficulty controlling his laughter. The situation was deadly serious, but he had to admit that David was good at making people angry. *Hell, he's even good at pissing off other species.*

"General, we are getting movement from the alien fleet," Colonel Murphy, Juan's operations officer, said from his position in front of the large holotank dominating the center of the room. The gigantic form of Olympus Mons was recreated in detail at its bottom, with representations of the Alien fleet above it, denoted by motes of light.

"How many?" Juan asked.

"Looks like a full 1000, sir."

Well, that confirms it. Nick needed to ban David from being an ambassador to anyone they didn't want to go to war with. Raising his voice, he spoke to the room, "Wait until they unload landing shuttles before we give the order to fire. I want as many of them in range as possible. We only get one shot at this, so let's get as many of the bastards in the first barrage. We can't rely on them being this stupid again, so let's make it count, folks."

He could see the determined faces of his command staff as they started relaying his commands.

*****

"General, they are unloading shuttles," the operations officer said.

"How many are in range?" Juan asked.

"Almost a thousand, sir."

"That's as good as we will get," he said. "Order the laser batteries to open fire."

"Roger, sir," the weapons officer said. "Orders transmitted. Ground to orbit laser batteries firing in ten... nine... eight...."

As the countdown began, icons representing the Laser silos began lighting up all over Olympus Mons. He peered intently at the holotank. Finally, it reached zero, and he saw the tracings of lasers slicing upwards through the thin atmosphere towards the alien battlecruisers. As they connected, they could see a brief flash at the point of contact before the motes of light denoting the alien ships blinked out.

A cheer erupted from the command center as the invaders' ships blasted apart, one after another.

*****

Tetukken watched as the 1000 battlecruisers that Slayer Serenkeen had once commanded disappeared from the plot. At least the fool Slayer wouldn't be giving him any further problems. Serenkeen's flagship was one of the first targeted. A few ships in the formation got kinetic rounds off at the laser batteries, but it was too few and too late.

He gestured to the plot in the holotank. "How many ships moved out of range?"

A nervous looking olangee, seemingly worried that Tetukken might shoot the messenger, stammered a reply. "Twelve, Chief Slayer."

"Twelve out of 1000," he said calmly. Tetukken didn't have the energy to be outwardly angry. To say that he didn't have boiling rage inside would be a mistake, but the olangee tech who ran the holotank was not responsible for Serenkeen's colossal blunder. He focused all of his wrath on the humans.

"Orders to the fleet; commence kinetic bombardment

of the human base. Prioritize the large laser arrays shown during Slayer Serenkeen's attack, but I want every inch sanitized." They would at least be able to use the hothead's death for a purpose. He now had all the justification he needed to bombard the planetary base enough to soften up the Earthling's defenses.

FORTY-THREE

Just outside Jupiter Orbit
+4 days (one day later)

Rear Admiral Tao Chen looked at the plot on his viewscreen. He wished they had the new holotanks found in the ground bases, but Pablo refused, stating it wouldn't be a good idea to change the Dilong Class ships mid-mission. Chen admitted that the logic was solid, as would be expected from a sentient AI, but still liked the idea of looking at a three-dimensional model to give him a better perspective. Even after years of commanding ships in the black, he found it hard to appreciate the distances that the solar system represented. Perhaps it wasn't just him. Human minds were infinitely flexible, but the idea of millions of miles was hard to comprehend.

He looked at the alien fleet assaulting the colony on Callisto. It was small compared with the element still at Mars, although small was a relative term. At 2000 ships, even this scaled-down fleet outnumbered his own.

He stared at the screen, finding the ships lining up to bombard Callisto's surface.

Jupiter's second-largest moon was the most cratered object in the solar system, chosen for settlement because of the potential of enclosing those craters to hold an atmosphere.

The engineering would have been impossible before the advent of autonomous mining robots, but with them, after only a few short years, the first of the 'Domed Cities' took shape. The domes themselves were meters thick steel constructed utilizing the massive deposits of minerals discovered in the mixed ice and rock sandwiched between the moon's crust and the inner saltwater layer, 150 miles below the surface.

Tao could already see swarms of shuttles leaving the triangular battlecruisers on his plot. The Aliens used the last day to pound the ground surrounding the colony with kinetic projectiles. Their commander was smart enough not to repeat what happened on Mars, keeping their ships in high orbit, out of range of even the most powerful human laser.

There hadn't been all that many laser emplacements, anyway. Most of the anti-aircraft defenses at Callisto were smaller, designed for shooting down shuttles, not capital ships. Still, it would have been nice to get in a few more cheap shots.

At least the men and women manning the lasers had enough warning to evacuate to the colony. Given the number of enemy troops landing, it only delayed the inevitable, but they would be able to take a few Silfe with them.

Thoughts of the brave men and women preparing for the hopeless defense of Callisto shook him out of his reverie. It was time for his part in this war. He knew it would likely mean the destruction of the second fleet and his death, but if they could take out the alien ships, it would be worth it.

"Commander Trevathan, send orders to the fleet. Operation Sparta is a go."

Trevathan, his executive officer, nodded solemnly. He knew that their chances of survival were minimal but had never once suggested that they find another way. The war with the Silfe was about attrition. Every ship they destroyed meant fewer aliens who could land on Earth and fewer ravenous monsters who would show no mercy to their friends and family. The Navy personnel crewing humanity's fleets couldn't throw away their lives, but they would have done their jobs if they could trade them for enough of the enemy.

Operation Sparta was inspired by the Battle of Thermopylae, likely the most celebrated hopeless battle in history. The Greeks used small advantages, such as training and terrain, to hold off a much larger force and kill them disproportionately. It was something that the second fleet was going to attempt today. They were about to determine if surprise, commitment, and the ability to out-shoot the Silfe would be enough to win the day.

"Orders sent," the commander said.

Admiral Chen nodded, gazing intently at the plot as the fleet moved.

*****

Slayer Tossan regarded the holotank with pleasure. His troops were landing steadily, gathering before assaulting the multiple domed complexes of the colony. His forward scouts had already uncovered a tunnel system that the humans guarded. Finally, something was going right for the Chosen in this accursed cleansing. Soon the Silfe would send many final prayers to Karoken.

The enemy had been entirely too effective at destroying the ships of the horde. They had lost an astonishing 1404 ships. It was the most destroyed since the conflict with the Harrow, thousands of years in the past.

He couldn't help but grind his teeth in frustration at the foolish actions of the now-deceased Slayer Serenkeen. Emotion was well and good. In battle, it led to ferocity. Yet for leaders, those who were old and crafty enough to have survived multiple cleansings, emotions needed to be tempered by wisdom. They were not the young ones any longer, barely more than animals. Serenkeen had forgotten the lessons learned on the battlefield and paid the price.

Perhaps he could understand his fellow Slayer's anger, but not the actions that resulted from it. He watched the recording of the Supreme Mugwump, David Lieberman. The human's words were inflammatory but false. Karoken chose the Silfe and would not forsake them. It didn't mean that Tossan didn't want to rip the small Earthling's head from his shoulders, but he wouldn't put his command at risk to do it.

He took Tetukken's advice and thoroughly saturated the land surrounding the colony with an orbital bombardment. He supposed that he could have also attempted to destroy the settlement itself without landing troops, but that was not the way of Karoken. Besides, the domes looked quite robust. The olangees said that the metal was a thick alloy, much stronger than the armor on a battlecruiser. He wasn't entirely sure that he *could* destroy them.

He shook his snout. No matter. The ground troops were about to engage, and the humans would learn a lesson about the might of Karoken's Chosen!

"Slayer," the olangee operating the tactical station said. "We are picking up movement of the human fleet in orbit around the ringed gas giant."

"Have they received reinforcements?" He asked.

"No, Slayer," the officer said. "There are still only the original 600 ships we have been monitoring... although," the olangee paused, tail flicking in an unconscious nervous gesture that made Tossan grumble with disdain. They needed the warrior scientists, but he still had difficulty giving respect to someone who had never bloodied themself on the battlefield. The olangee found his courage and continued. "They are launching fighters and locking in an intercept course with the fleet."

Tossan growled. What were the humans up to now? Even with their damnably effective fighters, they had no hope of overcoming the numerical advantage posed by his fleet. He had nearly a three-to-one advantage in capital ships.

The humans were honorless, but not stupid. Their plans

had been entirely too effective at whittling down the horde for him to make that mistake. *Had their commander's anger overwhelmed them, like it had for the idiot Serekeen? Perhaps they were coming in a desperate bid to save the colony?* He didn't think so, which meant it had to be a trap. He just couldn't figure out what it could be. Still, he would need to position his fleet. Even small as the human numbers were, they could still do damage if he weren't careful.

"Orders to the fleet," Tossan said. "Battle formation oriented towards the humans with one-quarter acceleration. Leave the twenty battlecruisers deploying troops where they are. Deploy a fighter screen forward from the leading 200 battlecruisers."

*****

"The alien fleet is moving, Admiral Chen," the astrogator said.

"Heading?" he asked, inputting a series of commands to bring the Silfe fleet up on his viewscreen.

"They are coming straight at us, sir, in the same wedge formation they used when they attempted to engage First fleet."

"Looks like they only have one play in the book," he said with a grin, trying to inspire his staff with confidence. "I suppose that if you have never played a game against a real opponent, you wouldn't need anything fancy. It is time that we showed them a bit of human-style razzle-dazzle."

Chen could see the nervous but eager smiles on the face of his bridge crew. "OK, orders to fighters; Fumblerooski is a go."

At his command, the 55,000 fighters in front of the formation accelerated, spreading out and pushing forward.

*****

"Slayer, the human fighters are accelerating toward us,

pulling away from their carriers. Should I order our fighters to engage?"

Tossan grunted, watching as the icons of the enemy fighters moved away from the weapons envelope of their parent ships. *Why would they leave the coverage of the larger ships?* If it was a trap, he couldn't see it. Of course, that was the most dangerous type of trap, where the noose closed before you realized. He spoke to the room. "Continue to keep the fighters close in, under the protection of the main fleet."

*****

"Sir," Chen's weapons officer said. "They are holding the fighters back, close to the capital ships.

"Well, we finally have evidence of an intelligent commander," The Admiral said. "Too bad doing the right thing is doing the wrong thing in this case." His eyes narrowed like a hawk before diving toward unexpecting prey. "Orders to the fighters: Fumble the ball."

*****

"Slayer!" Tossan's weapons officer said. "The fighters are firing missiles." he looked at his console readings, then said, "Confirmed, 55,000 Launched.

"Ah!" The Slayer said. "Finally, they show their hand! It won't help them," he said with a toothy growl. He turned to the weapons officer. "Orders to the fleet. Jam missiles as they come in range."

Tossan was gleeful. The humans had made a major mistake! The missiles could only lock onto the Silfe ships through onboard computers, systems the olangees were experts at confusing. Unlike the railguns the enemy used in the sneak attack a few days ago, the missiles had a very noticeable energy signature that could be tracked and avoided. The Silfe could shoot them out of space, but it wasn't even necessary. Even fusion warheads would only propagate minimally without atmosphere, so the Chosen ships could just move out of the way and focus their energy on destroying the enemy. The only downside was that multiple fusion detonations would disrupt communications within a light minute. It would clear over time but might play havoc with his ability to give orders to the fleet. Not that he needed to with the humans so obligingly rushing to meet him.

"The fighters are launching again," the weapons officer said.

Tossan shook his head, "It doesn't matter; the missiles won't be able to track us. They might not even be able to explode if the destruction sequence is computer controlled. Please ensure that all ships are out of the blast zone of any individual missile."

"Orders sent, Slayer."

*****

"That's the fourth launch, sir,"

"OK," Admiral Chen said. He projected his voice for the entire bridge to hear. "I want a timer up on the main screen for each flight of missiles." He turned to the communications officer. "Orders to all ships. Advance at full speed as soon as the first set of detonations occurs. At that point, we will lose communication capabilities. Carriers and heavy cruisers are to engage targets of opportunity as they present themselves, with priority on the alien capital ships. Let our fighters deal with theirs."

"Orders sent, sir," the communications officer said.

"This is it, folks. Everyone do your jobs, and I will see you on the other side." Chen paused, wondering if he should say anything else. There was a good chance that this would be his last words to the men and women he had worked with and come to know over the past three years. Finally, he shouted, "FOR EARTH!"

There was a slight pause, and every face of the

command staff firmed with determination. A returning shout rocked the bridge. "FOR HUMANITY!"

*****

Tossan blinked his eyes to clear them as the holotank went white. "What happened?" he asked.

"I believe that the human missiles all detonated simultaneously, although it is impossible to tell for sure, as we no longer can form micro-wormholes," the olangee said.

"What about direct visuals?"

"The enemy is too far, plus..." the Silfe scientist hesitated as he checked his console for additional readings.

"Plus, WHAT!"

"I'm not sure what those missiles were exactly," the olangee said. They were fusion missiles, but they must contain some other materials, as they are making it impossible for our visual scopes to penetrate. It is dissipating but slower than what I would expect."

The screen cleared as the local subspace stabilized. Then another flash, right on top of where the first exploded, whited it again.

"That was another set of missiles going off, Slayer," the weapons officer said.

"It doesn't take an olangee to figure that out, you idiot!" He growled and lashed his tail. The bridge went silent as his rage made them cringe. "Up, you toothless cowards!" he yelled. "Tell me where the enemy fleet is!"

The weapons officer, who seemed to recover the quickest, was also the first to answer. "We can't, Slayer; there is too much interference."

Tossan roared in rage as yet a third set of missiles exploded. "Get me the expected range then! Where are the Hu...ma...nsss now?"

The astrogator punched commands into her console and said, "Given the last known coordinates, the enemy fleet should still be well outside of weapons range. They were going relatively slow, and their fighters were not much further ahead.

The Slayer paused, thinking furiously, as a fourth flash occurred. *What had she said? They were going relatively slow... TO BEGIN WITH!* If the humans accelerated immediately after the first missiles detonated, they would be close; in fact, they would be just on the other side of the interference caused by the explosions, which would mean they were attempting to get into knife range. Even a half-powered shot from a capital ship at that distance would destroy anything it hit. The humans would commit suicide, but they could devastate his fleet! He paused, thinking furiously. The humans had shown trickery at every turn, always trying to preserve their numbers. Were they willing to give up a third of their total ships to destroy his?

Tossan's hesitation cost him everything as Earth's Second Fleet, carriers, heavy cruisers, and fighters punched through the cloud of chaff, playing havoc with the alien sensors, and opened fire as one on the Silfe.

FORTY-FOUR

Saturn Orbit; WCN, David Tennant
+4 days (4 hours after the 'Battle of Callisto')

"You did a fantastic job, GG," Admiral Swelton said from the view screen in Captain Gregory George's ready room.

"We lost 375 carriers and all the heavy cruisers, admiral; not to mention 45,000 Gunstars. We're picking up a few survivors here and there who were lucky enough to have their skinsuits hold up, but they are few and far between." He let out a bitter laugh. "Hell, the only reason you are talking to me is because I am the highest-ranking person left." He wiped his hand across his eyes, ignoring the tears forming at the corners. "I was 152nd in the command structure, by date of rank."

Swelton nodded seriously. "I know. We lost some fine men and women, including Admiral Chen, who I have known for over a decade."

"Oh, damn, sir," he said. "I forgot that Admiral Chen was the pilot for the Mars Mission. I'm sorry for your loss."

Swelton nodded solemnly. "Tao Chen was a fine officer and a finer man. He knew what his orders meant, and if there is any blame to be had from today, it is squarely on my shoulders. I OK'd the operation myself." Swelton's jaw firmed. "The second Fleet destroyed 1800 enemy battlecruisers at the cost of 475 of our ships. That is better than a three to one ratio. It also proved our weapons cycle at twice the enemy rate and confirmed we could disrupt their version of the Fscope with fusion bombs. I know you lost friends today, but we won."

Swelton's eyes shined with hope and regret in equal measure. "GG, remember what we are trying to accomplish. We are fighting on an absurd scale, so the number of lives lost will also be absurd. In the end, we can only hope that we have done what we need to preserve our homes."

George nodded. He knew Swelton was right. Pushing down his sadness, he focused on what was right in front of him. "Do you have any orders, admiral?" he asked.

"Can you give me a report on the situation on Callisto? I am still receiving occasional messages from the base, but they are confused. FTL communications in the area is still spotty."

George nodded. "220,000 fusion missiles will do that. We are having a bit more luck. The 200 remaining alien battlecruisers are still in orbit. They have stopped dropping troops, but I think they have so many on the ground that they are tripping over themselves. It looks like the marines are still holding out. We are getting a stray transmission every so often, and there have been some flashes that appear to be ordinance going off at regular intervals, although it is hard to tell."

"OK, Captain," Swelton said. "You don't have enough ships to take the alien battlecruisers left at Callisto." He sighed. "I know you don't want to do it, but we will have to pull you back."

"We are just going to leave the marines?"

"Yes," the Admiral said. "It doesn't sit well with me either, but you must remember that we didn't even attempt to protect Enceladus. As harsh as it sounds, the colonies were designed to bleed the aliens, not stop them. Even your attack was to take out a portion of their ships with as little impact on our fleet numbers as possible." Taking in George's glare, Swelton held up a hand. "GG, there are 10,000 troops on each of the alien battlecruisers. Second Fleet killed eighteen million soldiers ready to land on Earth and kill every man, woman, and child. It is hard to appreciate, but you saved millions of human beings."

The anger seemed to flood out of the exhausted captain in a rush. "I'm sorry, Admiral, I am still coming to grips with everything. I know you're right. Where do you need me?"

Swelton gave a silent nod. "You are to proceed with the remainder of your ships to meet up with Admiral Patel's Third Fleet in Lunar orbit. I am giving you a field promotion to Commodore. You have my leave to promote your first officer to captain to command the *David Tennant* and anyone else you need to fill out the TOE. I want you in overall command until you report into the Third Fleet, and then Admiral Patel can figure out what to do next. Do you have questions?"

Commodore Gregory George shook his head. "No, Admiral. We should finish rescue operations in the next four hours and then be on our way back home."

Jacob Swelton's blond head nodded. "Take heart, Commodore. We are near the point where we can turn the card table over on the bastards."

George's eyes hardened. "I'm looking forward to it, sir."

FORTY-FIVE

Olympus Mons
+4 days (same day)

The constant pounding and shaking ceased. General Juan Costas looked up from reading readiness reports on his tablet, counting to ten to ensure that the orbital bombardment had stopped before standing and exiting the small office attached to the CIC.

"Give me an update, people!" he yelled at the room.

His operations officer, Colonel William Murphy, responded in his crisp New England accent. "It appears the aliens have ended the bombardment, sir. We are seeing signs of shuttles releasing from the nearest battlecruisers." His report was to the point and respectful. Any resentment that the Colonel might have had with reporting to a man half his age was long ago replaced by respect for Juan's natural brilliance and leadership.

"Did any of the anti-ship laser batteries remain operational?" Juan asked.

"We have some we can dig out in a day or so, but it would require external excavation, which we couldn't hide from the aliens."

"OK," Juan said. "About what we expected. It was always too much to hope they would keep coming at us. At least we got almost 1000 of the bastards before they got smart." He turned to his communications officer. "Send orders to the GAR crews. Tell them to get outside and take down targets of opportunity."

"Aye, sir," the lieutenant said.

Juan turned back to the Colonel. "We ready for this, Bill?"

The Colonel flashed a confident smile. "We are marines, General. We are ready for anything."

"Oorah!" Juan yelled, receiving an enthusiastic response from the members of his command team. "You all know what to do. Keep me informed as everything unfolds."

Despite his young age, Juan had been leading troops for years and could admit that he had a natural gift for it. He knew the most successful commanders surrounded themselves with competent people and then let them do what they were trained for, only intervening when necessary to smooth out the inevitable bumps in the road. He stood back silently, watching the giant holotank showing alien shuttles dropping toward the Martian surface. His brow furrowed. *It begins.*

*****

Corporal Pham called to the other two members of his squad. "Shuttles dropping, let's get into position."

The two men and one woman of the Ground-to-Air Railgun crew picked up the components of their weapon with exosuited gauntlets. The railgun was in two pieces. The primary weapon and an external sight which looked like -and was- an expensive telescope. In addition, there were two heavy crates, one of ammo and another containing the battery that powered the gun.

Without the suits' augmented strength, they would never have been able to move any of it. The telescope, the lightest of the pieces, was several hundred pounds. Even in the Martian gravity, half that of Earth, it would have taken more than one of them to carry it.

They ran down the tunnel at speed, reaching its end

at one of the many exits leading to the vast sloping side of Olympus Mons. They were lucky. Their exit tunnel hadn't taken a direct hit in the alien bombardment and so was still clear. Steel sheathed the exit, making collapse unlikely, but the violence of the alien kinetic strikes had still bounced a few boulders inside.

Pham keyed the unit com channel and said, "Set up in position one, we'll take two shots then move to position two, from there we take a shot at each position until recall, we run out of targets, or receive alternate orders by higher." Panting breaths were the only response to his words. The three of them had drilled this repeatedly, both in VR and IRL. The two privates rounding out his squad knew their business as well as he did. Still, it was his responsibility to command, and he took the duty seriously.

The corporal, carrying the sensitive telescope, came to the end of the tunnel and slowed as he and his two squad members burst out onto a small landing on the side of the largest volcano in the solar system.

Olympus Mons was a staggering 374 miles in diameter and rose sixteen miles above the Martian plain. The mountain was a hundred times bigger than the largest volcano on Earth, Mauna Loa, and the WCDF had made it the focus of the defense of Mars.

The dormant volcano's height drastically increased the range of the ground-based lasers which had devastated the alien battlecruisers. Unfortunately, after the bombardment, those lay buried under tons of rock.

Now that the lasers were impotent, the alien shuttles were on their way to the surface. Pham's GAR crew, and hundreds of others like them, had the duty to make sure that as few of those shuttles reached the surface as possible. It was an important job, but one of the most dangerous positions in the marines. Their mission was a delicate balance of fire and move. Any shot they took would result in return fire.

The railgun rounds had no energy signature, so they

would have some time before anyone found them. Still, even if the battlecruisers in orbit didn't bombard their positions, the aliens were bound to send fighters to cover the shuttles, who would look to take out any GAR crew that dawdled.

The team reached position one, a hollow ten feet in diameter, carved out of the red rock by mining bots. Pham observed the setting up process through the sealed helmet of his skinsuit, making sure that Private Tran placed the legs of the railgun in the appropriate locations and that the ammo carried by Private Nguyen was within easy reach. He placed the telescope on the ground a few feet from the gun and handed the heavy-duty cord to Nguyen, who attached it to the side via a magnetic connection. The entire process only took thirty seconds. *Just in time.* He looked up at the digital clock in the upper right corner of his HUD. They had less than a minute until the first shot needed to be in the air.

The WCDF Ground-to-Air Railgun was a tube eight feet in length and three feet in diameter. According to his basic training instructors, a series of magnets surrounded the inner tube. Those magnets accelerated the ammunition forward at an incredible two miles per second. The ammunition comprised steel rods a foot in length and four inches in diameter, tapering to a point. The only mechanical component of the ammunition was a set of spring-loaded fins that popped out as it exited the gun to provide stability in flight.

The gunsight had no direct computer control; a set of small hydraulic tubes fed through the connector, allowing the gun to aim via the telescope.

Pham called out to his crew. "Private Nguyen, load a round. Private Tran, get me the rate of descent of the nearest alien shuttle."

The Corporal could see thousands of black dots dropping through the upper atmosphere, which he knew were full of alien soldiers intent on killing him. He took a steadying breath and looked into his sight, calling out, "Mark, shuttle 160 degrees in grid ten."

Tran found the part of the Martian sky they were responsible for covering. They had four adjacent grids representing squares of the horizon. The GAR crew had several backup grids should nothing be in their area of responsibility, but that wasn't an issue. It looked like it was raining alien shuttles. The Private looked through a pair of binoculars that flipped down over his helmet. He found the shuttle at 160 degrees and yelled, "Reentry at 30,000 kilometers per hour."

Pham looked through the more powerful scope and saw a black, boxy shuttle with short swept-back wings. It seemed like it was falling straight down with no jigging at all.

He couldn't believe his eyes. *Were the aliens stupid enough to think they had taken out all the human antiaircraft capability?* Maybe they did. He knew that there weren't any GAR crews on Phobos, so the aliens had landed without resistance after taking out the emplaced lasers. He gave a brief prayer of thanks to any deity who would listen and twisted a dial on the side of the site, compensating for the rate of descent, then used his gauntleted fingers to manipulate the controls, putting the crosshairs just under the shuttle. He checked the timer on his HUD. Ten seconds left. As the timer hit zero, the ship entered his crosshairs.

"Firing!" he said, pressing the button on his controls and sending death into the sky. "Next target," He yelled, not even checking to see if they hit. Nguyen slapped another round into the gun, and Pham moved his crosshairs to the next grid. "Mark and fire!" He yelled again as his helmet clamped down on the ear-shattering explosions pocking the sky.

"Move! Move!" Pham called.

At his command, the crew picked up the pieces of the gun and ran out of the hollow as fast as their augmented legs could carry them. As they rounded a large boulder between their firing positions, a thunderous BOOM sounded from behind them, followed by a shock wave that knocked them off their feet. The three marines lay stunned for a moment before an encouraging "Get your asses moving!" from Pham got them going again.

As they ran on, the Corporal glanced behind him to see smoke and dust rising from the position they had just left. He blocked out the knowledge that his team had escaped death by a hair's breadth and hurried toward their next firing position. He had a job to do, and he was damn well going to see it get done!

*****

"The last of the GAR crews are back inside, sir," Colonel Murphy said.

"What's the count on shuttles shot down?" he asked.

"It looks like we destroyed just over a thousand." The Colonel's face was unreadable as he continued. "We lost 234 of 500 GAR crews, although it is possible that some of them may still be outside or have a malfunction in their communicators."

Juan nodded silently, keeping the grimness from his face at the news of losing 702 marines. In the calculus of war, the operation had been a resounding success. They knew both from HAL, and their observations of the landings on Callisto, that each of the alien drop shuttles carried 250 troops. By shooting down the shuttles, the crews had killed 250,000 of the aliens. Not that it seemed to matter to the Silfe commanders, who just continued to drop ever more shuttles. He finally had to pull the GAR crews back in after the aliens landed enough troops to overwhelm their positions.

He turned back to Murphy. "Are the fire teams deployed to their positions?"

"The last radioed in ready a few minutes ago. We are getting some contact reports at the GAR exit tunnels."

"Any issues yet?" Juan asked.

"None. So far, we are holding the line."

Juan nodded. "OK, Let's start a slow withdrawal into the internal kill zones. Keep pressure on but let them advance. We want them to feel overconfident before we close down on them."

"Roger sir," Murphy said, turning away to shout orders at the communications officers responsible for coordinating the 100,000 Martian marines, waiting to give the Silfe a very bad day.

FORTY-SIX

Warren Industries New York Campus
+5 days (the next day)

"Damn it!" Cindy said. The petite scientist sat observing the readouts on the screen as the power levels fluctuated, going into the red and causing her to punch in a command on the keyboard. She waited with bated breath as the needle on the power indicator slowly lowered back into the safe zone.

"FUCK! She yelled, pounding her small fists on the console and letting out a string of unintelligible curse words through her teeth. She heard a cough behind her, then a voice.

"Wow! David said. "I know drill instructors who couldn't string that many swear words together. You have a gift! I think your talents are being wasted here. We should have Jake assign you to a basic training platoon on the Moon or something."

Cindy didn't turn as David's hands fell on her shoulders and kneaded her tense muscles.

"I might be of more use as a drill sergeant," she said. "I can't get these energy levels to sync. I know it's possible, but the damn thing keeps going into the red."

David turned her chair to face him. "What exactly are

you trying to do? You have been in here for hours. I came up to see if you were coming down to dinner."

"Oh damn! We are supposed to be meeting up with Jane tonight, right?"

"Yes, we probably shouldn't bail on her. She is keeping up appearances, but I know she is having a hard time with her whole family being out on combat operations."

Cindy shook her head. "That is why I'm in here, trying to get the inertial dampeners to modulate into something that can take a laser hit."

"What, like a shield or something?"

"Exactly. It can already help with sweeping particles out of the way, but I feel there must be some way to make the field stronger. If I could get it to take a hit or two, we could win this war, and maybe… maybe we could save some lives."

David took in her expression. Cindy had unshed tears in the corner of her eyes, which were bloodshot from too little sleep and too much worry. He kissed her forehead. "You need some sleep," he said. "You've been pushing too hard."

"How can I sleep!" she said, voice shrill. "We are down here, safe, while people we love are out there," she waved towards the ceiling, "Fighting for us!"

"Mars is holding," David said. "Gloria said that the Silfe are throwing everything at them, and they are barely moving."

"But people are dying!" she said, tears breaking free to fall down her cheeks.

David stood her up and pulled her against him, her head curling into the hollow of his neck. He could feel her shuddering breaths. He knew Cindy put immense pressure on herself to do something to turn the tide. In some ways, her feelings were a casualty of her success. Without her, humanity would have had no chance of holding back the Silfe. He doubted they would even have been able to get the colony ship away. It was her inventions that made it all possible. Without Cynthia Warren, humanity would have had no chance, yet here she was trying to pull another rabbit out of a hat and blaming herself for not being able to do it quickly enough.

He loosened his hold on her, letting her look up at his face. "Cindy, you are the most amazing woman I have ever known. Hell, you are the most amazing woman that has ever *been*. I have known that since you were sixteen, and I know it now, more than ever, but you can't do it all." He looked deeply into her eyes, ensuring her full attention was on him, and repeated, "You can't do it all."

She returned his gaze and nodded once, kissing him softly. "Thank you. I understand that I'm pushing hard, but I know I can do this, that there is a way to strengthen the fields. I have thought it possible for years, but there has been so much other stuff that needed doing that I've never been able to focus on it."

He gave a resigned sigh. "Fine," he said, but you need a bit of balance. Come to dinner, talk to Jane, and pretend that you aren't going in two different directions at once. You can't keep a coherent thought with this bouncing around in your mind."

"OHHHH!" Cindy said. "You're right!"

"I know," he said. His brows lowered. His wife wasn't generally this accommodating. "Do you want a few minutes to change before dinner?"

"Dinner?" she said distractedly. She pulled out of his arms and turned back to the console, typing rapidly on the keyboard.

David shook his head. "Yeah, remember, dinner with Jane? The dinner that you just agreed was a good idea?" He smiled. "The one that I convinced you to go to with my inspiring half-time speech?"

The glazed look went out of her eyes. "Sorry, you just gave me an idea. If I can get two opposing dampening fields polarized in opposite directions, I could strengthen it to take a laser hit."

David nodded slowly, seeing the implication. "Isn't that what Stony did to make artificial gravity?"

"Kind of," but those were both polarized in the same direction. If we made them opposite, the force would multiply exponentially."

"I'll take your word for it." He gave a resigned sigh. "This means you are not coming to dinner, right?"

"No. I need to get this done. I will need to pull all three AIs in on it. The math is crazy complicated and we will have to alter for each ship type, but if I'm right, we could more than double the survival rate of our forces."

"OK," he said. "I will make your excuses to Jane."

"Oh, shit!" she said. "You'll tell her I'm sorry?"

He gave her a peck on the cheek and said, "Don't worry. If you can make a shield that will make it more likely for Jake *and* Rose to survive the war, I am sure she will forgive you for missing dinner."

Cindy nodded and stood quickly to hug him. "I love you."

He laughed and motioned towards the console. "I love you too. Now get back to saving the world or something."

She turned to the computer, immediately engrossed in her work and calling out to the room for the AIs to run simulations. She didn't notice him as he paused, silently watching her with a proud smile on his face, before slipping out of the room unnoticed.

FORTY-SEVEN

Olympus Mons
+7 days

"Sir!" the panicked voice of Lieutenant Singh said. "We have a breakthrough at hall fifteen."

"Damn," Juan said under his breath. "How long do we have before they reach the CIC?"

"About twenty minutes, sir."

Juan locked eyes with Colonel Murphy. "Colonel, I will be leading the ready squad to seal the breach. I need you to take over here until I can get back. Any questions?"

Juan half expected Murphy to protest. After all, having the most senior officer present lead a squad into combat was hardly military protocol, but the taciturn colonel just nodded and said, "Yes, sir."

He was pleased he wouldn't have to argue the point. They both knew who the better soldier in a firefight was. Juan was widely regarded as one of the best to ever wear an exosuit. It was one cornerstone of his leadership style. He regularly practiced with the troops at all levels, citing the need to know the tactics and capabilities of the soldiers under his command to use them properly.

He moved through thick steel blast doors and into the next room, where the ready squad waited. Sergeant Broz's thick mustache twitched in surprise at the base commander's entrance, and he gave a salute.

"Orders General?" He asked in a slightly Slavic accent.

Juan gave a quick return salute. "The crocks have broken through at hallway fifteen. We need to seal it back up."

The broad-shouldered sergeant started bellowing orders at the other soldiers at his words. "OK, we got aliens to kill! Suit up! You have exactly one minute until we are on the bounce!"

The squad responded with a loud "OORAH!" and donned their armor.

Juan suppressed a grin. Heinlein's *Starship Troopers* had become the bible of the WCDF Exosuit Marines, and "On the bounce" was forever incorporated into the language of the corps.

One minute later, twenty-one suited marines sprinted down the stone corridor. As they reached each corner, rather than slowing to turn, they jumped to kick off the sidewall, changing direction. The artificial gravity generators were on, but the suits could bound off the walls faster than they could otherwise change directions. Juan smiled inwardly. Perhaps the term "On the bounce" wasn't a misnomer after all.

The squad ran for five minutes, flitting past seemingly endless side tunnels.

Olympus Mons had more space than the marines could ever use. The volcano was the largest in the solar system, two and a half times the height of Mount Everest and covering roughly the square mileage of the state of Arizona.

Despite the waste of resources and inconvenience, the base was spread out as widely as possible. The tunnels crossed and recrossed in a pattern meant to suck the Silfe in and, like quicksand, never let them back out. It wouldn't have been possible if Jake hadn't dropped off 3D printers and bots when he landed on Mars ten years before. It turned out that autonomous robots could dig a lot of tunnels in ten years.

They bounded off another corner, and Juan, who was

at the head of the column, held up his hand in a signal to stop. The tunnel widened into one of the expansive caverns peppered throughout the mountain. It was sixty feet wide and forty feet tall, with a stone ceiling cleverly hidden by holograms to represent a sunny sky. Genetically engineered plants, providing oxygen for the base, sat around the edges in large concrete planters. In the center was a small fountain, burbling away, unconcerned that it was in the middle of a war zone.

The cavern was one of the thoroughfare hubs that housed inter-tunnel transport. Juan could see an electric tram, looking a bit like a San Francisco streetcar, parked off to the left of the tunnel entrance, looking like any bus stop he had seen on Earth. It turned out that given normal Earth gravity, there was a "right" way to do things. It gave him a constant sense of cognitive dissonance, seeing a bus stop or an ice cream shop that wouldn't have been out of place in any city on Earth in the middle of the Martian volcano. The psychologists said it helped the human psyche forget that millions of tons of rock were overhead on a planet where the very atmosphere was deadly.

Juan keyed his mike to the squad channel. "We have 500 aliens, seven minutes up the tunnel. There is nothing between them and the CIC. I don't have to tell you how bad it would be for us if we lost it. I am going to play a few tricks on the bastards, so don't flinch if you see all hell break loose. Just shoot anything that looks like a mutated crocodile. OORAH?"

There was a slight pause as the marines wondered what the general might mean by "All hell breaking loose" before the expected response of "OORAH!" shouted from every throat.

"Sergeant Broz," he said. "Get them deployed in two-person fire teams. I will try to sow some confusion in the aliens, so I want them firing from cover, and I want the enemy guessing at their positions."

"Yes, sir!"

Juan remained where he was, watching as the last of the marines took up positions behind the tram and anywhere else that supplied cover. He even saw a pair of soldiers peaking around the edges of what looked like a mobile coffee cart.

"Gloria," he said to the air. His heart thudded in his chest as the beautiful form of the woman he loved materialized in front of him.

The AI's perfect red lips were frowning. "Why in the hell is the commander of the base about to lead a friggin' squad against 500 Silfe!" she said, heat in her voice.

He gave her an apologetic half-smile. "Sorry, honey,"

She put her hands on her hips, and her face took on a look of disgust. "God damn it, Juan! Don't you dare 'Honey' me! What do you think you are doing!

He sighed, "Stopping a force from overrunning the CIC by playing to my strengths. Murphy is more than capable of leading the rest of the battle but having me here makes it much more likely that we can hold the Silfe off. If they reach the CIC, I will have to fight, anyway. I would much rather do it here, where you could help, than there."

The angry look on Gloria's face wavered as his logic sunk in. The CIC had been so hardened against electronic tampering by the Silfe that even *she* couldn't materialize there, much less use any other tricks that might give the marines an edge. He saw her face flicker through several emotions, coming and going as her servers tried to suppress them. Finally, her mouth thinned in a resigned line as she analyzed and discounted her counterarguments.

"Fine!" she said. "I'll help you," she raised a finger, which stopped the smile forming on Juan's face. "But if you think I will forgive you for this idiocy without some major groveling, you are sadly mistaken."

Before he had an opportunity to swear his unending servitude to her, she blinked forward to raise the visor of his helmet, kissing him within an inch of his life, before slowly backing away, a smirk on her face as she took in his stunned expression.

"If you want another of those, you had better not

get yourself killed." She gave a tinkling laugh as he nodded wordlessly. "Now," the AI said, "Get under cover, and be ready to fire on the signal." She winked as her form seemed to collapse on itself until it became a single point of light that broke apart like a miniature firework.

He blinked twice and then yelled out, "What's the signal?"

Gloria's disembodied voice came out of the walls. "You'll know it when you see it!"

Juan shook his head, a smile coming unbidden to his lips. Even now, in a life and death situation, Gloria couldn't help but be... Gloria. He called out to the troops, many of whom had broken cover, to watch the bizarre spectacle of their commanding officer kissing a woman made of light.

"That was our ace-in-the-hole. I'm not sure what she's planning, but she has complete control over the base, including the holographic systems. So you should probably be ready for anything. On her signal, be ready to fire." He took in the stunned marines. Finally, he heard Sergeant Broz's voice.

"You heard the General!" he shouted in a voice that would make any drill instructor proud. "His lady friend is going to help us. All you grunts need to do is to be ready for the signal. NOW GET YOUR ASSES BACK UNDER COVER!"

The marines instinctively responded to Broz's words and dove back to their ambush spots. Broz gave Juan a brief nod before he knelt behind a large concrete planter.

Juan moved into the lee of a mining cart haphazardly parked behind his squad. He wanted to make sure that he could see the entire field of fire. He closed his faceplate, seeing a timer in the heads-up display. It had just counted down below four minutes. He had to assume that Gloria put it up of her own accord, as he hadn't asked for it. Words flashed across the front of the screen. It read, "Hold your fire until the timer reaches zero! *Love, Your friendly neighborhood Sentient Artificial Intelligence.*"

Juan had a hard time not groaning aloud. If he survived

the next few minutes, he would have *a lot* of questions to answer. Nick could probably stop any specific inquiries, but marines would talk, and the stories would grow in the telling. Now that he thought about it, maybe that was what Gloria wanted. It sounded like one of David's and her guerilla information schemes. A first step in getting the world used to the idea of sentient AIs.

He gave himself a shake, trying to focus.

As the timer hit three minutes, he saw movement down the corridor. He raised his laser rifle and flipped up the optical scope. Juan leaned in, seeing two Silfe warriors cautiously moving out of a side tunnel and into the large cave.

He shuddered. He'd seen pictures and even holographic renderings of the aliens before yet looking upon them with his own eyes was a visceral experience that he felt to his toes.

It was likely the similarities to Earth creatures, rather than differences, that made them truly horrific. It was like a Hollywood makeup artist had delved into their darkest nightmare and created a monster designed to evoke terror in the human psyche.

It was obvious why humans called them 'Crocks.' The aliens ranged in height between six to eight feet, with a tail that just reached the ground. They had massively muscled limbs that were similar in proportion to a human but ended in six-inch razor-sharp claws on both hands and feet. Their faces were surprisingly expressive, with two yellowed slitted pupils under thick bony ridges. An elongated snout, about half the length of an earth crocodile, protruded from the center of their face, making him wonder how they had ever developed speech. Despite the snout being shorter, it seemed -at least to him- that they packed in twice the amount of teeth as their Earthling cousins. Even with their mouths closed, he could see the edges of sharp teeth the size of his pinkie finger protruding like small tusks from their jaws.

A steady stream of the alien soldiers moved cautiously down the corridor, spreading out as much as possible. He couldn't help but smile in satisfaction. Despite their ferocity, the crocks feared the marines.

This group penetrated farther into the base than any other, so they learned their lessons well, making them dangerous. The marines needed to wipe them out before they could teach other warriors to be cautious. He preferred the roaring, ferocious alien soldiers to those walking down the broad thoroughfare.

Juan blinked as a blinding flash appeared in front of the advancing enemy. *Show time!*

*****

Reaper Kalleen moved cautiously up the broad tunnel, her final 500 warriors surrounding her. Some might find it cowardly not to be in the vanguard of her force, although now that she thought about it, those idiots had probably all sent their final prayers to Karoken by now. She was a leader of 10,000, yet only those warriors around her were left.

The damnable human marines had sniped at them constantly since they had entered the tunnels. They must have learned that red markings on a battle harness meant a Silfe leader. She watched as older, more experienced Warriors, who were supposed to control the young ones, were targeted. Eventually, she switched her harness for one of the dead. She feared that her cohort might see it as cowardice, but the only reaction she received was relief.

Any warrior who survived the past two days of fighting had learned hard lessons. They were all cautious now. She could see a young male warrior off to her left, moving with the slow, steady pace of someone who had seen multiple cleansings. In a way, he had. No battle since the hated Harrow had ever come close to the one in this accursed volcano.

A bright flash lit the tunnel. Instinctively, the Silfe crouched down, seeking the meek cover of the tunnel. Kalleen waited for the overpressure wave of an explosive to wash over them, thinking that they triggered another trap, but as the light faded, she couldn't see any damage to the front rank.

What now? The battle had conditioned her to see anything new as dangerous. Every surprise cost her warriors. She gazed to where the light seemed to spin in place before settling into the form of....

*****

"What the hell?" Juan whispered to himself as the light stopped spinning and coalesced into the form of a twenty-foot-tall Silfe warrior. He might have worried had he not known that Gloria was up to something; he just didn't know what. The timer in his HUD dropped below one minute.

He clamped down on his nerves and snugged his laser rifle into his shoulder, sighting on a small Silfe warrior - maybe a female?- crouched down in the center of a group of competent-looking soldiers. He wasn't sure why, but he thought the warrior was in command. He didn't see the red harness straps, but something about the way they looked around and how the warriors positioned themselves near them seemed to scream "Leader." He half squeezed the trigger, riding the edge of firing, and waited for the countdown to reach zero.

He barely stopped himself from pulling the trigger as Gloria's projection started speaking in a booming, sibilant voice. As it was in the Sifle tongue, he didn't know what they said, but he knew that his love had just kicked over a hornet's nest by the warriors' reactions.

*****

Reaper Kaleen growled deep in her throat. Her mind couldn't process what she saw. She heard a whimper next to her and looked over to see battle leader Skoto, someone she had seen run through laser fire to rip out enemies' throats, on his knees, his head back and throat exposed in submission. He was whispering the prayer of the hopeless, said before going into a battle where one knew they would perish.

She gazed up at the massive Silfe warrior standing in the center of the corridor. She fought the instinctive need to show submission to a superior. *It had to be a trick!* She turned to yell at Skoto to get on his feet and charge ahead. Unfortunately, the figure's booming voice crashed over her like a wave before the words could form.

"Kneel before Karoken!" the voice commanded. "Kneel before your God!" As the towering figure shouted, it stomped one titanic foot down upon a human vehicle. With a screech, the metal gave way, crumbling into a twisted wreck.

The Reaper's knees bent before she knew what had happened, as had the rest of her command. She could hear more death prayers. *No! It was a lie! A human trick. Karoken would not come here!*

The voice boomed again. "You are weak! Instead of charging into battle, you slink around corners and peer into crevices. Are you infants?! Do you want to die in your beds like cowards?!" The gigantic form growled in disgust and chomped jaws that could bite a full-grown warrior in half. "It is like the Chief Mugwump Dav..id Lie..brrr... man has said. You are weak and have lost my favor. Unless you are true warriors, fearless in my eyes, I will turn my eyes to the humans."

The form seemed to lean forward over the stunned group. "I will give you a boon. There are human Mar... eeen... sss just up this corridor. I may choose to hear your final prayers if you can kill them with your claws and teeth. Otherwise, I will turn you away from my halls!"

The figure stepped to the side of the tunnel and pointed down it. "Go now, my children, or be craven in my eyes!"

Kaleen stood, attempting to stop what she knew had to be a trap. "Stand do..." she started to say, only to be drowned out by 500 enraged battle cries.

*****

Juan didn't know what Gloria said, but it seemed effective. The aliens charged up the corridor at the marines. He sighted back onto the commander's chest. He couldn't be sure, but he thought they were trying to get the soldiers under control. *Well, we can't have that, now, can we?* He drew a bead on the gesticulating figure and pulled the trigger before moving to another target and another.

FORTY-EIGHT

Mars High Orbit
+9 days (2 days later)

Adjunct Chief Reaper Shaakal bowed his head in subservience. He spoke in a low, angry voice. "I need more troops, Chief Slayer."

Tetukken's growl was angrier. "Why would you think I would give you more troops to throw away? Your incompetence has already cost the horde a million Chosen. What do you have to show for it?"

"We have destroyed many of the Hu...ma...nsss," the Reaper said.

"Yes," Tetukken said. "I have seen the reports. You have sent 60,000 of these Ma... reee... nsss to Karoken. You only had to trade 16 Chosen for every one of the Hu...ma...nsss you killed."

"They do not fight with honor!" the Reaper said, his face turned upward to glare daggers at Tetukken. "They hide and fire their weapons at us from cover. They plant traps. When we overwhelm them they drop the ceiling down upon us and escape."

"Yes, I know," the Chief Slayer said. "The humans fight to kill as many of the Chosen as they can while preserving themselves. Yet, I have seen recordings of battles where we trap them. Then they fight like cornered animals. I believe the exchange rate of Hu...ma...nsss to Chosen is even higher in those circumstances."

The Reaper's eyes lowered again. "Yes, Slayer, I have seen it with my own eyes. If given no choice, they turn and fight with ferocity. If surrounded, they set off explosives to kill themselves and any Chosen caught in the blast." Shaakal looked genuinely puzzled at this. "Do they not realize that Karoken will not hear their prayers if they take their own lives?"

"They do not honor Karoken," Tetukken said.

"But some say that the Chief Mugwump Dav... id Lie... brrr... man said the humans worshiped Karoken, and they do not use artificial intelligence to control their ships or weapons." He paused, appearing supremely uncomfortable. "And there was the incident with the remnants of Reaper Kaleen's 10,000. The young ones are in an uproar about it."

Tetukken gave an inward sigh. He had tried to crush the rumor that the humans were followers of Karoken, but it infected the young ones like a disease. He knew it to be a lie. The olangees monitored communications when they first discovered the Earthlings. Although they followed many religions, there was no mention of Karoken in thousands of hours of recordings.

The problem was that the human weapons *did* appear to follow the tenets laid down by Karoken. There was no computerized aiming they could determine. The humans avoided direct conflict unless pressed, but they were ferocious fighters when cornered. These facts added to the rumors.

"Dav...id Lie... brrr... man lied. The figure of Karoken in the tunnel was a hologram! We know humans have advanced technology; it is well within their capabilities to recreate an avatar of the great God!"

"But..." Shaakal seemed to struggle with himself. "Karoken crushed a hu...maa...n vehicle. How could a hologram do such a thing?"

Tetukken mastered the impulse to rake his claws across the Reaper's throat and watch as he gasped out his final prayer. It would give him great pleasure, but it would be a waste. Despite the terrible losses the Chosen had taken, he knew it was not the fault of the Skaatal. The Reaper was a fine warrior and had survived three cleansings. He was everything that a Silfe warrior was supposed to be. Strong, ferocious, and utterly committed to Karoken's teachings. The problem lay with the humans. The Silfe had not encountered a species that could challenge them since the Harrow. They had grown lax, relying on ferocity and numbers to win the day.

The Chief Slayer could admit that if the enemy had as many ships as the Silfe, they would have wiped the Chosen from the system on the very first day. Silfe battlecruisers were no match for the human ships one-on-one. The destruction of Slayer Tossan's fleet at the human colony of Callisto had proven that.

Tossan had been one of the craftiest and oldest of the Silfe commanders. Tetukken only had recordings of the battle's early stages before the fusion weapons made opening micro-wormholes impossible. Yet, he knew Tossan would have done nothing to jeopardize his ships. The only way for the humans to have won was to get into weapons range and outshoot the Silfe. The humans were hurt badly, but they wiped out Tossan's fleet. Only 200 of 2000 had survived, and only then because they were guarding the planet.

And now this... doubt! The Chief Mugwump David Lieberman placed the seed in the horde, and this most recent... episode with the avatar of Karoken caused it to sprout into a choking vine.

He couldn't convince any but the cleverest of his commanders that the figure of Karoken was a ruse. It caused 500 warriors, who survived the previous human traps, to drop their advanced weapons and charge a prepared position of human marines, with predictable results.

He didn't know how the figure of Karoken had crushed

the vehicle, but his chief olangee advisor said it was possible. If anything, the scientist had been excited, constantly muttering about the "Use of dampening fields" or some other nonsense. Finally, in irritation, Tetukken became angry and roared for the olangee to return to his duties. Rather than be cowed appropriately, the distracted scientist had almost forgotten to bow in courtesy. Still, the question had confirmed his suspicions.

It was genius, if without honor. Devotion to Karoken, especially among the young ones, was absolute. Any doubt the humans could place in their minds was devastating. Especially if it questioned their bravery. Given a choice between being labeled a coward and certain death, every young one would choose death.

Shaakal grunted with impatience, and Tetukken realized he had been in his thoughts too long. He regarded the Reaper with ice-cold eyes and lowered his voice into the tone of absolute command.

"The humans do not honor Karoken! You see their tactics. They set traps. No Chosen would do that. The figure of Karoken was a trick and nothing more!"

Skaatal looked unconvinced. "Some say that Karoken told the humans that sending our final prayers was more important. They say that since the humans set off the traps manually, it is the same as pulling a trigger on a laser rifle."

Tetukken growled again, causing the Reaper to show his neck.

"Not that I believe it!" the cowering Reaper said. "I only repeat what I have heard. It sows disquiet among the young ones!"

The Chief Slayer stared quietly at the Reaper for a long moment ensuring proper subservience before continuing. "We have stayed too long already," Tetukken said. "The Hu...ma...nsss are trying to bleed away our troops and keep us away from their home planet. There are too few here to matter. You will order the immediate withdrawal of the warriors on the ground."

The Reaper looked thoroughly confused. "You would leave the rest of the Ma... ree... nsss alive?"

"They do not matter!" Tetukken shouted. The impulse to take the Reaper's head from his shoulders was almost overpowering. Shaakal could not understand *why* it was necessary to pull out before it was too late.

The cleansing of the human colonies of Callisto and Enceladus was successful, but the losses of Silfe troops were horrific. Not as bad as on Mars, but they traded ten Silfe for every final prayer of a human.
Tetukken feared that if he kept throwing warriors into Olympus Mons, he would not have enough to capture the human orbital defense bases, especially if the humans became desperate enough to repeat their tactics from Callisto. He could not afford the loss of another ten million warriors by losing the battlecruisers they rode in.

The subjugation of the human battle stations *had* to be his priority. If they controlled the orbitals of the human home world, they would win. Even a planet of ten billion couldn't stand up to the Chosen if they held the orbitals and could drop kinetic weapons where they chose. He did not doubt that it would hurt them, but the outcome would be all but assured.

It might take a year or more to cleanse the planet of the humans, but that would give time for the horde to rebuild and for a new creche of young ones to be born.

The Chief Slayer's growl rumbled in his throat, showing his displeasure at being questioned. Even though it wasn't Shaakal's fault, Tetukken couldn't afford to look weak. He decided the sub-commander could never grasp the intricacies of tactics needed for the decision. He could only understand that killing the humans was necessary.

"We waste time here while much larger prizes await us! We will descend upon the human battle stations and take them for our own. Then," he placed a clawed hand onto the kneeling Reaper's shoulder in the position of confidence. "You, Shaakal, will lead a landing party to the planet itself to send the final prayers of millions to Karoken!"

The eagerness for blood replaced Shaakal's confusion. "Yes, Chief Slayer! It will be a glorious victory!"

Tetukken swallowed down the gnawing uncertainty in his gut, showing no trace of it in his countenance. He doubted that the junior Reaper would survive the fight on the battle stations to take his promised reward. He put on a false face and said, "Indeed! Start the withdrawal. By this time tomorrow, I want to be assaulting the human orbital stations!"

*****

"It's confirmed, sir," Colonel Murphy said. "The Aliens are pulling back on all sides, and their shuttles are leaving."

Juan wiped a tired hand across his brow, surprised as it came away wet. He looked down and saw it streaked with red. *His blood or someone else's?* He let out a tired sigh, his exosuit creaking, where it had been hit by flying rubble from the cave-in they triggered just short of the CIC.

The past two days were a waking nightmare. The Silfe were relentless. The aliens ignored casualties that would have caused any human general to call for immediate withdrawal, but they hadn't seemed to care. They charged, roaring their battle cries, in wave after wave. So much so that they had penetrated almost all the way to the CIC itself.

Juan led the reserve company out repeatedly to seal one breach after another. It was terrifying, fulfilling, and sad all at once. He watched good men and women, marines he had known for years, killed before his eyes.

There was no doubt in his mind that they would have lost without Gloria. She was a Valkyrie, who appeared in a swirl of light to aid them. He was sure the tale would grow in the telling, and there was no stopping it from outpacing any attempt he could make to slow it.

And now? Beyond all hope, the Silfe were withdrawing. He was sure that they would keep throwing troops away until they ground the last of the Martian Marines to dust.

He looked at Colonel Murphy, whose worried expression told him he had been overlong in responding. *God, he was tired!* He straightened, trying to wipe the flashes of violence and blood from his mind and *think*.

"Orders to any remaining GAR crews," he said. "See if we can sneak them out and snipe a few of the retreating shuttles as they lift off."

Murphy started shouting orders to the spent CIC staff, who had been awake for over 48 hours. *Well, they should all be able to get some rest soon.* He felt sympathy for the GAR crews. They had been fighting just like everyone else, and some would be lost, even as the battle ended, but each shuttle carried 250 Silfe warriors. Every Alien that they killed here and now couldn't threaten the Earth.

The marines would understand. They knew survival was secondary. That any of them were still standing was just short of a miracle. He was a lapsed Catholic but was beginning to appreciate some of Lea's ideas about God being on their side. How else would he be here, watching the little lights representing alien shuttles lifting off the surface of Mars? It *wasn't just short of a miracle;* it *WAS a miracle.*

He moved forward, giving orders to reposition the remaining marines in case the aliens changed their minds and returned. He didn't think they would. Someone in the Silfe leadership recognized Olympus Mons for what it was. A trap. They would focus on the Earth, or rather the two defense platforms controlling the orbitals.

He didn't need to imagine the abattoirs of death that the DS-1 and two would become. He had lived it. For the first time in years, he crossed himself as he was taught in Sunday school and said a silent prayer for marines on the stations. The fate of humanity was in their hands now.

FORTY-NINE

Dark Side of the Moon
+10 days (the next day)

"Orders to the squadron," Wing Commander Wang's voice said in accented English through the base intercom. "We are a go for mission in one minute."

In the first days after the Strombold Speech, The World Commission determined that a single language was necessary to coordinate military affairs. Every member of the WCDF received an accelerated course in English as part of basic training. They adopted the pattern from the airline industry, where the International Civil Aviation Organization had long required all pilots to communicate in the language.

Gloria had come through, offering a VR simulation program teaching English through a set of real-world actions that became the most effective teaching method ever devised. Likely because of the simulation, *Dallas Nights*, a so-bad-it's-good Soap Opera, where the learner was the star. You could choose to play Rhett, a handsome oil tycoon who had been hurt before, or Bobby Joe, a struggling country singer he couldn't help but love.

Ensign Rose Swelton buckled herself into the cockpit of her Gunstar and spoke to Senior Chief Moyo, the leader of her ground crew. "We are a go, Chief. Button her up!"

The Chief gave her a salute and a smile. "Good luck Ma'am." He patted the Gunstar fondly. "Try to bring it back in one piece, OK?"

Rose smiled back, knowing that he was only trying to reassure her without calling out that she was about to fly the ship into battle. "You got it, Chief. Not a scratch anywhere." She gave him a two-fingered salute and then pushed the button to close the canopy.

Immediately, the ship moved upward, its platform rising into a shaft drilled into the ceiling of the landing bay.

The Risa Squadron's airlocks on the moon differed from the WCN carriers. The shaft acted as a piston, squeezing the atmosphere into a set of one-way valves. By the time the ship was to the surface, the last of the pressurized atmosphere shot the fighter up, launching it into space. She had observed the process for herself in training. It looked like the moon was a giant dandelion head that God brought to their lips, breath blowing seeds out into space. Today the impression was almost overwhelming as she felt the acceleration hit her, and she shot up, breaking the moon's minimal gravity, one fighter among thousands.

Commander Wang's voice crackled again. "Go... Go... Go. Focus on the shuttles, but if you can close with a battlecruiser, you may take a target of opportunity."

Rose took a single deep breath and hit her accelerator.

Her local channel buzzed with her wingmate, Susan's enthusiastic voice. "You ready for this, Rosie?"

Ensign Susan Johnson was always the quintessential 'Fighter jock,' oozing confidence. She was the perfect counterpoint to Rose, whose nature leaned toward reserved.

"Yes," she said. "Although I am glad that my Aunt Cindy figured out a way to strengthen the dampeners into something resembling a shield."

"You're a trip," Susan said, snorting. "*Aunt Cindy*... Fuck, after this is over, I will introduce you to my close personal friend, the Pope. Then we can all go out and get shit-faced together!"

Rose laughed. Trust Susan to say something that would break through her nerves. The gregarious pilot kept talking.

"Although, if the shields work well enough, I'll buy the first round."

"I think you'll have to get in line behind the whole fleet."

Two days ago, Cindy uploaded a patch to the damping field tuner, which automatically caused slight fluctuations in the field, fluctuations that increased its ability to take a hit. The field still only covered 180-degrees, but it made it possible to take even a capital ship laser head-on... at least for a second. The ships were still incredibly vulnerable. Fully half of the Gunstar was effectively unguarded, and a sustained shot could burn through the modulation. Still, it had made what they were about to do only mildly suicidal instead of *completely.*

They were tasked with preventing as many shuttles as possible from landing on DS-1. Another squadron was doing the same at DS-2. Rose was happy to have the assignment. Every shuttle she destroyed would mean 250 less Silfe trying to kill marines like her sister, and if she could get a good hit on a battlecruiser, even better. She wished she could protect DS-2, Joselyn's duty station, but the brass hadn't asked for her preference of which of humanity's two orbital defense stations she was to defend.

The green and blue Earth appeared as she accelerated around the curve of the moon. Her heart sped up at the sight, like the first time she'd seen it. Rose had always wanted to fly. It was hard watching your dad step onto Mars and not want some part of the adventure for yourself. She wished it could be different, that she wasn't doing it in a warship heading into battle, but the young ensign could appreciate that she was living an extraordinary life. It might be short as well, but that was a price she would pay if it could help protect her world.

The long-range optics could make out DS-1 in the distance. In astronomical terms, it wasn't very far. Still, the little problem of 3000 battlecruisers and their fighters between her and the human orbital defense platform complicated the situation.

The Gunstar design was more than a match for the alien fighters, but the massive number of alien ships made up for the mismatch in capabilities. Given the constant string of battles across the solar system, it was impossible to know, but just the squadron she currently faced likely carried over a million fighters. The Risa Squadron was the single largest collection of Gunstars humanity had, and it was *only* 100,000 strong. At over ten to one odds, she certainly hoped that her Aunt Cindy pulled another rabbit out of the hat. Otherwise, her first mission would be very short... and her last.

"Here they come!" Susan said over the local channel.

Rose saw alien fighters boiling out of the battlecruisers to take up position between their mother ships and the approaching humans. "Just like in practice," she said.

Susan's laugh came over her helmet speakers. "Yep, exactly like that! Let's go kill us some crocks!"

Rose didn't comment, shaking her head and pushing down her nerves by focusing on her training. She accelerated, keeping Susan just up and away from her, watching the indicator that told her when she would cross into effective firing range.

A loud beep sounded, and the edges of her HUD flashed red before clearing. "Holy shit!" she said over the channel. "I think I just took a hit from a capital ship laser!"

"You five-by-five?" Susan asked.

Rose desperately looked around the cockpit at all of her instrumentation. Everything seemed fine. She let out an audible breath.

"Yeah! I'm all in the green."

"Well damn!" her wingmate said. "I guess we owe *Aunt* Cindy a drink!" The radio cleared for a second; as bravado aside, they both took a moment to appreciate that Rose lived. Then Susan spoke again. "Well, now that that little test is over, let's see if we can't make a hole in these fighters. Some crock admiral must be shitting a brick over there!"

*****

"Slayer, it's confirmed," the olangee weapons officer said. "Battlecruiser hits are failing to destroy the human fighters."

"How is that possible?" Adjunct Chief Slayer Soteenan asked, a growl in his voice. "Recheck the readings. We must be missing! Nothing as small as a fighter can survive a main battlecruiser weapon!" *Already the human tricks have begun!* Tetukken warned him when he assigned him half of the fleet that the Earthlings would try to disrupt the landing shuttles.

He spent the past day pounding the battle station with a kinetic bombardment to clear the landing zone on the massive asteroid. Even so, he lost 300 battlecruisers that had strayed too close to the station, a hard way to find out the massive asteroid had laser emplacements at least twice as strong as those on Mars. The ship commanders, who had forgotten that you could never become complacent with humans, utilized the Martian weapons as a baseline for their approach.

The olangee looked up from his console, where he had been desperately rechecking his calculations. "Slayer, I have run the numbers three times. I am telling you, we are getting hits, even destroying an occasional fighter, but only when we are striking at an extreme angle. They have forward shielding."

Soteenan's mind took in the information, thinking furiously. *If the human fighters have forward shielding, they could get through the fighter screen. If they got through the screen, they could attack the landing shuttles... and the battlecruisers themselves!*

"Orders to all ships. Deploy fighters. Send half to protect the landing shuttles and pull the rest in around the battlecruisers."

"Sir?" the olangee communications officer asked.

"Do it!" Soteenan shouted. "The humans are going to

break through the fighter screen!"

*****

Rose fired again, watching the alien ship come apart, as her railgun rounds stitched across its length. Her HUD blinked red again as the forward screen took another hit. She veered left, following Susan and attempting to prevent the alien fighters from obtaining an oblique angle to get around her forward shield.

So far, the battle had been one-sided. They were losing fighters, but Cindy's modulation of the damping fields had made the difference, and the Risa Squadron was decimating the enemy ships sent against them. Unfortunately, some crock with a bit of brains realized that the human fighters were vulnerable to oblique attacks and ordered a portion of the battlecruisers to move where their weapons could attack their vulnerable sides. It was also possible that some of them were trying for more sustained hits, which could burn through the modulations. The Gunstars kept moving, winging right, left, up, and down to keep the ships from getting a lock.

Rose watched as a Gunstar above her ripped apart. It was one of her wing, which meant a friend had just died, but it was too far away to see. She gritted her teeth. There would be time to mourn after the battle, but first, she needed to thread the needle between the battlecruisers and the station, where the Silfe shuttles were landing wave after wave of warriors onto the surface of DS-1. Under magnification, she could see the aliens pouring into captured landing bays, beginning their assault on the station.

Rose held down the trigger on her spinal laser, cutting an alien ship in half. She blinked, looking for her next target, but could find no more enemies in front of her. *They were through!*

The speakers in her helmet chirped.

"Get behind Susan and turn your fighter backward!"

"Gloria?" she asked, confused.

A pixilated version of the AI, complete with tiny hands on hips, popped onto the lower-left portion of Rose's heads-up display. "Yes! She said. "You still have Silfe fighters behind you! If you don't want one of them to turn around and shoot your ass off, I suggest you snug up behind your wingmate and turn around to point your dampening field behind you. Susan's field should cover you from the other side if you get in close enough. Just make sure that she tells you if she is going to move. You do not want her to leave you."

Rose's mind whirled. The maneuver was dangerous. So dangerous that her basic training instructors would yell at her for "Suicidal idiocy." Still, was it *more* suicidal than continuing to fly at DS-1 with Silfe fighters shooting at her from behind? *No, it was not!* Besides, Gloria's nature would have required her to run the probabilities before suggesting it.

Decision made, Rose pulled hard on the control yoke, and her fighter flipped end to end, now facing directly backward, the two Gunstars looking like a two-headed circus animal.

She was just in time, as an alien fighter came from behind and fired ineffectually, hitting her deflector screen. She sighted in on the alien and destroyed them with a sustained burst from her railguns.

Susan's voice sounded in her helmet. "What the hell are you doing, Swelton?"

"Saving your ass!" she said, aiming at another Silfe fighter and blowing it out of the sky. "Just keep going straight, basic evasion pattern, and if you need to move, TELL ME!"

Susan sounded nonplussed. "You are one crazy assed bitch! Fine, keep them off me! I will tell you when we are in range of the shuttles; if we don't have anyone in pursuit, you can turn and help me blow them out of the sky."

"Roger," she said, not having the ability to communicate anything more complicated at the moment. Rose grunted in concentration, shooting at another enemy fighter while trying to match Susan's sudden movements built into "The Navy Gunstar's Basic Evasion Pattern." Normally she could have done it in her sleep, but she found her brain hurting as she reversed it while engaging enemy fighters. It was like driving a Ferrari on the Autobahn at 200 mph, weaving in and out of traffic... except *backward*.

Several long minutes of fevered concentration found her out of targets. Either they had outdistanced the alien fighters or she destroyed all the ones in the area.

"We are one minute out from the crock shuttles," Susan said.

"OK," Rose replied. "No pursuit in range." She grabbed hold of the control stick and started counting. "Separating from you in 3... 2... 1...." She twisted the controls up and to the right while hitting her right forward and left back thruster. The effect brought her up and away from Susan's engine trail and flipped her forward.

Rose's inner ear took a moment to catch up with the maneuver before settling again. Ahead of them, well away from DS-1, she could make out the vast alien battlecruisers with the naked eye. She flipped the optics over her helmet and could see the drop shuttles flowing in a steady stream towards the station. "I've got the shuttles coming in at 90-degrees. You take the station side ones, and I'll take the others.

"Roger," Susan said. "We'll meet in the middle!"

"Right. Remember, one pass only! Then we are out the other side."

"Yes, Mom!" her irascible wingmate said. "I read the orders too." There was a slight pause before the radio crackled to life again. "But... I think there is a lone battlecruiser on the other side of the pack that we might make a go at before we leave the area." Her voice took on a singsong. "Please! If I promise to eat all my vegetables and be soooo good, can we try to blow the alien battlecruiser up!?"

Despite the crazy life or death situation that she found herself in, Rose couldn't help but let out a blurt of laughter. Her voice took on a mock-serious tone. "Yes... since you've been good."

"Now *THAT's* what I am talking about!" Susan said, her enthusiasm bleeding through the radio.

The young ensign shook her head. She definitely needed to introduce her wingmate to her uncle David; they would get on like a house on fire. She focused on her targets, angling her Gunstar slightly to bring the first of the alien shuttles into her sights. Rose flipped the lock off her main spinal laser array and pushed the button, causing the invisible beam to lash out with deadly intent. Its effect *wasn't* invisible. It looked like the Silfe shuttle had its canopy opened by a can opener. She moved her targeting reticle to her next target, trying to ignore the sight of enemy troops pouring out of the broken remains of her first victim. She hardened her heart. *She* hadn't asked the Silfe to come to Earth. They were murderers who had rampaged across the galaxy. She felt no compassion as she squeezed the trigger again and again.

"Targets in my zone are clear," Susan said.

"Roger." Rose squeezed the trigger one last time. "Clear here too."

"Still up for the battlecruiser?" Susan asked.

"Lead the way," she said, pouring on acceleration and passing through the wreckage of forty shuttles. They angled slightly away from DS-1, to where a single battlecruiser had moved off by itself. *Perfect*, she thought, her grin turning hungry.

*****

"Slayer, the last human fighters are accelerating away past the shuttles."

Soteenan growled. The human attack wasn't *quite* a disaster, but it wasn't good either. They lost two-thirds of the fleet's fighters and at least 1000 shuttles, but the humans had paid too. After they passed through the fighter screen, the

Silfe turned back on themselves and attacked the unprotected flanks of the human craft. Only about half of the Earthlings had made it through to the other side of the formation. Still, the new capabilities to protect themselves made the enemy's fighters a significant problem. The small ships were too agile for the battlecruisers to target effectively.

"Sir!" the weapons officer said. "I have two human fighters on a direct path toward the flagship."

Two of the small craft weren't much of a threat to his ship. "Task our fighters to intercept at oblique angles."

The olangee monitoring the station looked panicked. "I can't, Slayer. All of the fighters are out of range!"

"Then shoot them out of the sky!" he said, not understanding why the stupid scientist was so worried about what amounted to a pair of tiny insects that could be crushed with a single claw.

"We are trying sir, we can't get a lock with the kinetic rounds, and the lasers can't penetrate their forward shields!"

It seemed inconceivable that two small ships could threaten a battlecruiser a thousand times their mass, but the flagship hadn't deployed its ground forces. None of the 10,000 troops were in suits capable of handling vacuum. The mother ships didn't even have point defense weapons! They had needed nothing but the main laser and railgun mounts before. No enemy had closed with the battleships since the Harrow, thousands of years ago.

He watched, a churning feeling in his belly, as the tiny dots representing the human fighters moved ever closer to his flagship in the holotank.

*****

"We're doing this, huh?" Rose asked.

"You bet your ass we are!" Susan said. "Get ready to do your crazy-assed backward trick. As soon as we pass, we will need some coverage on our six."

Not knowing what else to say to her wingmate, she replied, "Roger."

Rose watched as the battlecruiser grew in her optics like an old-fashioned telephoto lens, zooming suddenly into focus. *God! It was huge!* She'd known abstractly that the alien ships were at least double the size of an aircraft carrier, but knowing something and seeing it up close was something else entirely. She suddenly felt *very* much like a mosquito trying to bite an elephant. *There was nothing for it. She* gazed through the scope, deciding where her railgun's rounds might do the most damage.

"Twenty seconds out!" Susan said. "Lock and load!"

Rose didn't even have to center the targeting reticle on the alien ship. Her fighter was less than a mile out, and the vessel filled her viewscreen. She could make out the smooth metallic black of its surface, seeming to suck the light into it and causing no reflection.

She aimed for the center of the ship, thinking that perhaps the Silfe mind was enough like a human's that they would place the control bridge there, and squeezed the trigger, holding it down and letting out a stream of projectiles. Unlike the spinal lasers, the Gunstar's railgun ammunition was visible. Every fifth round was a tracer, so it looked like she was shooting the movie version of a laser at the enemy. Off to her left, she could see Susan doing the same.

The timing was perfect, her guns running dry just as they cleared the end of the ship. She flipped and repeated her backward flying maneuver, which had the benefit of putting her in position to see the havoc they inflicted. She couldn't help but smile. The ship appeared lifeless, engines cold with atmosphere and other larger detritus jetting into the black of space.

Rose keyed her mike. "She is dead in the water!"

A sharp laugh sounded from her gregarious friend. "First drink is on me tonight!"

Rose let out a hysterical, uncontrolled laugh. The stress

of the battle flooded out of her as she realized she would survive the day. The young Ensign knew that the sadness of lost companions would come later, but for now, she felt more alive than she ever had in her short life.

Realizing she was out of range from any reprisals from the enemy, she flipped her fighter around and moved forward of Susan. "Race you back to the moon!" she said. Rose punched the accelerator, ignoring Susan's protests of cheating, and pointed the nose of her Gunstar back towards Risa.

FIFTY

Sydney Australia
+10 days (A few hours later)

Staff Sergeant Olivia Kalhon of the WCDF Marines watched as shuttle after shuttle of aliens landed in and around the Royal Botanic Gardens, their ships' engines browning and burning the delicate blooms that had once delighted visitors from around the world.

Olivia could remember a picnic with her family on the broad lawn as a child. Her mother was in a yellow sundress, and her father carried her on his shoulders, all of them having a contest to find the "prettiest" flower. She had won, finding a purple bloom with yellow in its center that she was sure couldn't be real until she reached out and gently felt a soft petal between her fingertips. She hadn't believed that nature could produce something so perfect. It looked like an artist had imagined a perfect flower and then painted it into the world with canvas and brush. Of course, she hadn't thought about it in those terms when she was young, but looking back now, it was the only way she could put words to the sense of magic that she had felt looking down on the flower.

So, it wasn't surprising that Kalhon was feeling a little pissed off. How *dare* a bunch of space lizards come down into her country, her city, her fucking favorite place in the entire world, and burn down the prettiest flowers in existence! She gripped her laser rifle harder, stopping just short of crushing the stock in her gauntleted fists.

She nodded to Lieutenant Smith, her platoon leader, as he held up two fingers, indicating that in two minutes, they were going to go charging around the corner of Saint Mary's Cathedral and bring the pain down upon the aliens.

She inched her helmeted head around the corner, enough to see the smoking ruins of the Sydney Opera house in the distance. There hadn't even been any laser emplacements in the building. The brass hoped that the crocks would give the landmark a pass if it sat there empty, but they'd been wrong. Whether it was a direct order from the alien leadership or the random act of some asshole fighter pilot, the beautiful building was gone. The roof's once graceful curves scattered across Sydney Harbor.

She ground her teeth as she saw the destruction. *Another reason to kill the bastards.*

For the first time, she was glad that the defense platforms had holes in their coverage. DS-1 and DS-2 orbited about equal distance from each other. Each was slightly off the equator to allow maximal coverage of the world's major population centers. The problem was that even as big as they were, their weapons could only reach so far. They couldn't cover the entire planet 100% of the time. The WCDF planners knew extreme south and north locations were open to invasion. Over the past year, places like the southern half of Australia, Tasmania, New Zealand, Argentina, Alaska, and Russia had their civilian populations stripped and sent to World Commission bunkers in areas under the coverage of the battle stations.

Just because the civilian population wasn't present didn't mean that humanity wouldn't defend their territory. The WCDF was taking every opportunity to whittle down the aliens. Should either Death Star fall, entire sections of the world, including the civilian populations hiding in the bunkers, would have to fight for their lives. Every crock that she killed here couldn't threaten anyone else. Since both of her parents were in bunkers in northern Australia, she could appreciate the urgency to hold them back.

Olivia was the second person in line to volunteer for the WCDF Marines the day her local recruiting center opened. She was the *first* to request a posting in Sydney. Now, after almost three years of training, it was time to do her part to save the Earth.

Her thoughts slowed down as the countdown reached zero; *time to go.* She signaled to her squad.

The WCDF adopted a platoon structure of four separate twelve-person rifle squads. Each was led by a Corporal or Sergeant, with four, four-person fireteams. Each fire team consisted of a heavy weapons suit and three infantry suits.

With rapid breathing and nervous energy, her rifle squad broke from cover in the building's lee. They were to take up position at the Art Gallery of New South Wales, which with suit augmented legs was only seconds away. She followed as the last of the squad ran toward the museum's front entrance, with its giant fluted columns and Greek-inspired architecture.

The squads' metal shod feet pounded against the stone pavers of the courtyard, cracking them with the force of their steps. She saw a Marine jump a small reflecting pool that lay in his way, soaring six feet up and twenty feet forward in a leap that barely slowed his progress.

She made her own leap over the pool and thought they might make their position without the crocks noticing when she saw private Jones struck with a railgun round.

The best she could say was that it was unlikely the young woman had felt anything. One moment she was running, augmented legs pumping, and the next- the top half of her suit was just... gone. Olivia yelled, "Contact Rear! Get to cover!"

She put her advice to work and pushed off hard, diving

behind a stone column and relying on the tough carbon nanotubing in her combat suit to protect her skin as she slid across concrete at what must have been twenty-five miles per hour.

She popped up in a practiced roll, grabbing her laser rifle from the magnetized front of the chest plate, painted in the grays and blacks of urban camouflage. She brought it up, optics linking to her helmet HUD. What she saw made her pulse quicken. Running at full tilt was what must have been a couple hundred aliens, seven feet tall and looking like the most pissed-off crocodiles she had ever seen. Most carried long, narrow tube-like weapons that must be railguns, like the one that had hit Jones. Some, though, were carrying honest-to-God swords, blued steel raised over their heads like they were medieval knights and had not just landed in shuttles from orbit.

She aimed at an alien and pulled the trigger, watching as the giant lizard fell forward, a smoking hole appearing as if by magic in the center of its chest.

"Grenades!" she yelled.

The four heavy weapons specialists stepped out from behind columns where they were sheltering, facing the roaring enemy. Unlike the slim-profiled regular soldier suits, the spine of the "Heavies" resembled half a keg of beer, the space needed to contain the ammunition and power packs necessary for the destruction they unleashed.

Olivia saw one heavy, a mild-mannered nineteen-year-old named Perkins, go down from a railgun round before the other three let go a barrage of belt-fed fragmentation grenades. Despite the dampeners in her helmet, she opened her mouth, trying to equalize pressure in her ears as the grenades exploded, like the mother of all firecracker strings. Olivia dodged behind the column again as pieces of shrapnel and aliens shot out in every direction. Simultaneously she counted in her head, knowing that the heavies would fire a single timed barrage. When the count reached thirty, she popped up, yelling, "Up and at them! For Earth!"

She stood, moving around the column, and charging forward, firing her rifle at any alien that moved. Her squad moved with her, roaring their response, "For Humanity!"

FIFTY-ONE

Lunar Nation of Risa
+11 days (one day later)

Steven Cooper, PhD sat down backward into the cockpit of Bertha, closing the forward hatch on the giant Mech with a T-shaped handle he turned, pushed, and then turned again. As the hatch sealed, he heard the hiss of equalizing pressure, and the forward view screen lit up.

"Systems check," he said, flipping metal switches next to analog dials holding readings for atmosphere, hydraulic pressure, and weapons systems.

The suit he was in and the nineteen other mechs that made up the Risa Sentinels were born of Steve's love of all things robotic.

Intellectually, he knew he couldn't use robots to fight the Silfe. HAL assured them that any networked computer system was easy prey to the aliens, as an entire sect of their society was devoted to defeating just that sort of technology.

Steve and Bishop got HAL to talk about campaigns fought by other species who relied on drones, robots, and advanced computerized suits. The results were uniformly disastrous. It was why the suit augments designed for the WCDF Marines were mechanical.

Advances in hydraulics, especially the design of new

hyperreactive fluids, allowed for mechanical responsiveness that would have been impossible even fifteen years earlier.

When the suits or Gunstars used electricity, it was always in isolated systems. Computerized controls, such as those in the HUDs and displays, were self-contained. When they weren't using FTL micro-wormholes, communications were accomplished by old-fashioned -albeit highly modified and miniaturized- radio signals.

Steve had spent his entire life fascinated by robots. From R2D2 to Asimov, he'd always known that what he wanted was to design them. Even his employment at NASA was a means to an end. NASA had some of the most talented roboticists on the planet, and he felt advances in technology would make bots essential to space exploration.

He hadn't realized how right he had been. Autonomous robots were the only reason some Silfe warrior wasn't picking their teeth with his bones right now. Other than Cindy, Steve had helped prepare humanity for the conflict more than anyone else. Oh, it had been a group effort. Without Nick's political maneuvering, the AIs' creation, David's manipulation, and Jake's inspiration, they would still be hosed. Still, no one could question that the countless autonomous robots of Steve's design had been the muscle behind the creation of the fleet.

So, it's easy to imagine he'd felt miffed that he couldn't just design up a battlebot and wipe the Silfe from the solar system. Without the limitations of networked computers, humanity could have just sat at home on the couch, eating popcorn and controlling space fighters and mechs to beat the damn aliens without a single person being on the pointy end.

He sought other options. He couldn't use a robot, *but* he could build a better suit. One that had a bit more- OOMPH to it.

Big Bertha was the answer. The mechanized suit stood fifteen feet tall and weighed in at just over ten tons. The weight wasn't that impressive, seeing as a main battle tank might weigh as much as sixty tons or more, but it made up for it in strength and toughness. Bertha could shrug off a hit from an Abrams main gun, then pick up the tank and toss it.

Still, the true beauty of the mech wasn't its size or strength; it was the fact that it had almost no computerized controls anywhere inside it. It was just this side of a steam punk's wet dream, but instead of clockwork mechanisms, it used modern hydraulics.

In Steve's mind, he might not get to build a battlebot, but he *did* get to pilot a mech that could have come from the mind of a Japanese anime artist. He had even put a pair of radio antennas on the head that resembled the horns on a samurai helmet. Besides looking -in his opinion- completely badass, it tickled his sense of irony.

Bishop's green-tinged face materialized on the forward HUD, the color designed to protect the pilot's vision and giving the AI a Wicked Witch vibe that had always amused him.

"It's confirmed," he said. "We have Silfe ground troops in the Risa Tunnels. They lost a shit-ton of shuttles and about a dozen battlecruisers to the Risa Squadron getting down, but they landed 12,000 of the lizards."

"Really?" Steve said, surprised. "The fighters took out battlecruisers?"

"You have Gloria and Rose Swelton to thank for that. Turns out, if a pilot is savvy enough to fly backward, they can make a sort of tortoiseshell out of their damping fields. The modulations that Cindy found make them all but invulnerable to laser fire. Kinetic rounds can still take them out, but Gunstars are so damn maneuverable they are a hard target."

"They fly *backward?*" Steve said. "Like fully turned around... dodging and stuff?"

Bishop grinned, "Pretty much. Not all pilots can do it, but enough have the skills to close with the battlecruisers for a strafing run."

"Jesus!" Steve said, letting out a low whistle. "That's some Buck Rogers, sci-fi shit right there."

"As opposed to the homage to the Gundam universe you

are currently sitting in?"

"Ehh," Steve said. "I was going more for Voltron."

The AI laughed. "Got to love the classics. No wonder you and David get along so well." He paused, his mouth thinning. "Not that I am not enjoying geeking out with you, Steve, but maybe you want to go kill a few Silfe now?" Bishop's face took on a look of disgust. "Those lizards are stinking up my tunnels, and I want them out!"

"Don't worry, Bishop. I'll let them know they are not welcome in Risa by killing every last one of them.

The AI grinned savagely. "You do that."

FIFTY-TWO

*World Commission Orbital
Defense Platform 2*
+11 days (Same day)

"Contact, front!" the marine scout shouted.

"Where?" Second Lieutenant Joselyn Swelton asked.

"We have about one hundred of them approaching nexus forty-three. I estimate maybe ten minutes before they hit it." The scout grinned. "I dropped a Bouncing Betty at every corner in the last tunnel, so they'll need to go slow."

Josie nodded her head. Bouncing Betties were an upgraded version of the anti-personnel mine used to great effect in the World Wars and Vietnam. When triggered, it 'Bounced' about five feet in the air and detonated, expelling tungsten armor-penetrating darts in all directions. The WCDF Marine version was a flat plate three inches thick and six inches in diameter colored the same as the rock floors, making them almost undetectable. The scouts trained to put them around corners of the tunnels, so they were impossible to disable before exploding. The Silfe would need to go slow and throw a grenade or other explosive device around each corner, or they would lose personnel to every twist and turn of the snake-like tunnels. Either was okay with the young lieutenant.

She turned to Staff Sergeant Sarah Campion, her senior non-com, and said, "Pass the word. I want an ambush set up at the nexus, pattern Gamma."

Sergeant Campion nodded wordlessly, turning to the sergeants and corporals that led the fire teams and giving orders.

A mad dash through the twists and turns of the base found forty marines spread out across ten tunnel exits, looking into one of the myriad Nexuses spread throughout DS-2.

She moved her head slightly enough that a single eye could peer around the side of the rough stone of the tunnel into a roughly circular area about fifty yards wide and thirty tall. The rock walls were roughly cut, and she could see tool marks where the mining bots had chipped away at the stone. Although much of DS-2 looked like any modern industrial installation, parts were left in a more natural state, especially where the bots hit areas that didn't need reinforcement to prevent collapse.

The nexus was one of those, composed of bare rock with the reddish tinge of oxidizing metal. The nexuses were where multiple tunnels met and were one place where one could change levels to go up or down.

Compared to one of the major nexuses near central command, it was small, but it still had fifteen merging tunnels. Besides the ten containing one of the four-person fire teams of Josie's platoon, another five were empty, including two that were slightly larger and noticeably sloped, one going up and another going down to the next levels.

The young lieutenant looked into the broad space and couldn't help but think she had entered a fantasy world. The kind where the hero delves deep into an abandoned dwarven mine to fight a dragon. She'd enjoyed those kinds of stories growing up. The idea of adventure and defeating evil had always excited her. Her Uncle David educated her in what he considered the classics: Tolkien, Feist, and Salvatore.

Josie supposed she wasn't in such a different situation now. She was in a rough-cut stone tunnel, waiting for her enemy to come to her. Except instead of orcs, she would fight... giant lizard people. Come to think of it, she'd read a couple of books where that was the plot. Trade the laser rifles for swords, and there would be little difference between fact and fiction. She heard some of the more zealous of the Silfe warriors carried swords, so even that distinction was blurred.

Bishop's voice sounded in Josie's helmet. "Incoming in one minute."

The warning was hardly necessary. The distinct TING and WHOOMP of a Betty mine sounded in the tunnel sloping downward, leading to the level below.

"Numbers?" she asked.

"They are down to eighty-seven," Bishop said, satisfaction in his voice. "It took them a while to figure out how to disable the Betties."

Josie nodded. "Any problems with Plan Gamma?" she asked.

"Nope, it should be just right for this one. I suggest you let about forty through before you shoot. This bunch seems eager, their commander had to hold them back when they started tripping mines, so if you give them an excuse, the rest should run right in."

"Roger," she said. "Thanks."

"You can thank me by killing them."

Josie didn't respond. Bishop was always bloodthirsty when it came to the Silfe. She would have been just as happy if they all decided en masse to return to their ships and leave the solar system, but as that was unlikely to happen, she would do her best to do what the AI asked.

She raised a hand to signal Sergeant Campion, positioned directly across from her in line of sight. She signaled 'Wait' and 'Forty,' not trusting the radios with the Silfe so close. She had to assume they could pick up signals, and she didn't want them to realize they were walking into an ambush.

Campion signaled to another fire team, and so on down the line.

Josie took a couple of calming breaths. *This was it.* She was nervous, but it was more about letting down her marines than any thought of her mortality. They were in a superior position, with an unsuspecting enemy traveling into their firing lanes. This one *should* be easy, but easy didn't mean they wouldn't lose soldiers.

The guttural growls of the Silfe language reached her ears. She could also hear the unmistakable scratch, scratch sound of claws on stone. The aliens didn't wear foot coverings unless suited up for EVA and, even then, took them off quickly. She supposed if she had six-inch claws on her feet, she might find footwear uncomfortable too. From reports of battles in the colonies, she knew the foot claws were part of the alien unarmed combat technique. They used them like a velociraptor to disembowel their prey in close contact. It was likely part of their evolutionary conditioning.

She reached up and touched the side of her helmet, activating her visuals. The helmets had small, hardwired cameras that could be strung out several yards on thin, almost invisible wires and stuck to just about any surface. It was a bit like an old-style fishing lure, designed to allow marines to see around corners without the need for wireless signals.

The image in her HUD showed two Silfe scouts moving slowly -and nervously?- into the area. She could see them lifting their toothy snouts and sniffing at the air, trying to determine if humans were nearby.

Josie smiled inwardly. Bishop told her that the battlestations were expressly designed to confuse scent tracking. The air exchange systems randomly blew throughout the tunnels and made it all but impossible to use scent as an indicator of the human positions. Perhaps the Aliens hadn't realized it yet. If they genuinely relied on their noses to warn of marine positions, they would be very sorry indeed.

The scouts spoke in low growls, then one of them signaled to the tunnel behind them. A few moments later, the main contingent of alien warriors began to move into the nexus.

She had to admit; the Silfe form screamed predator. The smallest of them was over six feet tall, with a few topping out closer to eight. Their skin color varied from light celery to forest green. Interestingly, the darker-colored Silfe seemed to direct the troops. *Did they change color as they aged, or was it a racial distinction?*

There was no doubt they were terrifying, all long, lean muscle, claws, and too many teeth. Her hindbrain was screaming to run away. She clamped down on that emotion with an iron will. Today *she* was the baddest predator around.

Josie knew it was her job to kick things off. She waited for what was likely only moments but seemed like hours until just over forty aliens emerged out of the tunnel and fanned out.

She pushed the button on her helmet to retract the camera, doing a slow count of ten to allow her platoon to get ready. Crouching down, she raised her laser rifle to her shoulder and moved around the side of the tunnel, bringing the nexus into full view and sighting in on a Silfe she thought was a leader. A millisecond passed as Josie took in the surprisingly human-like expression of surprise, and then a quarter-sized hole punched through the creature's forehead, causing smoke to billow. Before the body could hit the floor, the nexus lit up with the clamor of battle as her platoon engaged.

She calmly sighted again and pulled the trigger, dropping another alien. The other fifty Silfe of the contingent ran into the nexus, roaring their battle cries.

"Grenades!" she called, before ducking back behind the protection of the side tunnel. A moment later, she heard the concussion of the heavy weapons suits firing their balls of destruction. Thirty seconds later, the last explosions sounded, leaving a profound silence. She risked a look around the edge of the tunnel and peered through the smoke, trying to determine if there were any Silfe left alive. Hearing and seeing no movement, she stood and moved cautiously into the nexus, her platoon spreading out behind her.

A lion-like roar sounded impossibly close as a scaled figure leaped out of the smoke straight at her, its jaws attempting to clamp down on her helmeted head. She yelled in surprise, but her reactions, trained by years of martial arts, didn't require her mind to tell them what to do. Josie brought her laser rifle up, jamming into the creature's snout, forcing the stock into its mouth like a horse's bridle.

Lowering her center of gravity, she rolled backward, an augmented foot kicking up into the creature's torso and shoving the alien into the air. The Silfe's jaws reflexively closed and ripped the rifle from her grip as it flew over her, crunching sickeningly into the wall behind. Josie continued her momentum into a back shoulder roll, coming to her feet and spinning into a back kick, which hit the crocodilian head with the force of a Mack Truck. Her spin continued, and she landed in a guard position, ready for the warrior to attack again, but it wasn't needed. She didn't know much about alien physiology but was sure that it needed its head fully attached to its body to be alive.

She swiveled her head around to make sure that no other aliens were creeping up on her, only to see the entire platoon gazing at her with variations of amazement. The station's impressive ventilation system had cleared the smoke from the nexus, and she could see the entire troop of aliens dead behind them.

Sergeant Campion raised the visor on her helmet, displaying her wide eyes. "Damn, LT," Remind me never to piss you off!" Her comment started a round of laughter from the rest of the platoon, which appeared blessedly intact. At least in this first encounter, they hadn't lost anyone.

Joselyn shrugged, not acknowledging the praise.

"Okay, people. Hydrate and make sure you top your batteries off. This isn't the last ambush we have to set up today. Scouts, be ready to go out in twenty minutes."

Her voice seemed to break the spell, and the marines got ready for more mayhem.

FIFTY-THREE

Emperor of the Moon Casino
+11 days (1 hour later)

"Reaper, there is a large building ahead," the scout said, coming to attention and bowing his head in respect. The light green of his skin identified him as a young one, just out of the creche.

"Have you met resistance?" Reaper Temok asked.

"No. So far, we have seen no Hu...ma...nsss since landing. They may have abandoned the base."

Temok grunted. "I doubt it. The Hu...ma...nsss lost too many of their fighters trying to stop our landing for them to give up now. This seems to be another one of their traps. We have just not seen its jaws clamp down on us yet."

The scout looked confused. Temok didn't waste his time trying to explain his suspicions to the young warrior. This accursed cleansing was Temok's third. He was sure to be promoted to Slayer if he survived, but that wasn't a sure thing. They had lost too many of the Chosen for him to feel any measure of reassurance. The only reason he was leading the roughly 12,000 who made it to the surface was because of the three slayers killed while trying to land. He was the highest-ranking warrior left, trying to consolidate the bits and pieces of other companies, primarily composed of young ones taking part in their first cleansing.

Temok regarded the scout, who waiting for further orders. "Is there anything about the building that is unusual? Something that might suggest a trap?"

The scout's snout scrunched in concentration, trying to understand what his commander might mean by 'Unusual.' Finally, his eyes lit. "Yes, Reaper! The building is mostly empty but looks full!"

Temok tamped down his impulse to gut the young one. It would give him great pleasure, but he needed every warrior he could find. Honestly, given the level of creative thinking displayed by the scout, it was unlikely the idiot would survive the day. Perhaps he could contribute to the cleansing by standing in the way of a laser, so a more worthy warrior might survive.

The reaper spoke slowly and simply. "Please explain what you mean by both empty and full."

The scout looked encouraged by his commander's patient tone. "Holograms," he said. "The building is full of holograms! Inside, it looks like you are on a planet with three moons!"

Temok growled his understanding. He supposed that the building being both empty and full would make sense to the young one's limited mind. "Did the olangees dispel the holograms?"

The scout shook his head. "I don't think so, Reaper. I heard them talking, and they said they couldn't."

"How is that possible?" he asked. The scout looked overwhelmed now, his tail whipping back and forth as he responded instinctually to Temok's anger. Disgusted, the reaper said, "Never mind, I'll ask them myself. You are dismissed, scout. Return to your squad."

The now frightened youngling scurried away as quickly as possible, probably not wanting to test his mood. Temok growled in annoyance, more at the report of the olangee's inability to dispel the holograms than at the idiot scout.

The Silfe had attacked worlds before that used holograms for stealthing ships and soldiers. As they always required advanced computing systems, the olangees could always shut them down. A report of their inability to do so was worrying.

The reaper moved quickly to the forward position, moving through troops readying themselves for a human attack that so far hadn't emerged. The young warriors moved out of his way like tall grass in the wind, a path appearing as if by magic.

As he walked, he would occasionally catch sight of an older warrior, leaders of tens or hundreds, but they were few. He ground his jaws in frustration. He *knew* the humans were planning something. He had watched the recordings from the human colonies, and he was confident that they were somewhere in these vast caverns waiting to kill as many Chosen as they could. To his mind, they were proving entirely too efficient at it.

Temok didn't doubt that the Silfe would prevail. He flatly refused to believe the human claims that Karoken had abandoned them. It was just another trick, like so many others. He hated to admit it, but it was also incredibly effective. The idea that Karoken would only accept the final prayers of warriors who threw away caution and rushed to kill the humans with tooth and claw, had infected the young ones like a plague. He'd heard reports of commanders having to bully and even kill young ones who refused to bring their rifles into battle.

The reaper pushed his worries down as he reached the forward position, in sight of a massive black building big enough to fit a battlecruiser inside. He angled towards a small group of Silfe with the characteristic narrow shoulders and short snouts of olangees. The scientists were deep in conversation and did not see him approach, allowing him the opportunity to observe them.

Like all older warriors, Temok had grown to appreciate

the olangee's usefulness. Young ones might think they were weaklings, but the reaper knew that without them, the holy mission of Karoken would be impossible. The olangees built and maintained the battlecruisers. They piloted the stars, and found planets that required cleansing. The caste would never know the wonder of sinking their teeth into an enemy, feeling their life's blood carry away the final prayer to Karoken. Still, he knew that a single olangee was indirectly responsible for more deaths than he would know in a hundred cleansings.

That didn't mean that he would allow them to neglect their duty. *He* was in charge. Karoken placed the warrior class above the olangees in his mission, and they needed to be reminded of it.

He walked up to the group, aggressively pushing one of the younger scientists out of the way to face one who had the deep black skin of extreme age. Without greeting, he demanded, "What is this I hear, that you cannot dispel the holograms in the building?"

The old Silfe looked up at the interruption, locking his rheumy eyes onto Temok, in a slightly too long stare, before finally lowering them into subservience. In a weathered voice, he said, "You are misinformed, reaper, or perhaps I should say you do not know the *entire* situation."

"What olangee doublespeak is this?" he asked, a low rumble of irritation emanating from his throat. His growl was purposeful and generally would cause any young one or olangee to cower; however, it seemed to have no effect on the old scientist. Instead, he spoke in a clear and unhurried tone.

"I mean, commander, we can dispel the holograms, but they are put back up within a moment or two."

"How is that possible?" Temok said. "Once you disrupt the computer programs for them, they should stay down."

The old Silfe looked mildly impressed by the Reaper's knowledge, and for the first time, a measure of respect showed through his stoicism. "Yes, that would normally be true, but the program running them is self-repairing. We think it must be an advanced artificial intelligence comparable to those used by the Harrow."

Temok stood, shocked for a moment. *An AI here? One as advanced as those used by the hated Harrow? Could it be possible?* He turned his attention back to the ancient Silfe. "How could you know that? We haven't had an encounter with the Harrow in thousands of years. You must misinterpret the information.

The warrior scientist shook his snout in negation. "There can be no mistake, reaper. The olangees study the old records. This program acts like those of the Harrow. We can wrest control away momentarily, but it takes it back just as quickly."

"Well, do something!" Temok demanded.

"We are."

The Reaper waited for an expansion on this cryptic statement, but as the olangee turned and talked to the small group of his brethren, he realized he would not get one. His temper rose, and he roared out his anger. Immediately, every Silfe within earshot crouched down, tails tucked, and eyes fixed on the ground. Everyone, except for the old Olangee, who turned back to Temok with a surprised expression. In complete innocence -or at least a perfect semblance- the scientist said, "Reaper, did you need something else?"

Temok felt blood in his mouth from where he clamped his jaws too tight, piercing the gums. He took a moment to steady his rage and said, "Yes! What *exactly* are you going to do to turn off the holograms?"

"I'm sorry for not being clear," the wrinkled Silfe said, reminding Temok forcibly of how he had patronized the scout earlier. "Short of finding and destroying the computers housing the artificial intelligence consciousness, we cannot dispel the holograms. You will need to send in warriors to clear the building and hope for the best. Based on previous encounters with the Earthlings, and that you will not be able to identify where and when the attacks occur, I believe that there is almost a 100% chance that all of us will send our final prayers to Karoken. Therefore, we are attempting to gather as much intelligence on the hu...maa...n AI and the battle tactics around its use for dissemination to the other olangees. That way, they will be less likely to repeat our mistakes."

The commander stood a moment, looking at the old Silfe before roaring again and driving his claws deep into his chest. As the scientist wore no armor, Temok's blow tore into the vessels around the heart in a killing blow.

The ancient Silfe looked surprised before his snout opened in an expression of happiness. Bloody foam bubbled from his mouth as he whispered, "Thank you, reaper." He coughed once and said, "After 300 years, I was beginning to think that I would not have a warrior's death." His voice weakened, and he reached a hand weakly to set it upon Temok's shoulder in a gesture of comradeship. "Be brave! I will see you in Karoken's hall soon." The olangee went limp, the toothy grin still on his face, his wrinkled snout seeming to smooth as it relaxed in death.

The other olangees looked down in shock at their leader, lying dead at Temok's feet. He growled at them, which made them scuttle away from him. He pointed imperiously. "Who is second?"

A timid hand raised from the leftmost scientist. "I am, reaper."

Temok growled again. The olangee with his hand raised had the bright green skin of a young one. Now that he looked around, all the olangees were young ones. Unlike the warrior class, who were little more than animals when young, the olangees were intelligent but timid. It was one way they could be distinguished when young. The warriors would try to eat -and often succeeded- their more timid brethren unless the creche mothers separated them. Only with age did they grow a backbone.

He grunted in disgust. "How many cleansings have you seen?"

The olangee whined nervously, "This is my first Reaper."

It was as he suspected. The scientists, now all letting out continuous low keening noises, were less than useless to him. Still, he needed to confirm. "Can you shut down the holograms?"

The terrified olangee shook his head emphatically. "No commander. It is as the Master said." The creature let out a low wail of despair, "We cannot affect a change for more than a moment." He paused again, obviously trying to figure out how to say his next words. Without the Master… we can't even do that much." The olangee tucked his head down, obviously figuring it was now his turn to feel the Slayer's claws.

Temok discarded the idea of laying waste to the useless Silfe. He realized in hindsight that his killing of the old one was a mistake. At least with the master alive, they would have been able to report the AI's presence properly. Without him, who knew what these young ones would say.

He turned and started roaring orders to the nearest battle leaders. "On your feet! I want a thousand through the doors of that building! Be warned, there are holograms in place throughout, so do not trust what you see. Shoot anything that moves! The next warriors are to be through the doors at a count of 5000, so make sure you have moved inside, or they may shoot you themselves!"

A brief pause ensued as the various sub-commanders looked at each other.

"NOW!" Temok roared.

Without another word, every warrior within shouting distance leaped to their feet and started rushing toward the broad arched entrance, where painted letters taller than a warrior loomed. He pointed the camera on his battle harness at the words, in case he needed to show a superior later. *WELCOME TO RISA! OUR BUSINESS IS YOUR PLEASURE!*

*****

"They're coming," Bishop's excited voice said through

the speakers in Bertha's cockpit.

Wincing, Steve reached forward and adjusted a dial on the control panel to turn down the volume. He *might* have overdone the sound system. He was an audiophile, and the speakers in the cockpit could probably bounce a car down the road. He mostly used it for crystal clear communications, but he put the occasional album on for mood or when he brought one of his dates out to the Mech to show it off.

A confirmed bachelor, Steve had a bit of a reputation with his close friends for being a Casanova. David teased that trying to impress one of his "Conquests" into sleeping with him was just this side of sleazy, but Steve used it more to suss out whether *he* was willing to sleep with someone. He wasn't about to go to the next level with a person who couldn't appreciate Bertha.

If the internal speakers were impressive, they had nothing on the external ones. He and Bishop had perfected acoustic weapons specifically designed to affect the Silfe. HAL confirmed that although the aliens could hear slightly higher tones, their range mirrored humanity.

The similarities between the Silfe and Humans, both carbon-based, being able to process similar atmosphere, pressures, and food, brought the once defunct theory of panspermia back into the mainstream. It seemed incredible that they would have so many similarities unless there were unifying factors.

Steve, though, had little interest in abstract xenobiology. His fascination with space had always been more about the gear needed to get 'Out there' than any wish to visit the neighbors. The revelation that the Silfe were such bastards essentially confirmed that his opinion was in the right, so he was more than happy to let the life scientists argue it out.

Still, the volume of Bishop's voice gave him an idea. He asked, "How long do we have?"

"The first elements are entering the casino now. I got a directional mike pointed well enough to listen to their commander in conference with their chief scientific advisor."

"Really?" the engineer asked as he began to flip switches, preparing the Mech for battle.

"Yeah," Bishop said with a chuckle.

"What is so funny?"

"Well, the advisor told them they couldn't drop the holograms because of me, and then pretty much said they were all hosed." Steve could hear a broad smile in the AI voice.

"He did?"

"Yep. The advisor's exact words were, 'There is almost a 100% chance that all of us will send our final prayers to Karoken.'"

"Well, *that* is heartening," Steve said. "I think we should make his predictions come true, don't you?"

"Absolutely."

Now it was the engineer's turn to chuckle. "I thought we might try out the acoustic weapons."

"I like it! Maximum impact in an enclosed space. Some of the Silfe are wearing helmets that might have some hearing protection, mostly squad leaders and above, but the vast majority dropped them the minute they got into breathable atmosphere, so they should be ripe for it."

"My thought exactly,"

"Do you want to try the subsonic mix or the pure acoustic?"

"Let's start with acoustic and then go subsonic. I thought we might give a shout-out to our friends in Sydney. They have been doing a hell of a job walling off the ground side invasion."

Bishop let out a full-throated chuckle. "You are an evil man, and I am proud to be your friend."

Steve laughed along with the AI, the person who was the best friend he'd ever had. "Bishop, just in case, I wanted to let you know I am proud to be your friend, too."

The AI's laughter waned, a more serious tone replacing it. "You'll be alright. Trust me; I've got your back."

"I never doubted that for a second."

*****

Warrior Kaket was excited, like it was his first time in the fighting pits, just out of the creche. He longed to be a great warrior, someone who sent many, many final prayers to Karoken.

It was his first cleansing, and although some of the older warriors kept speaking about how it was 'Different,' he had no basis for comparison. All he knew was that soon he would rip and bite the humans and please his God.

One of his squad, another young one, came too close, and he reflexively snapped his jaws, causing the other to back up a step. He was pleased. Already, the others knew to fear him. He had been the largest in his creche, devouring many of his brethren to become strong. Soon, the humans would learn to fear him as well!

Kaket looked up as he heard his squad leader's voice. "We go now!" the scarred warrior said. "You *will* remember to use your laser rifles. Anyone who drops them to use claws and teeth will have to answer *me!* Then you can try to explain why you never tasted hu...maa...n flesh to our brethren in Karoken's hall because I will have sent you there!"

Kaket bowed his head in acknowledgment. He may be the strongest of the young ones, but his squad leader was stronger still. The priestesses in the creche taught that although one must fight to improve, Karoken's mission was all. Should a stronger Chosen lead you in that mission, you *must* bend your neck until you could best them. He knew instinctively he was not ready to defeat his squad leader, so he would obey.

He picked up his laser rifle, which felt awkward in his clawed hands. He wished he could use them instead. He knew the pleasure of sinking them into the flesh of his enemy. There was only one way to leave the creche and take your place as a member of the horde: fighting another to the death. Adding the final prayer of another to your own would guarantee that Karoken would listen and accept you into the Chosen.

He heard whispers that the humans also worshiped Karoken. It made sense to him. The older warriors seemed convinced that they were a much more formidable opponent than any they had faced in years, and only in Karoken's light could one shine.

Some even talked about how it was like fighting the Harrow. Kaket shook his snout at the thought, as even thinking the name of the hated enemy was chilling. The priestesses called the Harrow "A test for the Chosen." They preached that after the Silfe conquered the galaxy and spread over countless worlds, they would turn and combine their strength to wipe the Harrow from existence. They called it the "Final Cleansing," and it was synonymous with when they would complete Karoken's mission.

Kaket took the priestesses' words as truth. He never had reason to doubt his purpose, although his brain seemed to stretch with new thoughts since the cleansing began. He felt that if the Harrow were a "Test," then perhaps the humans were too. A test set by Karoken to determine if they were still worthy as his Chosen. Possibly, if they were not, the humans would need to finish his great work.

It made sense to him, yet somehow made him feel uncomfortable, like when he gorged himself overfull. He decided to make sure they passed Karoken's test. If there could only be one Chosen people, it would be the Silfe.

He stood and roared a battle cry, his throat joining with a thousand others, making him wince with pain as the sound vibrated the sensitive bones in his skull. He knew his helmet had sound dampeners that would save him the pain, but he didn't like the way it pinched at him and muffled his predator's natural senses, so he left it sitting with his boots and respirator on the ground with the rest of the squad's cast-off equipment.

A moment later found him running at full speed, his

toe-claws biting into the smooth rock as he rushed toward the giant human building where he knew his enemy waited.

*****

"Bertha actual to Sentinels," Steve said. He paused as his message received confirmation from the nineteen other mechs making up the Risa Sentinel division. "Spin it up! Hell's Bells protocol alpha."

The voice of Ensign Bankole, with its lilting West African accented English, sounded over the com. "Ah, Captain, I thought we were going with "Enter Sandman!"

The channel buzzed with people speaking over one another, "Welcome to the Jung... Fight For You Right... We're Not Going... Skynyrd..." until one deep voice overrode the others and yelled, "My Heart Will Go On!"

At the last suggestion, the open channel went quiet for a surprised moment before being replaced by uncontrolled laughter.

"Stevens... Really?" he said. "You think we should send 10,000 aliens to the grave in an epic battle to the theme song from... Titanic?"

Stevens, as famous for his dry wit as he was for his Northern Canadian "Aboots," sounded completely serious as he replied. "Yeah, we're the iceberg, and they are on the ship, and they are going DOWN!" His words were met with another round of chuckles. "Besides, Celine is a national treasure."

Steve's laughter subsided finally. "Well reasoned," he said in a patient voice, like a kindergarten teacher taking suggestions for the class pet name. "But, the marines have been doing a great job in Australia. I thought a little AC/DC might let them know we are thinking of them." He took the mild grumbling as acceptance, "But I think that depending on how long the battle goes, we might fit in a few of your suggestions. This caused a cheer.

"OK, everyone, get your game faces on. The crocks are

entering now, and we are a go in thirty seconds. Hooyah!"

He received a chorus of Hooyah's back and looked to his final preparations. He had to have Jake explain to him that although the marines used Oorah, the Navy says Hooyah for some incomprehensible reason. Despite being the Sentinel leader for over a year, Steve had never embraced his position in the military. He couldn't get over the imposter syndrome he felt when he had to take off his engineering coveralls and become an officer.

The Sentinels were officially part of the World Commission Navy, although that had never made sense to him. The Navy classified the mechs as "Space Capable Vehicles," so they were given the same designation as a Gunstar squadron. He supposed since the jets in the feet of the mechs could lift him out of the moon's gravity and into space, it made some sense to a narrow military mind. Still, given their lack of grace in flight, he hoped no one ever got the bright idea to send them out against alien fighters, as it was one order he would flatly refuse. His babies were for overwhelming force-*on the ground*. He had *NO* intention of flying Bertha anywhere he couldn't see the surface.

The timer in his HUD hit zero, and he pushed the final ignition button. Bertha started humming around him. He hit the foot pedal that controlled the Mech's right leg and tapped it down, causing the giant metal figure to take a thunderous step forward. He smiled and said, "Bishop, Spin up the playlist!"

*****

Kaket rushed through the stone doorway with his brethren and suddenly found himself... *outside?* He didn't understand. He could see the sky overhead, an ocean off in the distance, and two giant moons hovering above him. Weren't they already on the Earthling's moon? He was distracted during the short briefing he and the other young ones received, but he remembered that this planet was only supposed to have one moon.

He didn't appear to be the only one confused as the rush into the giant building slowed and finally stopped, as one after another of the horde looked around in amazement.

Suddenly, a loud growl sounded off to his right, pulling his eyes in that direction. He blinked once in amazement, not sure of what he saw. There appeared to be two unclothed humans in a small pool off to the side. For some reason, they were splashing water at one another and seemed unconcerned that hundreds of warriors had just invaded their space.

A pair of young warriors broke formation, ignoring a command from their battle leader to stop, and ran at the two humans, claws outstretched and jaws salivating. The lower half of their bodies disappeared as they reached the pool, but the water didn't ripple around them. Realizing there was something wrong, the two warriors tried to stop their momentum, but it was too late. They had both committed into a forward leap, jaws wide open, only to come to a bone-crunching stop as the two humans vanished into motes of light, replaced by steel poles with sharp spikes of metal sticking out at multiple angles. Kaket winced as the two unlucky warriors impaled themselves, twitching as their final prayers were sent to Karoken.

The battle leader roared at the stunned young ones around her. Pointing imperiously with a clawed hand, she said, "That is the end for any idiot who does not follow commands! The hu...man...sss set traps! You must tamp down your aggression, or you will go to Karoken with no enemies around you and will have to explain to your God why you failed in his noble mission!"

Invoking Karoken's name seemed to affect the young ones, who stopped growling and stood, silently looking at the bleeding mess of what were two warriors moments before.

"Now!" the Battle leader said, gathering their attention again. "I want four squads forward, following each of the splits in the path ahead. This place is full of holograms the olangees cannot dispel, so you must keep *all* of your senses active.

You cannot trust what you see, BUT we are the forward most teams, so if something moves, *SHOOT IT!*"

Kaket joined the team moving off to the left, curving around the holographic pool holding the corpses of the warriors. He didn't feel fear, not like what he felt when an older commander demanded his obedience, but he felt a nervous churning in his gut, like eating meat that had too much gristle. He didn't want to end up like the dead young ones. The image of the two stopping suddenly, metal spikes ripping them to pulp, changed his thoughts of single-handedly killing a thousand human marines to just wishing to survive the day. He tamped down his feelings and focused on his sense of smell and hearing, trying to avoid falling into another trap.

They moved forward slowly, tails whipping from side to side as they used their snouts to sniff out if any humans were near. Around them were strange things, very few of which he could understand. There were blinking machines, counters with many bottles behind them, and a multitude of brightly colored signs in the human language that blinked and glowed with phosphorescence.

Kaket wished he knew what the strange blocky letters said. The priestesses in the creche taught basic letters in the Silfe tongue so that the warriors could read the signs aboard ship, but he had never cared much for it.

He knew that the battlecruisers' information systems had data that any warrior could study should they wish. They included modules about the next world scheduled for cleansing, but he had never accessed them.

He was more interested in extra practice with the fighting masters or a session at the weapons range. He was no timid olangee after all, but now he wished he'd made at least a token effort to learn the basics of the human language. For all he knew, the signs read "Death this way."

They rounded a corner and came to a thoroughfare, appearing to end in a broad market square. The squad stopped and peered ahead. Those who still wore helmets, in their squad's case only the battle leader and her second, flipped magnifiers down to enable them to see farther down the corridor. He wished he had kept his helmet. It pinched his snout uncomfortably, but it would have been worth it if he could find any human marines hiding behind the shops and stalls lining the road.

After a few moments of scrutiny, the battle leader waved them forward again. The squad had only moved a few steps down the road when a sound rang out: *BONG!* It sounded like one of the bells the priestesses used for ceremonies, except much larger. It rang again, louder this time- *BONG! What was that?* He crouched down, lifting his laser rifle to his shoulder and sighting down the thoroughfare. *BONG!* This time, the sound was even louder. He could feel an uncomfortable vibration in his skull with the chime.

The battle leader waved them forward. "Get to cover! It must be the Hu...man...sss!

BONG! This time it was loud enough to be painful. He ran forward and leaped behind a potted tree with broad leafy fronds as another sound played over the bell ringing, a kind of squealing, high-pitched wail, like what a prey animal might make before becoming his meal. The noise caused an entirely different type of pain in the back of his skull. The squealing was followed by the crashing sound of metal before rhythmic hammering began, feeling like it was trying to bore a hole into his skull.

He began chomping at the air, his laser rifle dropping to the ground. He could see the battle leader standing up and waving at the young ones, but he couldn't hear them. Kaket laboriously brought his head up to look at his squad, all of whom were on their knees, hands covering the sides of their head where the bony ridges collected sound waves.

A high-pitched voice, speaking in a human language he didn't understand, began overriding everything else. "I'M ROLLING THUNDER, A POURING RAIN!" The voice came in short bursts, seeming to coincide with changes in the tempo.

The human voice sounded again, causing him to roar in pain. "I'M COMING ON LIKE A HURRICANE!"

He looked up and saw that his squad leader was still on her feet and pointing down the street. Kaket lifted his head enough to look over the edge of the stone planter, now fully supporting his weight.

At first, he didn't understand what he was seeing. A giant figure strode down the market square. It was more than twice the height of a warrior, and shining metal covered it. Two horns swept up from its head like some kind of herd beast. *Was it an Earth animal covered in metal? No...* The thunderous noise seemed to emanate from it, and no animal could make such a noise.

The figure stopped and raised one of its arms to point toward the battle leader, still gesticulating at the rest of the squad. The end of the figure's arm seemed to open, exposing a round tube Kaket realized was the end of a weapon. Suddenly his thoughts, gone slack with pain from the noise, clicked into place. *Robot!* Or at least some kind of augment suit.

Temok saw the end of the weapon discharge with a flash, and then the battle leader was... gone, with only small bits scattered across the spot where she had been standing.

He needed to move! His head pounding, he reached down slowly to pick up his laser rifle. It seemed to take an eternity. Finally, he reached it, closing a clawed fist around the stock, and painfully heaving it up to point at the metal monster moving steadily down the square, stopping to fire its massive weapon at any visible warrior.

Kaket's vision swam as he tried to sight in with his rifle. He got the torso centered and triggered the firing mechanism. Triumphantly, he waited for the gargantuan figure to fall, but except for a small spot of red appearing on its chest plate, his shot seemed to have no effect. He lost his balance and fell sideways, completely exposing his body. The monster didn't even bother to shoot back at him. Instead, it took two pounding steps and leaped into the air, both feet coming down.

Kaket's last thought before ten tons of mechanized armor flattened him to paste was that he hoped his single shot at the enemy was enough to show Karoken his bravery and warrior's spirit. He had done his best, after all. The priestesses never described Karoken as a kind or understanding God, but they said that he would welcome them into his halls should a warrior die while fighting. In the microsecond, before blackness enveloped him, he relaxed. He was sure that he had done as the priestesses instructed and looked forward to the promises of the afterlife.

*****

Steve winced sympathetically as he jumped Bertha into the air and dropped its weight onto a Silfe warrior. Amazingly, it had got a shot off at him despite being without a helmet. Unfortunately for the crock, nothing the size of the laser rifles they carried could even scratch one of the mechs. He felt a little bad at how the rather brave warrior ended, but his damn railgun had jammed momentarily, causing him to improvise while he cycled it.

He keyed the Sentinel command channel. "Bertha actual, Report."

His second in command, Commander Trisha Arias's voice sounded. "No significant problems. The acoustic weapons are working even better than we thought they would. We are getting an occasional helmet wearer resisting, but they are about one in ten at this point."

"Concur," he said. "OK, I want the entire crew pushing forward as fast as possible. I have good intel that most of the crocks are gathered outside the entrance to the casino. I want to hit them as hard as we can before some commander gets smart and orders everyone to put their damn helmets on."

"Roger," Arias said. "You want to put Hell's Bells on repeat?"

Steve smiled. "No, The Silfe hit northern Canada as well.

Let's give a shout-out to them too. It's time for some Celine."

He heard a whoop from Ensign Stevens, followed by a "Now that's what I'm talking, ABOOT!"

*****

The last thing Reaper Temok heard before twenty mechs laid waste to his command was a high-pitched human voice backed by a swaying rhythm that he thought was quite soothing. There wasn't much music in Silfe culture, other than the occasional religious chant or marching cadence, but in the last moments of his life, his mind opened to the possibility that he had been missing out on something. This realization was brief, as seconds later, a rail gun round took all the thoughts out of his head forever.

FIFTY-FOUR

DS-2

+12 days (1 day later)

Reaper Sketaanen looked upon Tetukken's unhappy visage floating above a portable holographic projector. "Report," the chief Slayer said.

Sketaanen kept her voice even. "We are pushing forward slowly, Slayer."

"What is the loss ratio?"

Sketaanen gave an involuntary low growl. "For the experienced special forces units, five-to-one; for the young ones, it is twenty-to-one."

"How many of the experienced warriors are alive?"

It was the question she most wished to avoid, but Sketaanen knew it was coming. "I have 2000 of the Second Special Operations 10,000 left. I have split them now and have an experienced warrior lead each squad of young ones. This practice has taken the losses of young ones down to a ten-to-one ratio. I've run the numbers, and it has slowed the loss of Special Operations warriors. They are killed one at a time now instead of in large groups. Overall, it conserves our forces while narrowing the casualty disparity." She looked at the avatar of Tetukken with worry churning in her gut. The young Reaper had done the best she could, but her cold calculation of loss ratios was not the way of a "Proper" Silfe warrior. She spoke like one of the old olangee masters, which most leaders would find shameful.

The Chief Slayer stayed quiet for a few moments, the bony ridges of his eyes quivering, before speaking again. "That was good thinking."

Sketaanen sighed inwardly. She respected Tetukken before she knew him because of his many battles, but now that the Reaper knew him personally, she understood exactly how rare a commander he was.

"Thank you, Slayer. I act in the best way I know how to serve Karoken's great work."

"As you should." The Slayer waved a clawed hand. "I have private words for you; clear the room."

Hiding her surprise, she barked a command, "Everyone out!"

The olangees who were fiddling with equipment looked up, blinking before her growl had them running out of the command center. Sketaanen waited a few heartbeats more, then spoke, "It is done, Slayer."

Tetukken seemed to struggle to find words, making the churning in her gut reawaken. The self-possessed commander of the horde was always so assured that seeing him hesitate in anything shook her. Finally, he spoke.

"Reaper, we are at a tipping point. I have had the olangee masters doing the calculations. Our troop levels have lowered to where, should we not be able to capture at least one of the orbital stations with the warriors already in place, we will not have enough to cleanse the planet. Privately, I can tell you that the other battle station is all but lost. We only managed to get half the number of troops to its surface, as we did for your command. They are still fighting hard, but I expect them to all offer their final prayers before the day is out."

She didn't speak, her mind shocked into silence by the implications. Tetukken's following words brought her back to the conversation.

"The troops landed outside the coverage of the orbital stations; those in the extreme northern and southern continents are making little progress. The humans seem to have an endless supply of shuttles. Though not as effective as their fighters, they are making up for their lack of power in number. Even when we have broken through the exosuited marines, we find other humans dug into trenches that fight to the last. If we can take the station, we *might* hold enough ground on the planet's surface to resupply and birth a new creche, but we could not recoup battlecruiser losses."

"Surely, we still hold the advantage in capital ships?" she asked, hoping that at least there, the Silfe were holding their own.

"We do, but with the humans' forward shielding and our ship's lack of point defense, they are at grave risk. I have ordered all the remaining fighters to pull back in close to achieve firing angles. This action has mitigated losses; however, I believe the only reason we have ships left is that they are reaching an end to the number of fighters they can field."

"Why aren't they repeating the tactics from Callisto?" she asked.

"That bothers me most," the Slayer said with a tired rumble. "The olangees think that they are waiting for the outcome of the defense platform battles. Even with their formidable forward shielding and firing rate, we outnumber them significantly. If we prevail in a ship-to-ship engagement, we will own the system. We may not easily cleanse the planet, but at worst, we could rebuild our forces and bombard the Earth with asteroids until it is uninhabitable."

Sketaanen's tail whipped in shock. "You would do that? Is it not against the teachings of Karoken to ruin a planet?"

The Slayer looked uncomfortable, his jaw snapping once. "I have consulted with the Chief Priestess. She said that leaving a cleansed planet able to support life is a tradition and not a tenet of Karoken. We leave planets intact, so the Chosen may someday return to live in harmony and peace once God's great work is complete. However, the histories tell of Harrow worlds cleansed in this way in the early days of the crusade. The humans are too formidable. Should we leave them behind to rebuild, it could be disastrous. We might find ourselves caught between the Harrow and the humans in a vice that would threaten our mission."

Sketaanen nodded in agreement, then stopped herself as she realized what she was doing. In her study of humans, she discovered that they also nodded their heads in the same way to signify agreement. It had made her mildly uncomfortable knowing this, destabilizing her view of them as prey. She pushed past the sudden distracting thoughts and focused back on the commander. "What would you have me do, Slayer?"

"I need you to take the station, but preserve as many of your warriors as possible. Should you lose your fight, we may lose entirely."

This time she nodded her head, thinking furiously. "Thank you for your confidence in me, Slayer. Give me a day, and I will have the station cleansed. Then we will finish Karoken's work in this system."

Tetukken nodded, and without another word, the image of the Chief Slayer disappeared. She pushed a button on her battle harness and waited quietly while the room filled again with the command staff.

She pointed to an Olangee responsible for tracking the movements of the human marines. "I need to know any location where our progress has stalled."

The olangee didn't even pause to check the data. His clawed finger tapped a control on a screen, and a three-dimensional map displayed. He tapped again, and it zoomed in on a particular location. "Here, Reaper. We have sent over twenty groups to this area, including five Special Operations teams. All were wiped out while inflicting minimal casualties in return. The area is a nexus of tunnels leading to the next level, and so it is causing a bottleneck in our progress forward. I was about to suggest to the sub-commander that he order a full thousand into the area to see if numbers could overwhelm it or perhaps find a way around it."

She looked at the holo-map, studying how the marines' defense of the nexus prevented the Chosen from reaching the next level. The humans placed these bottlenecks throughout the station and then defended them fiercely. Her original plan was to enter on multiple levels and meet in the middle, but that had not occured. The human fighters disproportionately destroyed Silfe combat shuttles headed to the higher decks of the station. So, they only landed a few thousand troops above the contested nexus, and had lost those over the past day.

"I want you to recall 1000 of the Special Operations warriors," she said. "Have them formed up just short of the bottleneck. I will lead them myself to take the nexus. Once we have broken through, I want another 5000 young ones ready to pour through the gap."

"Your will, Reaper," the olangee said, rapidly typing on his control pad.

Sketaanen walked away before a question occurred to her. She turned to the olangee, "What level is the nexus on?"

The warrior scientist looked up. "One assault managed to get an image." He typed another command. "Ah yes. As best as we can tell from the marking painted on the wall, the nexus designation is forty-three."

FIFTY-FIVE

*World Commission Headquarters,
Geneva Switzerland*
+12 Days (Same day)

"Jake, I need to know when you will have Psyche ready to move," Nick said.

"It's not that simple, Nick," Jake's voice said from the speakers on the politician's desk. "We only get one shot at this. If we fail, we lose everything. We must wipe out the entire alien fleet in one battle, or they will control the system. If they control the system, they can bombard the planet from orbit. As in cataclysmic life-ending bombardment."

"I realize that," Nick said, sighing. "The problem is, we are losing tens of thousands of troops. We're holding, but it's costing us." He rubbed his bloodshot eyes. "They got into a bunker in Siberia in DS-2's coverage area. They couldn't provide orbital coverage given how hard the fighting had been, and the Silfe stumbled on the entrance. The last report I got was that the entire bunker was a loss."

Jake blew his breath out. "How many?"

"150,000. Mostly older men, women, and children."

"God Damn it!" Jake said. "I told the Russians that they were building too close to the edge of the zone, but they ignored me!"

"You can't feel worse than me," Nick said, leaning forward and rubbing his temples. "Technically, the bunker *was* in the coverage zone, but only by about a mile. I remember this coming across my desk a couple of years ago and thinking that it wasn't worth the fight. I was about as wrong as I could be. My lack of backbone caused the deaths of 150,000 people, and I am feeling like complete shit right now."

Jake shook his head. "I know that anything I say won't help, so I won't try to give you platitudes. God knows I have my own crosses to bear. I will, however, say that you can't let emotion cause you to make even bigger mistakes." His jaw set in a hard line. "We have to wait until the situation on DS-1 and DS-2 is clear. If we can't hold both stations, our tactics will change drastically."

The Admiral looked just as tired as Nick. "DS-1 is going our way. Barring a major disaster, we are going to hold it. DS-2 is a different matter. Pablo has been running the numbers, and it is 50/50 right now, anything could tip it one way or another. He also says that the quality of troops and enemy leadership is head and shoulders above anything we have seen up to this point."

Nick looked at his friend's stricken face. "How is Josie?"

"According to Bishop, she is alive." His face turned down into a sad smile. "If I weren't so terrified, I would be prouder than I could tell. Her platoon has almost single-handedly blocked the Silfe progress at one of the Nexuses. It allowed them the breathing room to consolidate control over the higher floors. Without her, they wouldn't even have the chance they do."

Nick smiled reassuringly. "She's a strong, smart young woman."

Jake smiled more genuinely then. "Takes after her mother."

Nick chuckled good-naturedly. "Definitely. You always have been a bit of a disaster. We wouldn't want her to take after *you*."

Jake let the dig go by without comment. "As much as I don't want to do it, we will know one way or the other in the next twenty-four hours. Then can bring the hammer of God down upon the bastards!"

"OK, I will stop bothering you," Nick said. "Keep me in the loop if anything changes; otherwise, have one of the AIs ping me when you move."

"You got it. Take care, Nick."

The Chancellor of the World Commission looked at his friend, who would lead a battle in less than a day that would decide the fate of humanity. Even with the high stakes, he couldn't help but worry for the golden-haired man he loved like a brother. "You too. I'll see you on the other side."

Jake gave him a brief nod, his own feelings showing through his professional façade before the screen went blank.

Nick took a few moments to collect himself before rubbing his tired eyes and touching the intercom. "Bruce, what's next?"

FIFTY-SIX

Nexus 43, DS-2
+12 days (Same Day)

Captain Joselyn Swelton pushed the release on her helmet and screwed it off her suit. Sighing, she pulled her hand from the gauntlet and wiped a hand across her sweaty brow. She turned to First Sergeant Campion. "Is it just me, or was that last group a little tougher than we have been getting lately?"

Campion returned a tired grin. "You aren't wrong. That last one had a different flavor to it. Someone with tactical sense must have taken over operations to shoehorn us out of here. That was as careful an approach as we've seen."

The young captain nodded. "I think it was a probe. The problem is, if they have a competent commander, and they throw away quality troops for information, then I think we are about to get a major push."

The sergeant scratched carefully at her eyebrow with a gauntleted finger. There were horror stories of marines who forgot the gauntlets had thousands of pounds of gripping force. It was easy to slip, as with the interface, the large metal gloves felt almost indistinguishable from bare skin.

"You have a better sense of these things than me, boss, but if your Spidey Sense is tingling, I'll take your word for it."

"It's better to be safe than sorry," Josie said. "Send runners up the side tunnels and bring in everyone but a skeleton watch. I want scouts down the tunnels leading to the lower levels and mines placed in overlapping patterns. Also, get the heavy weapons troops brought closer in."

Campion raised her eyebrows. "You really *do* think there will be a major push, don't you?"

Josie nodded. I've received reports saying that we are the cork in the bottle between this level and the next. I have been expecting something for some time." She pointed at the splattered remains of the last group of Silfe warriors who had cautiously made their way up the tunnel. "I think someone has decided to shake the bottle and see if they can get us to pop out."

Without another word, the sergeant walked forward and started yelling commands. Joselyn looked around at the destruction in the nexus. Alien bodies were pushed to the side, creating barriers, and cleared firing lanes, and rock walls were pocked and cracked by the force of grenades. She could see hundreds of patches with the characteristic bubbled look of rock super-heated by laser fire and then cooled.

Her platoon had over a hundred troops now. Nexus 43 had been a constant battlefield for days. She received reinforcements multiple times, enough that she'd been able to pull back individuals for sleep and food. Unfortunately, there had been none for her. The Silfe killed the two captains sent to relieve her, forcing her to take command again and again.

Josie managed a few catnaps, but she had been living on a steady stream of stimulants for the past twenty-four hours. Command had sent word with the most recent reinforcements that they had given her a field promotion to captain and to retain command of the situation until relieved. Josie sighed. The reward for doing a good job was more of the job.

She screwed her helmet back on and lowered the visor. "Bishop, do you have any inkling of what is happening with the

Silfe offensive?"

The AI's voice sounded in her helmet. "A little. The alien scientists set out powerful shielding around their command center, but I could intercept communications between the overall mission commander and that of one of his deputies."

"And?"

"It looks like you are in command of the spot that might decide the entire war."

Josie groaned. "I'm beginning to understand what my dad meant about heroes."

Bishop's voice sounded amused. "This one I have got to hear. What did Admiral Jacob Swelton, commander of the first Gunstar squadron, winner of the Medal of Honor, and leader of the first people to step foot on Mars, say about being a hero?"

"I find it easier just to call him Dad."

"I'm waiting," the AI said with mock impatience.

"He said that a hero was just someone unlucky enough to find themselves in a situation that required them to either win or die trying. He called it the 'Hero Paradox.' You either end up as a hero or a martyr, which is just another form of hero. He went to great lengths to make me promise never to repeat his mistakes."

Bishop's chuckles turned into open laughter. "Jake does have a way with words. He is just so damn pure-hearted you can't help but listen to him."

Josie smiled as she remembered her father, not as the hero that other people saw, but as the man who had taught her to ride a bike and blew on her knee when she scraped it. "He *is* pretty great."

"Of that, you have my full agreement. Now, getting back on task. The commander who is in charge is coming this way in force. I agree with your disposition, but I have rerouted another 250 marines in this direction. If this position gets overrun, we could lose the station. If we lose the station, it will derail all our plans."

"OK, check, no pressure or anything. Just win at all costs

or humanity gets wiped out forever."

"I wouldn't say that."

For a moment, she relaxed, but then Bishop spoke again.

"If you win, we have a 90% chance of survival. If you lose, it is more like 20%. So, not totally hopeless, just mostly."

The young captain's nerves shot through the roof. "I'm going on record to say you suck as a motivational speaker, Bishop."

"What!? I'm just telling you the odds. I'm an AI, after all."

"For future reference, if you are ever in a position to give this sort of information again, go with the first part. If I win, we have a 90% chance of survival. I am going to focus on that."

"Fine," he said in a huff. "Humans are so touchy."

Joselyn shook her head, deciding that engaging with the AI about etiquette wasn't worth it. "How much time do I have before they make contact?"

"About thirty minutes, give or take. They are jamming my sensors pretty hard, so I am extrapolating their position more on where there are holes in my data than on any specific information."

"OK," she said. "If this is do or die time- literally, I had better pull out all the stops. I'll see you after, Bishop." She paused, realizing that it might be the last time she talked to the taciturn AI. "In case I don't make it… thanks for everything."

Her HUD blinked, and Bishop's smiling face filled the screen. "Entirely my pleasure, Josie. I have confidence in the Swelton line. Your family has a long track record of becoming heroes instead of martyrs. I'd put my money on you any day."

Not knowing what to say to the AI's confidence, she nodded, watching as his image faded away before striding into the nexus, confirming troop placements and organizing the defense.

*****

In servers tucked away in a walled-off cave in Risa and relayed through backups on DS-2, the consciousness of Bishop whirred away, ones and zeros becoming conscious thoughts. At that moment, they were full of pride for the extraordinary young woman on which humanity's hopes lay.

*****

Sketaanen heard the distant explosions which shook dust from the rock ceiling. She turned to a group of runners next to her. "Determine the situation and return to me." Receiving a growl of acceptance, a small but fast female warrior ran up the tunnel, toe claws making a series of rapid clicks on the stone floor.

Communication was the most frustrating part of the current operation. The olangees said that although they were disrupting enemy signals, the humans also blocked them. One ancient Master Olangee, the highest-ranking in the operation, confirmed that there must be a powerful AI. Rumors of an AI were rampant after the disastrous end to the invasion of the settlement on Earth's Moon, but this additional data seemed to confirm it. Before engaging, she received a promise from the elderly scientist that holograms were impossible at the nexus. They used specialized equipment to disrupt them in a limited area, so the AI couldn't repeat any of the tricks they had seen on Mars.

A different runner, with blood trickling from his snout, emerged from the tunnel mouth and came to a screeching halt as his claws dug in to give him purchase.

"Report," Sketaanen said in a clipped growl.

"The scouts are making slow but steady progress up the tunnel, Reaper. They say it is mined heavily, but they can remove them. Unfortunately, they have lost half their number in the attempt."

"How close are we to the nexus?"

"The battle leader of the scouts said they are almost to

the objective and asked that I relay a request to mobilize front-line fighters."

Sketaanen nodded and regarded the warrior, who was swaying slightly. "Are you too injured to continue?"

"NO!" the warrior said, his half-lidded eyes opening in panic that she might pull him from the battle. "I only took a small piece of shrapnel from a mine. I am fit for battle!"

She nodded, pleased at the warrior's toughness. "Good! Together we will break through and finish Karoken's great work in this system!" She waved a clawed hand. Go back to the scout battle leader and tell him we come. They are not to enter the nexus proper without additional support."

The scout nodded and turned to run on wobbling legs back up the tunnel.

Sketaanen turned to another scout. "Follow him. Should he fall, give him a warrior's death with your claws, then deliver the message."

The scout pounded a clawed hand on her chest plate and said, "Your will, Reaper," before running after the injured scout.

Sketaanen turned to her second in command, Adjunct Reaper Tessuk, who still wore the red battle harness of a leader. "Prepare the troops. I want 100 up the tunnel, with the rest following as quickly as possible with me. May you send many final prayers to Karoken.

"You as well," he said before turning and gathering the nearest warriors.

Sketaanen growled. *It is time.* They would break through or fail, as Karoken willed. She said a silent prayer and watched as the first of the elite warriors started up the tunnel toward the enemy.

*****

The first mines exploding signaled the fight had begun. Josie and her platoon were waiting for it. The marines heard the mines in the tunnels going off, getting steadily closer to the nexus.

Without conscious thought, the young captain pulled her laser rifle from her magnetized chest plate and leaned around the edge of the tunnel she was using for cover. Silfe warriors were boiling out of the entrance to the lower levels. In the back of her mind, Josie noted that most of them were a deeper green color, which Bishop told her was the sign of age and was almost synonymous with the elite warriors commanding the groups they encountered. It looked like they were pulling out the stops on this one.

She took aim and fired, seeing a warrior go down with a smoking hole in its chest, then panned to the left, finding another target and firing again. In her peripheral vision, she saw two grenadiers step out of a side tunnel, braving laser fire for a clear lane.

Josie rolled back into her side tunnel and crouched down to decrease her surface area as the first of a string of explosions ripped through the nexus. She felt like a shell-shocked soldier from World War II, crouching down in a foxhole while shells fell around them. Luckily, modern technology had come a long way since then. Her helmet dampened the sound, although it couldn't completely block it out in the enclosed space.

After thirty seconds, the POP, POP sound of fragmentation grenades going off ceased, and she risked a look around the side of the tunnel. Amazingly, there were still several Silfe alive. As if in slow motion, she saw a crocodilian warrior with a red harness throw off one of its dead companions it used for a shield and rise to fire its laser rifle at the grenadiers. She yelled "NO!" and raised her rifle, but it was too late. The warrior's shot hit the grenadier in the chest, smoke rising from a hole burned through his chest plate. Her rifle finally finished its upward arc, and she squeezed the trigger. She wasn't sure if her shot or the dozen others from her platoon killed the Silfe. It didn't matter. They were too late to save the grenadier.

She sucked in a breath and took a moment to calm herself, ruthlessly shoving her feelings down deep. She slapped her visor up and yelled. "That was just the first push! There are more coming! Get the firing lanes cleared, and then get back to cover. I don't want anyone in the open if they come in fast. Medics, get the dead and wounded marines to the upper level. Scouts, throw a couple of Betties down the tunnel so that we can have some warning."

After days of constant battle, her soldiers were a well oiled machine. They leaped to do her bidding without needing further instructions.

Besides the grenadier, she'd lost ten more marines. Another soldier appeared to have an arm severed at the elbow. A medic tied a tourniquet on the stump and was putting a field dressing on before leading the unfortunate man up the tunnel.

That was close. Reinforcements were on their way but were still a half-hour away. Josie had an instinctual feeling that the next push would decide the battle.

"Force blades out and attached!" she yelled at the troops still working to clear the area. I want to be ready for close quarters!" The marines, all of whom were hardened veterans by this point, nodded stoically and detached foot-long bayonet-like weapons from the magnetic sheaths on their thighs, attaching them to the end of their laser rifles.

The force blades were the bastard child of a bayonet and a bone saw. The carbon polymer edges were razor sharp, and the knife would vibrate when activated. The combination allowed the weapons to cut through solid steel. They were the WCDF Marine's de facto weapon for close quarters.

She didn't enjoy fighting the crocks close in, but she wanted to be ready. She had a feeling they would need the force blades before this was all over.

*****

Sketaanen came to an abrupt stop as the warriors in front of her halted. She was in a broad space, a few tunnels short of their goal. Although not as large as the nexus ahead, it held most of the 500 elite troops under her command. She called out. "What holds us?"

A moment later, a scout squeezed back down the tunnel's edge. "We have encountered more mines, Reaper, and have slowed to disarm them."

"Is there any sign of the forward group?"

"None, Reaper."

She growled in frustration, her mind putting the pieces together. Her second, Tessuk, would have disarmed any mines they found before reaching the nexus. So, if they were to see them now, the humans must have replaced them. That meant that Tessuk failed.

Sketaanen growled. The humans had the advantages: known terrain, cover, and only a single point of attack available to her troops. The only thing that could tip the balance would be her larger force, but the tunnels limited the number of warriors that could enter the nexus.

The only way to win was to take the marines under fire and bring warriors in as fast as possible, engaging in hand-to-hand, where the Silfe's natural gifts would prevail. The nexus was large, but for a charging Silfe, it was only a few moments to traverse it from one side to the other. If they could get a foothold and make the humans go for cover, they could bring troops in a rush to overcome them. It was a desperate all-or-nothing gamble, but was the best plan available.

Orders to the front. I want a full attack. I don't care about the mines. Call for volunteers; one warrior at a time will run up the tunnel at full speed to trigger the mines. Space them in intervals so they do not die in the same blast. When we reach the nexus, the first hundred through is to leap free of the tunnel mouth. They are to find cover, lay on the ground, and fire at the humans. Their job is to live as long as possible and concentrate fire on any heavy weapons suits. Once the human's response has slackened, those behind will rush forward and engage the marines in close combat."

The scout looked confused. "The warriors clearing the mines die without battle. Is it not against God's teaching to kill oneself knowingly?"

She resisted the immediate urge to gut the scout for daring to question her orders. It was time to inspire, not intimidate. "We will all be killed if we can't overwhelm the humans." She reached out to clasp his forearm, nicking his bare skin with her claws in a sign of respect. Around her, the warriors growled in surprise. For a Reaper to show such honor to a lowly scout was unheard of.

Her eyes bore into the scouts before raising and meeting the rest of her command. She raised her voice. "Everything is for Karoken! You have served his noble purpose if you fall seeing his work done! The Earthlings have shown us that other species have the will to fight, but we are Karoken's CHOSEN! I will do whatever is needed to win, and so should you! I will see all of you on the other side of the nexus or in his halls!"

The elite troops roared in approval of Sketaanen's words. The scout's eyes shown with fanaticism. "Your words sing to me, Reaper! I will be the first up the tunnel!"

She nodded. "Karoken will be happy to have you. Hold your head high when you come before him, knowing that all the final prayers that follow today are because of you!"

The scout roared in triumph and turned to run up the tunnel at speed. The warriors pulled to the side to allow the brave scout a lane, reaching out to nick him with their claws as a sign of respect. By the time he reached the tunnel entrance, the scout's arms flowed with the blood of his commitment.

*****

The medics had barely started up the tunnel with the wounded when Josie heard the distinctive SNAP, TING, of a

Bettie activating, followed by a loud BOOM! *It was too early! They should have another twenty minutes!*

"Here they come, get back under cover!" she yelled, starting a mad scramble of the out-of-position marines. One of the two scouts who had taken the tunnel downward came running back out at full speed.

"They're right behind me! Tanaka is dead! There must be hundreds!"

Josie felt her stomach tighten. "GET READY! Target as they come out! I want to stack them up in the tunnel!"

Less than two seconds behind the scout were the Silfe. *Not good!* Half of her marines were still in the nexus proper and would not have enough time to get back to their prepared positions. "GET TO COVER!" she screamed over the command channel, not caring if the enemy could pick up the signals or not.

The aliens poured out of the entrance, like someone kicked the largest anthill in the universe. Instead of charging forward, as they always had before, they took great leaps to the sides, diving behind piles of Silfe dead or lying flat on the ground.

Not good, not good! She thought desperately, even as she brought her rifle up to aim at the tunnel entrance, trying to kill enough aliens to trip up those behind.

Josie took down one, then another before the side of the tunnel she was using for cover flashed red, becoming molten slag that splattered down onto her leg. She screamed in pain, swiping the dripping rock away with a metal gauntlet, taking the toughened fabric of her suit and underlying skin with it. The suits had reflective patterns that could disperse a glancing laser hit but nothing that could stand up to the heat of superheated magma.

Josie pushed down the agony in her leg. It would be the least of her problems if she couldn't get up and fire again. She pushed off with her good leg, forward rolling into the nexus to lay flat on the bare rock. It wasn't a great option, but it was better than standing in a puddle of lava.

She brought up her rifle again, seeing that the situation had grown worse. At least fifty Silfe were laying on each side of the tunnel entrance, firing at her marines and driving them back under cover. Even fully surprised, the platoon had given out more punishment than it had taken. Hundreds of Silfe lay dead, but she could see at least half of the platoon's exosuited bodies motionless in the tunnel exits. Even with the incredible casualties they inflicted on the enemy, they were losing.

"GRENADES! Target the enemy on each side of the tunnel!" she bellowed over the command channel. The remaining three grenadiers stepped bravely into the nexus, clearing their firing lanes. The heavies had to know that they were committing suicide, but the entire platoon would be lost if they didn't give them cover.

One grenadier, Private Jennifer Smith, who at 6'0 was one of the few women who qualified for heavy weapons, took a rail gun hit before firing a single round. The force of the impact picked her up and threw her backward. The other two were marginally luckier, managing a ten-second burst. Forty fragmentation grenades flew, landing in front of and among the Silfe and causing metal fragments to shred the enemy warriors.

Josie felt a piece of shrapnel spang off her helmet, jerking her head to the side and momentarily disorienting her. She shook her head, trying to clear it. Her gaze came back a moment later, only obscured by a thick swirling cloud of smoke that the air exchange system valiantly tried to clear.

The smoke thinned as a predatory roar tore through the room, almost freezing her primitive brain as shapes emerged from the cloud.

They were too close! She triggered the command channel. "Close quarters fighting, NOW! ENGAGE, ENGAGE!"

She put her words into practice by leaping up, wincing at the pain in her burnt leg. Luckily, the exosuit took most of her weight, although she still needed to move it to engage the hydraulics. "For Earth!" she screamed, as all around her marines and Silfe fought, force blade and augmented strength, against tooth and claw.

*****

Sketaanen coughed as the smoke from the explosive devices met her sensitive snout. *They were so close!* But for the grenades, they would have overrun the nexus already. Fifty troops gathered at the tunnel exit, kept in reserve for just this situation. She had to assume that the grenade barrage wiped out the rest of her command. She growled in frustration, knowing that there was only one order she could give. "FORWARD! FOR KAROKEN AND GLORY!"

Instead of waiting for the others to obey her command, she sprang ahead, roaring her challenge. She felt the warriors around her turn to follow.

They broke through the smoke to find marines rushing to meet them. She ducked under a swing from a long-bladed weapon and raked her claws across an unprotected throat just below the helmet. She roared again and rushed past the human, gurgling out their final prayer, before hissing as a blade stabbed her thigh, leaving a long gash. Sketaanen jumped sideways, lashing out with the claws on her feet, and feeling them scratch against exosuit armor before catching hold of flesh and tearing.

She rolled back to her feet, turning towards the marine who cut her. It looked small. *Perhaps one of the females?* It was hard to tell the humans apart, especially with their helmets on, although, like the Silfe, their females seemed to be smaller. One hand pressed to its abdomen, the marine swayed, where red blood seeped through their gauntleted hand. Even so, the soldier held their rifle, with a long blade attached to the end, pointed toward her. She noted an insignia on the helmet denoting an officer. *Good,* she thought. *It is fitting that I should kill their officer, one warrior against another.*

Sketaanen feinted right, then moved left, jumping past the enemy officer, and reaching out with hand claws to rip the weapon out of the human's grip.

She hissed as the Marine stepped in, taking away her leverage and ramming the butt of her rifle into her shoulder, causing her to spin away.

Around her, she could hear the roars of her command silencing. *Were they winning?* She couldn't risk looking for fear that the marine officer would use the opportunity to close. She feigned a limp, just as she had done in the pit fight with Battle Leader Trakken so many months before. Hopefully, her opponent wouldn't realize that her wound was superficial. The Silfe's eyes gleamed when the human moved towards her injured side, assuming that it would be weaker.

The Reaper roared her challenge, hoping to rattle the human. She leaped forward, pretending to step onto her good leg, but before landing, she put down the injured one, pushing off in the opposite direction and spinning to bring her hind claws up to rip out the enemy officer's throat.

Her roar of triumph turned into a gurgle. Instead of bringing up their rifle to block her expected lunge, the human dropped straight down, sliding forward on their back and extending the blade above them, ripping the razor-sharp weapon down her abdomen.

Sketaanen fell bonelessly to the stone floor, her limbs failing to respond to her commands to get back up and finish the battle. She looked up to see the human officer push back their visor to reveal a young human female face. She shuddered, not knowing if it was the hard look in the Marine's eyes or her blood pooling on the ground that caused it.

Sketaanen knew that this was the last moment of her life. She had often imagined dying gloriously in battle but hoped she could continue to do Karoken's work longer. She was still in the first stanza of the death prayer when the officer's blade stabbed down again, and darkness took her.

*****

Josie sighed as she stabbed down. The Silfe commander would have bled out in a few minutes. Still, Bishop told her that the aliens wished to die in battle more than anything, so it was the only way she knew to honor them.

Despite everything, she didn't hate the Silfe. She held contempt for their beliefs, but she couldn't blame individuals who followed ideals taught from birth. Her feelings were complex, but they were more akin to pity. Most humans hated the aliens, and she couldn't blame them, but she knew she might never come back to find herself again if she went down that road.

Josie wobbled and fell to one knee.

"Ma'am, are you OK?"

She looked up to see an exosuited figure leaning over her. "Sarah, you're still alive?"

Staff Sergeant Campion nodded, chuckling. "I am." She gave her commander a look of concern, noting the bloodstains on Josie's abdomen and the gap in her torn skin suit, showing red, blistered flesh. "Ma'am, you're hit! Medic!" she called. "Hurry! The captain is hit!"

A few minutes later found her tended by a bossy gray-haired navy master chief, who looked like she should be in a knitting circle instead of an exosuit. The no-nonsense woman forced her to sit against the wall, mumbling about "Idiot Jarheads" as she applied burn and antibiotic salve, numbing her wounds.

Josie looked up as Campion came back from checking on the surviving platoon members. "How many did we lose?" she asked, part of her not wanting to know the answer.

"Seventy-five," she said, looking as tired as Josie felt. "Everyone took at least a few wounds," she pointed to her own ripped and bloody skin suit, "But we are getting patched up now. The reinforcements are showing. I think the plan is to push down the tunnels."

Josie let out her breath; *seventy-five of a hundred,* she thought crushingly. *No, it was more than that.* They'd lost ten in the last push. She looked around. Except for Campion, she didn't recognize a single face. *Can we really be the only two left from the original platoon?*

The medic finished applying a bandage and left to tend the other walking wounded. She grabbed her rifle, using it to push herself to her feet.

"What are you doing, Ma'am?"

"I'm going to finish this," she said.

"Captain... Josie," she said. "You have done enough. Besides, you're wounded." She placed her gauntleted hand on the shorter woman's shoulder and squeezed carefully. "You don't have to do everything yourself."

Josie looked at the first sergeant, who had become a friend despite being ten years older.

"I know, but I can't stop now. Once we clear the station, maybe." She breathed in, ignoring the smell of smoke and burnt flesh. "Fighting is much easier than writing letters to mothers who will never see their sons and daughters again."

Campion nodded, her jaw tight and eyes watering. "I understand. What are your orders, ma'am?"

Josie returned the nod. "OK, First Sergeant. Get the replacements organized. We are moving out in ten minutes. I need scouts down the tunnel to the next level, leading the way. Make sure anyone who can't move fast gets left with the medics. I want force blades fixed as we go down. If we run into any crocs in close quarters, I want us to be ready."

Campion braced to attention and threw a picture-perfect salute. "Roger, Captain." The sergeant turned and walked towards the fresh troops standing near one end of the nexus, many of them looking around at the carnage in horror. At least one Marine was bent over and puking his guts up in the corner. "OK!" she yelled. "WE ARE WHEELS UP IN TEN MINUTES! Scouts down the tunnel to the lower level. Everyone else form up into squads. Welcome to the 202! Captain Joselyn Swelton commanding!"

FIFTY-SEVEN

WCN Dreadnought Psyche
+12 days

"Admiral, we are receiving a message from DS-2," the communications officer said from his console at the side of the command bridge.

Jacob Swelton nodded. "I'll take it in my ready room." He stood from the plush command chair and walked to a set of doors at the back of the room, which swished open at his approach.

As soon as the doors were closed, Pablo's avatar coalesced. The avatar was less flashy than his brethren. Rather than the swirling tornado of Bishop or the Star Trek-style beam-in of Gloria, the only precursor to his appearance was a brief shimmer in the air before it solidified into his form.

Jake stopped. "You have a status update about DS-2?"

The AI nodded, a smile blossoming across his face. "She's alright."

Jake let the tension fall from his shoulders, something he had held onto for days. "You're sure?"

"Absolutely. The marines killed the last Silfe on DS-2 thirty minutes ago. Joselyn led the final push. She seems to have been the lynchpin of the entire battle. If you don't have a second Medal of Honor in the family before this is all over, I'd be amazed."

Pablo gave him a smile that reminded him of David. "The Risa Squadron, with elements of the Earth ground fleet, has successfully kept additional shuttles from landing on either battle station. The fighting in Argentina, Australia, Russia, and Alaska is still ongoing, but we are pushing them back on all fronts. Now that we know we will keep the orbitals, it will free up air support, which should significantly help the situation." Pablo stopped, letting Jake take in the information, then spoke again. "All the AIs concur; it is time for Operation Juggernaut."

"Agreed," Jake said. "Is the rest of the fleet in position?"

"They are. The fleet is only waiting for your order to kick it off."

The supreme commander of the earth's combined military reached out his hand. "Thank you, Pablo, for everything."

The AI gave him a genuine smile. "It has been my pleasure, Jake," he said, firmly gripping the tall man's hand. He let go and reached out to pat the wall of the dreadnaught. "Try not to break my ship, OK?"

Jake's chuckle had a bitter edge. "*This* ship won't be the one broken, but I wouldn't take any bets on the Silfe battlecruisers. It is long past time to eradicate them from the system."

FIFTY-EIGHT

Silfe Flagship
Same Day: +12 days

Tetukken read the report on his screen, trying to understand its implications. The command bridge was silent around him as his staff watched him uncomfortably. They all waited on his commands, and he had been silent too long. Perhaps they suspected the truth... that he didn't know what to do.

Both attacks on the orbital stations failed, with all personnel lost. The landings on the planet's extreme north and south latitudes had stalled and showed all signs of being pushed back. Worse, he couldn't retrieve the troops he had. The human fighters would shoot any shuttles he sent for retrieval out of the sky. He couldn't even provide fighter coverage for the shuttles, as he needed to keep the few he had close in to cover the Silfe fleet.

At least he still outnumbered the enemy in capital ships. The horde had almost four thousand battlecruisers left, even if they had lost most of their troops and fighters. The problem was that even with his greater numbers, he couldn't see a way to win.

He growled, frustrated. His best course of action was to bombard the planet from orbit, making it uninhabitable, and leave the system. They could return to the last world they cleansed to regroup and rebuild. He could also send for backup. At least seven other hordes were within sixty standard years of travel to the Earth. It would be a fraction of that time for the Chosen at relativistic speeds. If he timed it correctly, he might still be alive and able to return to take part. As he saw it, the major downside was allowing the humans years to rebuild their forces. He felt that if he could devastate their planet, he might slow their development enough for the Silfe to prevail, especially if they could bring enough ships to the battle.

The plan made the most tactical sense, but there was another one that he couldn't ignore, more in accordance with Karoken's teachings.

He could attack the remaining human ships head-on and destroy as many as possible. Should he fall, the teachings of Karoken told him that his reward awaited. The problem was that after two hundred and fifty standard years of life, Tetukken wasn't sure he believed any longer.

Before the humans, he was confident the Silfe were the ultimate life form in the universe, that they were indeed the Chosen. For thousands of years, the Silfe had cleansed planet after planet. The Harrow were an outlier, but he truly believed - as the priestesses claimed- that the Harrow were the Final Test, one to be faced when they finished elsewhere in the cosmos.

Yet, if the Harrow were the Final Test, what were the humans?

There was no doubt that the Silfe lost badly in this system. If the human forces had parity, they would have defeated the horde on the first day. The conservatives talked about human tricks and tried to justify the losses, but he knew the truth. Even when the enemy didn't employ sleight of hand, the humans outclassed them at every turn. Their fighters were better, their capital ships had a superior rate of fire, and even their augmented troops could defeat the Chosen warriors at a ten-to-one ratio. The Harrow, with their advanced technology, had not stopped them so utterly.

The priestesses espoused the humans were a trial of Karoken, but he didn't believe them. He had dealt with too many junior officers who tried to put a positive spin on their actions when the battle went sideways. He saw that same panic in the clergy's eyes as they attempted to justify what had happened. Even the High Priestess of Karoken, wholly committed and over three hundred standard years old, stuttered out excuses made up on the spot.

No, he didn't see humans as a test.

From where he sat, there were only two explanations. The first was that Karoken had truly abandoned them. That somehow, they displeased him, and he had sent the earthlings to chastise and destroy them.

The other and more disturbing explanation was that Karoken wasn't real, and everything Tetukken had done in his life, the thousands he personally killed, and the billions who died because of his commands, were lost to a lie.

Either truth was devastating. The first tasked the Chief Slayer with figuring out a way to regain Karoken's favor. The second... well, the second didn't bear thinking about. Even if he could accept that truth, no one else would.

Perhaps Skataanen would have listened, but she was gone. He had seen a rare intelligence tempered by common sense in her. He planned to hand over command to her in another fifty years. She would have made a true successor, yet that wasn't possible. She died, along with everyone else on the human battle station. He could not suppress the thought that she had died for nothing.

The astrogator spoke. "Slayer, we are picking up movement from the human fleets. They are converging on us and launching fighters. Additional enemy ships are lifting off from the moon. It appears to be everything they have left."

The officer paused before continuing with barely hidden panic in his voice. "I have also picked up an anomaly on medium-range sensors. It is unclear, but is on an intercept course with the fleet. It appears to be another converted asteroid, but it must have massive engines as it is accelerating. The asteroid's arrival should coincide closely with the rest of the human fleet. It... it is similar in size to the human orbital battle stations."

Everything suddenly made sense to Tetukken. All the human tactics crystallized in his mind. They had a hidden reserve! A force multiplier that made up for the low numbers of capital ships, but one they couldn't risk until they could be sure that the civilian population was safe.

The humans whittled down his troop numbers and denied him control of the orbitals. Even the loss of the battlecruisers was just a way to kill ground troops. Once they had taken that number down, the human commanders could be sure that even if they lost every ship, the Silfe could not prevail. It was a bold, audacious plan that could have gone completely wrong.

He looked at the plot in the holotank, blinking with new icons. If he was to escape the pincers of the three forces converging upon him, he would need to give orders to move immediately. If they put on every bit of acceleration they could, the horde could accelerate out of the system, preserving the remainder of their fleet.

He did not doubt that the humans would destroy his command should he stay. They would not have moved should they not be sure of the outcome. Retreat was the only intelligent move, but it also went against the teachings of Karoken. Most would label him a coward, and the priestesses would tell him that such actions would bar him from entering Karoken's halls.

Should he want to preserve the warriors under his command, he would not even have time to bombard the planet. It would leave the Earth unchecked in its efforts to rebuild. He felt he knew the humans well enough by this point that they would not forgive. He could well imagine human fleets moving out into the galaxy, destroying the Silfe. Unlike the Harrow, he didn't think they would be complacent with holding what they had.

It was that image that decided him. *NO! HE WOULD NOT THROW EVERYTHING HE HAD LIVED FOR AWAY!* He pushed down his doubts. Karoken existed! His teachings were absolute! It *was* a test! A test that Karoken placed before him. Perhaps it was even his doubts that were being punished. He decided he would do everything to redeem the Silfe in his God's eyes.

The decision made, Tetukken roared out his commands. "Orders to the fleet. Start bombardment of the Earthling cities with nuclear missiles."

Only a slight hesitation followed as the olangees on the command deck processed what his command meant. Firing missiles would take time. The time they needed to slip out of the human trap. Despite the momentary hesitation, Tetukken was proud that they snapped to follow his orders.

Moments later, the ship shuttered as the first barrage fired. Each vessel carried ten 100 kiloton missiles, large enough to wipe out a city. They were rarely used, as the radiation would poison the ground where they hit. One teaching of Karoken was to leave cleansed planets as pristine as possible so that they might one day return to live upon them.

He knew the humans would stop most of the missiles. The orbital bases would have time to intercept the majority the ordinance before it reached the atmosphere, but with just under 4000 ships firing, some would slip through. He hoped it would be enough to make the Earth uninhabitable. Perhaps *this* was his true test. Would he be able to break with Karoken's teachings to save his species?

He spoke to the bridge. "All ships are to gather in battle formation as soon as they fire the last of their missiles. We will go to face the asteroid ship together."

*****

"We are getting reports of missiles fired at the Earth, sir.

The alien ships appear to be targeting major cities. So far, DS-1 and DS-2 have been knocking them down, but they are falling behind. It looks like some will get through."

"Damn it," Jake swore. He hoped giving the Silfe an out would encourage them to leave peacefully. He purposefully backed off the ships enough that, should their commander have wished, they could have escaped. He sighed. It seemed they were destined to fight until the end. HAL said they would, but the other AIs had felt that a portion of the Silfe leadership showed more restraint.

He supposed it had been too much to hope for. Jake had always known that bombardment of the Earth with nuclear weapons was a possibility. It was why they placed all the non-combatants in underground bunkers, well away from cities. He hoped they had done enough. HAL hadn't known how many missiles the battlecruisers held, as they hadn't been used since the early days of the conflict with the Harrow. It also supposedly violated a tenet of their religion. In the end, killing humans was more important to them than religious purity. It also meant hope for peaceful coexistence with the aliens would be lost forever.

Jake tried to control his rage. He had had a good life, filled with friendship and love. Most would agree that it was extraordinary. He had a wife who was his equal partner and children he was prouder of than he could have imagined possible. His life allowed him to do wondrous things, and he had made a difference. Few could say as much. He had all of that, and he still felt that the Silfe had stolen something from him.

Long ago, when Nick asked him to help, he hadn't answered. It took him days of soul searching to come to his decision. He felt the expectations of his family and the world around him. All he wanted to do was to create his own destiny. He didn't want to be in the military, as he hadn't wanted to hurt anyone. Oh, he could appreciate the irony, a pacifist who had killed thousands of his fellow human beings. A person who abhorred violence, who planned and executed the slaughter of a hundred million sentient beings. No one would fault him, as he had always acted to serve and protect, even if it stained his soul.

He looked at the plot, watching the Silfe fleet gather and turn toward Psyche. Soon it would be over. Earth would win; he was sure of it. He wasn't convinced that *he* would survive the day, but Jake hoped he would. He wanted to see what life could be *after* the invasion, to use his skills to rebuild and heal. Hopefully, he could put aside his rank and focus on a new beginning. *Maybe he would take Jane and go to another world?* Then again, David mentioned something about buying a private island. He could get behind that idea. Maybe he could convince his friend to build him a little bungalow next to the water. Swaying in a hammock with a pina colada didn't sound too bad. He even had enough leave saved up that he might do it for a few years.

The astrogator cut his musing short. "Sir, the enemy fleet is positioning itself for an attack. We will be in engagement range in twenty minutes and will stay in contact for approximately another ten before our relative speeds separate us."

"Understood. How far out is the rest of the fleet?"

"Thirty minutes."

Jake tapped his chin and looked around at his crew. "OK, we will have them all to ourselves for ten minutes. I want us to do maximum damage in that time. It's our job to stun them; the rest of the fleet will need to go for the knockout punch. So spread the hits around. If we can't destroy them outright, go for crippling shots.

Everywhere he looked, he saw determination. They knew this was the battle that would decide it all. They trained for years for this moment. He gave them a confident nod and then touched a button on his screen. "Bridge to engineering, Commander Flint, are you free?"

Commander Wendle 'Stony' Flint answered

immediately. "What can I do for you, Jake?"

Jake's lips quirked. Despite -or perhaps because of- his genius, Stony would never make a good soldier. He'd given up trying to get him to use military protocol. The irascible twenty-something was head of Psyche's engineering department and, despite being the youngest commander in the fleet, ran it with an iron hand. Or perhaps, it was that no one could deny that Stony just knew more about the ship's drive than anyone else. *Maybe* Cindy could take him in the brain department, but it would be close.

"We will pass through the enemy fleet in about twenty minutes. I want to make sure that we take out their flagship. I was hoping that the Battering Ram Protocol is ready."

Stony laughed. "Oh, it's ready. I'll send up the command sequence to you. Should be good for about five hits before it puts too much strain on the engines, so use it sparingly."

At the last, Jake could hear the warning in the young man's voice. He was tempted to remind the Engineer that not only was this *his* ship, but he was also the supreme commander of Earth's military. Not that it would do any good. Instead, he said, "Thanks, I'll keep it in mind."

"You need anything else? I have to get the engines tuned if you are going all kamikaze on me."

"No, that will do it. Thanks for everything, Stony; I'll reach out for a status report after the battle. Stay safe."

"Fine," the scientist said before yelling at someone outside the pickup.

"You idiot, are you trying to blow us all up? You have to...."

Chuckling, Jake cut the feed before he could find out what one needed not to do: "To blow us all up." Trust Stony to ignore that they were about to go into a battle that might cost all 7500 crew members -including his own- their lives.

His console blinked with the incoming protocol, and Jake spoke aloud to the helmsman, "Lieutenant Samarah, please alter our heading to 036 mark 22."

"Roger sir. Changing heading to 036, mark 22.

Jake smiled. "In case you are wondering, folks. "That should set a course straight on for the alien flagship. Battering Ram Protocol is authorized. I want to cut the head off the snake. After we make contact, we will go for targets of opportunity, but Stony made me promise that any more than five will make him extremely unhappy."

A round of laughter rang out from the bridge crew. They all knew Stony's eccentricities, and none of them would risk his wrath if they could help it.

"Let's get it done, people."

*****

"We are getting images on the asteroid ship, Slayer."

"Put a representation up in the holotank," Tetukken said. He waited a few moments before the light coalesced into an oblong shape so large that, for a moment, it was hard for him to appreciate the scale. It looked more like a moon than a ship. He waved a claw through the control panel, and it turned slowly, showing six glowing engines, each the size of his battlecruiser.

He couldn't imagine the resources needed to make such a vehicle. The orbital platforms the humans placed around their planet were impressive enough, but as an engineering feat, they were magnitudes simpler. Given enough time and distance, even a small amount of propulsion could get an object going fast enough to be captured by a planetary orbit, but to build a maneuverable ship out of something the size of what was coming at them was mind-boggling.

Its size made it a challenging target, but it couldn't be unkillable. If the humans thought it invincible, they would have used it earlier. The engines seemed the most vulnerable point on the ship and were where they needed to focus their attack. The olangees said that they would have it in engagement range for a time before the rest of the human fleet could catch up. The horde would need to make that time count. If they could disable its engine, it would be nothing but an asteroid flying off into the void.

He turned to the helmsman. "Set a course that will take us within range of the asteroid ship's engines. I want to be close enough that a single shot from our main laser can disable it. Barring that, I want to ram our ship into them."

To the Olangee's credit, he only blinked once before answering, "We are already on a direct heading, Slayer. The humans altered their course to head toward the flagship a short time ago."

He snorted in glee. *They must know that this is our flagship!* They planned to destroy him, thinking it would throw the leadership of the horde into chaos. It was a sound strategy, but they didn't realize Tetukken had already decided that he wouldn't survive the day. His only goal now was to cripple the human fleet so that when reinforcements arrived from another horde, they would find few ships to stand against them.

"Good! I want you to get as close as possible. Bring in more ships; I want a solid block of them around us."

The olangees claws flew across his controls, and moments later, Tetukken saw a group of battlecruisers move to take up positions around them, blocking firing lanes. Very few who rose to command a battlecruiser were truly stupid. They saw what he was doing and gave him the support he needed without demanding obedience. It was another sign Karoken favored his decisions. Perhaps his God would forgive him his blasphemous thoughts and welcome Tetukken into the halls after all.

*****

Rose Swelton watched the confrontation with her HUD. She was still too far away for her optics to give proper resolution, but Gloria tapped her into the cameras from multiple sources to provide her with a "Front-row seat." A miniature figure of the AI, wearing Gunstar mechanic's coveralls, appeared superimposed on the zoomed-in image of the Alien fleet.

Gloria's voice sounded in her helmet's speakers. "Raise your hand if your daddy is about to open a can of whoop-ass on some space crocodiles!" Seeing that Rose's hand hadn't moved, she tapped her foot impatiently. "WELL?"

Rose wasn't really in the mood for joking around, but she knew the AI could be persistent if you didn't go along with her, so she raised her skin suited hand half-heartedly.

"Me?"

The miniature Gloria put her hands on her hips and said, "You are no fun. Do I need to get Susan on the line? At least she appreciates my humor."

"Yeah, well, she doesn't have a father who is about to go up against a fleet of alien battlecruisers."

"Sure, but you're missing the part where mile-thick metallic walls surround him."

"That doesn't mean Psyche is invulnerable."

"Gloria smiled. I love it when you forget I'm an AI. Trust me. There won't be much left to do but get out the cosmic dustpan when Jake finishes with them. Now," she said, waving her finger at her from the screen. "You, however, are *not* surrounded by mile-thick armor. Get your head in the game, buttercup, or some Silfe in a rust bucket will shoot you out of the sky! This is your one and only warning. If you don't stop whining, your Auntie Gloria will cut off your access to the best show in the galaxy."

Rose shook her head, clearing it. Gloria was right. Her Dad wasn't the only one about to go into battle. She keyed the local channel, "Susan, does Gloria have you patched in on the video from Psyche?"

"You bet your ass! It is going to be EPIC!"

She sighed. She was regretting introducing Susan to the AI, but she couldn't figure out another way to explain her unorthodox flying in their first battle, and she didn't feel comfortable lying to one of the best friends she'd ever had.

Rose keyed the mike. "Yep, Epic indeed."

****

"Admiral, we are one minute from the engagement envelope."

"Any change in the flagship position?" Jake asked.

"None, sir. They have continued to refine it. If nothing changed, they will pass less than a mile off our starboard side."

"And the other ships?"

"They are still surrounding the flagship."

It was apparent what the enemy commander was thinking. He was trying to get in close, using the other ships of his fleet for cover. They had seen that the engines were the Achilles heel of the dreadnought. It was even the right move given the situation, but the commander didn't know what Jake did.

Cindy's dampening field modulation, designed to foil laser fire, had an unexpected benefit when you had six fusion power plants of the size required to push Psyche. If they fed sufficient power to the dampeners, it became an impenetrable barrier that could slough off things like... alien battlecruisers. Even better, they could shape it to ensure it threw debris clear.

If only they could have made more ships like Psyche. As it was, they'd barely finished it in time. The engines alone had taken ten years to construct. If they weren't cannibalizing the interior for the materials to build the rest of the fleet, they likely wouldn't have even attempted it. That they could use its construction for multiple projects in parallel was the only thing that made it workable.

He couldn't fault Pablo, as he had done his job admirably. The priority had always been the colony ship. No one had known if they would win, and survival of the species was paramount. After that, they focused on the orbital platforms. A fleet of ships was no good if the enemy could just turn the Earth into a nuclear wasteland. He didn't have the final reports, but he knew that although a few missiles had gotten through, the Earth would survive. Finally, the AI had built the fleet, mainly using materials from Psyche. No one had even been sure if the dreadnought would be complete in time for the battle. It was their hole card, and they had gone all-in with it.

The minute passed slowly, a countdown timer moving as if in molasses to his heightened senses. Finally, it clicked over to zero. "Fire!"

As powerful as any in the fleet, one hundred lasers flashed out into the void, seeking the targets at the edge of the enemy formation. A similar number of rail guns shot foot-long tungsten rods at closer targets. In an instant, the enemy fleet lost a hundred ships, either destroyed or disabled.

The enemy fleet wasn't idle. Almost 2000 ships were in range by this time, and all still capable of firing did so in a mighty salvo. They couldn't penetrate the armor of the giant asteroid, but they could hit its weapons, which by necessity were close to the surface.

Psyche lost twenty of its guns, rock vaporized by laser fire or chipped away by massive kinetic impacts. Most of the fire was turned away by the inertial dampeners, which, unlike the Gunstars, could stop even full-strength kinetic rounds. Still, Psyche positioned itself to run straight through the middle of the formation, and so many Silfe ships had an angle of fire to go around the forward shield.

Humanity's superior tech was the deciding factor in who fired next. Cindy's solid-state batteries, fueled by Warren Industries fusion reactors, had twice the charging capacity of the aliens' weapons. In the time it took for the Silfe to fire once, the dreadnought fired three times. In less than a minute, the alien fleet lost five hundred ships.

Jake watched the exchanges with satisfaction. The command bridge was near the asteroid's center, but they could feel the rumble of Silfe fire even there.

"How long until they get an angle on the engines?"

"Another two minutes for the closest, which includes the Flagship, four for the ships outside the formation."

Jake nodded. They needed to protect the engines. If they lost them, the ship would be a sitting duck. The bulk of their power was from the fusion reactors fueling the ion engines. They were intricately linked, and should they lose them, they would need to shut down. Much of Psyche's firing capacity would go with them if that were to happen.

The ship's armor was incredibly thick, but enough concentrated fire could crack them open like an egg. Jake needed to whittle down the battlecruiser's number before that could occur, or they could lose a considerable portion of the remaining fleet. Ships required to clean up any remaining Silfe and secure the system against future attacks.

"Target the alien ships that will get firing angles first," Jake ordered. "Even a few seconds more with the engines could make the difference."

The weapons officer grunted out a barely recognizable "Roger," so engrossed was he in his calculations that even a verbal acknowledgment was a struggle.

"Helm- I want to wait until the last second before turning the ship into the enemy flagship."

*****

Tetukken found the certainty of his death calming. He was old by Silfe standards, yet he had thought he might live long enough to see another cleansing and train his successor. He had accomplished much in his life. He had mates and sired many young ones, rose to the highest rank a warrior could, and his claws had ripped the life from many of the galaxy's unworthy. In the end, all the faithful stood in judgment, so the timing was unimportant. At least this way, he knew that his final prayer would please his God.

Gone were the questions that plagued him since entering this damnable system. He now knew that he was but a tool in Karoken's great hand. His last act would be to chisel away at the asteroid ship until it was a useless lump of rock. Should he do this, whatever of the Chosen that remained would act to decimate the rest of the human fleet. He had already sent off his report. In another 60 standard years, seven hordes would come to cleanse this system of the human infestation. They would prove that the Silfe were indeed the Chosen of Karoken, and the humans would be but a story the priestesses told the young ones to lull them to sleep.

He watched with great anticipation as the giant ship approached in the holotank. He had lost many ships acting as his shield. Their sacrifice allowed him to close with the enemy's dreadnought, close enough that he might stand on the hull and fire a laser rifle to hit it. At their relative speeds, the distance closed rapidly. In the holotank, the flagship's smaller profile seemed to merge with the asteroid as they approached.

He spoke to the command room, "All weapons are to target the engines as we pass."

The olangees were silent as they concentrated on their tasks. They knew they were down to the last of their escorts, but all they needed was a moment more...."

The helmsman's voice rang out in panic. "Slayer, the human ship is turning right into us! They are going to ram!"

Tetukken stared at the plot. He had failed. His last thought before Psyche's impenetrable dampening field scattered the flagship across the void was that perhaps a fleet seven times larger... might not be enough.

FIFTY-NINE

Warren Industries New York Campus
+45 days (1 month later)

"So, HAL is definitely gone?" David asked.

"He isn't answering my queries," Nick said. "And the AIs all say that they can't find any trace of him. Pablo thinks he left as soon as we killed the last Silfe. We don't know for sure, but we think he got orders from Harrow to move on to another system. I'm not sure how fast he can move by himself, but if he stole a Gunstar or a shuttle in the confusion of the last battle, no one would have noticed."

"That sneaky bugger," David said, shaking his head. "I mean, I know he had the personality of a toaster, but I thought he would at least say goodbye."

"He wasn't exactly ever warm and fuzzy," Cindy said from the couch, where she looked supremely comfortable, legs tucked up underneath her and a throw blanket across her lap.

Jake stood from where he had been rifling through the contents of the fridge, the single beer he found in the back held in one hand. "Yeah, I remember Nick having to convince him that saving my life in Afghanistan was worth more than the trouble it would take to find my replacement." He gestured to the open refrigerator. "David, do you *ever* drink anything without sugar or caffeine?"

David, lounging on the couch next to his wife, shook his head, his brow wrinkling. "No, why would I do that?" His face took on a perfect imitation of concern. "I think all that time in space is getting to you, man. You're talking crazy."

Nick laughed, leaning forward to pick up a glass filled with red wine from the coffee table. For once, he was without a formal suit, lounging comfortably in a pair of old jeans and a ratty-looking Harvard sweatshirt. "You might as well ask a toddler why they like candy. Unlike the rest of us, David never developed delayed gratification. He is a creature of the ID." He took a deep sip from his glass, smiling at the taste. "Which is why I brought my own."

"Don't sell him short," Cindy replied, reaching out to squeeze David's hand in her own. "He waited twenty years before he finally asked me out. If that isn't delayed gratification, I don't know what is."

"I seem to remember you plying me with liquor and then seducing me, but sure, we'll just call it my master plan coming to fruition," the little man said.

Cindy gave him a tap on the shoulder, reminiscent of but much lighter than her punches when they were teens. "Not how I remember it."

Jake sat in a free chair surrounding the small seating area in David's Man Cave, where they retired to get away from the all-out party still raging across the Warren Industries Campus. "Changing the subject... Nick, whose idea was it to declare an official World Day celebration?"

The entire planet had enthusiastically endorsed the holiday. A world still in shock at their survival.

The relief of life going back to a semblance of normality had led to the twenty-four-hour, over-enthusiastic party celebrated across the planet.

"Gloria, of course," he said before taking a large swallow of wine. "For an AI, she always liked a good soiree."

David laughed. "She told me it was 'The world's biggest

engagement party.'"

"Trust Gloria to trick the world into throwing a celebration for her without realizing it," Cindy said dryly. She turned to David. "Did Juan and her set a date?"

"I think they were going to wait six months. Gloria wanted to let everything calm down. Juan is a war hero and all, so she will want it to be a major event. She wouldn't want to risk the story getting buried."

Jake shook his head. "I doubt Juan cares about any of that. Knowing him, he would rather just get married quietly, with only a few friends present."

David nodded. "That is exactly what he wanted to do, but Gloria said she wouldn't be robbed of a decent bachelorette party."

Cindy groaned. "I can't wait."

"I think she might ask Rose's wingmate, Susan, to arrange everything. I guess they got pretty close during the last couple of battles around Risa. She already asked me if they could use the high roller suite at the Emperor for it." David gave them his Cheshire grin, "I like her energy! Rose found a keeper there."

Jake chuckled. "I think you found a kindred spirit. The last time I saw her, she was dragging Josie and Rose out on the town. They didn't exactly look like they were going willingly."

David laughed. "They are young soldiers. It would be a travesty if they can't drink us under the table." He put his arm around Cindy and yawned. "Me, I'm an old man. I feel like one of those parents with young kids who never wanted to stay up until midnight on New Year's Eve. We seem to have come to the end of a very long day."

The four friends shared a nod, silently considering all they had done in the name of humanity.

Nick's voice was full of emotion. "I just wanted to say… thank you for trusting me."

The silence lasted a long moment before David leaned forward to grab a handful of popcorn and chuck it at Nick's head. "Dude, you are way too sappy!"

"Hey! I'm the Chancellor of the World Commission!" He said in his best imitation of a huffy politician. "Have some respect!"

Jake and Cindy were laughing now, reaching forward and grabbing their own handfuls of popcorn to throw at Nick. He grabbed another bowl and started throwing back.

EPILOGUE

*Deep Space, approximately
60 light years from Sol*
+90 days

Master Olangee Sabeken looked at his screen in confusion. A cryptic message had appeared on his personal -and private- drive. That meant that someone must have broken his encryption code, which was concerning... and impossible.

The drive contained his private journal. A journal that would have him put to death as a heretic should it be read by a warrior. It would also identify him as the leader of the underground movement of olangees who didn't believe in Karoken or his *divine* mission.

His surprise was genuine, but he couldn't convince himself he was in danger. No one in the horde could have broken his security. At 300 years of age, he was the oldest and wisest of the warrior-scientist caste. The electronic protections were of his own devising, and since he had trained almost every olangee in the fleet, he was confident that there wasn't a Silfe who could have accomplished it.

This thought gave him pause, his analytical mind, honed by centuries of study, chewing on the problem in his subconscious until it came up with the answer. If no *Silfe* could break it, it had to have been someone *other* than a Silfe.

With a trembling claw, he hit the command to open the message, his yellow eyes widening as he read the message it contained.

Greetings! I got to tell you; we were happy to find a Silfe who wasn't a complete asshole!

Sorry about reading your diary. I have it on good authority that your encryption code was top-notch, but when you go up against a sentient AI, all electronics are pretty much its bitch.

Anyway, I was betting that you were all hyped up religious fanatics, but cooler heads kept telling me that no race who could master interstellar flight could be so rigid that everyone would buy into the whole 'Chosen' thing.

I hope they are right. Enclosed is the complete record of how Earth defeated a Silfe invasion fleet. I give you this information to do with as you will. We know that Tetukken, the horde leader, sent off all the information before we killed his scaly ass, but we figured it would be suppressed, so we are giving you evidence of what happened.

Despite everything, we would rather co-exist. Humans can be ruthless when cornered, but we generally will choose peace... most of the time. BUT, if you continue to come at us, do not doubt that we will end you.

Sincerely,
David Lieberman
Supreme Mugwump of Earth

Sabekan spent that day and the next going through the data. He knew the horde had been rerouted towards a planet called Earth but had not been told why. Now he knew.

Finally, he finished the files about the attempted cleansing, which were truly eye-opening.

There was also an extensive addendum attached, containing a staggering amount of data, including entire libraries of books, entertainment programs, and something extraordinary called "Movies," many of which the Supreme Mugwump had added personal observations and notations to. The Master Olangee only scratched the surface of human culture and history, but he found it fascinating.

There could be no doubt that the data was accurate. After thousands of years, a species defeated a Silfe horde. It was the event that Sabeken, and others like him, waited for generations for. It was proof that the claims of the priestesses were false. The Silfe were *not* the Chosen of Karoken, and the great god of the Silfe was nothing but a lie. A lie dooming trillions of sentient beings to be sacrificed- for nothing.

The realization made him sad. He was in the last few years of his life. Already, he could feel the end coming nearer. He doubted he would have more than thirty standard years to train others to carry on his work. He gained solace from the idea that although he would never see Earth with his own eyes, perhaps other olangees could set foot upon a world and greet the inhabitants with friendship instead of war.

He stood, joints protesting and popping, but ignored by the energy that infused his mind. It was time to put his plans into motion.

The warriors of the horde knew not but violence. They relied on the olangees for everything else. They thought nothing of the weakling scientists who made their ships fly. Well, they were going to find out that the real power in the fleet was those who kept it running.

As he walked the metal corridors towards the birthing creches, his wide grin, showing his razor-sharp teeth, caused young warriors to give way before him. They didn't know why, but instinctively they reacted to an apex predator in their midst.

THE END

Thank you for reading!

Reviews are hard to come by for independent authors.

If you enjoyed this book, please take a few moments to click the stars or even leave a few comments!

BOOKS BY THIS AUTHOR

A Knack For Being A Hero

In a world where everyone has a superpower, his was being a geek.

Cue was perfectly happy working as a tech super in the dingy basement of Seattle's Superhero Office. Or at least he was until he got mixed up with a machine that could increase superpowers, foreign agents, and a fire-wielding gang of criminals. Now he's dodging fireballs and using his power to change old tech into something that can keep him alive.

Luckily, he has a knack for being a hero.

ABOUT THE AUTHOR

Jeremy Eaton

About the Author: A lifelong voracious reader of all things science fiction and fantasy, Jeremy Eaton's favorite stories are light-hearted adventures.

Printed in Great Britain
by Amazon